Joan of the
Sword Hand

by

S. R. Crockett

Joan of the Sword Hand
by S. R. Crockett

ISBN: 978-93-62764-26-3

Published by

DOUBLE 9 BOOKS

2/13-B, Ansari Road
Daryaganj, New Delhi – 110002
info@double9books.com
www.double9books.com
Tel. 011-40042856

ABOUT THE AUTHOR

Samuel Rutherford Crockett was a Scottish novelist who published under the pen name "S. R. Crockett". He was born on September 24, 1859, in Little Duchrae, Balmaghie, Kirkcudbrightshire, Galloway, as the illegitimate son of dairymaid Annie Crocket. His Cameronian grandparents nurtured him on the tenanted farm until the family relocated to Cotton Street, Castle Douglas in 1867 (later fictionalized as Cairn Edward). In 1876, he obtained the Galloway bursary at Edinburgh University, where he earned an MA. He began his journalistic career in 1877 to support his bursary by writing for journals. He left the university in April 1879 without receiving a diploma. From 1879 to 1881, he traveled throughout Europe as a tutor before returning to Edinburgh's New College to prepare for the ministry. The Crocketts had four children: Maisie Rutherford, Philip Hugh Barbour, George Milner, and Margaret Douglas, all of whom appeared in his children's stories. In 1906, the family relocated from Bank House in Penicuik to Torwood House in Peebles, but Crockett spent much of the year overseas and made frequent trips back to Galloway. In 1886, he released a volume of poetry under the alias Ford Brereton, titled Dulce Cor (Latin for Sweet Heart). Dulce Cor is a ruined abbey in Galloway. In the late 1880s, he was a regular contributor to The Christian Leader magazine, edited by W.H. Wylie.

CONTENTS

CHAPTER I
THE HALL OF THE GUARD

Loud rang the laughter in the hall of the men-at-arms at Castle Kernsberg. There had come an embassy from the hereditary Princess of Plassenburg, recently established upon the throne of her ancestors, to the Duchess Joan of Hohenstein, ruler of that cluster of hill statelets which is called collectively Masurenland, and which includes, besides Hohenstein the original Eagle's Eyrie, Kernsberg also, and Marienfield.

Above, in the hall of audience, the ambassador, one Leopold von Dessauer, a great lord and most learned councillor of state, sat alone with the young Duchess. They were eating of the baked meats and drinking the good Rhenish up there. But, after all, it was much merrier down below with Werner von Orseln, Alt Pikker, Peter Balta, and John of Thorn, though what they ate was mostly but plain ox-flesh, and their drink the strong ale native to the hill lands, which is called Wendish mead.

"Get you down, Captains Jorian and Boris," the young Duchess had commanded, looking very handsome and haughty in the pride of her twenty years, her eight strong castles, and her two thousand men ready to rise at her word; "down to the hall of guard, where my officers send round the wassail. If they do not treat you well, e'en come up and tell it to me."

"Good!" responded the two soldiers of the Princess of Plassenburg, turning them about as if they had been hinged on the same stick, and starting forward with precisely the same stiff hitch from the halt, they made for the door.

"But stay," Joan of Hohenstein had said, ere they reached it, "here are a couple of rings. My father left me one or two such. Fit them upon your fingers, and when you return give them to the maidens of your choice. Is there by chance such an one, Captain Jorian, left behind you at Plassenburg?"

"Aye, madam," said Jorian, directing his left eye, as he stood at attention, a little slantwise in the direction of his companion.

"What is her name?"

"Gretchen is her name," quoth the soldier.

"And yours, Captain Boris?"

The second automaton, a little slower of tongue than his companion, hesitated a moment.

"Speak up," said his comrade, in an undergrowl; "say 'Katrin.'"

"Katrin!" thundered Captain Boris, with bluff apparent honesty.

"It is well," said the Duchess Joan; "I think no less of a sturdy soldier for being somewhat shamefaced as to the name of his sweetheart. Here is a ring apiece which will not shame your maidens in far Plassenburg, as you walk with them under the lime-trees, or buy ribbons for them in the booths that cluster about the Minster walls."

The donor looked at the rings again. She espied the letters of a posy upon them.

"Ha!" she cried, "Captain Boris, what said you was the name of your betrothed?"

"Good Lord!" muttered Boris lowly to himself, "did I not tell the woman even now?—Gretchen!"

"Hut, you fool!" Jorian's undergrowl came to his ear, "Katrin—not Gretchen; Gretchen is mine."

"I mean Katrin, my Lady Duchess," said Boris, putting a bold face on the mistake.

The young mistress of the castle smiled. "Thou art a strange lover," she said, "thus to forget the name of thy mistress. But here is a ring with a K writ large upon it, which will serve for thy Katherina. And here, Captain Jorian, is one with a G scrolled in Gothic, which thou wilt doubtless place with pride upon the finger of Mistress Gretchen among the rose gardens of Plassenburg."

"Good!" said Jorian and Boris, making their bows together; "we thank your most gracious highness."

"Back out, you hulking brute!" the undertone came again from Jorian; "she will be asking us for their surnames if we bide a moment longer. Now then, we are safe through the door; right about, Boris, and thank Heaven she had not time for another question, or we were men undone!"

And with their rings upon their little fingers the two burly captains went down the narrow stair of Castle Kernsberg, nudging each other jovially in the dark places as if they had again been men-at-arms and no captains, as in the old days before the death of Karl the Usurper and the coming back of the legitimate Princess Helene into her rights.

Being arrived at the hall beneath they soon found themselves the centre of a hospitable circle. Gruff, bearded Wendish men were these officers of the young Duchess; not a butterfly youngling or a courtly carpet knight among them, but men tanned like shipmen of the Baltic, soldiers mostly who had served under her father Henry, foraging upon occasion as far as the Mark in one direction and into Bor-Russia in the other, men grounded and compacted after the hearts of Jorian and Boris.

It was small wonder that amid such congenial society the ex-men-at-arms found themselves presently very much at home. Scarcely were they seated when Jorian began to brag of the gift the Duchess had given him for the maiden of his troth.

"And Boris here, that hulking cobold, that Hans Klapper upon the housetops, had well-nigh spoiled the jest; for when her ladyship asked him a second time in her sweet voice for the name of his 'betrothed,' he must needs lay his tongue to 'Gretchen,' instead of 'Katrin,' as he had done at the first!"

Then all suddenly the bearded, burly officers of the Duchess Joan looked at each other with a little scared expression on their faces, through which gradually glimmered up a certain grim amusement. Werner von Orseln, the eldest and gravest of all, glanced round the full circle of his mess. Then he looked back at the two captains of the embassy guard of Plassenburg with a pitying glance.

"And you lied about your sweethearts to the Duchess Joan?" he said.

"Ha, ha! Yes! I trow yes," quoth Jorian jovially. "Wine may be dear, but this ring will pay the sweets of many a night!"

"Ha, ha! It will, will it?" said Werner, the chief captain, grimly.

"Aye, truly," echoed Boris, the mead beginning to work nuttily under his steel cap, "when we melt this—ha, ha!—Katrin's jewel, we'll quaff many a beaker. The Rhenish shall flow-ow-ow! And Peg and Moll and Elisabet shall be there—yes, and many a good fellow-ow-ow——"

"Shut the door!" quoth Werner, the chief captain, at this point. "Sit down, gentlemen!"

But Jorian and Boris were not to be so easily turned aside.

"Call in the ale-drawer—the tapster, the pottler, the over-cellarer, whatever you call him. For we would have more of his vintage. Why, is this a night of jewels, and shall we not melt them? We may chance to get another for a second mouthful of lies to-morrow morning. A good duchess as ever was—a soft princess, a princess most gullible is this of yours, gentlemen of the Eagle's Nest, kerns of Kernsberg!"

"Sit down," said Werner yet more gravely. "Captains Jorian and Boris, you do not seem to know that you are no longer in Plassenburg. The broom bush does not keep the cow betwixt Kernsberg and Hohenstein. Here are no Tables of Karl the Miller's Son to hamper our liege mistress. Do you know that you have lied to her and made a jest of it?"

"Aye," cried Jorian, holding his ring high; "a sweet, easy maid, this of yours, as ever was cozened. An easy service yours must be. Lord! I could feather my nest well inside a year—one short year with such a mistress would do the business. Why, she will believe anything!"

"So," said Werner von Orseln grimly, "you think so, do you, Captains Boris and Jorian, of the embassy staff? Well, listen!"

He spoke very slowly, leaning towards them and punctuating his meaning upon the palm of his left hand with the fingers of his right. "If I, Werner of Orseln, were now to walk upstairs, and in so many words tell my lady, 'the sweet, easy princess,' as you name her, Joan of the Sword Hand, as we are proud — —"

"*Joan of the Sword Hand! Hoch!*"

The men-at-arms at the lower table, the bearded captains at the high board, the very page boys lounging and scuffling in the niches, rose to their feet at the name, pronounced in a voice of thunder-pride by Chief Captain Werner.

"Joan of the Sword Hand! *Hoch!* Hent yourselves up, Wends! Up, Plassenburg! Joan of the Sword Hand! Our Lady Joan! *Hoch!* And three times *hoch*!"

The hurrahs ran round the oak-panelled hall. Jorian and Boris looked at each other with surprise, but they were stout fellows, and took matters, even when most serious, pretty much as they came.

"I thank you, gentlemen, on behalf of my lady, in whose name I command here," said Werner, bowing ceremoniously to all around, while the others settled themselves to listen. "Now, worthy soldiers of Plassenburg," he went on, "be it known to you that if (to suppose a case which will not happen) I were to tell our Lady Joan what you have confessed to us here and boasted of—that you lied and double lied to her—I lay my life and the lives of these good fellows that the pair of you would be aswing from the corner gallery of the Lion's Tower in something under five minutes."

"Aye, and a good deed it were, too!" chorussed the round table of the guard hall. "Heaven send it, the jackanapes! To rail at our Duchess!"

Jorian rose to his feet. "Up, Boris!" he cried; "no Bor-Russian, no kern of Hohenstein that ever lived, shall overcrow a captain of the armies of Plassenburg and a soldier of the Princess Helene—Heaven bless her! Take your ring in your hand, Boris, for we will go up straightway, you and I. And we will tell the Lady Duchess Joan that, having no sweetheart of legal standing, and no desire for any, we choused her into the belief that we would bestow her rings upon our betrothed in the rose-gardens of Plassenburg. Then will we see if indeed we shall be aswing in five minutes. Ready, Boris?"

"Aye, thrice ready, Jorian!"

"About, then! Quick march!"

A great noise of clapping rose all round the hall as the two stout soldiers set themselves to march up the staircase by which they had just descended.

"Stand to the doors!" cried Werner, the chief captain; "do not let them pass. Up and drink a deep cup to them, rather! To Captains Jorian and Boris of Plassenburg, brave fellows both! Charge your tankards. The mead of Wendishland shall not run dry. Fill them to the brim. A caraway seed in each for health's sake. There! Now to the honour and long lives of our guests. Jorian and Boris—*hoch*!"

"*Jorian and Boris—hoch!*"

The toast was drunk amid multitudinous shoutings and handshakings. The two men had stopped, perforce, for the doors were in the hands of the soldiers of the guard, and the pike points clustered thick in their path. They turned now in the direction of the high table from which they had risen.

"Deal you so with your guests who come on embassy?" said Jorian, smiling. "First you threaten them with hanging, and then you would make them drunk with mead as long in the head as the devil of Trier that deceived the Archbishop-Elector and gat the holy coat for a foot-warmer!"

"Sit down, gentlemen, and I also will sit. Now, hearken well," said Werner; "these honest fellows of mine will bear me out that I lie not. You have done bravely and spoken up like good men taken in a fault. But we will not permit you to go to your deaths. For our Lady Joan—God bless her!—would not take a false word from any—no, not if it were on Twelfth Night or after a Christmas merry-making. She would not forgive it from your old Longbeard upstairs, whose business it is—that is, if she found it out. 'To the gallows!' she would say, and we—why then we should sorrow for having to hasten the stretching of two good men. But what would you, gentlemen? We are her servants and we should be obliged to do her will. Keep your rings, lads, and keep also your wits about you when the Duchess questions you again. Nay, when you return to Plassenburg, be wise, seek out a Gretchen and a Katrin and bestow the rings upon them—that is, if ever you mean again to stand within the danger of Joan of the Sword Hand in this her castle of Kernsberg."

"Gretchens are none so scarce in Plassenburg," muttered Jorian. "I think we can satisfy a pair of them—but at a cheaper price than a ring of rubies set in gold!"

CHAPTER II
THE BAITING OF THE SPARHAWK

"Bring in the Danish Sparhawk, and we will bait him!" said Werner. "We have shown our guests but a poor entertainment. Bring in the Sparhawk, I say!"

At this there ensued unyoked merriment. Each stout lad, from one end of the hall to the other, undid his belt as before a nobler course and nudged his fellow.

"'Ware, I say, stand clear! Here comes the Wild Boar of the Ardennes, the Wolf of Thuringia, the Bear from the Forests of Bor-Russia! Stand clear—stand clear!" cried Werner von Orseln, laughing and pretending to draw a dagger to provide for his own safety.

The inner door which led from the hall of the men-at-arms to the dungeons of the castle was opened, and all looked towards it with an air of great amusement and expectation.

"Now we shall have some rare sport," each man said to his neighbour, and nodded.

"The baiting of the Sparhawk! The Sparhawk comes!"

Jorian and Boris looked with interest in the direction of the door through which such a remarkable bird was to arrive. They could not understand what all the pother could be about.

"What the devil——?" said Jorian.

And, not to be behindhand, "What the devil——?" echoed Boris. For mostly these two ran neck and neck from drop of flag to winning-post.

Through the black oblong of the dungeon doorway there came a lad of seventeen or eighteen, tall, slim, dark-browed, limber. He walked between a pair of men-at-arms, who held his wrists firmly at either side. His hands were chained together, and from between them dangled a spiked ball that clanked heavily on the floor as he stumbled forward rather than walked into the room. He had black hair that waved from his forehead in a backward sweep, a nose of slightly Roman shape, which, together with his bold eagle's eyes, had obtained him the name of the Spar or Sparrow-hawk. And on his face, handsome enough though pale, there was a look of haughty disdain and fierce indignation such as one may see in the demeanour of a newly prisoned bird of prey, which hath not yet had time to forget the blue empyrean spaces and the stoop with half-closed wings upon the quarry trembling in the vale.

"Ha, Sparhawk!" cried Werner, "how goes it, Sparhawk? Any less bold and peremptory than when last we met? Your servant, Count Maurice von Lynar! We pray you dance for us the Danish dance of shuffle-board, Count Maurice, if so your Excellency pleases!"

The lad looked up the table and down with haughty eyes that deigned no answer.

Werner von Orseln turned to his guests and said, "This Sparhawk is a little Dane we took on our last excursion to the north. It is only in that direction we can lead the foray, since you have grown so law-abiding and strong in Plassenburg and the Mark. His uncles and kinsfolk were all killed in the defence of Castle Lynar, on the Northern Haff. We know not which of these had also the claim of fatherhood upon him. At all events, his grandad had a manor there, and came from the Jutland sand-dunes to build a castle upon the Baltic shores. But he had better have stayed at home, for he would not pay the Peace Geld to our Henry. So the Lion roared, and we went to Castle Lynar and made an end—save of this spitting Sparhawk, whom our master would not let us kill, and whom now we keep with clipped wings for our sport."

The lad listened with erected head and haughty eyes to the tale, but answered not a word.

"Now," cried Werner, with his cup in his hand and his brows bent upon the youth, "dance for us as you used to do upon the Baltic, when the maids came in fresh from their tiring and the newest kirtles were donned. Dance, I say! Foot it for your life!"

The lad Maurice von Lynar stood with his bold eyes upon his tormentors. "Curs of Bor-Russia," he said at last, in speech that trembled with anger, "you may vex the soul of a Danish gentleman with your aspersions, you may wound his body, but you will never be able to stand up to him in battle. You will never be worthy to eat or drink with him, to take his hand in comradeship, or to ride a tilt with him. Pigs of the sty you are, man by man of you—Wends and boors, and no king's gentlemen."

"Bravo!" said Boris, under his breath, "that is none so dustily said for a junker!"

"Silence with that tongue of yours!" muttered his mate. "Dost want to be yawing out of that window presently, with the wind spinning you about and about like a capon on a jack-spit? They are uncanny folk, these of the woman's castle—not to trust to. One knows not what they may do, nor where their jest may end."

"Hans Trenck, lift this springald's pretty wrist-bauble!" said Werner.

A laughing man-at-arms went up, his partisan still over his shoulder, and laying his hand upon the chain which depended between the manacled wrists of the boy Maurice, he strove to lift the spiked ball.

"What!" cried Werner, "canst thou, pap-backed babe, not lift that which the noble Count Maurice of Lynar has perforce to carry about with him all day long? Down with your weapon, man, and to it like an apothecary compounding some blister for stale fly-blown rogues!"

At the word the man laid down his partisan and lifted the ball high between his two hands.

"Now dance!" commanded Werner von Orseln, "dance the Danish milkmaid's coranto, or I will bid him drop it on your toes. Dost want them jellied, man?"

"Drop, and be damned in your low-born souls!" cried the lad fiercely. "Untruss my hands and let me loose with a sword, and ten yards clear on the floor, and, by Saint Magnus of the Isles, I will disembowel any three of you!"

"You will not dance?" said Werner, nodding at him.

"I will see you fry in hell fire first!"

"Down with the ball, Hans Trenck!" cried Werner. "He that will not dance at Castle Kernsberg must learn at least to jump."

The man-at-arms, still grinning, lifted the ball a little higher, balancing it in one hand to give it more force. He prepared to plump it heavily upon the undefended feet of young Maurice.

"'Ware toes, Sparhawk!" cried the soldiers in chorus, but at that moment, suddenly kicking out as far as his chains allowed, the boy took the stooping lout on the face, and incontinently widened the superficial area of his mouth. He went over on his back amid the uproarious laughter of his fellows.

"Ha! Hans Trenck, the Sparhawk hath spurred you, indeed! A brave Sparhawk! Down went poor Hans Trenck like a barndoor fowl!"

The fellow rose, spluttering angrily.

"Hold his legs, some one," he said, "I'll mark his pretty feet for him. He shall not kick so free another time."

A couple of his companions took hold of the boy on either side, so that he could not move his limbs, and Hans again lifted high the ball.

"Shall we stand this? They call this sport!" said Boris; "shall I pink the brutes?"

"Sit down and shut your eyes. Our Prince Hugo will harry this nest of thieves anon. For the present we must bear their devilry if we want to escape hanging!"

"Now then, for marrow and mashed trotters!" cried Hans, spitting the blood from the split corners of his mouth.

"*Halt!*"

CHAPTER III
JOAN DRAWS FIRST BLOOD

The word of command came full and strong from the open doorway of the hall.

Hans Trenck came instantly to the salute with the ball in his hand. He had no difficulty in lifting it now. In fact, he did not seem able to let it down. Every man in the hall except the two captains of Plassenburg had risen to his feet and stood as if carved in marble.

For there in the doorway, her slim figure erect and exceedingly commanding, and her beautiful eyes shining with indignation, stood the Duchess Joan of Hohenstein.

"Joan of the Sword Hand!" said Jorian, enraptured. "Gott, what a wench!"

In stern silence she advanced into the hall, every man standing fixed at attention.

"Good discipline!" said Boris.

"Shut your mouth!" responded Jorian.

"Keep your hand so, Hans Trenck," said their mistress; "give me your sword, Werner! You shall see whether I am called Joan of the Sword Hand for naught. You would torture prisoners, would you, after what I have said? Hold up, I say, Hans Trenck!"

And so, no man saying her nay, the girl took the shining blade and, with a preliminary swish through the air and a balancing shake to feel the elastic return, she looked at the poor knave fixed before her in the centre of the hall with his wrist strained to hold the prisoner's ball aloft at the stretch of his arm. What wonder if it wavered like a branch in an uncertain wind?

"Steady there!" said Joan.

And she drew back her arm for the stroke.

The young Dane, who, since her entrance, had looked at nothing save the radiant beauty of the figure before him, now cried out, "For Heaven's sake, lady, do not soil the skirts of your dress with his villain blood. He but obeyed his orders. Let me be set free, and I will fight him or any man in the castle. And if I am beaten, let them torture me till I am carrion fit only to be thrown into the castle ditch."

The Duchess paused and leaned on the sword, holding it point to the floor.

"By whose orders was this thing done?" she demanded.

The lad was silent. He disdained to tell tales even on his enemies. Was he not a gentleman and a Dane?

"By mine, my lady!" said Werner von Orseln, a deep flush upon his manly brow.

The girl looked severely at him. She seemed to waver. "Good, then!" she said, "the Dane shall fight Werner for his life. Loose him and chafe his wrists. Ho! there—bring a dozen swords from the armoury!"

The flush was now rising to the boy's cheek.

"I thank you, Duchess," he said. "I ask no more than this."

"Faith, the Sparhawk is not tamed yet," said Boris; "we shall see better sport ere all be done!"

"Hold thy peace," growled Jorian, "and look."

"Out into the light!" cried the young Duchess Joan, pointing the way with Werner's sword, which she still held in her hand. And going first she went forth from the hall of the soldiery, down the broad stairs, and soon through a low-arched door with a sculptured coat-of-arms over it, out into the quadrangle of the courtyard.

"And now we will see this prisoner of ours, this cock of the Danish marches, make good his words. That, surely, is better sport than to drop caltrops upon the toes of manacled men."

Werner followed unwillingly and with deep flush of shame upon his brow.

"My lady," he said, going up to his mistress, "I do not need to prove my courage after I have served Kernsberg and Hohenstein for thirty-eight years—or well-nigh twice the years you have lived—fought for you and your father and shed my blood in a score of pitched battles, to say nothing of forays. Of course I will fight, but surely this young cockerel might be satisfied to have his comb cut by younger hands."

"Was yours the order concerning the dropping of the ball?" asked the Duchess Joan.

The grey-headed soldier nodded grimly.

"I gave the order," he said briefly.

"Then by St. Ursula and her boneyard, you must stand to it!" cried this fiery young woman. "Else will I drub you with the flat of your own sword!"

Werner bowed with a slightly ironic smile on his grizzled face.

"As your ladyship wills," he said; "I do not give you half obedience. If you say that I am to get down on my knees and play cat's cradle with the Kernsberg bairns, I will do it!"

Joan of the Sword here looked calmly at him with a certain austerity in her glance.

"Why, of course you would!" she said simply.

Meanwhile the lad had been freed from his bonds and stood with a sword in his hand suppling himself for the work before him with quick little guards and feints and attacks. There was a proud look in his eyes, and as his glance left the Duchess and roved round the circle of his foes, it flashed full, bold, and defiant.

Werner turned to a palish lean Bohemian who stood a little apart.

"Peter Balta," he said, "will you be my second? Agreed! And who will care for my honourable opponent?"

"Do not trouble yourself—that will arrange itself!" said Joan to her chief captain.

With that she flashed lightfoot into one of the low doors which led into the flanking turrets of the quadrangle, and in a tierce of seconds she was out again, in a forester's dress of green doublet and broad pleated kirtle that came to her knee.

"I myself," she said, challenging them with her eyes, "will be this young man's second, in this place where he has so many enemies and no friends."

As the forester in green and the prisoner stood up together, the guards murmured in astonishment at the likeness between them.

"Had this Dane and our Joan been brother and sister, they could not have favoured each other more," they said.

A deep blush rose to the youth's swarthy face.

"I am not worthy," he said, and kept his eyes upon the lithe figure of the girl in its array of well-fitting velvet. "I cannot thank you!" he said again.

"Tut," she answered, "worthy—unworthy—thank—unthank—what avail these upon the mountains of Kernsberg and in the Castle of Joan of the Sword Hand? A good heart, a merry fight, a quick death! These are more to the purpose than many thanks and compliments. Peter Balta, are you seconding Werner? Come hither. Let us try the swords, you and I. Will not these two serve? Guard! Well smitten! There, enough. What, you are touched on the sword arm? Faith, man, for the moment I forgot that it was not you and I who were to drum. This tickling of steel goes to my head like wine and I am bound to forget. I am sorry—but, after all, a day or two in a sling will put your arm to rights again, Peter. These are good swords. Now then, Maurice von Lynar—Werner. At the salute! Ready! Fall to!"

The burly figure of the Captain Werner von Orseln and the slim arrowy swiftness of Maurice the Dane were opposed in the clear shadow of the quadrangle, where neither had any advantage of light, and the swords of their seconds kept them at proper distance according to the fighting rules of the time.

"I give the Sparhawk five minutes," said Boris to Jorian, after the first parry. It was little more than formal and gave no token of what was to follow. Yet for full twenty minutes Werner von Orseln, the oldest sworder of all the north, from the marshes of Wilna to the hills of Silesia, could do nothing but stand on the defensive, so fierce and incessant were the attacks of the young Dane.

But Werner did not give back. He stood his ground, warily, steadfastly, with a half smile on his face, a wall of quick steel in front of him, and the point of his adversary's blade ever missing him an inch at this side, and coming an inch short upon that other. The Dane kept as steadily to the attack, and made his points as much by his remarkable nimbleness upon his feet as by the lightning rapidity of his sword-play.

"The Kernsberger is playing with him!" said Boris, under his breath.

Jorian nodded. He had no breath to waste.

"But he is not going to kill him. He has not the Death in his eye!" Boris spoke with judgment, for so it proved. Werner lifted an eyebrow for the fraction of a second towards his mistress. And then at the end of the next rally his sword just touched his young adversary on the shoulder and the blood answered the thrust, staining the white underdoublet of the Dane.

Then Werner threw down his sword and held out his hand.

"A well-fought rally," he said; "let us be friends. We need lads of such metal to ride the forays from the hills of Kernsberg. I am sorry I baited you, Sparhawk!"

"A good fight clears all scores!" replied the youth, smiling in his turn.

"Bring a bandage for his shoulder, Peter Balta!" cried Joan. "Mine was the cleaner stroke which went so near your great muscle, but Werner's is somewhat the deeper. You can keep each other company at the dice-box these next days. And, as I warrant neither of you has a Lübeck guilder to bless yourself with, you can e'en play for love till you wear out the pips with throwing."

"Then I am not to go back to the dungeon?" said the lad, one reason of whose wounding had been that he also lifted his eyes for a moment to those of his second.

"To prison—no," said Joan; "you are one of us now. We have blooded you. Do you take service with me?"

"I have no choice—your father left me none!" the lad replied, quickly altering his phrase. "Castle Lynar is no more. My grandfather, my father, and my uncles are all dead, and there is small service in going back to Denmark, where there are more than enough of hungry gentlemen with no wealth but their swords and no living but their gentility. If you will let me serve in the ranks, Duchess Joan, I shall be well content!"

"I also," said Joan heartily. "We are all free in Kernsberg, even if we are not all equal. We will try you in the ranks first. Go to the men's quarters. George the Hussite, I deliver him to you. See that he does not get into any more quarrels till his arm is better, and curb my rascals' tongues as far as you can. Remember who meddles with the principal must reckon with the second."

CHAPTER IV
THE COZENING OF THE AMBASSADOR

The next moment Joan had disappeared, and when she was seen again she had assumed the skirt she had previously worn over her dress of forester, and was again the sedate lady of the castle, ready to lead the dance, grace the banquet, or entertain the High State's Councillor of Plassenburg, Leopold von Dessauer.

But when she went upstairs she met on the middle flight a grey-bearded man with a skull cap of black velvet upon his head. His dress also was of black, of a distinguishing plain richness and dignity.

"Whither away, Ambassador?" she cried gaily at the sight of him.

"To see to your principal's wound and that of the other whom your sword countered in the trial bout!"

"What? You saw?" said the Duchess, with a quick flush.

"I am indeed privileged not to be blind," said Dessauer; "and never did I see a sight that contented me more."

"And you stood at the window saying in your heart (nay, do not deny it) 'unwomanly—bold—not like my lady the Princess of Plassenburg. She would not thus ruffle in the courtyard with the men-at-arms!'"

"I said no such thing," said the High Councillor. "I am an old man and have seen many fair women, many sweet princesses, each perfect to their lovers, some of them even perfect to their lords. But I have never before seen a Duchess Joan of Hohenstein."

"Ambassador," cried the girl, "if you speak thus and with that flash of the eye, I shall have to bethink me whether you come not as an ambassador for your own cause."

"I would that I were forty years younger and a prince in my own right, instead of a penniless old baron. Why, then, I would not come on any man's errand—no, nor take a refusal even from your fair lips!"

"I declare," said the Duchess Joan impetuously, "you should have no refusal from me. You are the only man I have ever met who can speak of love and yet be tolerable. It is a pity that my father left me the evil heritage that I must wed the Prince of Courtland or lose my dominions!"

At the sound of the name of her predestined husband a sudden flashing thought seemed to wake in the girl's breast.

"My lord," she said, "is it true that you go to Courtland after leaving our poor eagle's nest up here on the cliffs of the Kernsberg?"

Von Dessauer bowed, smiling at her. He was not too old to love beauty and frankness in women. "It is true that I have a mission from my Prince and Princess to the Prince of Courtland and Wilna. But— —"

Joan of the Sword clasped her hands and drew a long breath.

"I would not ask it of any man in the world but yourself," she said, "but will you let me go with you?"

"My dear lady," said Dessauer, with swift deprecation, "to go with the ambassador of another power to the court and palace of the man you are to marry—that were a tale indeed, salt enough even for the Princes of Ritterdom. As it is— —"

The Duchess looked across at Dessauer with great haughtiness. "As it is, they talk more than enough about me already," she said. "Well—I know, and care not. I am no puling maid that waits till she is authorised by a conclave of the empire before she dares wipe her nose when she hath a cold in the head. Joan of the Sword Hand cares not what any prince may say— from yours of Plassenburg, him of the Red Axe, to the fat Margraf George."

"Oh, our Prince, he says naught, but does much," said Dessauer. "He hath been a rough blade in his time, but Karl the Miller's son mellowed him, and by now his own Princess hath fairly civilised him."

"Well," said Joan of the Sword, with determination, "then it is settled. I am coming with you to Courtland."

A shade of anxiety passed over Dessauer's countenance. "My lady," he answered, "you let me use many freedoms of speech with you. It is the privilege of age and frailty. But let me tell you that the thing is plainly foolish. Hardly under the escort of the Empress herself would it be possible for you to visit, without scandal, the court of the Prince of Courtland and Wilna. But in the train of an envoy of Plassenburg, even if that ambassador be poor old Leopold von Dessauer, the thing, I must tell you, is frankly impossible."

"Well, I am coming, at any rate!" said Joan, as usual rejecting argument and falling back upon assertion. "Make your count with that, friend of mine, whether you are shocked or no. It is the penalty a respectable diplomatist has to pay for cultivating the friendship of lone females like Joan of Hohenstein."

Von Dessauer held up his hands in horror that was more than half affected.

"My girl," he said, "I might be your grandfather, it is true, but do not remind me of it too often. But if I were your great-great-grandfather the thing you propose is still impossible. Think of what the Margraf George and his chattering train would say!"

"Think of what every fathead princeling and beer-swilling ritter from here to Basel would say!" cried Joan, with her pretty nose in the air. "Let them say! They will not say anything that I care the snap of my finger for. And in their hearts they will envy you the experience—shall we say the privilege?"

"Nay, I thought not of myself, my lady," said Dessauer, "for an old man, a mere anatomy of bones and parchment, I take strange pleasure in your society—more than I ought, I tell you frankly. You are to me more than a daughter, though I am but a poor baron of Plassenburg and the faithful servant of the Princess Helene. It is for your own sake that I say you cannot come to Wilna with me. Shall the future Princess of Courtland and Wilna ride in the train of an ambassador of Plassenburg to the palace in which she is soon to reign as queen?"

"I said not that I would go as the Duchess," Joan replied, speaking low. "You say that you saw me at the fight in the courtyard out there. If you will not have the Duchess Joan von Hohenstein, what say you to the Sparhawk's second, Johann the Squire?"

Dessauer started.

"You dare not," he said; "why, there is not a lady in the German land, from Bohemia to the Baltic, that dares do as much."

"Ladies," flashed Joan—"I am sick for ever of hearing that a lady must not do this or that, go here or there, because of her so fragile reputation. She may do needlework or embroider altar-cloths, but she must not shoot with a pistolet or play with a sword. Well, I am a lady; let him counter it who durst. And I cannot broider altar-cloths and I will not try—but I can shoot with any man at the flying mark. She must have a care for her honour, which (poor, feckless wretch!) will be smirched if she speaks to any as a man speaks to his fellows. Faith! For me I would rather die than have such an egg-shell reputation. I can care for mine own. I need none to take up my quarrel. If any have a word to say upon the repute of Joan of the Sword Hand—why, let him say it at the point of her rapier."

The girl stood up, tall and straight, her head thrown back as it were at the world, with an exact and striking counterpart of the defiance of the young Dane in the presence of his enemies an hour before. Dessauer stood wavering. With quick tact she altered her tone, and with a soft accent and in a melting voice she added, "Ah, let me come. I will make such a creditable squire all in a suit of blue and silver, with just a touch of nutty juice upon my face that my old nurse knows the secret of."

Still Dessauer stood silent, weighing difficulties and chances.

"I tell you what," she cried, pursuing her advantage, "I will see the man I am to marry as men see him, without trappings and furbelows. And if you will not take me, by my faith! I will send Werner there, whom you saw fight the Dane, as my own envoy, and go with him as a page. On the honour of Henry the Lion, my father, I will do it!"

Von Dessauer capitulated. "A wilful woman"—he smiled—"a wilful, wilful woman. Well, I am not responsible for aught of this, save for my own weakness in permitting it. It is a madcap freak, and no good will come of it."

"But you will like it!" she said. "Oh, yes, you will like it very much. For, you see, you are fond of madcaps."

CHAPTER V
JOHANN THE SECRETARY

Ten miles outside the boundary of the little hill state of Kernsberg, the embassage of Plassenburg was met by another cavalcade bearing additional instructions from the Princess Helene. The leader was a slender youth of middle height, the accuracy of whose form gave evidence of much agility. He was dark-skinned, of an olive complexion, and with closely cropped black hair which curled crisply about his small head. His eyes were dark and fine, looking straightly and boldly out upon all comers.

With him, as chiefs of his escort, were those two silent men Jorian and Boris, who had, as it was reported, ridden to Plassenburg for instructions. None of those who followed Dessauer had ever before set eyes upon this youth, who came with fresh despatches, and, in consequence, great was the consternation and many the surmises as to who he might be who stood so high in favour with the Prince and Princess.

But his very first words made the matter clear.

"Your Excellency," he said to the Ambassador, "I bring you the most recent instructions from their Highnesses Hugo and Helene of Plassenburg. They sojourn for the time being in the city of Thorn, where they build a new palace for themselves. I was brought from Hamburg to be one of the master-builders. I have skill in plans, and I bring you these for your approval and in order to go over the rates of cost with you, as Treasurer of Plassenburg and the Wolfsmark."

Dessauer took, with every token of deference, the sheaf of papers so carefully enwrapt and sealed with the seal of Plassenburg.

"I thank you for your diligence, good master architect," he said; "I shall peruse these at my leisure, and, I doubt not, call upon you frequently for explanations."

The young man rode on at his side, modestly waiting to be questioned.

"What is your name, sir?" asked Dessauer, so that all the escort might hear.

"I am called Johann Pyrmont," said the youth promptly, and with engaging frankness; "my father is a Hamburg merchant, trading to the Spanish ports for oil and wine, but I follow him not. I had ever a turn for drawing and the art of design!"

"Also for having your own way, as is common with the young," said the Ambassador, smiling shrewdly. "So, against your father's will, you apprenticed yourself to an architect?"

The young man bowed.

"Nay, sir," he said, "but my good father could deny me nothing on which I had set my mind."

"Not he," muttered Dessauer under his breath; "no, nor any one else either!"

So, bridle by jingling bridle, they rode on over the interminable plain till Kernsberg, with its noble crown of towers, became first grey and afterwards pale blue in the utmost distance. Then, like a tall ship at sea, it sank altogether out of sight. And still they rode on through the marshy hollows, round innumerable little wildfowl-haunted lakelets, and so over the sandy, rolling dunes to the city of Courtland, where was abiding the Prince of that rich and noble principality.

It had been a favourite scheme of dead princes of Courtland to unite to their fat acres and populous mercantile cities the hardy mountaineers and pastoral uplands of Kernsberg. But though Wilna and Courtland were infinitely more populous, the Eagle's Nest was ill to pull down, and hitherto the best laid plans for their union had invariably fallen through. But there had come to Joan's father, Henry called the Lion, and the late Prince Michael of Courtland a better thought. One had a daughter, the other a son. Neither was burdened with any law of succession, Salic or other. They held their domains by the free tenure of the sword. They could leave their powers to whomsoever they would, not even the Emperor having the right to say, "What doest thou?" So with that frank carelessness of the private feelings of the individual which has ever distinguished great politicians, they decreed that, as a condition of succession, their male and female heirs should marry each other.

This bond of Heritage-brotherhood, as it was called, had received the sanction of the Emperor in full Diet, and now it wanted only that the Duchess Joan of Hohenstein should be of age, in order that the provinces might at last be united and the long wars of highland and lowland make an end.

The scheme had taken everything into consideration except the private character of the persons principally affected, Prince Louis of Courtland and the young Duchess Joan.

As they came nearer to the ancient city of Courtland, it spread like a metropolis before the eyes of the embassy of the Prince and Princess of Plassenburg. The city stretched from the rock whereon the fortress-palace was built, along a windy, irregular ridge. Innumerable crow-stepped gables were set at right angles to the street. The towers of the minster rose against the sky at the lower end, and far to the southward the palace of the Cardinal Archbishop cast peaked shadows from its many towers, walled and cinctured like a city within a city.

It was a far-seen town this of Courtland, populous, prosperous, defenced. Its clear and broad river was navigable for any craft of the time, and already it threatened to equal if not to outstrip in importance the free cities of the Hanseatic League—so far, at least, as the trade of the Baltic was concerned.

Courtland had long been considered too strong to be attacked, save from the Polish border, while the adhesion of Kernsberg, and the drafting of the Duchess's hardy fighting mountaineers into the lowland armies would render the princedom safe for many generations.

Pity it was that plans so far-reaching and purposes so politic should be dependent upon the whims of a girl!

But then it is just such whims that make the world interesting.

It was the last day of the famous tournament of the Black Eagle in the princely city of Courtland. Prince Louis had sent out an escort to bring in the travellers and conduct them with honour to the seats reserved for them. The Ambassador and High Councillor of Plassenburg must be received with all observance. He had, he gave notice, brought a secretary with him. For so the young architect was now styled, in order to give him an official position in the mission.

The Prince had also sent a request that, as this was the day upon which all combatants wore plain armour and jousted unknown, for that time being the Ambassador should accept other escort and excuse him coming to receive him in person. They would meet at dinner on the morrow, in the great hall of the palace.

The city was arrayed in flaming banners, some streaming high from the lofty towers of the cathedral, while others (in streets into which the wind came only in puffs) more languidly and luxuriously unfolded themselves, as the Black Eagle on its ground of white everywhere took the air. All over the city a galaxy of lighter silk and bunting, pennons, bannerettes, particoloured streamers of the national colours danced becking and bowing from window and roof-tree.

Yet there was a curious silence too in the streets, as they rode towards the lists of the Black Eagle, and when at last they came within hearing of the hum of the thousands gathered there, they understood why the city had seemed so unwontedly deserted. The Courtlanders surrounded the great oval space of the lists in clustered myriads, and their eyes were bent inwards. It was the crisis of the great *mêlée*. Scarcely an eye in all that assembly was turned towards the strangers, who passed quite unobserved to their reserved places in the Prince's empty box. Only his sister Margaret, throned on high as Queen of Beauty, looked down upon them with interest, seeing that they were men who came, and that one at least was young.

It was a gay and changeful scene. In the brilliant daylight of the lists a hundred knights charged and recharged. Those who had been unhorsed drew their swords and attacked with fury others of the enemy in like case. The air resounded with the clashing of steel on steel.

Fifty knights with white plumes on their helmets had charged fifty wearing black, and the combat still raged. The shouts of the people rang in the ears of the ambassador of Plassenburg and his secretary, as they seated themselves and looked down upon the tide of combat over the flower-draped balustrades of their box.

"The blacks have it!" said Dessauer after regarding the *mêlée* with interest. "We have come in time to see the end of the fray. Would that we had also seen the shock!"

And indeed the Blacks seemed to have carried all before them. They were mostly bigger and stronger built men, knights of the landward provinces, and their horses, great solid-boned Saxon chargers, had by sheer weight borne their way through the lighter ranks of the Baltic knights on the white horses.

Not more than half a dozen of these were now in saddle, and all over the field were to be seen black knights receiving the submission of knights whose broken spears and tarnished plumes showed that they had succumbed in the charge to superior weight of metal. For, so soon as a knight yielded, his steed became the property of his victorious foe, and he himself was either carried or limped as best he could to the pavilion of his party, there to remove his armour and send it also to the victor—to whom, in literal fact, belonged the spoils.

Of the half-dozen white knights who still kept up the struggle, one shone pre-eminent for dashing valour. His charger surged hither and thither through the crowd, his spear was victorious and unbroken, and the boldest opponent thought it politic to turn aside out of his path. Set upon by more than a score of riders, he still managed to evade them, and even when all his side had submitted and he alone remained—at the end of the lists to which he had been driven, he made him ready for a final charge into the scarce broken array of his foes, of whom more than twenty remained still on horseback in the field.

But though his spear struck true in the middle of his immediate antagonist's shield and his opponent went down, it availed the brave white knight nothing. For at the same moment half a score of lances struck him on the shield, on the breastplate, on the vizor bars of his helmet, and he fell heavily to the earth. Nevertheless, scarcely had he touched the ground when he was again on his feet. Sword in hand, he stood for a moment unscathed and undaunted, while his foes, momentarily disordered by the energy of the charge, reined in their steeds ere they could return to the attack.

"Oh, well ridden!" "Greatly done!" "A most noble knight!" These were the exclamations which came from all parts of the crowd which surged about the barriers on this great day.

"I would that I were down beside him with a sword in my hand also!" said the young architect, Master Johann Pyrmont, secretary of the embassage of Plassenburg.

"'Tis well you are where you are, madcap, sitting by an old man's side, instead of fighting by that of a young one," growled Dessauer. "Else then, indeed, the bent would be on fire."

But at this moment the Princess Margaret, sister of the reigning Prince, rose in her place and threw down the truncheon, which in such cases stops the combat.

"The black knights have won," so she gave her verdict, "but there is no need to humiliate or injure a knight who has fought so well against so many. Let the white knight come hither—though he be of the losing side. His is the reward of highest honour. Give him a steed, that he may come and receive the meed of bravest in the tourney!"

The knights of the black were manifestly a little disappointed that after their victory one of their opponents should be selected for honour. But there was no appeal from the decision of the Queen of Love and Beauty. For that day she reigned alone, without council or diet imperial.

The black riders had therefore to be contented with their general victory, which, indeed, was indisputable enough.

The white knight came near and said something in a low voice, unheard by the general crowd, to the Princess.

"I insist," she said aloud; "you must unhelm, that all may see the face of him who has won the prize."

Whereat the knight bowed and undid his helmet. A closely-cropped fair-haired head was revealed, the features clearly chiselled and yet of a grave and massive beauty, the head of a marble emperor.

"My brother—you!" cried Margaret of Courtland in astonishment.

The voice of the Princess had also something of disappointment in it. Clearly she had wished for some other to receive the honour, and the event did not please her. But it was otherwise with the populace.

"The young Prince! The young Prince!" cried the people, surging impetuously about the barriers. "Glory to the noble house of Courtland and to the brave Prince."

The Ambassador looked curiously at his secretary. That youth was standing with eyes brilliant as those of a man in fever. His face had paled even under its dusky tan. His lips quivered. He straightened himself up as brave and generous men do when they see a deed of bravery done by another, or like a woman who sees the man she loves publicly honoured.

"The Prince!" said Johann Pyrmont, in a voice hoarse and broken; "it is the Prince himself."

And on his high seat the State's Councillor, Leopold von Dessauer, smiled well pleased.

"This turns out better than I had expected," he muttered. "God Himself favours the drunkard and the madcap. Only wise men suffer for their sins— aye, and often for those of other people as well."

CHAPTER VI
AN AMBASSADOR'S AMBASSADOR

After the tourney of the Black Eagle, Leopold von Dessauer had gone to bed early, feeling younger and lighter than he had done for years. Part of his scheme for these northern provinces of his fatherland consisted in gradual substitution of a few strong states for many weak ones. For this reason he smiled when he saw the eyes of his secretary shining like stars.

It would yet more have rejoiced him had he known how uneasy lay that handsome head on its pillow. Aye, even in pain it would have pleasured him. For Von Dessauer was lying awake and thinking of the strange chances which help or mar the lives of men and women, when a sudden sense of shock, a numbness spreading upwards through his limbs, the rising of rheum to his eyes, and a humming in his ears, announced the approach of one of those attacks to which he had been subject ever since he had been wounded in a duel some years before—a duel in which his present Prince and his late master, Karl the Miller's Son, had both been engaged.

The Ambassador called for Jorian in a feeble voice. That light-sleeping soldier immediately answered him. He had stretched himself out, wrapped in a blanket for all covering, on the floor of the antechamber in Dessauer's lodging. In a moment, therefore, he presented himself at the door completely dressed. A shake and a half-checked yawn completed his inexpensive toilet, for Jorian prided himself on not being what he called "a pretty-pretty captainet."

"Your Excellency needs me?" he said, standing at the salute as if it had been the morning guard changing at the palace gate.

"Give me my case of medicine," said the old man; "that in the bag of rough Silesian leather. So! I feel my old attack coming upon me. It will be three days before I can stir. Yet must these papers be put in the hands of the Prince early this morning. Ah, there is my little Johann; I was thinking about her—him, I mean. Well, he shall have his chance. This foul easterly wind may yet blow us all good!"

He made a wry face as a twinge of pain caught him. It passed and he resumed.

"Go, Jorian," he said, "tap light upon his chamber door. If he chance to be in the deep sleep of youth and health—not yet distempered by thought and love, by old age and the eating of many suppers—rap louder, for I must see him forthwith. There is much to set in order ere at nine o'clock he must adjourn to the summer palace to meet the Prince."

So in a trice Jorian was gone and at the door of the architect-secretary, he of the brown skin and Greekish profile.

Johann Pyrmont was, it appeared, neither in bed nor yet asleep. Instead, he had been standing at the window watching the brighter stars swim up one by one out of the east. The thoughts of the young man were happy thoughts. At last he was in the capital city of the Princes of Courtland. His many days' journey had not been in vain. Almost in the first moment he had seen the noble youthful Prince and his sister, and he was prepared to like them both. Life held more than the preparation of plans and the ordering of bricklayers at their tasks. There was in it, strangely enough, a young man with closely cropped head whom Johann had seen storm through the ranks of the fighting-men that day, and afterwards receive the guerdon of the bravest.

Though what difference these things made to an architect of Hamburg town it was difficult (on the face of things) to perceive. Nevertheless, he stood and watched the east. It was five of a clear autumnal morning, and a light chill breath blew from the point at which the sun would rise.

A pale moon in her last quarter was tossed high among the stars, as if upborne upon the ebbing tide of night. Translucent greyness filled the wide plain of Courtland, and in the scattered farms all about the lights, which signified early horse-tending and the milking of kine, were already beginning to outrival the waning stars. Orion, with his guardian four set wide about him, tingled against the face of the east, and the electric lamp of Sirius burnt blue above the horizon. The lightness and the hope of breathing morn, the scent of fields half reaped, the cool salt wind from off the sea, filled the channels of the youth's life. It was good to be alive, thought Johann Pyrmont, architect of Hamburg, or otherwise.

Jorian rapped low, with more reverence than is common from captains to secretaries of legations. The young man was leaning out of the window and did not hear. The ex-man-at-arms rapped louder. At the sound Johann Pyrmont clapped his hand to the hip where his sword should have been.

"Who is there?" he asked, turning about with keen alertness, and in a voice which seemed at once sweeter and more commanding than even the most imperious master-builder would naturally use to his underlings.

"I—Jorian! His Excellency is taken suddenly ill and bade me come for you."

Immediately the secretary opened the door, and in a few seconds stood at the old man's bedside.

Here they talked low to each other, the young man with his hand laid tenderly on the forehead of his elder. Only their last words concern us at present.

"This will serve to begin my business and to finish yours. Thereafter the sooner you return to Kernsberg the better. Remember the moon cannot long be lost out of the sky without causing remark."

The young man received the Ambassador's papers and went out. Dessauer took a composing draught and lay back with a sigh.

"It is humbling," he said to Jorian, "that to compose young wits you must do it through the heart, but in the case of the old through the stomach."

"'Tis a strange draught *he* hath gotten," said the soldier, indicating the door by which the secretary had gone forth. "If I be not mistaken, much water shall flow under bridge ere his sickness be cured."

As soon as he had reached his own chamber Johann laid the papers upon the table without glancing at them. He went again to the window and looked across the city. During his brief absence the stars had thinned out. Even the moon was now no brighter than so much grey ash. But the east had grown red and burned a glorious arch of cool brightness, with all its cloud edges teased loosely into fretted wisps and flakes of changeful fire. The wind began to blow more largely and stately before the coming of the sun. Johann drew a long breath and opened wide both halves of the casement.

"To-day I shall see the Prince!" he said.

It was exactly nine of the clock when he set out for the palace. He was attired in the plain black dress of a secretary, with only the narrowest corded edge and collar of rough-scrolled gold. The slimness of his waist was filled in so well that he looked no more than a well-grown, clean-limbed stripling of twenty. A plain sword in a scabbard of black leather was belted to his side, and he carried his papers in his hand sealed with seals and wrapped carefully about with silken ties. Yet, for all this simplicity, the eyes of Johann Pyrmont were so full of light, and his beauty of face so surprising, that all turned to look after him as he went by with a free carriage and a swing to his gait.

Even the market girls ran together to gaze after the young stranger. Maids of higher degree called sharply to each other and crowded the balconies to look down upon him. But through the busy morning tumult of the streets Johann Pyrmont walked serene and unconscious. Was not he going to the summer palace to see the Prince?

At the great door of the outer pavilion he intimated his desire to the officer in charge of the guard.

"Which Prince?" said the officer curtly.

"Why," answered the secretary, with a glad heart, "there is but one—he who won the prize yesterday at the tilting!"

"God's truth!—And you say true!" ejaculated the guardsman, starting. "But who are you who dares blurt out on the steps of the palace of Courtland that which ordinary men—aye, even good soldiers—durst scarcely think in their own hearts?"

"I am secretary of the noble Ambassador of Plassenburg, and I come to see the Prince!"

"You are a limber slip to be so outspoken," said the man; "but remember that you could be right easily broken on the wheel. So have a care of those slender limbs of yours. Keep them for the maids of your Plassenburg!"

And with the freedom of a soldier he put his hand about the neck of Johann Pyrmont, laying it upon his far shoulder with the easy familiarity of an elder, who has it in his power to do a kindness to a younger. Instinctively Johann slipped aside his shoulder, and the officer's hand after hanging a moment suspended in the air, fell to his side. The Courtlander laughed aloud.

"What!" he cried, "is my young cock of Plassenburg so mightily particular that he cannot have an honest soldier's hand upon his shoulder?"

"I am not accustomed," said Johann Pyrmont, with dignity, "to have men's hands upon my shoulder. It is not our Plassenburg custom!"

The soldier laughed a huge earth-shaking laugh of merriment.

"Faith!" he cried, "you are early begun, my lad, that men's hands are so debarred. 'Not our custom!' says he. Why, I warrant, by the fashion of your countenance, that the hands of ladies are not so unwelcome. Ha! you blush! Here, Paul Strelitz, come hither and see a young gallant that blushes at a word, and owns that he is more at home with ladies than with rough soldiers."

A great bearded Bor-Russian came out of the guard-room, stretching himself and yawning like one whose night has been irregular.

"What's ado? what is't, that you fret a man in his beauty sleep?" he said. "Oh, this young gentleman! Yes, I saw him yesterday, and the Princess Margaret saw him yesterday, too. Does he go to visit her so early this morning? He loses no time, i' faith! But he had better keep out of the way of the Wasp, if the Princess gives him many of those glances of hers, half over her shoulder—you know her way, Otto."

At this the first officer reiterated his jest about his hand on Johann's shoulder, being of that mighty faction which cannot originate the smallest joke without immediately wearing it to the bone.

The secretary began to be angry. His temper was not long at the longest. He had not thought of having to submit to this when he became a secretary.

"I am quite willing, sir captain," he said, with haughty reserve, "that your hand should be—where it ought to be—on your sword handle. For in that case my hand will also be on mine, and very much at your service. But in my country such liberties are not taken between strangers!"

"What?" cried Otto the guardsman, "do men not embrace one another when they meet, and kiss each other on either cheek at parting? How then, so mighty particular about hands on shoulders? Answer me that, my young secretary."

"For me," said Johann, instantly losing his head in the hotness of his indignation, "I would have you know that I only kiss ladies, or permit them to kiss me!"

The Courtlander and the Bor-Russian roared unanimously.

"Is he not precious beyond words, this youngling, eh, Paul Strelitz?" cried the first. "I would we had him at our table of mess. What would our commander say to that? How he would gobble and glower? 'As for me, I only kiss ladies!' Can you imagine it, Paul?"

But just then there came a clatter of horse's hoofs across the wide spaces of the palace front, into which the bright forenoon sun was now beating, and a lady of tall figure and a head all a-ripple with sunny, golden curls dashed up at a canter, the stones spraying forward and outward as she reined her horse sharply with her hands low.

"The Princess Margaret!" said the first officer. "Stand to it, Paul. Be a man, secretary, and hold your tongue."

The two officers saluted stiffly, and the lady looked about for some one to help her to descend. She observed Johann standing, still haughtily indignant, by the gate.

"Come hither!" she said, beckoning with her finger.

"Give me your hand!" she commanded.

The secretary gave it awkwardly, and the Princess plumped rather sharply to the ground.

"What! Do they not teach you how to help ladies to alight in Plassenburg?" queried the Princess. "You accompany the new ambassador, do you not?"

"You are the first I ever helped in my life," said Johann simply. "Mostly— —"

"What! I am the first? You jest. It is not possible. There are many ladies in Plassenburg, and I doubt not they have noted and distinguished a handsome youth like you."

The secretary shook his head.

"Not so," he said, smiling; "I have never been so remarked by any lady in Plassenburg in my life."

The Courtlander, standing stiff at the salute, turned his head the least fraction of an inch towards Paul Strelitz the Bor-Russian.

"He sticks to it. Lord! I wish that I could lie like that! I would make my fortune in a trice," he muttered. "'As for me, I only kiss ladies!' Did you hear him, Paul?"

"I hear him. He lies like an archbishop—a divine liar," muttered the Bor-Russian under his breath.

"Well, at any rate," said the Princess, never taking her eyes off the young man's face, "you will be good enough to escort me to the Prince's room."

"I am going there myself," said the secretary curtly.

"Certainly they do not teach you to say pretty things to ladies," answered the Princess. "I know many that could have bettered that speech without stressing themselves. Yet, after all, I know not but I like your blunt way best!" she added, after a pause, again smiling upon him.

As she took the young man's arm, a cavalier suddenly dashed up on a smoking horse, which had evidently been ridden to his limit. He was of middle size, of a figure exceedingly elegant, and dressed in the highest fashion. He wore a suit of black velvet with yellow points and narrow braidings also of yellow, a broad golden sash girt his waist, his face was handsome, and his mustachios long, fierce, and curling. His eye glittered like that of a snake, with a steady chill sheen, unpleasant to linger upon. He swung from his horse, casting the reins to the nearest soldier, who happened to be our Courtland officer Otto, and sprang up the steps after the Princess and her young escort.

"Princess," he said hastily, "Princess Margaret, I beg your pardon most humbly that I have been so unfortunate as to be late in my attendance upon you. The Prince sent for me at the critical moment, and I was bound to obey. May I now have the honour of conducting you to the summer parlour?"

The Princess turned carelessly, or rather, to tell it exactly, she turned her head a little back over her shoulder with a beautiful gesture peculiar to herself.

"I thank you," she said coldly, "I have already requested this gentleman to escort me. I shall not need you, Prince Ivan."

And she went in, bending graciously and even confidingly towards the secretary, on whose arm her hand reposed.

The cavalier in banded yellow stood a moment with an expression on his face at once humorous and malevolent.

He gazed after the pair till the door swung to and they disappeared. Then he turned bitterly towards the nearest officer.

"He gazed after the pair till the door swung to."

"Tell me," he said, "who is the lout in black, that looks like a priest-cub out for a holiday?"

"He is the secretary of the embassy of Plassenburg," said Otto the guardsman, restraining a desire to put his information in another form. He did not love this imperious cavalier; he was a Courtlander and holding a Muscovite's horse. The conjunction brought something into his throat.

"Ha," said the young man in black and yellow, still gazing at the closed door, "I think I shall go into the rose-garden; I may have something further to say to the most honourable the secretary of the embassy of Plassenburg!" And summoning the officer with a curt monosyllable to bring his horse, he mounted and rode off.

"I wonder he did not give me a silver groat," said the Courtlander. "The secretary sparrow may be dainty and kiss only ladies, but this Prince of Muscovy has not pretty manners. I hope he does not marry the Princess after all."

"Not with her goodwill, I warrant," said Paul Strelitz; "either you or I would have a better chance, unless our Prince Ludwig compel her to it for the good of the State!"

"Prince Wasp seemed somewhat disturbed in his mind," said the Courtlander, chuckling. "I wish I were on guard in the rose-garden to see the meeting of Master Prettyman and his Royal Highness the Hornet of Muscovy!"

CHAPTER VII
H.R.H. THE PRINCESS IMPETUOSITY

The Princess Margaret spoke low and confidentially to the secretary of embassy as they paced along. Johann Pyrmont felt correspondingly awkward. For one thing, the pressure of the Princess's hand upon his arm distracted him. He longed to have her on his other side.

"You are noble?" she said, with a look down at him.

"Of course!" said the secretary quickly. The opposite had never occurred to him. He had not considered the pedigree of travelling merchants or Hamburg architects.

The Princess thought it was not at all of course, but continued—

"I understand—you would learn diplomacy under a man so wise as the High Councillor von Dessauer. I have heard of such sacrifices. My brother, who is very learned, went to Italy, and they say (though he only laughs when I ask him) worked with his hands in one of the places where they print the new sort of books instead of writing them. Is it not wonderful?"

"And he is so brave," said the secretary, whose interest suddenly increased; "he won the tournament yesterday, did he not? I saw you give him the crown of bay. I had not thought so brave a man could be learned also."

"Oh, my brother has all the perfections, yet thinks more of every shaveling monk and unfledged chorister than of himself. I will introduce you to him now. I am a pet of his. You will love him, too—when you know him, that is!"

"Devoutly do I hope so!" said the secretary under his breath.

But the Princess heard him.

"Of course you will," she said gaily; "I love him, therefore so will you!"

"An agreeable princess—I shall get on well with her!" thought Johann Pyrmont. Then the attention of his companion flagged and she was silent and distrait for a little, as they paced through courts and colonnades which to the secretary seemed interminable. The Princess silently indicated the way by a pressure upon his arm which was almost more than friendly.

"We walk well together," she said presently, rousing herself from her reverie.

"Yes," answered the secretary, who was thinking that surely it was a long way to the summer parlour, where he was to meet the Prince.

"I fear," said the Princess Margaret quaintly, "that you are often in the habit of walking with ladies! Your step agrees so well with mine!"

"I never walk with any others," the secretary answered without thought.

"What?" cried the Princess, quickly taking away her hand, "and you swore to me even now that you never helped a lady from her horse in your life!"

It was an *impasse*, and the secretary, recalled to himself, blushed deeply.

"I see so few ladies," he stammered, in a tremor lest he should have betrayed himself. "I live in the country—only my maid——"

"Heaven's own sunshine!" cried the Princess. "Have the pretty young men of Plassenburg maids and tirewomen? Small wonder that so few of them ever visit us! No blame that you stay in that happy country!"

The secretary recovered his presence of mind rapidly.

"I mean," he explained, "the old woman Bette, my nurse, who, though now I am grown up, comes every night to see that I have all I want and to fold my clothes. I have no other women about me."

"You are sure that Bette, who comes for your clothes and to see that you have all you want, is old?" persisted the Princess, keeping her eyes sharply upon her companion.

"She is so old that I never remember her to have been any younger," replied the secretary, with an air of engaging candour.

"I believe you," cried the outspoken Princess; "no one can lie with such eyes. Strange that I should have liked you from the first. Stranger that in an hour I should tell you so. Your arm!"

The secretary immediately put his hand within the arm of the Princess Margaret, who turned upon him instantly in great astonishment.

"Is that also a Plassenburg custom?" she said sharply. "Was it old Bette who taught you thus to take a lady's arm? It is otherwise thought of in our ignorant Courtland!"

The young man blushed and looked down.

"I am sorry," he said; "it is a common fashion with us. I crave your pardon if in aught I have offended."

The Princess Margaret looked quizzically at her companion.

"I' faith," she said, "I have ever had a curiosity about foreign customs. This one I find not amiss. Do it again!"

And with her own princessly hand she took Johann's slender brown fingers and placed them upon her arm.

"These are fitter for the pen than for the sword!" she said, a saying which pleased the owner of them but little.

The Courtlander Otto, who had been on guard at the gate, had meantime been relieved, and now followed the pair through the corridors to the summer palace upon an errand which he had speciously invented.

At this point he stood astonished.

"I would that Prince Wasp were here. We should see his sting. He is indeed a marvel, this fellow of Plassenburg. Glad am I that he does not know little Lenchen up in the Kaiser Platz. No one of us would have a maid to his name, if this gamester abode in Courtland long and made the running in this style!"

The Princess and her squire now went out into the open air. For she had led him by devious ways almost round the entire square of the palace buildings. They passed into a thick avenue of acacias and yews, through the arcades of which they walked silently.

For the Princess was content, and the secretary afraid of making any more mistakes. So he let the foreign custom go at what it might be worth, knowing that if he tried to better it, ten to one a worse thing might befall.

"I have changed my mind," said the Princess, suddenly stopping and turning upon her companion; "I shall not introduce you to my brother. If you come from the Ambassador, you must have matters of importance to speak of. I will rest me here in an arbour and come in later. Then, if you are good, you shall perhaps be permitted to reconduct me to my lodging, and as we go, teach me any other pleasant foreign customs!"

The secretary bowed, but kept his eyes on the ground.

"You do not say that you are glad," cried the Princess, coming impulsively a step nearer. "I tell you there is not one youth——but no matter. I see that it is your innocence, and I am not sure that I do not like you the better for it."

Behind an evergreen, Otto the Courtlander nearly discovered himself at this declaration.

"His innocence—magnificent Karl the Great! His Plassenburger's innocence—God wot! He will not die of it, but he may be the death of me. Oh, for the opinion of Prince Wasp of Muscovy upon such innocence."

"Come," said the Princess, holding out her hands, "bid me goodbye as you do in your country. There is the Prince my brother's horse at the door. You must hasten, or he will be gone ere you do your message."

At this the heart of the youth gave a great leap.

"The Prince!" he cried, "he will be gone!" And would have bolted off without a word.

"Never mind the Prince—think of me," commanded the Princess, stamping her foot. "Give me your hand. I am not accustomed to ask twice. Bid me goodbye."

With his eyes on the white charger by the door the secretary hastily took the Princess by both hands. Then, with his mind still upon the departing Prince, he drew her impulsively towards him, kissed her swiftly upon both cheeks, and finished by imprinting his lips heartily upon her mouth!

Then, still with swift impulse and an ardent glance upward at the palace front, he ran in the direction of the steps of the summer palace.

The Princess Margaret stood rooted to the ground. A flush of shame, anger, or some other violent emotion rose to her brow and stayed there.

Then she called to mind the straightforward unclouded eyes, the clear innocence of the youth's brow, and the smile came back to her lips.

"After all, it is doubtless only his foreign custom," she mused. Then, after a pause, "I like foreign customs," she added, "they are interesting to learn!"

Behind his tree the Courtlander stood gasping with astonishment, as well he might.

"God never made such a fellow," he said to himself. "Well might he say he never kissed any but ladies. Such abilities were lost upon mere men. An hour's acquaintance—nay, less—and he hath kissed the Princess Margaret upon the mouth. And she, instead of shrieking and calling the guard to have the insulter thrust into the darkest dungeon, falls to musing and smiling. A devil of a secretary this! Of a certainty I must have little Lenchen out of town!"

CHAPTER VIII
JOHANN IN THE SUMMER PALACE

At the door of the summer palace not a soul was on guard. A great quiet surrounded it. The secretary could hear the gentle lapping of the river over the parapet, for the little pavilion had been erected overhanging the water, and the leaves of the linden-trees rustled above. These last were still clamorous with the hum of bees, whose busy wings gave forth a sort of dull booming roar, comparable only to the distant noise of breakers when a roller curls slowly over and runs league-long down the sandy beach.

It was with a beating heart that Johann Pyrmont knocked.

"Enter!" said a voice within, with startling suddenness.

And opening the door and grasping his papers, the secretary suddenly found himself in the presence of the hero of the tournament.

The Prince was standing by a desk covered with books and papers. In his hand he held a quill, wherewith he had been writing in a great book which lay on a shelf at his elbow. For a moment the secretary could not reconcile this monkish occupation with his idea of the gallant white-plumed knight whom he had seen flash athwart the lists, driving a clean furrow through the hostile ranks with his single spear.

But he remembered his sister's description, and looked at him with the reverence of the time for one to whom all knowledge was open.

"You have business with me, young sir?" said the Prince courteously, turning upon the youth a regard full of dignity and condescension. The knees of Johann Pyrmont trembled. For a full score of moments his tongue refused its office.

"I come," he said at last, "to convey these documents to the noble Prince of Courtland and Wilna." He gained courage as he spoke, for he had carefully rehearsed this speech to Dessauer. "I am acting as secretary to the Ambassador—in lieu of a better. These are the proposals concerning alliance between the realms proposed by our late master, the Prince Karl, before his death; and now, it is hoped, to be ratified and carried out between Courtland and Plassenburg under his successors, the Princess Helene and her husband."

The tall fair-haired Prince listened carefully. His luminous and steady eyes seemed to pierce through every disguise and to read the truth in the heart of the young architect-secretary. He took the papers from the hand of Johann Pyrmont, and laid them on a desk beside him, without, however, breaking the seals.

"I will gladly take charge of such proposals. They do as much credit, I doubt not, to the sagacity of the late Prince, your great master, as to the kindness and good-feeling of our present noble rulers. But where is the Ambassador? I had hoped to see High Councillor von Dessauer for my own sake, as well as because of the ancient kindliness and correspondence that there was between him and my brother."

"His brother," thought the secretary. "I did not know he had a brother—a lad, I suppose, in whom Dessauer hath an interest. He is ever considerate to the young!" But aloud he answered, "I grieve to tell you, my lord, that the High Councillor von Dessauer is not able to leave his bed this morning. He caught a chill yesterday, either riding hither or at the tourney, and it hath induced an old trouble which no leech has hitherto been skilful enough to heal entirely. He will, I fear, be kept close in his room for several days."

"I also am grieved," said the Prince, with grave regret, seeing the youth's agitation, and liking him for it. "I am glad he keeps the art to make himself so beloved. It is one as useful as it is unusual in a diplomatist!"

Then with a quick change of subject habitual to the man, he said, "How found you your way hither? The corridors are both confusing and intricate, and the guards ordinarily somewhat exacting."

The tall youth smiled.

"I was in the best hands," he said. "Your sister, the Princess Margaret, was good enough to direct me, being on her way to her own apartment."

"Ah!" muttered the Prince, smiling as if he knew his sister, "this is the way to the Princess's apartments, is it? The Moscow road to Rome, I wot!"

He said no more, but stood regarding the youth, whose blushes came and went as he stood irresolute before him.

"A modest lad," said the Prince to himself; "this ingenuousness is particularly charming in a secretary of legation. I must see more of him."

Suddenly a thought crossed his mind.

"Why, did I not hear that you came to us by way of Kernsberg?" he said.

The blushes ceased and a certain pallor showed under the tan which overspread the young man's face as the Prince continued to gaze fixedly at him. He could only bow in assent.

"Then, doubtless, you would see the Duchess Joan?" he continued. "Is she very beautiful? They say so."

"I do not think so. I never thought about it at all!" answered the secretary. Suddenly he found himself plunged into deep waters, just as he had seen the port of safety before him.

The Prince laughed, throwing back his head a little.

"That is surely a strange story to bring here to Courtland," he said, "whither the lady is to come as a bride ere long! Especially strange to tell to me, who— —"

"I ask your pardon," said Johann Pyrmont; "your Highness must bear with me. I have never done an errand of such moment before, having mostly spent my life among soldiers and ("he was on his guard now") in a fortress. For diplomacy and word-play I have no skill—no, nor any liking!"

"You have chosen your trade strangely, then," smiled the Prince, "to proclaim such tastes. Wherefore are you not a soldier?"

"I am! I am!" cried Johann eagerly; "at least, as much as it is allowed to one of my—of my strength to be."

"Can you fence?" asked the Prince, "or play with the broad blade?"

"I can do both!"

"Then," continued his inquisitor, "you must surely have tried yourself against the Duchess Joan. They say she has wonderful skill. Joan of the Sword Hand, I have heard her called. You have often fenced with her?"

"No," said the secretary, truthfully, "I have never fenced with the Duchess Joan."

"So," said the Prince, evidently in considerable surprise; "then you have certainly often seen her fence?"

"I have never seen the Duchess fence, but I have often seen others fence with her."

"You practise casuistry, surely," cried the Prince. "I do not quite follow the distinction."

But, nevertheless, the secretary knew that the difference existed. He would have given all the proceeds and emoluments of his office to escape at this moment, but the eye of the Prince was too steady.

"I doubt not, young sir," he continued, "that you were one of the army of admirers which, they say, continually surrounds the Duchess of Hohenstein!"

"Indeed, you are in great error, my lord," said Johann Pyrmont, with much earnestness and obvious sincerity; "I never said one single word of love to the Lady Joan—no, nor to any other woman!"

"No," said a new voice from the doorway, that of the Princess Margaret, "but doubtless you took great pleasure in teaching them foreign customs. And I am persuaded you did it very well, too!"

The Prince left his desk for the first time and came smilingly towards his sister. As he stooped to kiss her hand, Johann observed that his hair seemed already to be thin upon the top of his head.

"He is young to be growing bald," he said to himself; "but, after all" (with a sigh), "that does not matter in a man so noble of mien and in every way so great a prince."

The impulsive Princess Margaret scarcely permitted her hand to be kissed. She threw her arms warmly about her brother's neck, and then as quickly releasing him, she turned to the secretary, who stood deferentially looking out at the window, that he might not observe the meeting of brother and sister.

"I told you he was my favourite brother, and that you would love him, too," she said. "You must leave your dull Plassenburg and come to Courtland. I, the Princess, ask you. Do you promise?"

"I think I shall come again to Courtland," answered the secretary very gravely.

"This young man knows the Duchess Joan of Hohenstein," said the Prince, still smiling quietly; "but I do not think he admires her very greatly— an opinion he had better keep to himself if he would have a quiet life of it in Courtland!"

"Indeed," said the Princess brusquely. "I wonder not at it. I hear she is a forward minx, and at any rate she shall never lord it over me. I will run away with a dog-whipper first."

"Your husband would have occasion for the exercise of his art, sister mine!" said the Prince. "But, indeed, you must not begin by misliking the poor young maid that will find herself so far from home."

"Oh," cried the Princess, laughing outright, "I mislike her not a whit. But there is no reason in the world why, because you are all ready to fall down and worship, this young man or any other should be compelled to do likewise."

And right princess-like she looked as she pouted her proud little lips and with her foot patted the polished oak.

"But," she went on again to her brother, "your poor beast out there hath almost fretted himself into ribands by this time. If you have done with this noble youth, I have a fancy to hear him tell of the countries wherein he has sojourned. And, in addition, I have promised to show him the carp in the ponds. You have surely given him a great enough dose of diplomatics and canon law by this time. You have, it seems to me, spent half the day in each other's society."

"On the contrary," returned the Prince, smiling again, but going towards the desk to put away the papers which Dessauer's secretary had brought—"on the contrary, we talked almost solely about women—a subject not uncommon when man meets man."

"But somewhat out of keeping with the dignity of your calling, my brother!" said the Princess pointedly.

"And wherefore?" he said, turning quickly with the papers still in his hand. "If to guide, to advise, to rule, are of my profession, surely to speak of women, who are the more important half of the human race, cannot be foreign to my calling!"

"Come," she said, hearing the words without attending to the sense, "I also like things foreign. The noble secretary has promised to teach me some more of them!"

The tolerant Prince laughed. He was evidently accustomed to his sister's whims, and, knowing how perfectly harmless they were, he never interfered with them.

"A good day to you," he said to the young man, by way of dismissal. "If I do not see you again before you leave, you must promise me to come back to the wedding of the Duchess Johanna. In that event you must do me the honour to be my guest on that occasion."

The red flooded back to Johann's cheek.

"I thank you," he said, bowing; "I *will* come back to the wedding of the Duchess Joan."

"And you promise to be my guest? I insist upon it," continued the kindly Prince, willing to gratify his sister, who was smiling approval, "I insist that you shall let me be your host."

"I hope to be your guest, most noble Prince," said the secretary, looking up at him quickly as he went through the door.

It was a singular look. For a moment it checked and astonished the Prince so much that he stood still on the threshold.

"Where have I seen a look like that before?" he mused, as he cast his memory back into the past without success. "Surely never on any man's face?"

Which, after all, was likely enough.

Then putting the matter aside as curious, but of no consequence, the Prince rode away towards that part of the city from which the towers of the minster loomed up. A couple of priests bowed low before him as he passed, and the people standing still to watch his broad shoulders and erect carriage, said one to the other, "Alas! alas! the truest Prince of them all—to be thus thrown away!"

And these were the words which the secretary heard from a couple of guards who talked at the gate of the rose-garden, as they, too, stood looking after the Prince.

"Wait," said Johann Pyrmont to himself; "wait, I will yet show them whether he is thrown away or not."

CHAPTER IX
THE ROSE GARDEN

The rose garden of the summer palace of Courtland was a paradise made for lovers' whisperings. Even now, when the chills of autumn had begun to blow through its bowers, it was over-clambered with late-blooming flowers. Its bowers were creeper-tangled. Trees met over paths bedded with fallen petals, making a shade in sunshine, a shelter in rain, and delightful in both.

It was natural that so fair a Princess, taking such a sudden fancy to a young man, should find her way where the shade was deepest and the labyrinth most entangled.

But this secretary Johann of ours, being creditably hard of heart, would far rather have hied him straight back to old Dessauer with his news. More than anything he desired to be alone, that he might think over the events of the morning.

But the Princess Margaret had quite other intentions.

"Do you know," she began, "that I might well have lodged you in a dungeon cell for that which in another had been dire insolence?"

They were pacing a long dusky avenue of tall yew-trees. The secretary turned towards her the blank look of one whose thoughts have been far away. But the Princess rattled on, heedless of his mood.

"Nevertheless, I forgive you," she said; "after all, I myself asked you to teach me your foreign customs. If any one be to blame, it is I. But one thing I would impress upon you, sir secretary: do not practise these outland peculiarities before my brothers. Either of them might look with prejudice upon such customs being observed generally throughout the city. I came back chiefly to warn you. We do not want that handsome head of yours (which I admit is well enough in its way, as, being a man, you are doubtless aware) to be taken off and stuck on a pole over the Strasburg Gate!"

It was with an effort that the secretary detached himself sufficiently from his reveries upon the interview in the summer palace to understand what the Princess was driving at.

"All this mighty pother, just because I kissed her on the cheek," he thought. "A Princess of Courtland is no such mighty thing—and why should I not?—Oh, of course, I had forgotten again. I am not now the person I was."

But how can we tell with what infinite condescension the Princess took the young man's hand and read his fortune, dwelling frowningly on the lines of love and life?

"You have too pretty a hand for a man," she said; "why is it hard here and here?"

"That is from the sword grip," said the secretary, with no small pride.

"Do you, then, fence well? I wish I could see you," she cried, clapping her hands. "How splendid it would be to see a bout between you and Prince Wasp—that is, the Prince Ivan of Muscovy, I mean. He is a great fencer, and also desires to be a great friend of mine. He would give something to be sitting here teaching me how they take hands and bid each other goodbye in Bearland. They rub noses, I have heard say, a custom which, to my thinking, would be more provocative than satisfactory. I like your Plassenburg fashion better."

Whereat, of course there was nothing for it but that the secretary should arouse himself out of his reverie and do his part. If the Princess of Courtland chose to amuse herself with him, well, it was harmless on either side—even more so than she knew. Soon he would be far away. Meanwhile he must not comport himself like a puking fool.

"I think in somewise it were possible to improve upon the customs even of Plassenburg," said the Princess Margaret, after certain experiments; "but tell me, since you say that we are to be friends, and I have admitted your plea, what is your fortune? Nay, do you know that I do not even know your name—at least, not from your own lips."

For, headlong as she had proved herself in making love, yet a vein of Baltic practicality was hidden beneath the princess's impetuosity.

"My father was the Count von Löen, and I am his heir!" said the secretary carefully; "but I do not usually call myself so. There are reasons why I should not."

Which there were, indeed—grave reasons, too.

"Then you are the Count von Löen?" said the Princess. "I seem to have heard that name somewhere before. Tell me, are you the Count von Löen?"

"I am certainly the heir to that title," said the secretary, grilling within and wishing himself a thousand miles away.

"I must go directly and tell my brother. He will be back from the cathedral by this time. I am sure he did not know. And the estates—a little involved, doubtless, like those of most well-born folk in these ill days? Are they in your sole right?"

"The estates are extensive. They are not encumbered so far as I know. They are all in my own right," explained the newly styled Count with perfect truth. But within he was saying, "God help me! I get deeper and deeper. What a whirling chaos a single lie leads one into! Heaven give me speedy succour out of this!" And as he thought of his troubles, the noble count, the swordsman, the learned secretary, could scarce restrain a desire to break out into hysterical sobbing.

A new thought seemed to strike the Princess as he was speaking.

"But so young, so handsome," she murmured, "so apt a pupil at love!" Then aloud she said, "You are not deceiving me? You are not already betrothed?"

"Not to any woman!" said the deceitful Count, picking his words with exactness.

The gay laugh of the Princess rang out prompt as an echo.

"I did not expect you to be engaged to a man!" she cried. "But now conduct me to the entrance of my chambers" (here she reached him her hand). "I like you," she added frankly, looking at him with unflinching eyes. "I am of the house of Courtland, and we are accustomed to say what we think—the women of us especially. And sooner than carry out this wretched contract and marry the Prince Wasp, I will do even as I said to my brother, I will run away and wed a dog-whipper! But perhaps I may do better than either!" she said in her heart, nodding determinedly as she looked at the handsome youth before her, who now stood with his eyes downcast upon the ground.

They were almost out of the yew-tree walk, and the voice of the Princess carried far, like that of most very impulsive persons. It reached the ears of a gay young fashionable, who had just dismounted at the gate which led from the rose garden into the wing of the palace inhabited by the Princess Margaret and her suite.

"Now," said the Princess, "I will show you how apt a pupil I make. Tell me whether this is according to the best traditions of Plassenburg!" And taking his face between her hands she kissed him rapidly upon either cheek and then upon the lips.

"There!" she said, "I wonder what my noble brothers would say to that! I will show them that Margaret of Courtland can choose both whom she will kiss and whom she will marry!"

And flashing away from him like a bright-winged bird she fled upward into her chambers. Then, somewhat dazed by the rapid succession of emotions, Johann the Secretary stepped out of the green gloom of the yew-tree walk into the broad glare of the September sun and found himself face to face with Prince Wasp.

CHAPTER X
PRINCE WASP

Now Ivan, Prince of Muscovy, had business in Courtland very clear and distinct. He came to woo the Princess Margaret, which being done, he wished to be gone. There was on his side the certainty of an excellent fortune, a possible succession, and, in any case, a pretty and wilful wife. But as he thought on that last the Wasp smiled to himself. In Moscow there were many ways, once he had her there, of taming the most wilful of wives.

As to the inheritance—well, it was true there were two lives between; but one of these, in Prince Ivan's mind, was as good as nought, and the other——In addition, the marriage had been arranged by their several fathers, though not under the same penalty as that which threatened the Prince of Courtland and Joan Duchess of Hohenstein.

Prince Wasp had not favourably impressed the family at the palace. His manners had the strident edge and blatant self-assertion of one who, unlicensed at home, has been flattered abroad, deferred to everywhere, and accustomed to his own way in all things. Nevertheless, Ivan had managed to make himself popular with the townsfolk, on account of the largesse which he lavished and the custom which his numerous suite brought to the city. Specially, he had been successful in attaching the rabble of the place to his cause; and already he had headed off two other wooers who had come from the south to solicit the smiles of the Princess Margaret.

"So," he said, as he faced the secretary, now somewhat compositely styled—Johann, Count von Löen, "so, young springald, you think to court a foolish princess. You play upon her with your pretty words and graceful compliments. That is an agreeable relaxation enough. It passes the time better than fumbling with papers in front of an escritoire. Only—you have in addition to reckon with me, Ivan, hereditary Prince of Muscovy."

And with a sweep of his hand across his body he drew his sword from its sheath.

The sword of the young secretary came into his hand with equal swiftness. But he answered nothing. A curious feeling of detachment crept over him. He had held the bare sword before in presence of an enemy, but never till now unsupported.

"I do you the honour to suppose you noble," said Prince Wasp, "otherwise I should have you flogged by my lacqueys and thrown into the town ditch. I have informed you of my name and pretensions to the hand of the Princess Margaret, whom you have insulted. I pray you give me yours in return."

"I am called Johann, Count von Löen," answered the secretary as curtly as possible.

"Pardon the doubt which is in my mind," said the Prince of Muscovy, with a black sneering bitterness characteristic of him, "but though I am well versed in all the noble families of the north, and especially in those of Plassenburg, where I resided a full year in the late Prince's time, I am not acquainted with any such title."

"Nevertheless, it is mine by right and by birthright," retorted the secretary, "as I am well prepared to maintain with my sword in the meantime. And, after, you can assure yourself from the mouth of the High State's Councillor Dessauer that the name and style are mine. Your ignorance, however, need not defer your chastisement."

"Follow me, Count von Löen," said the Prince; "I am too anxious to deal with your insolence as it deserves to quarrel as to names or titles, legal or illegitimate. My quarrel is with your fascinating body and prettyish face, the beauty of which I will presently improve with some good Northland steel."

And with his lithe and springy walk the Prince of Muscovy passed again along the alleys of the rose garden till he reached the first open space, where he turned upon the secretary.

"We are arrived," he said; "our business is so pressing, and will be so quickly finished, that there is no need for the formality of seconds. Though I honour you by crossing my sword with yours, it is a mere formality. I have such skill of the weapon, as I daresay report has told you, that you may consider yourself dead already. I look upon your chastisement no more seriously than I might the killing of a fly that has vexed me with its buzzing. Guard!"

But Johann Pyrmont had been trained in a school which permitted no such windy preludes, and with the fencer's smile on his face he kept his silence. His sword would answer all such boastings, and that in good time.

And so it fell out.

From the very first crossing of the swords Prince Wasp found himself opposed by a quicker eye, a firmer wrist, a method and science infinitely superior to his own. His most dashing attack was repelled with apparent ease, yet with a subtlety which interposed nothing but the most delicate of guards and parries between Prince Ivan and victory. This gradually infuriated the Prince, till suddenly losing his temper he stamped his foot in anger and rushed upon his foe with the true Muscovite fire.

Then, indeed, had Johann need of all his most constant practice with the sword, for the sting of the Wasp flashed to kill as he struck straight at the heart of his foe.

But lo! the blade was turned aside, the long-delayed answering thrust glittered out, and the secretary's sword stood a couple of handbreadths in the boaster's shoulder.

With an effort Johann recovered his blade and stood ready for the ripost; but the wound was more than enough. The Prince staggered, cried out some unintelligible words in the Muscovite language, and pitched forward slowly on his face among the trampled leaves and blown rose petals of the palace garden.

"The Prince staggered."

The secretary grew paler than his wont, and ran to lift his fallen enemy. But, all unseen, other eyes had watched the combat, and from the door by which they had entered, and from behind the trees of the surrounding glade, there came the noise of pounding footsteps and fierce cries of "Seize him! Kill him! Tear him to pieces! He has slain the good Prince, the friend of the people! The Prince Ivan is dead!"

And ere the secretary could touch the body of his unconscious foe, or assure himself concerning his wound, he found himself surrounded by a yelling crowd of city loafers and gallows'-rats, many of them rag-clad, others habited in heterogeneous scraps of cast-off clothing, or articles snatched from clothes-lines and bleaching greens—long-mourned, doubtless, by the good wives of Courtland.

The secretary eyed this unkempt horde with haughty scorn, and his fearless attitude, as he striped his stained sword through his handkerchief and threw the linen away, had something to do with the fact that the rabble halted at the distance of half-a-dozen yards and for many minutes contented themselves with hurling oaths and imprecations at him. Johann Pyrmont kept his sword in his hand and stood by the body of his fallen foe in disdainful silence till the arrival of fresh contingents through the gate aroused the halting spirit of the crowd. Knives and sword-blades began to gleam here and there in grimy hands where at first there had been only staves and chance-snatched gauds of iron.

"At him! Down with him! He can only strike once!" These and similar cries inspirited the rabble of Courtland, great haters of the Plassenburg and the Teutonic west, to rush in and make an end.

At last they did come on, not all together, but in irregular undisciplined rushes. Johann's sword streaked out this way and that. There was an answering cry of pain, a turmoil among the assailants as a wounded man whirled his way backward out of the press. But this could not last for long. The odds were too great. The droning roar of hate from the edges of the crowd grew louder as new and ever newer accretions joined themselves to its changing fringes.

Then suddenly came a voice. "Back, on your lives, dogs and traitors! Germans to the rescue! Danes, Teuts, Northmen to the rescue!"

Following the direction of the sound, Johann saw a young man drive through the press, his sword bare in his hand, his eyes glittering with excitement. It was the Danish prisoner of the guard-hall at Kernsberg, that same Sparhawk who had fought with Werner von Orseln.

The crowd stared back and forth betwixt him and that other whom he came to succour. Far more than ever his extraordinary likeness to the secretary appeared. Apparent enough at any time, it was accentuated now by similarity of clothing. For, like Johann Pyrmont, the Sparhawk was attired in a black doublet and trunk hose of scholastic cut, and as they stood back to back, little difference could be noted between them, save that the newcomer was a trifle the taller.

"Saint Michael and all holy angels!" cried the leader of the crowd, "can it be that there are scores of these Plassenburg black crows in Courtland, slaying whom they will? Here be two of them as like as two peas, or a couple of earthen pipkins from the same potter's wheel!"

The Dane flung a word over his shoulder to his companion.

"Pardon me, your grace," said the Sparhawk, "if I stand back to back with you. They are dangerous. We must watch well for any chance of escape."

The secretary did not answer to this strange style of address, but placed himself back to back with his ally, and their two bright blades waved every way. Only that of Johann Pyrmont was already reddened well-nigh half its length.

A second time the courage of the crowd worked itself up, and they came on.

"Death to the Russ, to the lovers of Russians!" cried the Sparhawk, and his blade dealt thrusts right and left. But the pressure increased every moment. Those behind cried, "Kill them!" For they were out of reach of those two shining streaks of steel. Those before would gladly have fallen behind, but could not for the forward thrust of their friends. Still the ring narrowed, and the pair of gallant fighters would doubtlessly have been swept away had not a diversion come to alter the face of things.

Out of the gate which led to the wing of the palace occupied by the Princess Margaret burst a little company of halberdiers, at sight of whom the crowd gave suddenly back. The Princess herself was with them.

"Take all prisoners, and bring them within," she cried. "Well you know that my brother is from home, or you dare not thus brawl in the very precincts of the palace!"

And at her words the soldiers advanced rapidly. A further diversion was caused by the Sparhawk suddenly cleaving a way through the crowd and setting off at full speed in the direction of the river. Whereupon the rabble, glad to combine personal safety with the pleasures of the chase, took to their heels after him. But, light and unexpected in motion as his namesake, the Sparhawk skimmed down the alleys, darted sideways through gates which he shut behind him with a clash of iron, and finally plunged into the green rush of the Alla, swimming safe and unhurt to the further shore, whither, in the absence of boats at this particular spot, none could pursue him.

CHAPTER XI
THE KISS OF THE PRINCESS MARGARET

The Princess and her guard were left alone with the secretary and the unconscious body of the Prince of Muscovy.

"Sirrah," she cried severely to the former, "is this the first use you make of our hospitality, thus to brawl in the street underneath my very windows with our noble guest the Prince Ivan? Take him to my brother's room, and keep him safely there to await our lord's return. We shall see what the Prince will say to this. And as for this wounded man, take him to his own apartments, and let a surgeon be sent to him. Only not in too great a hurry!" she added as an afterthought to the commander of her little company of palace guards.

So, merely detailing half a dozen to carry the Prince to his chambers, the captain of the guard conducted the secretary to the very room in which an hour before he had met the brother of the Princess. Here he was confined, with a couple of guards at the door. Nor had he been long shut up before he heard the quick step of the Princess coming along the passage-way. He could distinguish it a long way off, for the summer palace was built mostly of wood, and every sound was clearly audible.

"So," she said, as soon as the door was shut, "you have killed Prince Wasp!"

"I trust not," said the secretary gravely; "I meant only to wound him. But as he attacked me I could not do otherwise than defend myself."

"Tut," cried the Princess, "I hope you have killed him. It will be good riddance, and most like the Muscovites will send an army—which, with your Plassenburg to help us, will make a pretty fight. It serves him right, in any event, for Prince Wasp must always be thrusting his sting into honest folk. He will be none the worse for some of his own poison applied at a rapier's point to keep him quiet for some few days."

But Johann was not in a mood to relish the jubilation of the Princess. He grew markedly uneasy in his mind. Every moment he anticipated that the Prince would return. A trial would take place, and he did not know what might not be discovered.

The Princess Margaret delivered him from his anxiety.

"The laws are strict against duelling," she continued. "The Prince Ivan is in high favour with my elder brother, and it will be well that you should be seen no more in Courtland—for the present, that is. But in a little the Prince Wasp will die or he will recover. In either case the affair will blow over. Then you will come back to teach me more foreign customs."

She smiled and held out her hand. Johann kissed it, perhaps without the fervour which might have been expected from a brisk young man thus highly favoured by the fairest and sprightliest of princesses.

"To-night," she went on, "there will be a boat beneath that window. It will be manned by those whom I can trust. A ladder of rope will be thrown to your casement. By it you will descend, and with a good horse and a sufficient escort you can ride either to Plassenburg—or to Kernsberg, which is nearer, and tell Joan of the Sword Hand that her sister the Princess Margaret sends you to her. I will give you a letter to the minx, though I am sure I shall not like her. She is so forward, they say. But be ready at the hour of midnight. Who was that youth who fled as we came up?"

"A Danish knight who came hither in our train from Kernsberg," replied Johann. "But for him I should have been lost indeed!"

"I must have a horse also for him!" cried the Princess. "He will surely be on the watch and join you, knowing that his danger is as great as yours. Hearken—they are mourning for their precious Prince Wasp. To-morrow they will howl louder if by good hap he goes home to—purgatory!"

And through the open windows came a sound of distant shoutings as they carried the wounded Prince to his lodgings.

"Now," said the Princess, "for the present fare you well—in the colder fashion of Courtland this time, for the sake of the guards at the door. But remember that you are more than ever plighted to me to be my instructor, dear Count von Löen!"

She went to the door, and with her fingers on the handle she turned her about with a pretty vixenish expression. "I am so glad you stung the Wasp. I love you for it!" she said.

But after she had vanished with these words the secretary grew more and more downcast in spirit. Even this naïve declaration of affection failed to cheer him. He sat down and gave himself up to the most melancholy anticipations.

At six a servitor silently entered with a well-chosen and beautifully cooked meal, of which the secretary partook sparingly. At seven it grew dark, and at ten all was quiet in the city. The river rushed swiftly beneath, and the noise of it, as the water lapped against the foundations of the summer palace, helped to disguise the sound of oars, as the boat, a dark shadow upon greyish water, detached itself from the opposite shore and approached the window from whose open casement Johann Pyrmont looked out.

A low whistle came from underneath, and presently followed the soft reeving *whisk* of a coil of rope as it passed through the window and fell at his feet. The secretary looked about for something to fasten it to, and finally decided upon the iron uprights of the great desk at which the Prince had stood earlier in the day.

No sooner was this done than Johann set his foot on the top round and began to descend. It was with a sudden emptiness at the pit of the stomach and a great desire to cry out for some one to hold the ladder steady that the secretary found himself swaying over the dark water. The boat seemed very far away, a mere spot of blackness upon the river's face.

"The Secretary found himself swaying over the dark water."

But presently, and while making up his mind to practise the gymnastic of rope ladders quietly at home, he made out a man holding the ladder, while two others with grappled boat-hooks kept the boat steady fore and aft.

A shrouded figure sat in the stern. The secretary seemed rather to find himself in a boat which rose swiftly to meet him than to descend into it. He was handed from one to the other of the rowers till he reached the shrouded figure in the stern, out of the folds of whose enveloping cloak a small warm hand shot forth and pulled him down upon the seat.

"Draw this corner about you, Count," a low voice whispered; and in another moment Johann found himself under the shelter of one cloak with that daring slip of nobility, the Princess Margaret of Courtland.

"I was obliged to come; there is no danger. These fellows are of my household and devoted to me. I did not dare to risk anything going wrong. Besides, I am a princess, and—why need not I say it?—I wanted to come. I wanted to see you again, though, indeed, there is small chance of that in such a night. And 'tis as well, for I am sure my hair is blown every way about my face."

"The horses are over there," she added after a pause; "we are almost at the shore now—alas, too quickly! But I must not keep you. I want you to come back the sooner. And remember, if Prince Wasp gets better and worries me too much, or my brother is unkind and insists upon marrying me to the Bear, I will take one or two of these fellows and come to seek you at Plassenburg, so make your reckoning with that, Sir Count von Löen. As I said, what is the use of being a princess if you cannot marry whom you will? Most, I know, marry whom they are told; but then they have not the spirit of a Baltic weevil, let alone that of Margaret of Courtland."

They touched the shore almost at the place where the Sparhawk had landed in the morning when he escaped from the city rabble, and a stone's-throw further up the bank they found the horses waiting, ready caparisoned for the journey.

Two men were, by the Princess's orders, to accompany Johann.

But with great thoughtfulness she had provided a fourth horse for the companion who, equally with himself, was under the ban of the law for wounding the lieges of the Prince of Courtland within the precincts of the palace.

"He cannot have gone far," said the Princess. "He would certainly conceal himself till nightfall in the first convenient hiding-place. He will be on the look-out for any chance to release you."

And the event proved the wisdom of her prophecy. For as soon as he had distinguished the slim figure of the secretary landing from the boat the Sparhawk appeared on the crest of the hill, though for the moment he was still unseen by those below.

"Goodbye! For the present, goodbye, dear Princess," said Johann, with his heart in his voice. "God knows, I can never thank or repay you. My heart is heavy for that. I am unworthy of all your goodness. It is not as you think— —"

He paused for words which might warn without revealing his secret; but the Princess, never long silent, struck in.

"Let there be no talk of parting except for the moment," she said. "Go, you are my knight. Perhaps one day, if you do not forget me, I may be yet far kinder to you!"

And with a most tender kiss and a little sob the Princess sent her lover, more and more downcast and discouraged by reason of her very kindness, upon his way. So much did his obvious depression affect Margaret of Courtland, that after the secretary, with one of the men-at-arms leading the spare horse, had reached the top of the river bank, she suddenly bade the rowers wait a moment before casting loose from the land.

"Your sword! Your sword!" she called aloud, risking any listener in her eagerness; "you have forgotten your sword."

Now it chanced that the Sparhawk had already come up with the little party of travellers. He kissed the hand of Johann Pyrmont, placed him on his beast, and was preparing to mount his steed with a glad heart, when the voice from beneath startled him.

"Do not trouble, I will bring the sword," said the Sparhawk to Johann, with his usual impetuosity, putting the reins into the secretary's hands. And without a moment's hesitation he flung himself down the bank. The Princess had leaped nimbly ashore, and was standing with the sheathed sword in her hand.

When she saw the figure came bounding towards her down the pebbly bank, she gave a little cry, and dropping the scabbard, threw her arms impulsively about the Sparhawk's neck.

"I could not let you go like that—without ever telling you that I loved you—really, I mean," she whispered, while the youth stood petrified with astonishment, without sound or motion. "I will marry none but you— neither Prince Ivan nor another. A woman should not tell a man that, I know, lest he despise her; but a princess may, if the man dare not tell her."

"And what answered you?" asked the secretary of his companion, as they rode together through the night out on their road to Kernsberg.

"Why, I said nothing—speech was not needed," quoth the Dane coolly.

"She kissed you?"

"Well," said the Sparhawk, "I could not help that, could I?"

"But what said you to that?"

"Why, of course, I kissed her back again, as a man ought!" he made answer.

"Poor Princess," mused the secretary; "it is more than I could ever have done for her!" Aloud he said, "But you do not love her—you had not seen her before! Why then did you kiss her?"

For these things are hidden from women.

The Dane shrugged his shoulders in the dark.

"Well, I take what the gods send," he replied. "She was a pretty girl, and her Princess-ship made no difference in her kissing so far as I could see. I serve you to the death, my Lady Duchess; but if a princess loves me by the way—why, I am ready to indulge her to the limit of her desirings!"

"You are indeed an accommodating youth," sighed the secretary, and forthwith returned to his own melancholy thoughts.

And ever as they rode westward they heard all around them the rustle of corn in the night wind. Stacks of hay shed a sweet scent momently athwart their path, and more than once fruit-laden branches swept across their faces. For they were passing through the garden of the Baltic, and its fresh beauty was never fresher than on that September night when these four rode out of Courtland towards the distant blue hills on which was perched Kernsberg, built like an eagle's nest on a crag overfrowning the wealthier plain.

At the first boundaries of the group of little hill principalities the two soldiers were dismissed, suitably rewarded by Johann, to carry the news of safety back to their wayward and impulsive mistress. And thence-forward the Sparhawk and the secretary rode on alone.

At the little châlet among the hills where the Duchess Joan had so suddenly disappeared they found two of her tire-maidens and an aged nurse impatiently awaiting their mistress. To them entered that composite and puzzling youth the ex-architect and secretary of the embassy of Plassenburg, Johann, Count von Löen. And wonder of wonders, in an hour afterwards Joan of the Sword Hand was riding eagerly towards her capital city with her due retinue, as if she had merely been taking a little summer breathing space at a country seat.

Her entrance created as little surprise as her exit. For as to her exits and entrances alike the Duchess consulted no man, much less any woman. Werner von Orseln saluted as impassively as if he had seen his mistress an hour before, and the acclamations of the guard rang out as cheerfully as ever.

Joan felt her spirits rise to be once more in her own land and among her own folk. Nevertheless, there was a new feeling in her heart as she thought of the day of her marriage, when the long-planned bond of brotherhood-heritage should at last be carried out, and she should indeed become the mistress of that great land into which she had ventured so strangely, and the bride of the Prince—her Prince, the most noble man on whom her eyes had ever rested.

Then her thoughts flew to the Princess who had delivered her out of peril so deadly, and her soul grew sick and sad within her, not at all lest her adventure should be known. She cared not so much about that now. (Perhaps some day she would even tell him herself when—well, *after*!)

But since she had ridden to Courtland, Joan, all untouched before, had grown suddenly very tender to the smarting of another woman's heart.

"It is in no wise my fault," she told herself, which in a sense was true.

But conscience, being a thing not subject to reason, dealt not a whit the more easily with her on that account.

It was six months afterwards that the Sparhawk, who had been given the command of a troop of good Hohenstein lancers, asked permission to go on a journey.

He had been palpably restless and uneasy ever since his return, and in spite of immediate favour and the prospect of yet further promotion, he could not settle to his work.

"Whither would you go?" asked his mistress.

"To Courtland," he confessed, somewhat reluctantly, looking down at the peaked toe of his tanned leather riding-boot.

"And what takes you to Courtland?" said Joan; "you are in danger there. Besides, even if you could, would you leave my service and engage with some other?"

"Nay, my lady," he burst out, "that will not I, so long as life lasts. But—but the truth is"—he hesitated as he spoke—"I cannot get out of my mind the Princess who kissed me in the dark. The like never happened before to any man. I cannot forget her, do what I will. No, nor rest till I have looked upon her face."

"Wait," said Joan. "Only wait till the spring and it is my hap to ride to Courtland for my marriage day. Then I promise you you shall see somewhat of her—the Lord send that it be not more than enough!"

So through many bitter winter days the Sparhawk abode at the castle of Kernsberg, ill content.

CHAPTER XII
JOAN FORSWEARS THE SWORD

It was not in accordance with etiquette that two such nobly born betrothed persons, to be allied for reasons of high State policy, should visit each other openly before the day of marriage; but many letters and presents had at various times come to Kernsberg, all bearing witness to the lover-like eagerness of the Prince of Courtland and of his desire to possess so fair a bride, especially one who was to bring him so coveted a possession as the hill provinces of Kernsberg and Hohenstein.

Amongst other things he had forwarded portraits of himself, drawn with such skill as the artists of the Baltic at that time possessed, of a man in armour, with a countenance of such wooden severity that it might stand (as the Duchess openly declared) just as well for Werner, her chief captain, or any other man of war in full panoply.

"But," said Joan within herself, "what care I for armour black or armour white? Mine eyes have seen—and my heart does not forget."

Then she smiled and for a while forgot the coming inevitable disappointment of the Princess Margaret, which troubled her much at other times.

The winter was unusually long and fierce in the mountains of Kernsberg that year, and even along the Baltic shores the ice packed thicker and the snow lay longer by a full month than usual.

It was the end of May, and the full bursting glory of a northern spring, when at last the bridal cavalcade wound down from the towers of the Castle of Kernsberg. Four hundred riders there were, every man arrayed like a prince in the colours of Hohenstein—four fairest maids to be bridesmaids to their Duchess, and as many matrons of rank and years to bring their mistress with dignity and discretion to her new home. But the people and the rough soldiers openly mourned for Joan of the Sword Hand. "The Princess of Courtland will not be the same thing!" they said.

And they were right, for since the last time she rode out Joan had thought many thoughts. Could it be that she was indeed that reckless maid who once had vowed that she would go and look once at the man her father had bidden her marry, and then, if she did not like him, would carry him off and clap him into a dungeon till he had paid a swinging ransom? But the knight of the white plume, and the interview she had had with a certain Prince in the summer palace of Courtland, had changed all that.

Now she would be sober, grave—a fit mate for such a man. Almost she blushed to recall her madcap feats of only a year ago.

As they approached the city, and each night brought them closer to the great day, Joan rode more by herself, or talked with the young Dane, Maurice von Lynar, of the Princess Margaret—without, however, telling him aught of the rose garden or the expositions of foreign customs which had preceded the duel with the Wasp.

The heart of the Duchess beat yet faster when at last the day of their entry arrived. As they rode toward the gate of Courtland they were aware of a splendid cavalcade which came out to receive them in the name of the Prince, and to conduct them with honour to the palace prepared for them.

In the centre of a brilliant company rode the Princess Margaret, in a well-fitting robe of pale blue broidered with crimson, while behind and about her was such a galaxy of the fashion and beauty of a court, that had not Joan remembered and thought on the summer parlour and the man who was waiting for her in the city, she had almost bidden her four hundred riders wheel to the right about, and gallop straight back to Kernsberg and the heights of rustic Hohenstein.

At sight of the Duchess's party the Princess alighted from off her steed with the help of a cavalier. At the same moment Joan of the Sword Hand leaped down of her own accord and came forward to meet her new sister.

The two women kissed, and then held each other at arm's length for the luxury of a long look.

The face of the Princess showed a trace of emotion. She appeared to be struggling with some recollection she was unable to locate with precision.

"I hope you will be very happy with my brother," she faltered; then after a moment she added, "Have you not perchance a brother of your own?"

But before Joan could reply the representative of the Prince had come forward to conduct the bride-elect to her rooms, and the Princess gave place to him.

But all the same she kept her eyes keenly about her, and presently they rested with a sudden brightness upon the young Dane, Maurice von Lynar, at the head of his troop of horse. He was near enough for her to see his face, and it was with a curious sense of strangeness that she saw his eyes fixed upon herself.

"He is different—he is changed," she said to herself; "but how—wait till we get to the palace, and I shall soon find out!"

And immediately she caused it to be intimated that all the captains of troops and the superior officers of the escort of the Duchess Joan were to be entertained at the palace of the Princess Margaret.

So that at the moment when Joan was taking a first survey of her chambers, which occupied one entire wing of the Palace of the Princes of Courtland, Margaret the impetuous had already commanded the presence of the Count von Löen, one of the commanders of the bridal escort.

The young officer entrusted with the message returned almost immediately, to find his mistress impatiently pacing up and down.

"Well?" she said, halting at the upper end of the reception-room and looking at him.

"Your Highness," he said, "there is no Count von Löen among the officers of Kernsberg!"

Margaret of Courtland stamped her foot.

"I expected as much," she said. "He shall pay for this. Why, man, I saw him with my own eyes an hour ago—a young man, slender, sits erect in his saddle, of a dark allure, and with eyes like those of an eagle."

A flush came over the youth's face.

"Does he look like the brother of the Duchess Joan?" he said.

"That is the man—Count von Löen or no. That is the man, I tell you. Bring him immediately to me."

The young officer smiled.

"Methinks he will come readily enough. He started forward as if to follow me when first I told my message. But when I mentioned the name of the Count von Löen he stood aside in manifest disappointment."

"At all events, bring him instantly!" commanded the Princess.

The officer bowed low and retired.

The Princess Margaret smiled to herself.

"It is some more of their precious State secrets," she said. "Well—I love secrets, and I can keep them too; but only my own, or those that are told to me. And I will make my gentleman pay for playing off his Counts von Löen on me!"

Presently she heard heavy footsteps approaching the door.

"Come in—come in straightway," she said in a loud, clear voice; "I have a word to speak with you, Sir Count—who yet deny that you are a count. And, prithee, to how many silly girls have you taught the foreign fashions of linked arms, and all that most pleasant ceremony of leave-taking in Kernsberg and Plassenburg?"

Then the Sparhawk had his long-desired view in full daylight of the woman whose lips, touched once under cloud of night, had dominated his fancy and enslaved his will during all the weary months of winter.

Also he had before him, though he knew it not, a somewhat difficult and complicated explanation.

CHAPTER XIII
THE SPARHAWK IN THE TOILS

The Princess Margaret was standing by the window as the young man entered. Her golden curls flashed in the late sunshine, which made a kind of haze of light about her head as she turned the resentful brilliance of her eyes upon Maurice von Lynar.

"Is it a safe thing, think you, Sir Count, to jest with a princess in her own land and then come back to flout her for it?"

Maurice understood her to refer to the kiss given and returned in the darkness of the night. He knew not of how many other indiscretions he was now to bear the brunt, or he had turned on the spot and fled once more across the river.

"My lady," he said, "if I offended you once, it was not done intentionally, but by mistake."

"By mistake, sir! Have a care. I may have been indiscreet, but I am not imbecile."

"The darkness of the night——" faltered von Lynar, "let that be my excuse."

"Pshaw!" flashed the Princess, suddenly firing up; "do you not see, man, that you cannot lie yourself out of this? And, indeed, what need? If *I* were a secretary of embassy, and a princess distinguished me with her slightest favour, methinks when next I came I would not meanly deny her acquaintance!"

Von Lynar was distressed, and fortunately for himself his distress showed in his face.

"Princess," he said, standing humbly before her, "I did wrong. But consider the sudden temptation, the darkness of the night——"

"The darkness of the night," she said, stamping her foot, and in an instinctively mocking tone; "you are indeed well inspired. You remind me of what I ventured that you should be free. The darkness of the night, indeed! I suppose that is all that sticks in your memory, because you gained something tangible by it. You have forgotten the walk through the corridors of the Palace, all you taught me in the rose garden, and—and—how apt a pupil you said I was. Pray, good Master Forgetfulness, who hath forgotten all these things, forgotten even his own name, tell me what you did in Courtland eight months ago?"

"I came—I came," faltered the Sparhawk, fearful of yet further committing himself, "I came to find and save my dear mistress."

"Your—dear—mistress?" The Princess spoke slowly, and the blue eyes hardened till they overtopped and beat down the bold black ones of Maurice von Lynar; "and you dare to tell me this—me, to whom you swore that you had never loved woman in the world before, never spoken to them word of wooing or compliment! Out of my sight, fellow! The Prince, my brother, shall deal with you."

Then all suddenly her pride utterly gave way. The disappointment was too keen. She sank down on a silk-covered ottoman by the window side, sobbing.

"Oh, that I could kill you now, with my hands—so," she said in little furious jerks, gripping at the pillow; "I hate you, thus to put a shame upon me—me, Margaret of Courtland. Could it have been for such a thing as you that I sent away the Prince of Muscovy—yes, and many others—because I could not forget you? And after all——!"

Now Maurice von Lynar was not quick in discernment where woman was concerned, but on this occasion he recognised that he was blindly playing the hand of another—a hand, moreover, of which he could not hope to see the cards. He did the only thing which could have saved him with the Princess. He came near and sank on one knee before her.

"Madam," he said humbly and in a moving voice, "I beseech you not to be angry—not to condemn me unheard. In the sense of being in love, I never loved any but yourself. I would rather die than put the least slight upon one so surpassingly fair, whose memory has never departed from me, sleeping or waking, whose image, dimly seen, has never for a moment been erased from my heart's tablets."

The Princess paused and lifted her eyes till they dwelt searchingly upon him. His obvious sincerity touched her willing heart.

"But you said just now that you came to Courtland to see 'your dear mistress?'"

The young man put his hand to his head.

"You must bear with me," he said, "if perchance for a little my words are wild. I had, indeed, no right to speak of you as my dear mistress."

"Oh, it was of me that you spoke," said the Princess, smiling a little; "I begin to understand."

"Of what other could I speak?" said the shameless Von Lynar, who now began to feel his way a little clearer. "I have indeed been very ill, and when I am in straits my head is still unsettled. Oftentimes I forget my very name, so sharp a pang striking through my forehead that I dote and stare and forget all else. It springs from a secret wound that at the time I knew nothing of."

"Yes—yes, I remember. In the duel with the Wasp—in the yew-tree walk it happened. Tell me, is it dangerous? Did it well-nigh cost you your life?"

The youth modestly hung down his head.

This sudden spate of falsehood had come upon him, as it were, from the outside.

"If the truth will not help me," he muttered, "why, I can lie with any man. Else wherefore was I born a Dane? But, by my faith, my mistress must have done some rare tall lying on her own account, and now I am reaping that which she hath sown."

As he kneeled thus the Princess bent over him with a quizzical expression on her face.

"You are sure that you speak the truth now? Your wound is not again causing you to dote?"

"Nay," said the Sparhawk; "indeed, 'tis almost healed."

"Where was the wound?" queried the Princess anxiously.

"There were two," answered Von Lynar diplomatically; "one in my shoulder at the base of my neck, and the other, more dangerous because internal, on the head itself."

"Let me see."

She came and stood above him as he put his hand to the collar of his doublet, and, unfastening a tie, he slipped it down a little and showed her at the spring of his neck Werner von Orseln's thrust.

"And the other," she said, covering it up with a little shudder, "that on the head, where is it?"

The youth blushed, but answered valiantly enough.

"It never was an open wound, and so is a little difficult to find. Here, where my hand is, above my brow."

"Hold up your head," said the Princess. "On which side was it? On the right? Strange, I cannot find it. You are too far beneath me. The light falls not aright. Ah, that is better!"

She kneeled down in front of him and examined each side of his head with interest, making as she did so, many little exclamations of pity and remorse.

"I think it must be nearer the brow," she said at last; "hold up your head—look at me."

Von Lynar looked at the Princess. Their position was one as charming as it was dangerous. They were kneeling opposite to one another, their faces, drawn together by the interest of the surgical examination, had approached very close. The dark eyes looked squarely into the blue. With stuff so inflammable, fire and tow in such immediate conjunction, who knows what conflagration might have ensued had Von Lynar's eyes continued thus to dwell on those of the Princess?

But the young man's gaze passed over her shoulder. Behind Margaret of Courtland he saw a man standing at the door with his hand still on the latch. A dark frown overspread his face. The Princess, instantly conscious that the interest had gone out of the situation, followed the direction of Von Lynar's eyes. She rose to her feet as the young Dane also had done a moment before.

Maurice recognised the man who stood by the door as the same whom he had seen on the ground in the yew-tree walk when he and Joan of the Sword Hand had faced the howling mob of the city. For the second time Prince Wasp had interfered with the amusements of the Princess Margaret.

That lady looked haughtily at the intruder.

"The lady looked haughtily at the intruder."

"To what," she said, "am I so fortunate as to owe the unexpected honour of this visit?"

"I came to pay my respects to your Highness," said Prince Wasp, bowing low. "I did not know that the Princess was amusing herself. It is my ill-fortune, not my fault, that I interrupted at a point so full of interest."

It was the truth. The point was decidedly interesting, and therein lay the sting of the situation, as probably the Wasp knew full well.

"You are at liberty to leave me now," said the Princess, falling back on a certain haughty dignity which she kept in reserve behind her headlong impulsiveness.

"I obey, madam," he replied; "but first I have a message from the Prince your brother. He asks you to be good enough to accompany his bride to the minster to-morrow. He has been ill all day with his old trouble, and so cannot wait in person upon his betrothed. He must abide in solitude for this day at least. Your Highness is apparently more fortunate!"

The purpose of the insult was plain; but the Princess Margaret restrained herself, not, however, hating the insulter less.

"I pray you, Prince Ivan," she said, "return to my brother and tell him that his commands are ever an honour, and shall be obeyed to the letter."

She bowed in dignified dismissal. Prince Wasp swept his plumed hat along the floor with the profundity of his retiring salutation, and in the same moment he flashed out his sting.

"I leave your Highness with less regret because I perceive that solitude has its compensations!" he said.

The pair were left alone, but all things seemed altered now. Margaret of Courtland was silent and distrait. Von Lynar had a frown upon his brow, and his eyes were very dark and angry.

"Next time I must kill the fellow!" he muttered. He took the hand of the Princess and respectfully kissed it.

"I am your servant," he said; "I will do your bidding in all things, in life or in death. If I have forgotten anything, in aught been remiss, believe me that it was fate and not I. I will never presume, never count on your friendship past your desire, never recall your ancient goodness. I am but a poor soldier, yet at least I can faithfully keep my word."

The Princess withdrew her hand as if she had been somewhat fatigued.

"Do not be afraid," she said a little bitterly, "I shall not forget. *I* have not been wounded in the head! *Only in the heart!*" she added, as she turned away.

CHAPTER XIV
AT THE HIGH ALTAR

When Maurice von Lynar reached the open air he stood for full five minutes, light-headed in the rush of the city traffic. The loud iteration of rejoicing sounded heartless and even impertinent in his ear. The world had changed for the young Dane since the Count von Löen had been summoned by the Princess Margaret.

He cast his mind back over the interview, but failed to disentangle anything definite. It was a maze of impressions out of which grew the certainty that, safely to play his difficult part, he must obtain the whole confidence of the Duchess Joan.

He looked about for the Prince of Muscovy, but failed to see him. Though not anxious about the result, he was rather glad, for he did not want another quarrel on his hands till after the wedding. He would see the Princess Margaret there. If he played his cards well with the bride, he might even be sent for to escort her.

So he made his way to the magnificent suite of apartments where the Duchess was lodged. The Prince had ordered everything with great consideration. Her own horsemen patrolled the front of the palace, and the Courtland guards were for the time being wholly withdrawn.

It seemed strange that Joan of the Sword Hand, who not so long ago had led many a dashing foray and been the foremost in many a brisk encounter, should be a bride! It could not be that once he had imagined her the fairest woman under the sun, and himself, for her sake, the most miserable of men. Thus do lovers deceive themselves when the new has come to obliterate the old. Some can even persuade themselves that the old never had any existence.

The young Dane found the Duchess walking up and down on the noble promenade which faces the river to the west. For the water curved in a spacious elbow about the city of Courtland, and the summer palace was placed in the angle.

Maurice von Lynar stood awhile respectfully waiting for the Duchess to recognise him. Werner, John of Thorn, or any of her Kernsberg captains would have gone directly up to her. But this youth had been trained in another school.

"Joan of Hohenstein stood, looking out upon the river."

Joan of Hohenstein stood a while without moving, looking out upon the river. She thought with a kind of troubled shyness of the morrow, oft dreamed of, long expected. She saw the man whom she was not known ever to have seen—the noble young man of the tournament, the gracious Prince of the summer parlour, courteous and dignified alike to the poor secretary of embassy and to his sister the Princess Margaret of Courtland. Surely there never was any one like him—proudly thought this girl, as she looked across the river at the rich plain studded with far-smiling farms and fields just waking to life after their long winter sleep.

"Ah, Von Lynar, my brave Dane, what good wind blows you here?" she cried. "I declare I was longing for some one to talk to." A consciousness of need which had only just come to her.

"I have seen the Princess Margaret," said the youth slowly, "and I think that she must mistake me for some other person. She spoke things most strange to me to hear. But fearing I might meddle with affairs wherewith I had no concern, I forebore to correct her."

The eyes of the Duchess danced. A load seemed suddenly lifted off her mind.

"Was she very angry?" she queried.

"Very!" returned Von Lynar, smiling in recognition of her smile.

"What said the Princess?"

"First she would have it that my name and style were those of the Count Von Löen. Then she reproached me fiercely because I denied it. After that she spoke of certain foreign customs she had been taught, recalled walks through corridors and rose gardens with me, till my head swam and I knew not what to answer."

Joan of the Sword Hand laughed a merry peal.

"The Count von Löen, did she say?" she meditated. "Well, so you are the Count von Löen. I create you the Count von Löen now. I give you the title. It is mine to give. By to-morrow I shall have done with all these things. And since as the Count von Löen I drank the wine, it is fair that you, who have to pay the reckoning, should be the Count von Löen also."

"My family is noble, and I am the sole heir—that is, alive," said Maurice, a little drily. To his mind the grandson of Count von Lynar, of the order of the Dannebrog, had no need of any other distinction.

"But I give you also therewith the estates which pertain to the title. They are situated on the borders of Reichenau. I am so happy to-night that I would like to make all the world happy. I am sorry for all the folk I have injured!"

"Love changes all things," said the Dane sententiously.

The Duchess looked at him quickly.

"You are in love—with the Princess Margaret?" she said.

The youth blushed a deep crimson, which flooded his neck and dyed his dusky skin.

"Poor Maurice!" she said, touching his bowed head with her hand, "your troubles will not be to seek."

"My lady," said the youth, "I fear not trouble. I have promised to serve the Princess in all things. She has been very kind to me. She has forgiven me all."

"So—you are anxious to change your allegiance," said the Duchess. "It is as well that I have already made you Count von Löen, and so in a manner bound you to me, or you would be going off into another's service with all my secrets in your keeping. Not that it will matter very much—after to-morrow!" she added, with a glance at the wing of the palace which held the summer parlour. "But how did you manage to appease her? That is no mean feat. She is an imperious lady and quick of understanding."

Then Maurice von Lynar told his mistress of his most allowable falsehoods, and begged her not to undeceive the Princess, for that he would rather bear all that she might put upon him than that she should know he had lied to her.

"Do not be afraid," said the Duchess, laughing, "it was I who tangled the skein. So far you have unravelled it very well. The least I can do is to leave you to unwind it to the end, my brave Count von Löen."

So they parted, the Duchess to her apartment, and the young man to pace up and down the stone-flagged promenade all night, thinking of the distracting whimsies of the Princess Margaret, of the hopelessness of his love, and, most of all, of how daintily exquisite and altogether desirable was her beauty of face, of figure, of temper, of everything!

For the Sparhawk was not a lover to make reservations.

The morning of the great day dawned cool and grey. A sunshade of misty cloud overspread the city and tempered the heat. It had come up with the morning wind from the Baltic, and by eight the ships at the quays, and the tall beflagged festal masts in the streets through which the procession was to pass, ran clear up into it and were lost, so that the standards and pennons on their tops could not be seen any more than if they had been amongst the stars.

The streets were completely lined with the folk of the city of Courtland as the Princess Margaret, with the Sparhawk and his company of lances clattering behind her, rode to the entrance of the palace where abode the bride-elect.

"Who is that youth?" asked Margaret of Courtland of Joan, as they came out together; she looked at the Dane—"he at the head of your first troops? He looks like your brother."

"He has often been taken for such!" said the bride. "He is called the Count von Löen!"

The Princess did not reply, and as the two fair women came out arm in arm, a sudden glint of sunlight broke through the leaden clouds and fell upon them, glorifying the white dress of the one, and the blue and gold apparel of the other.

The bells of the minster clanged a changeful thunder of brazen acclaim as the bride set out for the first time (so they told each other on the streets) to see her promised husband.

"'Twas well we did not so manage our affairs, Hans," said a fishmonger's wife, touching her husband's arm archly.

"Yea, wife," returned the seller of fish; "whatever thou beest, at least I cannot deny that I took thee with my eyes open!"

They reached the Rathhaus, and the clamour grew louder than ever. Presently they were at the cathedral and making them ready to dismount. The bells in the towers above burst forth into yet more frantic jubilation. The cannons roared from the ramparts.

The Princess Margaret had delayed a little, either taking longer to her attiring, or, perhaps, gossiping with the bride. So that when the shouts in the wide Minster Place announced their arrival, all was in readiness within the crowded church, and the bridegroom had gone in well-nigh half an hour before them. But that was in accord with the best traditions.

Very like a Princess and a great lady looked Joan of Hohenstein as she went up the aisle, with Margaret of Courtland by her side. She kept her eyes on the ground, for she meant to look at no one and behold nothing till she should see—that which she longed to look upon.

Suddenly she was conscious that they had stopped in the middle of a vast silence. The candles upon the great altar threw down a golden lustre. Joan saw the irregular shining of them on her white bridal dress, and wondered that it should be so bright.

There was a hush over all the assembly, the silence of a great multitude all intent upon one thing.

"My brother, the Prince of Courtland!" said the voice of the Princess Margaret.

Slowly Joan raised her eyes—pride and happiness at war with a kind of glorious shame upon her face.

But that one look altered all things.

She stood fixed, aghast, turned to stone as she gazed. She could neither speak nor think. That which she saw almost struck her dead with horror.

The man whom his sister introduced as the Prince of Courtland was not the knight of the tournament. He was not the young prince of the summer palace. He was a man much older, more meagre of body, grey-headed, with an odd sidelong expression in his eyes. His shoulders were bent, and he carried himself like a man prematurely old.

And there, behind the altar-railing, clad in the scarlet of a prince of the Church, and wearing the mitre of a bishop, stood the husband of her heart's deepest thoughts, the man who had never been out of her mind all these weary months. He held a service book in his hand, and stood ready to marry Joan of Hohenstein to another.

The man who was called Prince of Courtland came forward to take her hand; but Joan stood with her arms firmly at her sides. The terrible nature of her mistake flashed upon her and grew in horror with every moment. Fate seemed to laugh suddenly and mockingly in her face. Destiny shut her in.

"Are you the Prince of Courtland?" she asked; and at the sound of her voice, unwontedly clear in the great church, even the organ appeared to still itself. All listened intently, though only a few heard the conversation.

"I have that honour," bowed the man with the bent shoulders.

"Then, as God lives, I will never marry you!" cried Joan, all her soul in the disgust of her voice.

"Be not disdainful, my lady," said the bridegroom mildly; "I will be your humble slave. You shall have a palace and an establishment of your own, an it like you. The marriage was your father's desire, and hath the sanction of the Emperor. It is as necessary for your State as for mine."

Then, while the people waited in a kind of palpitating uncertainty, the Princess Margaret whispered to the bride, who stood with a face ashen pale as her own white dress.

Sometimes she looked at the Prince of Courtland, and then immediately averted her eyes. But never, after the first glance, did Joan permit them to stray to the face of him who stood behind the altar railings with his service book in his hand.

"Well," she said finally, "I *will* marry this man, since it is my fate. Let the ceremony proceed!"

"I thank you, gracious lady," said the Prince, taking her hand and leading his bride to the altar. "You will never regret it."

"No, but you will!" muttered his groomsman, the Prince Ivan of Muscovy.

The full rich tones of the prince bishop rose and fell through the crowded minster as Joan of Hohenstein was married to his elder brother, and with the closing words of the episcopal benediction an awe fell upon the multitude. They felt that they were in the presence of great unknown forces, the action and interaction of which might lead no man knew whither.

At the close of the service, Joan, now Princess of Courtland, leaned over and whispered a word to her chosen captain, Maurice von Lynar, an action noticed by few. The young man started and gazed into her face; but, immediately commanding his emotion, he nodded and disappeared by a side door.

The great organ swelled out. The marriage procession was re-formed. The prince-bishop had retired to his sacristy to change his robes. The new Princess of Courtland came down the aisle on the arm of her husband.

Then the bells almost turned over in their fury of jubilation, and every cannon in the city bellowed out. The people shouted themselves hoarse, and the line of Courtland troops who kept the people back had great difficulty in restraining the enthusiasm which threatened to break all bounds and involve the married pair in a whirling tumult of acclaim.

In the centre of the Minster Place the four hundred lances of the Kernsberg escort had formed up, a serried mass of beautiful well-groomed horses, stalwart men, and shining spears, from each of which the pennon of their mistress fluttered in the light wind.

"Ha! there they come at last! See them on the steps!" The shouts rang out, and the people flung their headgear wildly into the air. The line of Courtland foot saluted, but no cheer came from the array of Kernsberg lances.

"They are sorry to lose her—and small wonder. Well, she is ours now!" the people cried, congratulating one another as they shook hands and the wine gurgled out of the pigskins into innumerable thirsty mouths.

On the steps of the minster, after they had descended more than half-way, the new Princess of Courtland turned upon her lord. Her hand slipped from his arm, which hung a moment crooked and empty before it dropped to his side. His mouth was a little open with surprise. Prince Louis knew that he was wedding a wilful dame, but he had not been prepared for this.

"Now, my lord," said the Princess Joan, loud and clear. "I have married you. The bond of heritage-brotherhood is fulfilled. I have obeyed my father to the letter. I have obeyed the Emperor. I have done all. Now be it known to you and to all men that I will neither live with you nor yet in your city. I am your wife in name. You shall never be my husband in aught else. I bid you farewell, Prince of Courtland. Joan of Hohenstein may marry where she is bidden, but she loves where she will."

The horse upon which she had come to the minster stood waiting. There was the Sparhawk ready to help her into the saddle.

Ere one of the wedding guests could move to prevent her, before the Prince of Courtland could cry an order or decide what to do, Joan of the

Sword Hand had placed herself at the head of her four hundred lances, and was riding through the shouting streets towards the Plassenburg gate.

The people cheered as she went by, clearing the way that she might not be annoyed. They thought it part of the day's show, and voted the Kernsbergers a gallant band, well set up and right bravely arrayed.

So they passed through the gate in safety. The noble portal was all aflutter with colour, the arms of Hohenstein and Courtland being quartered together on a great wooden plaque over the main entrance.

As soon as they were clear the Princess Joan turned in her saddle and spake to the four hundred behind her.

"We ride back to Kernsberg," she cried. "Joan of the Sword Hand is wed, but not yet won. If they would keep her they must first catch her. Are you with me, lads of the hills?"

Then came back a unanimous shout of "Aye—to the death!" from four hundred throats.

"Then give me a sword and put the horses to their speed. We ride for home. Let them catch us who can!"

And this was the true fashion of the marrying of Joan of the Sword Hand, Duchess of Hohenstein, to the Prince Louis of Courtland, by his brother Conrad, Cardinal and Prince of Holy Church.

CHAPTER XV
WHAT JOAN LEFT BEHIND

After the departure of his bride, the Prince of Courtland stood on the steps of the minster, dazed and foundered by the shame which had so suddenly befallen him. Beneath him the people seethed tumultuously, their holiday ribands and maypole dresses making as gay a swirl of colour as when one looks at the sun through the facets of a cut Venetian glass. Prince Louis's weak and fretful face worked with emotion. His bird-like hands clawed uncertainly at his sword-hilt, wandering off over the golden pouches that tasselled his baldric till they rested on the sheath of the poignard he wore.

"Bid the gates be shut, Prince!" The whisper came over his shoulder from a young man who had been standing all the time twisting his moustache. "Bid your horsemen bit and bridle. The plain is fair before you. It is a long way to Kernsberg. I have a hundred Muscovites at your service, all well mounted—ten thousand behind them over the frontier if these are not enough! Let no wench in the world put this shame upon a reigning Prince of Courtland on his wedding-day!"

Thus Ivan of Muscovy, attired in silk, banded of black and gold, counselled the disdained Prince Louis, who stood pushing upward with two fingers the point of his thin greyish beard and gnawing the straggling ends between his teeth.

"I say, 'To horse and ride, man!' Will you dare tell this folk of yours that you are disdained, slighted at the very church door by your wedded wife, cast off and trodden in the mire like a bursten glove? Can you afford to proclaim yourself the scorn of Germany? How it will run, that news! To Plassenburg first, where the Executioner's Son will smile triumphantly to his witch woman, and straightway send off a messenger to tickle the well-larded ribs of his friend the Margraf George with the rare jest."

The Prince Louis appeared to be moved by the Wasp's words. He turned about to the nearest knight-in-waiting.

"Let us to horse—every man of us!" he said. "Bid that the steeds be brought instantly."

The banded Wasp had further counsels to give.

"Give out that you go to meet the Princess at a rendezvous. For a pleasantry between yourselves, you have resolved to spend the honeymoon at a distant hunting-lodge. Quick! Not half a dozen of all the company caught the true import of her words. You will tame her yet. She will founder her horses in a single day's ride, while you have relays along the road at every castle, at every farm-house, and your borders are fifty good miles away."

Beneath, in the square, the court jesters leaped and laughed, turning somersaults and making a flying skirt, like that of a morrice dancer, out of the long, flapping points of their parti-coloured blouses. The streets in front of the cathedral were alive with musicians, mostly in little bands of three, a harper with his harp of fourteen strings, his companion playing industriously upon a Flute-English, and with these two their 'prentice or servitor, who accompanied them with shrill iterance of whistle, while both his hands busied themselves with the merry tuck of tabour.

In this incessant merrymaking the people soon forgot their astonishment at the sudden disappearance of the bride. There was, indeed, no understanding these great folk. But it was a fine day for a feast—the pretext a good one. And so the lasses and lads joked as they danced in the lower vaults of the town house, from which the barrels had been cleared for the occasion.

"If thou and I were thus wedded, Grete, would you ride one way and I the other? Nay, God wot, lass! I am but a tanner's 'prentice, but I'd abide beside thee, as close as bark by hide that lies three years in the same tan-pit—aye, an' that I would, lass!"

Then Gretchen bridled. "I would not marry thee, nor yet lie near or far, Hans; thou art but a boy, feckless and skill-less save to pole about thy stinking skins—faugh!"

"Nay, try me, Grete! Is not this kiss as sweet as any civet-scented fop could give?"

At the command of the Prince the trumpets rang out again the call of "Boot-and-saddle!" from the steps of the cathedral. At the sound the grooms, who were here and there in the press, hasted to find and caparison the horses of their lords. Meanwhile, on the wide steps the Prince Louis fretted, dinting his nails restlessly into his palms and shaking with anger and disappointment till his deep sleeves vibrated like scarlet flames in a veering wind.

Suddenly there passed a wave over the people who crowded the spacious Dom Platz of Courtland. The turmoil stilled itself unconsciously.

The many-headed parti-coloured throng of women's tall coifs, gay fluttering ribands, men's velvet caps, gallants' white feathers that shifted like the permutations of a kaleidoscope, all at once fixed itself into a sea of white faces, from which presently arose a forest of arms flourishing kerchiefs and tossing caps. To this succeeded a deep mouth-roar of burgherish welcome such as the reigning Prince had never heard raised in his own honour.

"Conrad—Prince Conrad! God bless our Prince-Cardinal!"

The legitimate ruler of Courtland, standing where Joan had left him, with his slim-waisted Muscovite mentor behind him, half-turned to look. And there on the highest place stood his brother in the scarlet of his new dignity as it had come from the Pope himself, his red biretta held in his hand, and his fair and noble head erect as he looked over the folk to where on the slope above the city gates he could still see the sun glint and sparkle on the cuirasses and lanceheads of the four hundred riders of Kernsberg.

But even as the Prince of Courtland looked back at his brother, the whisper of the tempter smote his ear.

"Had Prince Conrad been in your place, and you behind the altar rails, think you that the Duchess Joan would have fled so cavalierly?"

By this time the young Cardinal had descended till he stood on the other side of the Prince from Ivan of Muscovy.

"You take horse to follow your bride?" he queried, smiling. "Is it a fashion of Kernsberg brides thus to steal away?" For he could see the grooms bringing horses into the square, and the guards beating the people back with the butts of their spears to make room for the mounting of the Prince's cavalcade.

"Hark—he flouts you!" came the whisper over the bridegroom's shoulder; "I warrant he knew of this before."

"You have done your priest's work, brother," said Louis coldly, "e'en permit me to go about that of a prince and a husband in my own way."

The Cardinal bowed low, but with great self-command held his peace, whereat Louis of Courtland broke out in a sudden overboiling fury.

"This is your doing!" he cried; "I know it well. From her first coming my bride had set herself to scorn me. My sister knew it. You knew it. You smile as at a jest. The Pope's favour has turned your head. You would have all—the love of my wife, the rule of my folk, as well as the acclaim of these city swine. Listen—'The good Prince Conrad! God save the noble Prince!' It is worth while living for favour such as this."

"Brother of mine," said the young man gently, "as you know well, I never set eyes upon the noble Lady Joan before. Never spoke word to her, held no communication by word or pen."

"Von Dessauer—his secretary!" whispered Ivan, dropping the suggestion carefully over his shoulder like poison distilled into a cup.

"You were constantly with the old fox Dessauer, the envoy of Plassenburg—who came from Kernsberg, bringing with him that slim secretary. By my faith, now, when I think of it, Prince Ivan told me last night he was as like this madcap girl as pea to pea—some fly-blown base-born brother, doubtless!"

Conrad shook his head. His brother had doubtless gone momentarily distract with his troubles.

"Nay, deny it not! And smile not either—lest I spoil the symmetry of that face for your monkish mummery and processions. Aye, if I have to lie under ten years' interdict for it from your friend the most Holy Pope of Rome!"

"Do not forget there is another Church in my country, which will lay no interdict upon you, Prince Louis," laughed Ivan of Muscovy. "But to horse—to horse—we lose time!"

"Brother," said the Cardinal, laying his hand on Louis's arm, "on my word as a knight—as a Prince of the Church—I knew nothing of the matter. I cannot even guess what has led you thus to accuse me!"

The Princess Margaret came at that moment out of the cathedral and ran impetuously to her favourite brother.

He put out his hand. She took it, and instead of kissing his bishop's ring, as in strict etiquette she ought to have done, she cried out, "Conrad, do you know what that glorious wench has done? Dared her husband's authority at the church door, leaped into the saddle, whistled up her men, cried to all these Courtland gallants, 'Catch me who can!' And lo! at this moment she is riding straight for Kernsberg, and now our Louis must catch her. A glorious wedding! I would I were by her side. Brother Louis, you need not frown, I am nowise affrighted at your glooms! This is a bride worth fighting for. No puling cloister-maid this that dares not raise her eyes higher than her bridegroom's knee! Were I a man, by my faith, I would never eat or drink, neither pray nor sain me, till I had tamed the darling and brought her to my wrist like a falcon to a lure!"

"So, then, madam, you knew of this?" said her elder brother, glowering upon her from beneath his heavy brows.

"Nay!" trilled the gay Princess, "I only wish I had. Then I, too, would have been riding with them—such a jest as never was, it would have been. Goodbye, my poor forsaken brother! Joy be with you on this your bridal journey. Take Prince Ivan with you, and Conrad and I will keep the kingdom against your return, with your prize gentled on your wrist."

So smiling and kissing her hand the Princess Margaret waved her brother and Prince Ivan off. The Prince of Courtland neither looked at her nor answered. But the Muscovite turned often in his saddle as if to carry with him the picture she made of saucy countenance and dainty figure as she stood looking up into the face of the Cardinal Prince Conrad.

"What in Heaven's name is the meaning of all this—I do not understand in the least?" he was saying.

"Haste you and unrobe, Brother Con," she said; "this grandeur of yours daunts me. Then, in the summer parlour, I will tell you all!"

CHAPTER XVI
PRINCE WASP'S COMPACT

"I cannot go back to Courtland dishonoured," said Prince Louis to Ivan of Muscovy, as they stood on the green bank looking down on the rushing river, broad and brown, which had so lately been the Fords of Alla. The river had risen almost as it seemed upon the very heels of the four hundred horsemen of Kernsberg, and the ironclad knights and men-at-arms who followed the Prince of Courtland could not face the yeasty swirl of the flood.

"They stood ... looking down at the rushing river."

Prince Ivan, left to himself, would have dared it.

"What is a little brown water?" he cried. "Let the men leave their armour on this side and swim their horses through. We do it fifty times a month in Muscovy in the springtime. And what are your hill-fed brooks to the full-bosomed rivers of the Great Plain?"

"It is just because they are hill-fed that we know them and will not risk our lives. The Alla has come down out of the mountains of Hohenstein. For four-and-twenty hours nothing without wing may pass and repass. Yet an hour earlier and our Duchess had been trapped on the hither side even as we. But now she will sit and laugh up there in Kernsberg. And—I cannot go back to Courtland without a bride!"

Prince Ivan stood a moment silent. Then his eyes glanced over his companion with a certain severe and amused curiosity. From foot to head they scanned him, beginning at the shoes of red Cordovan leather, following upwards to the great tassel he wore at his poignard; then came the golden girdle about his waist, the flowered needlework at his wrists and neck, and the scrutiny ended with the flat red cap on his head, from which a white feather nodded over his left eye.

Then the gaze of Prince Ivan returned again slowly to the pointed red shoes of Cordovan leather.

If there was anything so contemptuous as that eye-blink in the open scorn of all the burghers of Courtland, Prince Louis was to be excused for any hesitation he might show in facing his subjects.

The matter of Prince Wasp's meditation ran somewhat thuswise: "Thou man, fashioned from a scullion's nail-paring, and cocked upon a horse, what can I make of thee? Thou, to have a country, a crown, a wife! Gudgeon eats stickleback, jack-pike eats gudgeon and grows fat, till at last the sturgeon in his armour eats him. I will fatten this jack. I will feed him like the gudgeons of Kernsberg and Hohenstein, then take him with a dainty lure indeed, black-tipped, with sleeves gay as cranes' wings, and answering to the name of 'my lady Joan.' But wait—I must be wary, and have a care lest I shadow his water."

So saying within his heart, Prince Wasp became exceedingly thoughtful and of a demure countenance.

"My lord," he said, "this day's work will not go well down in Courtland, I fear me!"

Prince Louis moved uneasily, keeping his regard steadily upon the brown turmoil of the Alla swirling beneath, whereas the eyes of Ivan were never removed from his friend's meagre face.

"Your true Courtlander is more than half a Muscovite," mused Prince Wasp, as if thinking aloud; "he wishes not to be argued with. He wants a master, and he will not love one who permits himself to be choused of a wife upon his wedding-day!"

Prince Louis started quickly as the Wasp's sting pricked him.

"And pray, Prince Ivan," he said, "what could I have done that I left undone? Speak plainly, since you are so prodigal of smiles suppressed, so witty with covert words and shoulder-tappings!"

"My Louis," said Prince Wasp, laying his hand upon the arm of his companion with an affectation of tenderness. "I flout you not—I mock you not. And if I speak harshly, it is only that I love not to see you in your turn flouted, mocked, scorned, made light of before your own people!"

"I believe it, Ivan; pardon the heat of my hasty temper!" said the Prince of Courtland. The watchful Muscovite pursued his advantage, narrowing his eyes that he might the better note every change on the face of the man whom he held in his toils. He went on, with a certain resigned sadness in his voice—

"Ever since I came first to Courtland with the not dishonourable hope of carrying back to my father a princess of your house, none have been so amiable together as you and I. We have been even as David and Jonathan."

The Prince Louis put out a hand, which apparently Ivan did not see, for he continued without taking it.

"Yet what have I gained either of solid good or even of the lighter but not less agreeable matter of my lady's favour? So far as your sister is concerned, I have wasted my time. If I consider the union of our peoples, already one in heart, your brother works against us both; the Princess Margaret despises me, Prince Conrad thwarts us. He would bind us in chains and carry us tinkling to the feet of his pagan master in Rome!"

"I think not so," answered Prince Louis—"I cannot think so of my brother, with all his faults. Conrad is a brave soldier, a good knight—though, as is the custom of our house, it is his lot to be no more than a prince-bishop!"

The Wasp laughed a little hard laugh, clear and inhuman as the snap and rattle of Spanish castanets.

"Louis, my good friend, your simplicity, your lack of guile, do you wrong most grievous! You judge others as you yourself are. Do you not see that Conrad your brother must pay for his red hat? He must earn his cardinalate. Papa Sixtus gives nothing for nothing. Courtland must pay

Peter's pence, must become monkish land. On every flake of stockfish, every grain of sturgeon roe, every ounce of marled amber, your Holy Father must levy his sacred dues. And the clear ambition of your brother is to make you chief cat's-paw pontifical upon the Baltic shore. Consider it, good Louis."

And the Prince of Muscovy twirled his moustache and smiled condescendingly between his fingers. Then, as if he thought suddenly of something else and made a new calculation, he laughed a laugh, quick and short as the barking of a dog.

"Ha!" he cried, "truly we order things better in my country. I have brothers, one, two, three. They are grand dukes, highnesses very serene. One of them has this province, another this sinecure, yet another waits on my father. My father dies—and I—well, I am in my father's place. What will my brothers do with their serene highnesses then? They will take each one the clearest road and the shortest for the frontier, or by the Holy Icon of Moscow, there would very speedily be certain new tablets in the funeral vault of my fathers."

The Prince of Courtland started.

"This thing I could never imagine of Conrad my brother. He loves me. At heart he ever cared but for his books, and now that he is a priest he hath forsworn knighthood, and tournaments, and wars."

"Poor Louis," said Ivan sadly, "not to see that once a soldier always a soldier. But 'tis a good fault, this generous blindness of the eyes. He hath already the love of your people. He has won already the voice that speaks from every altar and presbytery. The power to loose and bind men's consciences is in his hand. In a little, when he has bartered away your power for his cardinal's hat, he may be made a greater than yourself, an elector of the empire, the right-hand man of Papa Sixtus, as his uncle Adrian was before him. Then indeed your Courtland will underlie the tinkle of Peter's keys!"

"I am sure that Conrad would do nothing against his fatherland or to the hurt of his prince and brother!" said Prince Louis, but he spoke in a wavering voice, like one more than half convinced.

"Again," continued Ivan, without heeding him, "there is your wife. I am sure that if he had been the prince and you the priest—well, she had not slept this night in the Castle of Kernsberg!"

"Ivan, if you love me, be silent," cried the tortured Prince of Courtland, setting his hand to his brow. "This is the mere idle dreaming of a fool. How learned you these things? I mean how did the thoughts enter into your mind?"

"I learned the matter from the Princess Margaret, who in the brief space of a day became your wife's confidante!"

"Did Margaret tell it you?"

The Prince Ivan laughed a short, self-depreciatory laugh.

"Nay, truly," he said, smiling sadly, "you and I are in one despite, Louis. Your wife scorns you—me, my sweetheart. Did Margaret tell me? Nay, verily! Yet I learned it, nevertheless, even more certainly because she denied it so vehemently. But, after all, I daresay all will end for the best."

"How so?" demanded Prince Louis haughtily.

"Why, I have heard that your Papa at Rome will do aught for money. Doubtless he will dissolve this marriage, which indeed is no more than one in name. He has done more than that already for his own nephews. He will absolve your brother from his vows. Then you can be the monk and he the king. There will be a new marriage, at which doubtless you shall hold the service book and he the lady's hand. Then we shall have no ridings back to Kernsberg, with four hundred lances, at a word from a girl's scornful mouth. And the Alla down there may rise or fall at its pleasure, and neither hurt nor hinder any!"

The Prince of Courtland turned an angry countenance upon his friend, but the keen-witted Muscovite looked so kindly and yet so sadly upon him that after awhile the severity of his face relaxed as it had been against his will, and with a quick gesture he added, "I believe you love me, Ivan, though indeed your words are no better than red-hot pincers in my heart."

"Love you, Louis?" cried Prince Ivan. "I love you better than any brother I have, though they will never live to thwart me as yours thwarts you— better even than my father, for you do not keep me out of my inheritance!"

Then in a gayer tone he went on.

"I love you so much that I will pledge my father's whole army to help you, first to win your wife, next to take Hohenstein, Kernsberg, and Marienfeld. And after that, if you are still ambitious, why—to Plassenburg and the Wolfmark, which now the Executioner's Son holds. That would make a noble kingdom to offer a fair and wilful queen."

"And for this you ask?"

"Only your love, Louis—only your love! And, if it please you, the alliance with that Princess of your honourable house, of whom we spoke just now!"

"My sister Margaret, you mean? I will do what I can, Ivan, but she also is wilful. You know she is wilful! I cannot compel her love!"

The Prince Ivan laughed.

"I am not so complaisant as you, Louis, nor yet so modest. Give me my bride on the day Joan of the Sword Hand sleeps in the palace of Courtland as its princess, and I will take my chance of winning our Margaret's love!"

CHAPTER XVII
WOMAN'S WILFULNESS

Joan rode on, silent, a furlong before her men.

Behind her sulked Maurice von Lynar. Had any been there to note, their faces were now strangely alike in feature, and yet more curiously unlike in expression. Joan gazed forward into the distance like a soul dead and about to be reborn, planning a new life. Maurice von Lynar looked more like a naughty schoolboy whom some tyrant Fate, rod-wielding, has compelled to obey against his will.

Yet, in spite of expression, it was Maurice von Lynar who was planning the future. Joan's heart was yet too sore. Her tree of life had, as it were, been cut off close to the ground. She could not go back to the old so soon after her blissful year of dreams. There was to be no new life for her. She could not take up the old. But Maurice—his thoughts were all for the Princess Margaret, of the ripple of her golden hair, of her pretty wilful words and ways, of that dimple on her chin, and, above all, of her threat to seek him out if—but it was not possible that she could mean that. And yet she looked as though she might make good her words. Was it possible? He posed himself with this question, and for half an hour rode on oblivious of all else.

"Eh?" he said at last, half conscious that some one had been speaking to him from an infinite distance. "Eh? Did you speak, Captain von Orseln?"

Von Orseln grunted out a little laugh, almost silently, indeed, and expressed more by a heave of his shoulders than by any alteration of his features.

"Speak, indeed? As if I had not been speaking these five minutes. Well nigh had I stuck my poignard in your ribs to teach you to mind your superior officer. What think you of this business?"

"Think?" the Sparhawk's disappointment burst out. "Think? Why, 'tis past all thinking. Courtland is shut to us for twenty years."

"Well," laughed Von Orseln, "who cares for that? Castle Kernsberg is good enough for me, so we can hold it."

"Hold it?" cried Maurice, with a kind of joy in his face; "do you think they will come after us?"

Von Orseln nodded approval of his spirit.

"Yes, little man, yes," he said; "if you have been fretting to come to blows with the Courtlanders you are in good case to be satisfied. I would we had only these lumpish Baltic jacks to fear."

Even as they talked Castle Kernsberg floated up like a cloud before them above the blue and misty plain, long before they could distinguish the walls and hundred gables of the town beneath.

But no word spoke Joan till that purple shadow had taken shape as stately stone and lime, and she could discern her own red lion flying abreast of the banner of Louis of Courtland upon the topmost pinnacle of the round tower.

Then on a little mound without the town she halted and faced about. Von Orseln halted the troop with a backward wave of the hand.

"Men of Hohenstein," said the Duchess, in a clear, far-reaching alto, "you have followed me, asking no word of why or wherefore. I have told you nothing, yet is an explanation due to you."

There came the sound as of a hoarse unanimous muttering among the soldiers. Joan looked at Von Orseln as a sign for him to interpret it.

"They say that they are Joan of the Sword Hand's men, and that they will disembowl any man who wants to know what it may please you to keep secret."

"Aye, or question by so much as one lifted eyebrow aught that it may please your Highness to do," added Captain Peter Balta, from the right of the first troop.

"I said that our Duchess could never live in such a dog's hole as their Courtland," quoth George the Hussite, who, before he took service with Henry the Lion, had been a heretic preacher. "In Bohemia, now, where the pines grow——"

"Hold your prate, all of you," growled Von Orseln, "or you will find where hemp grows, and why! My lady," he added, altering his voice as he turned to her, "be assured, no dog in Kernsberg will bark an interrogative at you. Shall our young Duchess Joan be wived and bedded like some little burgheress that sells laces and tape all day long on the Axel-strasse? Shall the daughter of Henry the Lion be at the commandment of any Bor-Russian boor, an it like her not? Shall she get a burr in her throat with breathing the raw fogs of the Baltic? Not a word, most gracious lady! Explain nothing.

Extenuate nothing. It is the will of Joan of the Sword Hand—that is enough; and, by the word of Werner von Orseln, it shall be enough!"

"It is the will of Joan of the Sword Hand! It is enough!" repeated the four hundred lances, like a class that learns a lesson by rote.

A lump rose in Joan's throat as she tried to shape into words the thoughts that surged within. She felt strangely weak. Her pride was not the same as of old, for the heart of a woman had grown up within her—a heart of flesh. Surely that could not be a tear in her eye? No; the wind blew shrewdly out of the west, to which they were riding. Von Orseln noted the struggle and took up his parable once more.

"The pact is carried out. The lands united—the will of Henry the Lion done! What more? Shall the free Princess be the huswife of a yellow Baltic dwarf? When we go into the town and they ask us, we will say but this, 'Our Lady misliked the fashion of his beard!' That will be reason good and broad and deep, sufficient alike for grey-haired carl and prattling bairn!"

"I thank you, noble gentlemen," said Joan. "Now, as you say, let us ride into Kernsberg."

"And pull down that flag!" cried Maurice, pointing to the black Courtland Eagle which flew so steadily beside the coronated lion of Kernsberg and Hohenstein.

"And pray, sir, why?" quoth Joan of the Sword Hand. "Am I not also Princess of Courtland?"

From woman's wilfulness all things somehow have their beginning. Yet of herself she is content with few things (so that she have what she wants), somewhat Spartan in fare if let alone, and no dinner-eating animal. Wine, tobacco, caviare, Strasburg goose-liver—Epicurus's choicest gifts to men of this world—are contemned by womankind. Left to their own devices, they prefer a drench of sweet mead or hydromel laced with water, or even of late the China brew that filters in black bricks through the country of the Muscovite. Nevertheless, to woman's wantings may be traced all restraints and judgments, from the sword flaming every way about Eden-gate to the last merchant declared bankrupt and "dyvour" upon the exchange flags of Hamburg town. Eve did not eat the apple when she got it. She hasted to give it away. She only wanted it because it had been forbidden.

So also Joan of Hohenstein desired to go down with Dessauer that she might look upon the man betrothed to her from birth. She went. She looked, and, as the tale tells, within her there grew a heart of flesh. Then, when the stroke fell, that heart uprose in quick, intemperate revolt. And what might have issued in the dull compliance of a princess whose life was settled for her, became the imperious revolt of a woman against an intolerable and loathsome impossibility.

So in her castle of Kernsberg Joan waited. But not idly. All day long and every day Maurice von Lynar rode on her service. The hillmen gathered to his word, and in the courtyard the stormy voices of George the Hussite and Peter Balta were never hushed. The shepherds from the hills went to and fro, marching and countermarching, wheeling and charging, porting musket and thrusting pike, till all Kernsberg was little better than a barracks, and the maidens sat wet-eyed at their knitting by the fire and thought, "Well for Her to please herself whom she shall marry—but how about us, with never a lad in the town to whistle us out in the gloaming, or to thumb a pebble against the window-lattice from the deep edges of the ripening corn?"

But there were two, at least, within the realm of the Duchess Joan who knew no drawbacks to their joy, who rubbed palm on palm and nudged each other for pure gladness. These (it is sad to say) were the military *attachés* of the neighbouring peaceful State of Plassenburg. Yet they had been specially cautioned by their Prince Hugo, in the presence of his wife Helene, the hereditary Princess, that they were most carefully to avoid all international complications. They were on no account to take sides in any quarrel. Above all they must do nothing prejudicial to the peace, neutrality, and universal amity of the State and Princedom of Plassenburg. Such were these instructions.

They promised faithfully.

But, their names being Captains Boris and Jorian, they now rubbed their hands and nudged each other. They ought to have been in their chamber in the Castle of Kernsberg, busily concocting despatches to their master and mistress, giving an account of these momentous events.

Instead, how is it that we find them lying on that spur of the Jägernbergen which overlooks the passes of Alla, watching the gathering of the great storm which in the course of days must break over the domains of the Duchess Joan—who had refused and slighted her wedded husband, Louis, Prince of Courtland?

Being both powerfully resourceful men, long lean Boris and rotund Jorian had found a way out of the apparent difficulty. There had come with them from Plassenburg a commission written upon an entire square of sheepskin by a secretary and sealed with the seal of Leopold von Dessauer, High Councillor of the United Princedom and Duchy, bearing that "In the name of Hugo and Helene our well-loved lieges Captains Boris and Jorian are empowered to act and treat," and so forth. This momentous deed was tied about the middle with a red string, and presented withal so courtly and respectable an appearance to the uncritical eyes of the ex-men-at-arms themselves, that they felt almost anything excusable which they might do in its name.

Before leaving Kernsberg, therefore, Boris placed this great red-waisted parchment roll in his bed, leaning it angle-wise against his pillow. Jorian tossed a spare dagger with the arms of Plassenburg beside it.

"There—let the civil power and the military for once lie down together!" he said. "We delegate our authority to these two during our absence!"

To the silent Plassenburgers who had accompanied them, and who now kept their door with unswerving attention, Boris explained himself briefly.

"Remember," he said, "when you are asked, that the envoys of Plassenburg are ill—ill of a dangerous and most contagious disease. Also, they are asleep. They must on no account be waked. The windows must be kept darkened. It is a great pity. You are desolated. You understand. The first time I have more money than I can spend you shall have ten marks!"

The men-at-arms understood, which was no wonder, for Boris generally contrived to make himself very clear. But they thought within them that their chances of financial benefit from their captain's conditional generosity were worth about one sole stiver.

So these two, being now free fighting-men, as it were, soldiers of fortune, lay waiting on the slopes of the Jägernbergen, talking over the situation.

"A man surely has a right to his own wife!" said Jorian, taking for the sake of argument the conventional side.

"*Narren-possen*, Jorian!" cried Boris, raising his voice to the indignation point. "Clotted nonsense! Who is going to keep a man's wife for him if he cannot do it himself? And he a prince, and within his own city and fortress, too. She boxed his ears, they say, and rode away, telling him that if he wanted her he might come and take her! A pretty spirit, i' faith! Too good for such a dried stockfish of the Baltic, with not so much soul as a speckled flounder on his own mud-flats! Faith! if I were a marrying man, I would run off with the lass myself. She ought at least to be a soldier's wife."

"The trouble is that so far she feels no necessity to be any one's wife," said Jorian, shifting his ground.

"That also is nonsense," said Boris, who, spite his defence of Joan, held the usual masculine views. "Every woman wishes to marry, if she can only have first choice."

"There they come!" whispered Jorian, whose eyes had never wandered from the long wavering lines of willow and alder which marked the courses of the sluggish streams flowing east toward the Alla.

Boris rose to his feet and looked long beneath his hand. Very far away there was a sort of white tremulousness in the atmosphere which after a while began to give off little luminous glints and sparkles, as the sea does when a shaft of moonlight touches it through a dark canopy of cloud.

Then there arose from the level green plain first one tall column of dense black smoke and then another, till as far as they could see to the left the plain was full of them.

"God's truth!" cried Jorian, "they are burning the farms and herds' houses. I thought they had been Christians in Courtland. But these are more like Duke Casimir's devil's tricks."

Boris did not immediately answer. His eyes were busy seeing, his brain setting in order.

"I tell you what," he said at last, in a tone of intense interest, "these are no fires lighted by Courtlanders. The heavy Baltic knights could never ride so fast nor spread so wide. The Muscovite is out! These are Cossack fires. Bravo, Jorian! we shall yet have our Hugo here with his axe! He will never suffer the Bear so near his borders."

"Let us go down," said Jorian, "or we shall miss some of the fun. In two good hours they will be at the fords of the Alla!"

So they looked to their arms and went down.

"What do you here? Go back!" shouted Werner von Orseln, who with his men lay waiting behind the floodbanks of the Alla. "This is not your quarrel! Go back, Plassenburgers!"

"We have for the time being demitted our office," Boris exclaimed. "The envoys of Plassenburg are at home in bed, sick of a most sanguinary fever. We offer you our swords as free fighting-men and good Teuts. The Muscovites are over yonder. Lord, to think that I have lived to forty-eight and never yet killed even one bearded Russ!"

"You may mend that record shortly, to all appearance, if you have luck!" said Von Orseln grimly. "And this gentleman here," he added, looking at Jorian, "is he also in bed, sick?"

"My sword is at your service," said the round one, "though I should prefer a musketoon, if it is all the same to you. It will be something to do till these firebrands come within arm's length of us."

"I have here two which are very much at your service, if you know how to use them!" said Werner.

The men-at-arms laughed.

"We know their tricks better than those of our sweethearts!" they said, "and those we know well!"

"Here they be, then," said Von Orseln. "I sent a couple of men spurring to warn my Lady Joan, and I bade them leave their muskets and bandoliers till they came back, that they might ride the lighter to and from Kernsberg."

Boris and Jorian took the spare pieces with a glow of gratitude, which was, however, very considerably modified when they discovered the state in which their former owners had kept them.

"Dirty Wendish pigs," they said (which was their favourite malediction, though they themselves were Wend of the Wends). "Were they but an hour in our camp they should ride the wooden horse with these very muskets tied to their soles to keep them firmly down. Faugh!"

And Jorian withdrew his finger from the muzzle, black as soot with the grease of uncleansed powder.

Looking up, they saw that the priest with the little army of Kernsberg was praying fervently (after the Hussite manner, without book) for the safety of the State and person of their lady Duchess, and that the men were listening bareheaded beneath the green slope of the water-dyke.

"Go on cleaning," said Boris; "this is some heretic function, and might sap our morality. We are volunteers, at any rate, as well as the best of good Catholics. We do not need unlicensed prayers. If you have quite done with that rag stick, lend it to me, Jorian!"

CHAPTER XVIII
CAPTAINS BORIS AND JORIAN
PROMOTE PEACE

Now this is the report which Captains Boris and Jorian, envoys (very) extraordinary from the Prince and Princess of Plassenburg to the reigning Duchess of Hohenstein, made to their home government upon their return from the fords of the Alla.

They wrote it in collaboration, on the usual plan of one working and the other assisting him with advice.

Jorian, being of the rotund and complaisant faction, acquiesced in the proposal that he should do the writing. But as he never got beyond "To our honoured Lord and Lady, Hugo and Helene, these——" there needs not to be any particularity as to his manner of acting the scribe. He mended at a pen till it looked like a brush worn to the straggling point. He squared his elbows suddenly and overset the inkhorn. He daubed an entire folio of paper with a completeness which left nothing to the imagination.

Then he remembered that he knew where a secretary was in waiting. He would go and borrow him. Jorian re-entered their bedroom with a beaming smile, and the secretary held by the sleeve to prevent his escape. Both felt that already the report was as good as written. It began thus:—

"With great assiduity (a word suggested by the secretary) your envoys remembered your Highnesses' princely advice and command that we should involve ourselves in no warfare or other local disagreement. So when we heard that Hohenstein was to be invaded by the troops of the Prince of Courtland we were deeply grieved.

"Nevertheless, judging it to be for the good of our country that we should have a near view of the fighting, we left worthy and assured substitutes in our place and room——"

"The parchment commission with a string round his belly!" explained Jorian, in answer to the young secretary's lifted eyebrow; "there he is, hiding behind the faggot-chest."

"Get on, Boris," quoth Jorian, from the settee on which he had thrown himself; "it is your turn to lie."

"Good!" says Boris. And did it as followeth:—

"We left our arms behind us——"

"Such as we could not carry," added Jorian under his breath. The secretary, a wise youth—full of the new learning and of talk concerning certain books printed on paper and bound all with one *druck* of a great machine like a cheese-press—held his pen suspended over the paper in doubt what to write.

"Do not mind him," said Boris. "*I* am dictating this report."

"Yes, my lord!" replied the secretary from behind his hand.

"We left our arms and armour behind us, and went out to make observations in the interest of your Highnesses' armies. Going down through the woods we saw many wild swine, exceeding fierce. But having no means of hunting these, we evaded them, all save one, which misfortunately met its death by falling against a spear in the hands of Captain Boris, and another, also of the male sex, shot dead by Jorian's pistol, which went off by accident as it was passing."

"I have already written that your arms were left at home, according to your direction," said the secretary, who was accustomed to criticise the composition of diplomatic reports.

"Pshaw!" growled Boris, bending his brow upon such superfluity of virtue; "a little thing like that will never be noticed. Besides, a man must carry something. We had no cannon or battering rams with us, therefore we were unarmed—to all intents and purposes, that is."

The secretary sighed. Verily life (as Von Orseln averred) must be easy in Plassenburg, if such stories would pass with the Prince. And now it seemed as if they would.

"We found the soldiers of the Duchess Joan waiting at the fords of the Alla, which is the eastern border of their province. There were not many of them, but all good soldiers. The Courtlanders came on in myriads, with Muscovites without number. These last burned and slew all in their path. Now the men of Hohenstein are good to attack, but their fault is that they are not patient to defend. So it came to pass that not long after we arrived at the fords of the Alla, one Werner von Orseln, commander of the soldiers of the Duchess, ordered that his men should attack the Courtlanders in front. Whereupon they crossed the ford, when they should have stayed behind their shelter. It was bravely done, but had better have been left undone.

"Remembering, however, your orders and our duty, we advanced with him, hoping that by some means we might be able to promote peace.

"This we did. For (wonderful as it may appear) we convinced no fewer than ten Muscovites whom we found sacking a farm, and their companions, four sutlers of Courtland, that it was wrong to slay and ravish in a peaceful country. In the heat of the argument Captain Boris received a bullet through his shoulder which caused us for the time being to cease our appeal and fall back. The Muscovites, however, made no attempt to follow us. Our arguments had been sufficient to convince them of the wickedness of their deed. We hope to receive your princely approval of this our action—peace being, in our opinion, the greatest blessing which any nation can enjoy. For without flattery we may say that if others had argued with equal persuasiveness, the end would have been happier.

"Then, being once more behind the flood-dykes of the Alla, Captain Jorian examined the hurt of Captain Boris which he had received in the peace negotiations with the Muscovites. It was but a flesh wound, happily, and was soon bound up. But the pain of it acted upon both your envoys as an additional incentive to put a stop to the horrors of war.

"So when a company of the infantry of Courtland, with whom we had hitherto had no opportunity of wrestling persuasively, attacked the fords, wading as deep as mid-thigh, we took upon us to rebuke them for their forwardness. And accordingly they desisted, some retreating to the further shore, while others, finding the water pleasant, remained, and floated peacefully down with the current.

"This also, in some measure, made for peace, and we humbly hope for the further approval of your Highnesses, when you have remarked our careful observance of all your instructions.

"If only we had had with us our several companies of the Regiment of Karl the Miller's Son to aid us in the discussion, more Cossacks and Strelits might have been convinced, and the final result have been different. Nevertheless, we did what we could, and were successful with many beyond our hopes.

"But the men of Hohenstein being so few, and those of Courtland with their allies so many, the river was overpassed both above and below the fords. Whereupon I pressed it upon Werner von Orseln that he should retreat to a place of greater hope and safety, being thus in danger on both flanks.

"For your envoys have a respect for Werner von Orseln, though we grieve to report that, being a man of war from his youth up, he does not display that desire for peace which your good counsels have so deeply implanted in our breasts, and which alone animates the hearts of Boris and Jorian, captains in the princely guard of Plassenburg."

"Put that in, till I have time to think what is to come next!" said Boris, waving his hand to the secretary. "We are doing pretty well, I think!" he added, turning to his companion with all the self-conscious pride of an amateur in words.

"Let us now tell more about Von Orseln, and how he would in no wise listen to us!" suggested Jorian. "But let us not mix the mead too strong! Our Hugo is shrewd!"

"This Werner von Orseln (be it known to your High Graciousnesses) was the chief obstacle in the way of our making peace—except, perhaps, those Muscovites with whom we were unable to argue, having no opportunity. This Werner had fought all the day, and, though most recklessly exposing himself, was still unhurt. His armour was covered with blood and black with powder after the fashion of these wild hot-bloods. His face also was stained, and when he spoke it was in a hoarse whisper. The matter of his discourse to us was this:—

"'I can do no more. My people are dead, my powder spent. They are more numerous than the sea-sands. They are behind us and before, also outflanking us on either side.'

"Then we advised him to set his face to Hohenstein and with those who were left to him to retreat in that direction. We accompanied him, bearing in mind your royal commands, and eager to do all that in us lay to advance the interests of amity. The enemy fetched a compass to close us in on every side.

"Whereupon we argued with them again to the best of our ability. There ensued some slight noise and confusion, so that Captain Boris forgot his wound, and Captain Jorian admits that in his haste he may have spoken uncivilly to several Bor-Russian gentry who thrust themselves in his way. And for this unseemly conduct he craves the pardon of their Highnesses Hugo and Helene, his beloved master and mistress. However, as no complaint has been received from the enemy's headquarters, no breach of friendly relations may be apprehended. Captain Boris is of opinion that the Muscovite boors did not understand Captain Jorian's Teuton language. At least they were not observed to resent his words.

"In this manner were the invaders of Hohenstein broken through, and the remnant of the soldiers of the Duchess Joan reached Kernsberg in safety—a result which, we flatter ourselves, was as much due to the zeal and amicable persuasiveness of your envoys as to the skill and bravery of Werner von Orseln and the soldiers of the Duchess.

"And your humble servants will ever pray for the speedy triumph of peace and concord, and also for an undisturbed reign to your Highnesses through countless years. In token whereof we append our signatures and seals.

"Boris

"Jorian."

"Is not that last somewhat overstrained about peace and concord and so forth?" asked Jorian anxiously.

"Not a whit—not a whit!" cried Boris, who, having finished his composition, was wholly satisfied with himself, after the manner of the beginner in letters. "Our desire to promote peace needs to be put strongly, in order to carry persuasion to their Highnesses in Plassenburg. In fact, I am not sure that it has been put strongly enough!"

"I am troubled with some few doubts myself!" said Jorian, under his breath.

And as the secretary jerked the ink from his pen he smiled.

CHAPTER XIX
JOAN STANDS WITHIN HER DANGER

So soon as Werner von Orseln returned to Castle Kernsberg with news of the forcing of the Alla and the overwhelming numbers of the Muscovite hordes, the sad-eyed Duchess of Hohenstein became once more Joan of the Sword Hand.

Hitherto she had doubted and feared. But now the thought of Prince Wasp and his Muscovite savages steadied her, and she was here and there, in every bastion of the Castle, looking especially to the gates which commanded the roads to Courtland and Plassenburg.

Her one thought was, "Will *he* be here?"

And again she saw the knight of the white plume storm through the lists of Courtland, and the enemy go down before him. Ah, if only— —!

The invading army must have numbered thirty thousand, at least. There were, all told, about two thousand spears in Kernsberg. Von Orseln, indeed, could easily have raised more. Nay, they would have come in of themselves by hundreds to fight for their Duchess, but the little hill town could not feed more. Yet Joan was not discouraged. She joked with Peter Balta upon the louts of Courtlanders taking the Castle which Henry the Lion had fortified. The Courtlanders, indeed! Had not Duke Casimir assaulted Kernsberg in vain, and even the great Margraf George threatened it? Yet still it remained a virgin fortress, looking out over the fertile and populous plain. But now what were left of the shepherds had fled to the deep-bosomed mountains with their flocks. The cattle were hidden in the thickest woods; only the white farm-houses remained tenantless, silently waiting the coming of the spoiler. And, stripped for combat, Castle Kernsberg looked out towards the invader, the rolling plain in front of it, and behind the grim intricate hill country of Hohenstein.

When Werner von Orseln and Peter Balta met the invader at the fords of the Alla, Maurice von Lynar and Alt Pikker had remained with Joan, nominally to assist her dispositions, but really to form a check upon the impetuosity of her temper.

Now Von Orseln was back again. The fords of the Alla were forced, and the fighting strength of Kernsberg united itself in the Eagle's Nest to make its final stand.

Aloft on the highest ramparts there was a terrace walk which the Sparhawk much affected, especially when he was on guard at night. It looked towards the east, and from it the first glimpse of the Courtlanders would be obtained.

In the great hall of the guard they were drinking their nightly toast. The shouting might have been heard in the town, where at street corners were groups of youths exercising late with wooden spears and mimic armour, crying "Hurrah, Kernsberg!"

They changed it, however, in imitation of their betters in the Castle above.

"Joan of the Sword Hand! Hoch!"

The shout went far into the night. Again and yet again it was repeated from about the crowded board in the hall of the men-at-arms and from the gloomy streets beneath.

"Captain Boris was telling a story."

When all was over, the Sparhawk rose, belted his sword a hole or two tighter, set a steel cap without a visor upon his head, glanced at Werner von Orseln, and withdrew, leaving the other captains to their free-running jest and laughter. Captain Boris of Plassenburg was telling a story with a countenance more than ordinarily grave and earnest, while the table round rang with contagious mirth.

The Sparhawk found the high terrace of the Lion Tower guarded by a sentry. Him he removed to the foot of the turret-stair, with orders to permit no one save Werner von Orseln to pass on any pretext.

Presently the chief captain's step was heard on the stone turnpike.

"Ha, Sparhawk," he cried, "this is cold cheer! Why could we not have talked comfortably in hall, with a beaker of mead at one's elbow?"

"The enemy are not in sight," said the Sparhawk gloomily.

"Well, that is bad luck," said Werner; "but do not be afraid, you will have your chance yet—indeed, all you want and a little over—in the way of killing of Muscovites."

"I wanted to speak with you on a matter we cannot mention elsewhere," said Maurice von Lynar.

The chief captain stopped in his stride, drew his cloak about him, rested his thigh on a square battlement, and resigned himself.

"Well," he said, "youth has ever yeasty brains. Go on."

"I would speak of my lady!" said the youth.

"So would most mooncalves of your age!" growled Werner; "but they do not usually bring their commanding officers up to the housetops to do it!"

"I mean our lady, the Duchess Joan!"

"Ah," said Werner, with the persiflage gone out of his tone, "that is altogether another matter!"

And the two men were silent for a minute, both looking out into the blackness where no stars shone or any light twinkled beyond the walls of the little fortified hill town.

At last Maurice von Lynar spoke.

"How long can we hold out if they besiege us?"

"Two months, certainly—with luck, three!"

"And then?"

Werner von Orseln shrugged his shoulders, but only said, "A soldier never anticipates disaster!"

"And what of the Duchess Joan?" persisted the young man.

"Why, in the same space of time she will be dead or wed!" said Von Orseln, with an affectation of carelessness easily seen through.

The young man burst out, "Dead she may be! I know she will never be wife to that Courtland Death's-head. I saw it in her eyes that day in their cathedral, when she bade me slip out and bring up our four hundred lances of Kernsberg."

"Like enough," said Werner shortly. "I, for one, set no bounds to any woman's likings or mislikings!"

"We must get her away to a place of safety," said the young man.

Von Orseln laughed.

"Get her? Who would persuade or compel our lady? Whither would she go? Would she be safer there than here? Would the Courtlander not find out in twenty-four hours that there was no Joan of the Sword Hand in Kernsberg, and follow on her trail? And lastly—question most pertinent of all—what had you to drink down there in hall, young fellow?"

The Sparhawk did not notice the last question, nor did he reply in a similarly jeering tone.

"We must persuade her—capture her, compel her, if necessary. Kernsberg cannot for long hold out against both the Muscovite and the Courtlander. Save good Jorian and Boris, who will lie manfully about their fighting, there is no help for us in mortal man. So this is what we must do to save our lady!"

"What? Capture Joan of the Sword Hand and carry her off? The mead buzzes in the boy's head. He grows dotty with anxiety and too much hard ale. 'Ware, Maurice—these battlements are not over high. I will relieve you, lad! Go to bed and sleep it off!"

"Von Orseln," said the youth, with simple earnestness, not heeding his taunts, "I have thought deeply. I see no way out of it but this. Our lady will eagerly go on reconnaissance if you represent it as necessary. You must take ten good men and ride north, far north, even to the edges of the Baltic, to a place I know of, which none but I and one other can find. There, with a few trusty fellows to guard her, she will be safe till the push of the times is over."

The chief captain was silent. He had wholly dropped his jeering mood.

"There is nothing else that I can see for it," the young Dane went on, finding that Werner did not speak. "Our Joan will never go to Courtland alive. She will not be carried off on Prince Louis' saddle-bow, as a Cossack might carry off a Circassian slave!"

"But how," said Von Orseln, meditating, "will you prevent her absence being known? The passage of so large a party may easily be traced and remembered. Though our folk are true enough and loyal enough, sooner or later what is known in the Castle is known in the town, and what is known in the town becomes known to the enemy!"

Maurice von Lynar leaned forward towards his chief captain and whispered a few words in his ear.

"Ah!" he said, and nodded. Then, after a pause for thought, he added, "That is none so ill thought on for a beardless younker! I will think it over, sleep on it, and tell you my opinion to-morrow!"

The youth tramped to and fro on the terrace, muttering to himself.

"Good-night, Sparhawk!" said Von Orseln, from the top of the corkscrew stair, as he prepared to descend; "go to bed. I will send Alt Pikker to command the house-guard to-night. Do you get straightway between the sheets as soon as maybe. If this mad scheme comes off you will need your beauty-sleep with a vengeance! So take it now!"

"At any rate," the chief captain growled to himself, "you have set a pretty part for me. I may forthwith order my shroud. I shall never be able to face my lady again!"

CHAPTER XX
THE CHIEF CAPTAIN'S TREACHERY

The Duchess Joan was in high spirits. It had been judged necessary, in consultation with her chief officers, to ride a reconnaissance in person in order to ascertain whether the advancing enemy had cut Kernsberg off towards the north. On this matter Von Orseln thought that her Highness had better judge for herself. Here at last was something definite to be done. It was almost like the old foraying days, but now in a more desperate cause.

Ten days before, Joan's maidens and her aged nurse had been sent for safety into Plassenburg, under escort of Captains Boris and Jorian as far as the frontier—who had, however, returned in time to accompany the party of observation on their ride northward.

No one in all Castle Kernsberg was to know of the departure of this cavalcade. Shortly before midnight the horses were to be ready under the Castle wall. The Sparhawk was appointed to command the town during Von Orseln's absence. Ten men only were to go, and these picked and sifted riders—chosen because of their powers of silence—and because, being unmarried, they had no wives to worm secrets out of them. Sweethearts they might have, but then, in Kernsberg at least, that is a very different thing.

Finally, having written to their princely master in Plassenburg, that they were leaving on account of the war—in which, as envoys extraordinary, they did not desire to be further mixed up—Captains Boris and Jorian made them ready to accompany the reconnaissance. It proved to be a dark and desperate night of storm and rain. The stars were ever and anon concealed by the thick pall of cloud which the wind from the south drove hurtling athwart them. Joan herself was in the highest spirits. She wore a long blue cloak, which completely concealed the firmly knit slender figure, clad in forester's dress, from prying eyes.

As for Werner von Orseln, that high captain was calm and grave as usual, but the rest of the ten men were plainly nervous, as they fingered their bridle-reins and avoided looking at each other while they waited in readiness to mount.

With a clatter of hoofs they were off, none in the Castle knowing more than that Werner the chief captain rode out on his occasions. A townsman or two huddled closer among his blankets as the clatter and jingle of the horses mingled with the sharp volleying of the rain upon his wind-beaten lattice, while the long *whoo* of the wind sang of troublous times in the twisted chimneys overhead.

Joan, as the historian has already said, was in high spirits.

"Werner," she cried, as soon as they were clear of the town, "if we strike the enemy to-night, I declare we will draw sword and ride through them."

"*If* we strike them to-night, right so, my lady!" returned Werner promptly.

But he had the best of reasons for knowing that they would not strike any enemy that night. His last spy from the north had arrived not half an hour before they started, having ridden completely round the enemy's host.

Joan and her chief captain rode on ahead, Von Orseln glancing keenly about him, and Joan riding free and careless, as in the old days when she overpassed the hills to drive a prey from the lands of her father's enemies.

It was grey morning when they came to a goatherd's hut at the top of the green valley. Already they had passed the bounds of Hohenstein by half a dozen miles. The goatherd had led his light-skipping train to the hills for the day, and the rude and chaotic remains of his breakfast were still on the table. Boris and Jorian cleared these away, and, with the trained alacrity of seasoned men-at-arms, they placed before the party a breakfast prepared with speed out of what they had brought with them and those things which they had found to their hand by foraging in the larder of the goatherd—to wit, sliced neat's-tongue dried in the smoke, and bread of fine wheat which Jorian had carried all the way in a net at his saddle-bow. Boris had charge of the wine-skins, and upon a shelf above the door they found a great butter-pot full of freshly made curded goats' milk, very delicious both to taste and smell.

Of these things they ate and drank largely, Joan and Von Orseln being together at the upper end of the table. Boris and Jorian had to sit with them, though much against their wills, being (spite of their sweethearts) more accustomed to the company of honest men-at-arms than to the practice of dainty eating in ladies' society.

Joan undertook to rally them upon their loves, for whose fair fingers, as it has been related in an earlier chapter, she had given them rings.

"And how took your Katrin the ring, Boris?" she said, looking at him past the side of her glass. For Jorian had bethought him to bring one for the

Duchess, the which he cleansed and cooled at the spring without. As for the others, they all drank out of one wooden whey-cog, as was most fitting.

"Why, she took it rarely," said honest Boris, "and swore to love me more than ever for it. We are to be married upon my first return to Plassenburg."

"Which, perhaps, is the reason why you are in no hurry to return thither, seeing that you stopped short at the frontier last week?" said the Duchess shrewdly.

"Nay, my lady, that grieved me sore—for, indeed, we love each other dearly, Katrin and I," persisted Captain Boris, thinking, as was his custom, to lie himself out of it by dint of the mere avoirdupois of asseveration.

"That is the greater marvel," returned the lady, smiling upon him, "because when last I spoke with you concerning the matter, her name was not Katrin, but Gretchen!"

Boris was silent, as well he might be, for even as he lied he had had some lurking suspicion of this himself. He felt that he could hope to get no further by this avenue.

The lady now turned to Jorian, who, having digested the defeat and shame of Boris, was ready to be very indignant at his companion for having claimed his sweetheart.

"And you, Captain Jorian," she said, "how went it with you? Was your ring well received?"

"Aye, marry," said that gallant captain, "better than well. Much better! Never did I see woman so grateful. Katrin, whom this long, wire-drawn, splenetic fool hath lyingly claimed as his (by some trick of tongue born of his carrying the malmsey at his saddle-bow)—Katrin, I say, did kiss and clip me so that my very soul fainted within me. She could not make enough of the giver of such a precious thing as your Highness's ring?"

Jorian in his own estimation was doing very well. He thought he could yet better it.

"Her eyes sparkled with joy. Her hands twitched—she could not keep them from turning the pretty jewel about upon her finger. She swore never to part with it while life lasted——"

"Then," said Joan, smiling, "have no more to do with her. She is a false wench and mansworn. For do not I see it upon the little finger of your left hand at this moment? Nay, do not turn the stone within. I know my gift, and will own it even if your Katrin (was it not?) hath despised it. What say you now to that, Jorian?"

"My lady," faltered Jorian, striving manfully to recover himself, "when I came again in the honourable guise of an ambassador to Kernsberg, Katrin gave it back again to me, saying, 'You have no signet ring. Take this, so that you be not ashamed among those others. Keep it for me. I myself will place it on your finger with a loving kiss.'"

"Well done, Captain Jorian, you are a somewhat better liar than your friend. But still your excuses should accord better. The ring I gave you is not a signet ring. That Katrin of yours must have been ignorant indeed."

With these words Joan of the Sword Hand rose to her feet, for the ex-men-at-arms had not so much as a word to say.

"Let us now mount and ride homeward," she said; "there are no enemy to be found on this northerly road. We shall be more fortunate upon another occasion."

Then Werner Von Orseln nerved himself for a battle more serious than any he had ever fought at the elbow of Henry the Lion of Hohenstein.

"My lady," he said, standing up and bowing gravely before her, "you see here eleven men who love you far above their lives, of whom I am the chief. Two others also there are, who, though not of our nation, are in heart joined to us, especially in this thing that we have done. With all respect, your Highness cannot go back. We have come out, not to make a reconnaissance, but to put your Grace in a place of safety till the storm blows over."

The Duchess had slowly risen to her feet, with her hand on the sword which swung at her belt.

"You have suddenly gone mad, Werner!" she said; "let us have no more of this. I bid you mount and ride. Back to Kernsberg, I say! Ye are not such fools and traitors as to deliver the maiden castle, the Eagle's Nest of Hohenstein, into the hands of our enemies?"

"Nay," said Von Orseln, looking steadily upon the ground, "that will we not do. Kernsberg is in good hands, and will fight bravely. But we cannot hold out with our few folk and scanty provender against the leaguer of thirty thousand. Nevertheless we will not permit you to sacrifice yourself for our sakes or for the sake of the women and children of the city."

Joan drew her sword.

"Werner von Orseln, will you obey me, or must I slay you with my hand?" she cried.

The chief captain yet further bowed his head and abased his eyes.

"We have thought also of this," he made answer. "Me you may kill, but these that are with me will defend themselves, though they will not strike one they love more than their lives. But man by man we have sworn to do this thing. At all hazards you must abide in our hands till the danger is overpast. For me (this he added in a deeper tone), I am your immediate officer. There is none to come between us. It is your right to slay me if you will. Mine is the responsibility for this deed, though the design was not mine. Here is my sword. Slay your chief captain with it if you will. He has faithfully served your house for five-and-thirty years. 'Tis perhaps time he rested now."

And with these words Werner von Orseln took his sword by the point and offered the hilt to his mistress.

Joan of the Sword Hand shook with mingled passion and helplessness, and her eyes were dark and troublous.

"Put up your blade," she said, striking aside the hilt with her hand; "if you have not deserved death, no more have I deserved this! But you said that the design was not yours. Who, then, has dared to plot against the liberty of Joan of Hohenstein?"

"I would I could claim the honour," said Werner the chief captain; "but truly the matter came from Maurice von Lynar the Dane. It is to his mother, who after the death of her brother, the Count von Lynar, continued to dwell in a secret strength on the Baltic shore, that we are conducting your Grace!"

"Maurice von Lynar?" exclaimed Joan, astonished. "He remains in Castle Kernsberg, then?"

"Aye," said Werner, relieved by her tone, "he will take your place when danger comes. In morning twilight or at dusk he makes none so ill a Lady Duchess, and, i' faith, his 'sword hand' is brisk enough. If the town be taken, better that he than you be found in Castle Kernsberg. Is the thing not well invented, my lady?"

Werner looked up hopefully. He thought he had pleaded his cause well.

"Traitor! Supplanter!" cried Joan indignantly; "this Dane in my place! I will hang him from the highest window in the Castle of Kernsberg if ever I win back to mine own again!"

"My lady," said Werner, gently and respectfully, "your servant Von Lynar bade me tell you that he would as faithfully and loyally take your place now as he did on a former occasion!"

"Ah," said Joan, smiling wanly with a quick change of mood, "I hope he will be more ready to give up his privileges on this occasion than on that!"

She was thinking of the Princess Margaret and the heritage of trouble upon which, as the Count von Löen, she had caused the Sparhawk to enter.

Then a new thought seemed to strike her.

"But my nurse and my women—how can he keep the imposture secret? He may pass before the stupid eyes of men. But they——"

"If your Highness will recollect, they have been sent out of harm's way into Plassenburg. There is not a woman born of woman in all the Castle of Kernsberg!"

"Yes," mused Joan, "I have indeed been fairly cozened. I gave that order also by the Dane's advice. Well, let him have his run. We will reeve him a firm collar of hemp at the end of it, and maybe for Werner von Orseln also, as a traitor alike to his bread and his mistress. Till then I hope you will both enjoy playing your parts."

The chief captain bowed.

"I am content, my lady," he said respectfully.

"Now, good jailers all," cried Joan, "lead on. I will follow. Or would you prefer to carry me with you handcuffed and chained? I will go with you in whatsoever fashion seemeth good to my masters!"

She paused and looked round the little goatherd's hut.

"Only," she said, nodding her head, "I warn you I will take my own time and manner of coming back!"

There was a deep silence as the men drew their belts tighter and prepared to mount and depart.

"About that time, Jorian," whispered Boris as they went out, "you and I will be better in Plassenburg than within the bounds of Kernsberg—for our health's sake and our sweethearts', that is!"

"Good!" said Jorian, dropping the bars of his visor; "but for all that she is a glorious wench, and looks her bravest when she is angry!"

CHAPTER XXI
ISLE RUGEN

They had travelled for six hours through high arched pines, their fallen needles making a carpet green and springy underfoot. Then succeeded oaks, stricken a little at top with the frosts of years. Alternating with these came marshy tracts where alder and white birch gleamed from the banks of shallow runnels and the margins of black peaty lakes. Anon the broom and the gorse began to flourish sparsely above wide sand-hills, heaved this way and that like the waves of a mountainous sea.

The party was approaching that no-man's-land which stretches for upwards of a hundred miles along the southern shores of the Baltic. It is a land of vast brackish backwaters connected with the outer sea by devious channels often half silted up, but still feeling the pulse of the outer green water in the winds which blow over the sandy "bills," bars, and spits, and bring with them sweet scents of heather and wild thyme, and, most of all, of the southernwood which grows wild on the scantily pastured braes.

It was at that time a beautiful but lonely country—the 'batable land of half a dozen princedoms, its only inhabitant a stray hunter setting up his gipsy booth of wattled boughs, heaping with stones a rude fireplace, or fixing a tripod over it whereon a pottinger was presently a-swing, in some sunny curve of the shore.

At eventide of the third day of their journeying the party came to a great morass. Black decaying trunks of trees stood up at various angles, often bristling with dead branches like *chevaux-de-frise*. The horses picked their path warily through this tangle, the rotten sticks yielding as readily and silently as wet mud beneath their hoofs. Finally all dismounted except Joan, while Werner von Orseln, with a rough map in his hand, traced out the way. Pools of stagnant black water had to be evaded, treacherous yellow sands tested, bridges constructed of the firmer logs, till all suddenly they came out upon a fairylike little half-moon of sand and tiny shells.

Here was a large flat-bottomed boat, drawn up against the shore. In the stern a strange figure was seated, a man, tall and angular, clad in jerkin and trunks of brown tanned leather, cross-gartered hose of grey cloth, and home-made shoon of hide with the hair outside. He wore a black skull cap, and his head had the strange, uncanny look of a wild animal. It was not at the first glance nor yet at the second that Boris and Jorian found out the cause of this curious appearance.

Meanwhile Werner von Orseln was putting into his hand some pledge or sign which he scrutinised carefully, when Jorian suddenly gripped his companion's arm.

"Look," he whispered, "he's got no ears!"

"Nor any tongue!" responded Boris, staring with all his eyes at the prodigy.

And, indeed, the strange man was pointing to his mouth with the index finger of his right hand and signing that they were to follow him into the boat which had been waiting for them.

Joan of the Sword Hand had never spoken since she knew that her men were taking her to a place of safety. Nor did her face show any trace of emotion now that Werner von Orseln, approaching cap in hand, humbly begged her to permit him to conduct her to the boat.

But the Duchess leapt from her horse, and without accepting his hand she stepped from the little pier of stone beside which the boat lay. Then walking firmly from seat to seat she reached the stern, where she sat down without seeming to have glanced at any of the company.

Werner von Orseln then motioned Captains Boris and Jorian to take their places in the bow, and having bared his head he seated himself beside his mistress. The wordless earless man took the oars and pushed off. The boat slid over a little belt of still water through a wilderness of tall reeds. Then all suddenly the wavelets lapped crisp and clean beneath her bottom, and the wide levels of a lake opened out before them. The ten men left on the shore set about building a fire and making shelters of brushwood, as if they expected to stay here some time.

The tiny harbour was fenced in on every side with an unbroken wall of lofty green pines. The lower part of their trunks shot up tall and straight and opened long vistas into the black depths of the forest. The sun was setting and threw slant rays far underneath, touching with gold the rank marish growths, and reddening the mouldering boles of the fallen pines.

The boat passed almost noiselessly along, the strange man rowing strongly and the boat drawing steadily away across the widest part of the still inland sea. As they thus coasted along the gloomy shores the sun went down and darkness came upon them at a bound. Then at the far end of the long tunnel, which an hour agone had been sunny glades, they saw strange flickering lights dancing and vanishing, waving and leaping upward—will-o'-the-wisps kindled doubtless from the stagnant boglands and the rotting vegetation of that ancient northern forest.

The breeze freshened. The water clappered louder under the boat's quarter. Breaths born of the wide sea unfiltered through forest dankness visited more keenly the nostrils of the voyagers. They heard ahead of them the distant roar of breakers. Now and then there came a long and gradual roll underneath their quarter, quite distinct from the little chopping waves of the fresh-water *haff*, as the surface of the mere heaved itself in a great slope of water upon which the boat swung sideways.

After a space tall trees again shot up overhead, and with a quick turn the boat passed between walls of trembling reeds that rustled against the oars like silk, emerged on a black circle of water, and then, gliding smoothly forward, took ground in the blank dark.

As the broad keel grated on the sand, the Wordless Man leapt out, and, standing on the shore, put his hands to his mouth and emitted a long shout like a blast blown on a conch shell. Again and again that melancholy ululation, with never a consonantal sound to break it, went forth into the night. Yet it was so modulated that it had obviously a meaning for some one, and to put the matter beyond a doubt it was answered by three shrill whistles from behind the rampart of trees.

Joan sat still in the boat where she had placed herself. She asked no question, and even these strange experiences did not alter her resolution.

Presently a light gleamed uncertainly through the trees, now lost behind brushwood and again breaking waveringly out.

A tall figure moved forward with a step quick and firm. It was that of a woman who carried a swinging lantern in her hand, from which wheeling lights gleamed through a score of variously coloured little plates of horn. She wore about her shoulders a great crimson cloak which masked her shape. A hood of the same material, attached at the back of the neck to the cloak, concealed her head and dropped about her face, partially hiding her features.

Standing still on a little wooden pier she held the lantern high, so that the light fell directly on those in the boat, and their faces looked strangely white in that illumined circle, surrounded as it was by a pent-house of tense blackness—black pines, black water, black sky.

"Follow me!" said the woman, in a deep rich voice—a voice whose tones thrilled those who heard them to their hearts, so full and low were some of the notes.

Joan of the Sword Hand rose to her feet.

"I am the Duchess of Hohenstein, and I do not leave this boat till I know in what place I am, and who this may be that cries 'Follow!' to the daughter of Henry the Lion!"

The tall woman turned without bowing and looked at the girl.

"I am the mother of Maurice von Lynar, and this is the Isle Rugen!" she said simply, as if the answer were all sufficient.

CHAPTER XXII
THE HOUSE ON THE DUNES

The woman in the crimson cloak waited for Joan to be assisted from the boat, and then, without a word of greeting, led the way up a little sanded path to a gate which opened in a high stone wall. Through this she admitted her guests, whereupon they found themselves in an enclosure with towers and battlements rising dimly all round. It was planted with fragrant bushes and fruit trees whose leaves brushed pleasantly against their faces as they walked in single file following their guide.

Then came a long grey building, another door, small and creaking heavily on unaccustomed hinges, a sudden burst of light, and lo! the wanderers found themselves within a lighted hall, wherein were many stands of arms and armour, mingled with skins of wild animals, wide-spreading many-tined antlers, and other records of the chase.

The woman who had been their guide now set down her lantern and allowed the hood of her cloak to slide from her head. Werner and his two male companions the captains of Plassenburg, fell back a little at the apparition. They had expected to see some hag or crone, fit companion of their wordless guide.

Instead, a woman stood before them, not girlish certainly, nor yet in the first bloom of her youth, but glorious even among fair women by reason of the very ripeness of her beauty. Her hair shone full auburn with shadows of heavy burnt-gold upon its coils. It clustered about the broad low brow in a few simple locks, then, sweeping back round her head in loose natural waves, it was caught in a broad flat coil at the back, giving a certain statuesque and classic dignity to her head.

The mother of that young paladin, their Sparhawk? It seemed impossible. This woman was too youthful, too fair, too bountiful in her gracious beauty to be the mother of such a tense young yew-bow as Maurice von Lynar.

Yet she had said it, and women do not lie (affirmatively) about such a matter. So, indeed, at heart thought Werner von Orseln.

"My lady Joan," she said, in the same thrilling voice, "my son has sent me word that till a certain great danger is overpast you are to abide with me here on the Isle Rugen. I live alone, save for this one man, dumb Max Ulrich, long since cruelly maimed at the hands of his enemies. I can offer you no suite of attendants beyond those you bring with you. Our safety depends on the secrecy of our abode, as for many years my own life has done. I ask you, therefore, to respect our privacy, as also to impose the same upon your soldiers."

The Duchess Joan bowed slightly.

"As you doubtless know, I have not come hither of my own free will," she answered haughtily; "but I thank you, madam, for your hospitality. Rest assured that the amenity of your dwelling shall not be endangered by me!"

The two looked at each other with that unyielding "at-arm's-length" eyeshot which signifies instinctive antipathy between women of strong wills.

Then with a large gesture the elder indicated the way up the broad staircase, and throwing her own cloak completely off she caught it across her arm as it dropped, and so followed Joan out of sight.

Werner von Orseln stood looking after them a little bewildered. But the more experienced Boris and Jorian exchanged significant glances with each other.

Then Boris shook his head at Jorian, and Jorian shook his head at Boris. And for once they did not designate the outlook by their favourite adjective.

Nevertheless, instinct was so strong that, as soon as the women had withdrawn themselves upstairs, the three captains seized the lantern and started towards the door to make the round of the defences. The Wordless Man accompanied them unasked. The square enclosure in which they found themselves seemed liker an old fortified farmhouse or grange than a regular castle, though the walls were thick as those of any fortress, being loopholed for musketry, and (in those days of bombards few and heavy) capable of standing a siege in good earnest against a small army.

The doors were of thick oak crossed in all directions with strengthening iron. The three captains examined every barred window with keen professional curiosity, and, coming to another staircase in a distant part of the house, Von Orseln intimated to the dumb man that they wished to examine it. In rapid pantomime he indicated to them that there was an ascending flight of steps leading round and round a tower till a platform was reached, from which (gazing out under his hand and making with his finger the shape of battlements) he gave them to understand that an extensive prospect was to be enjoyed.

With an inward resolve to ascend that stair and look upon that prospect at an early hour on the morrow, the three captains returned through the hall into a long dining-room vaulted above with beams of solid oak. Curtains were drawn close all about the walls. In the recesses were many stands of arms of good and recent construction, and opening a cupboard with the freedom of a man-at-arms, Boris saw ramrods, powder and shot horns arranged in order, as neatly as though he had done it himself, than which no better could be said.

In a little while the sound of footsteps descending the nearer staircase was heard. The Wordless Man moved to the door and held it open as Joan came in with a proud high look on her face. She was still pale, partly with travel and partly from the seething indignant angers of her heart. Von Lynar's mother entered immediately after her guest, and it needed nothing more subtle than Werner von Orseln's masculine acumen to discern that no word had been spoken between them while they were alone.

With a queenly gesture the hostess motioned her guest to the place of honour at her right hand, and indicated that the three soldiers were to take their places at the other side of the table. Werner von Orseln moved automatically to obey, but Jorian and Boris were already at the sideboard, dusting platters and making them ready to serve the meal.

"I thank you, madam," said Jorian. "Were we here as envoys of our master, Prince Hugo of Plassenburg, we would gladly and proudly sit at meat with you. But we are volunteers, and have all our lives been men-at-arms. We will therefore assist this good gentleman to serve, an it please you to permit us!"

The lady bowed slightly and for the first time smiled.

"You have, then, accompanied the Lady Duchess hither for pleasure, gentlemen? I fear Isle Rugen is a poor place for that!" she said, looking across at them.

"Aye and no!" said Jorian; "Kernsberg is, indeed, no fit dwelling-place for great ladies just now. The Duchess Joan will indeed be safer here than elsewhere till the Muscovites have gone home, and the hill-folk of Hohenstein have only the Courtlanders to deal with. All the same, we could have wished to have been permitted to speak with the Muscovite in the gate!"

"My son remains in Castle Kernsberg?" she asked, with an upward inflection, an indescribable softness at the same time overspreading her face, and a warmth coming into the grey eyes which showed what this woman might be to those whom she really loved.

"He keeps the Castle, indeed—in his mistress's absence and mine," said Werner. "He will make a good soldier. Our lady has already made him Count von Löen, that he may be the equal of those who care for such titles."

A strange flash as of remembrance and emotion passed over the face of their hostess.

"And your own title, my lord?" she asked after a little pause.

"I am plain Werner von Orseln, free ritter and faithful servant of my mistress the Duchess Joan, as I was also of her father, Henry the Lion of Hohenstein!"

He bowed as he spoke and continued, "I do not love titles, and, indeed, they would be wasted on an ancient grizzle-pate like me. But your son is young, and deserves this fortune, madam. He will doubtless do great honour to my lady's favour."

The eyes of the elder lady turned inquiringly to those of Joan.

"I have now no faithful servants," said the young Duchess at last, breaking her cold silence; "I have only traitors and jailers about me."

With that she became once more silent. A painful restraint fell upon the three who sat at table, and though their hostess and Werner von Orseln partook of the fish and brawn and fruit which their three servitors set before them in silver platters, it was but sparingly and without appetite.

All were glad when the meal was over and they could rise from the table. As soon as possible Boris and Jorian got outside into the long passage which led to the kitchen.

"Ha!" cried Boris, "I declare I would have burst if I had stayed in there another quarter hour! It was solemn as serving Karl the Great and his longbeards in their cellar under the Hartz. I wonder if they are going to keep it up all the time after this fashion!"

"And this is pleasure," rejoined Jorian gloomily; "not even a good rousing fight on the way. And then—why, prayers for the dead are cheerful as dance-gardens in July to that festal board. Good Lord! give me the Lady Ysolinde and the gnomes we fought so long ago at Erdberg. This stiff sword-handed Joan of theirs freezes a man's internals like Baltic ice."

"Jorian," said Boris, solemnly lowering his voice to a whisper, "if that Courtland fellow had known what we know, he would have been none so eager to get her home to bed and board!"

"Ice will melt—even Baltic ice!" said Jorian sententiously.

"Yes, but greybeard Louis of Courtland is not the man to do the melting!" retorted Boris.

"But I know who could!" said Jorian, nodding his head with an air of immense sagacity.

Boris went on cutting brawn upon a wooden platter with a swift and careful hand. The old servitor moved noiselessly about behind them, with feet that made no more noise than those of a cat walking on velvet.

"Who?" said Boris, shortly.

The door of the kitchen opened slightly and the tall woman stood a moment with the latch in her hand, ready to enter.

"Our Sparhawk could melt the Baltic ice!" said Jorian, and winked at Boris with his left eye in a sly manner.

Whereupon Boris dropped his knife and, seizing Jorian by the shoulders, he thrust him down upon a broad stool.

Then he dragged the platter of brawn before him and dumped the mustard pot beside it upon the deal table with a resounding clap.

"There!" he cried, "fill your silly mouth with that, Fatsides! 'Tis all you are good for. I have stood a deal of fine larded ignorance from you in my time, but nothing like this. You will be saying next that my Lady Duchess is taking a fancy to you!"

"She might do worse!" said Jorian philosophically, as he stirred the mustard with his knife and looked about for the ale tankard.

CHAPTER XXIII
THE FACE THAT LOOKED INTO JOAN'S

The chamber to which the Duchess Joan was conducted by her hostess had evidently been carefully prepared for her reception. It was a large low room, with a vaulted roof of carven wood. The work was of great merit and evidently old. The devices upon it were mostly coats-of-arms, which originally had been gilded and painted in heraldic colours, though neglect through long generations had tarnished the gold leaf and caused the colours to peel off in places. Here and there, however, were shields of more recent design, but in every case the motto and scutcheon of these had been defaced. At both ends of the room were windows, through whose stained glass Joan peered without result into blank darkness. Then she opened a little square of panes just large enough to put her head through and saw a walk of lofty poplars silhouetted against the sky, dark towers of leaves all a-rustle and a-shiver from the zenith to the ground, as a moaning and sobbing wind drew inward and whispered to them of the coming storm.

Then Joan shut the window and looked about her. A table with a little *prie-Dieu* stood in the corner, screened by a curtain which ran on a brazen rod. A Roman Breviary lay open on a velvet-covered table before the crucifix. Joan lifted it up and her eyes fell on the words: "*By a woman he overcame. By a woman he was overcome. A woman was once his weapon. A woman is now become the instrument of his defeat. He findeth that the weak vessel cannot be broken.*"

"Nor shall it!" said Joan, looking at the cross before her; "by the strength of Mary the Mother, the weak vessel shall not be broken!"

She turned her about and examined with interest the rest of the room which for many days was to be her own. The bed was low and wide, with sheets of fine linen folded back, and over all a richly embroidered coverlet. At the further end of the chamber was a fireplace, with a projecting hood of enamelled brick, looking fresh and new amid so much that was centuries old. Oaken panels covered the walls, opening mostly into deep cupboards. The girl tried one or two of these. They proved to be unlocked and were filled with ancient parchments, giving forth a faintly aromatic smell, but without a particle of dust upon their leaves. The cleanliness of everything within the chamber had been scrupulously attended to.

For a full hour Joan walked the chamber with her hands clasped behind her back, thinking how she was to return to her well-beloved Kernsberg. Her pride was slowly abating, and with it her anger against those faithful servants who had risked her favour to convey her beyond the reach of danger. But none the less she was resolved to go back. This conflict must not take place without her. If Kernsberg were captured, and Maurice von Lynar found personating his mistress, he would surely be put to death. If he fell into Muscovite hands that death would be by torture.

At all hazards she would return. And to this problem she turned her thoughts, knitting her brows and working her fingers nervously through each other.

She had it. There was a way. She would wait till the morrow and in the meantime—sleep.

As she stooped to blow out the last candle, a motto on the stem caught her eye. It ran round the massive silver base of the candelabra in the thick Gothic characters of a hundred years before. Joan took the candle out of its socket and read the inscription word by word—

"DA PACEM, DOMINE, IN DIEBUS NOSTRIS"

It was her own scroll, the motto of the reigning dukes of Hohenstein—a strange one, doubtless, to be that of a fighting race, but, nevertheless, her father's and her own.

Joan held the candle in her hand a long time, looking at it, heedless of the wax that dripped on the floor.

What did her father's motto, the device of her house, upon this Baltic island, far from the highlands of Kernsberg? Had these wastes once belonged to men of her race? And this woman, who so regally played the mistress of this strange heritage, who was she? And what was the secret of the residence of one in this wilderness who, by her manner, might in her time have queened it in royal courts?

And as Joan of Hohenstein blew out the candle she mused in her heart concerning these things.

The Duchess Joan slept soundly, her dark boyish head pillowed on the full rounded curves of an arm thrown behind her. On the little velvet-covered table beside the bed lay her belt and its dependent sword, a faithful companion in its sheath of plain black leather. Under the pillow, and within instant reach of her right hand, was her father's dagger. With it, they said, Henry the Lion had more than once removed an enemy who stood in his way, or more honourably given the *coup de grâce* to a would-be assassin.

Without, the mood of the night had changed. The sky, which had hitherto been of favourable aspect, save for the green light in the north as they rowed across the waters of the Haff, was now overflowed by thin wisps of cloud tacking up against the wind. Towards the sea a steely blue smother had settled down along the horizon, while the thunder growled nearer like a roll of drums beaten continuously. The wind, however, was not regular, but came in little puffs and bursts, now warm, now cold, from every point of the compass.

But still Joan slept on, being tired with her journey.

In their chamber in the wing which looks towards the north the three captains lay wrapped in their several mantles, Jorian and Boris answering each other nasally, in alternate trumpet blasts, like Alp calling to Alp. Werner von Orseln alone could not sleep, and after he had sworn and kicked his noisy companions in the ribs till he was weary of the task, he rose and went to the window to cast open the lattice. The air within felt thick and hot. He fumbled long at the catch, and in the unwholesome silence of the strange house the chief captain seemed to hear muffled feet going to and fro on the floor above him. But of this he thought little. For strange places were familiar to him, and any sense of danger made but an added spice in his cup of life.

At last he worried the catch loose, the lattice pane fell sagging inwards on its double hinge of skin. As Werner set his face to the opening quick flashes of summer lightning flamed alternately white and lilac across the horizon, and he felt the keen spit of hailstones in his face, driving level like so many musket balls when the infantry fires by platoons.

Above, in the vaulted chamber, Joan turned over on her bed, murmuring uneasily in her sleep. A white face, which for a quarter of an hour had been bent down to her dark head as it lay on the pillow, was suddenly retracted into the blackness at the girl's slight movement.

Again, apparently reassured, the shadowy visage approached as the young Duchess lay without further motion. Without the storm broke in a burst of appalling fury. The pale blue forks of the lightning flamed just outside the casement in flash on continuous flash. The thunder shook the house like an earthquake.

Suddenly, and for no apparent reason, Joan's eyes opened, and she found herself looking with bewilderment into a face that bent down upon her, a white face which somehow seemed to hang suspended in the dark above her. The features were lit up by the pulsing lightning which shone in the wild eyes and glittered on a knife-blade about the handle of which were clenched the tense white fingers of a hand equally detached.

A quick icy thrill chilled the girl's marrow, darting like a spear through her body. But Joan of Hohenstein was the true seed of Henry the Lion. In a moment her right hand had grasped the sword beside her pillow. Her left, shooting upward, closed on the arm which held the threatening steel. At the same time she flung herself forward, and with the roaring turmoils of the storm dinning in her ears she grappled something that withstood her in the interspace of darkness that had followed the flashes. Joan's spring had been that of the couchant young wild cat. Almost without rising from her bed she had projected herself upon her enemy. Her left hand grasped the wrist so tightly that the blade fell to the ground, whereupon Joan of the Sword Hand shifted her grasp upwards fiercely till she felt her fingers sink deep in the soft curves of a woman's throat.

Then a shriek, long and terrible, inhuman and threatening, rang through the house. A light began to burn yellow and steady through the cracks of the chamber door, not pulsing and blue like the lightning without. Presently, as Joan overbore her assailant upon the floor, the door opened, and glancing upwards she saw the Wordless Man stand on the threshold, a candle in one hand and a naked sword in the other.

The terrible cry which had rung in her ears had been his. At sight of him Joan unclasped her fingers from the throat of the woman and rose slowly to her feet. The old man rushed forward and knelt beside the prostrate body of his mistress.

At the same moment there came the sound of quick footsteps running up the stairway. The door flew open and Werner von Orseln burst in, also sword in hand.

"What is the meaning of this?" he shouted. "Who has dared to harm my lady?"

Joan did not answer, but remained standing tall and straight by the hooded mantel of the fireplace. As was her custom, before lying down she had clad herself in a loose gown of white silk which on all her journeys she carried in a roll at her saddle-bow.

She pointed to the mother of Maurice von Lynar, who lay on the floor, still unconscious, with the dumb man kneeling over her, chafing her hands and murmuring unintelligible tendernesses, like a mother crooning over a sick child.

But the face of the chief captain grew stern and terrible as he saw on the floor a knife of curious design. He stooped and lifted it. It was a Danish *tolle knife*, the edge a little curved outward and keen as a razor.

CHAPTER XXIV
THE SECRET OF THERESA VON LYNAR

"Go down and bring a cup of wine!" commanded Joan as soon as he appeared. And Werner von Orseln, having glanced once at his mistress where she stood with the point of her sword to the ground and her elbow on the corner of the mantel, turned on his heel and departed without a word to do her bidding.

Meanwhile the Wordless Man had raised his mistress up from the ground. Her eyes slowly opened and began to wander vaguely round the room, taking in the objects one by one. When they fell on Joan, standing erect by the fireplace, a spasm seemed to pass across her face and she strove fiercely but ineffectually to rise.

"Carry your mistress to that couch!" said the young Duchess, pointing to the tumbled bed from which a few minutes before she had so hastily launched herself.

The dumb man understood either the words or the significant action of Joan's hand, for he stooped and lifted Von Lynar's mother in his arms. Whilst he was thus engaged Werner came in quickly with a silver cup in his hand.

Joan took it instantly and going forward she put it to the lips of the woman on the bed. Her hair had escaped from its gathered coils and now flowed in luxuriant masses of red-gold over her shoulders and showered itself on either side of the pillow before falling in a shining cataract to the floor.

Putting out her hands the woman took the cup and drank of it slowly, pausing between the draughts to draw long breaths.

"I must have strength," she said. "I have much to say. Then, Joan of Hohenstein, yourself shall judge between thee and me!"

The fluttering of the lightning at the window seemed to disturb her, for as Joan bowed her assent slightly and sternly, the tall woman kept looking towards the lattice as if the pulsing flame fretted her. Joan moved her hand slightly without taking her eyes away, and the chief captain, used to such silent orders from his mistress, strode over to the window and pulled the curtains close. The storm had by this time subsided to a rumble, and only round the edges of the arras could a faint occasional glow be seen, telling of the turmoil without. But a certain faint tremulousness pervaded all the house, which was the Baltic thundering on the pebbly beaches and shaking the walls to their sandy foundations.

The colour came slowly back to the woman's pale face, and, after a little, she raised herself on the pillows. Joan stood motionless and uncompromising by the great iron dogs of the chimney.

"You are waiting for me to speak, and I will speak," said the woman. "You have a double right to know all. Shall it be told to yourself alone or in the presence of this man?"

She looked at Von Orseln as she spoke.

"I have no secrets in my life," said Joan; "there is nothing that I would hide from him. *Save one thing!*" She added the last words in her heart.

"I warn you that the matter concerns yourself very closely," answered the woman somewhat urgently.

"Werner von Orseln is my chief captain!" answered Joan.

"It concerns also your father's honour!"

"He was my father's chief captain before he was mine, and had charge of his honour on twenty fields."

Gratefully and silently Von Orseln lifted his mistress's hand to his lips. The tall woman on the bed smiled faintly.

"It is well that your Highness is so happy in her servants. I also have one who can hold his peace."

She pointed to the Wordless Man, who now stood with the candelabra in his hand, mute and immutable by his mistress's bedhead, as if watching that none should do her harm.

There was an interval of silence in the room, filled up by the hoarse persistent booming of the storm without and the shuddering shocks of the wind on the lonely house. Then the woman spoke again in a low, distinct voice.

"Since it is your right to know my name, I am Theresa von Lynar—who have also a right to call myself 'of Hohenstein'—and your dead father's widow!"

In an instant the reserve of Joan's sternly equal mind was broken up. She dropped her sword clattering on the floor and started angrily forward towards the bed.

"It is a lie most foul," she cried; "my father lived unwed for many years—nay, ever since my mother's death, who died in giving me life, he never so much as looked on woman. It is a thing well known in the Duchy!"

The woman did not answer directly.

"Max Ulrich, bring the silver casket," she said, taking from her neck a little silver key.

The Wordless Man, seeing her action, came forward and took the key. He went out of the room, and after an interval which seemed interminable he returned with a peculiarly shaped casket. It was formed like a heart, and upon it, curiously worked in gold and precious stones, Joan saw her father's motto and the armorial bearings of Hohenstein.

The woman touched a spring with well-practised hand, the silver heart divided, and a roll of parchment fell upon the bed. With a strange smile she gave it to Joan, beckoning her with an upward nod to approach.

"I give this precious document without fear into your hands. It is my very soul. But it is safe with the daughter of Henry the Lion."

Joan took the crackling parchment. It had three seals attached to it and the first part was in her father's own handwriting.

> *"I declare by these presents that I have married, according to the customs of Hohenstein and the laws of the Empire, Theresa von Lynar, daughter of the Count von Lynar of Jutland. But this marriage shall not, by any of its occasions or consequents, affect the succession of my daughter Joanna to the Duchy of Hohenstein and the Principalities of Kernsberg and Marienfeld. To which we subscribe our names as conjointly agreeing thereto in the presence of his High Eminence the Cardinal Adrian, Archbishop of Cologne and Elector of the Holy Roman Empire."*

Then followed the three signatures, and beneath, in another handwriting, Joan read the following: —

> "*These persons, Henry Duke of Hohenstein and Theresa von Lynar, were married by me subject to the above conditions mutually agreed upon in the Church of Olsen near to the Kurische Haff, in the presence of Julius Count von Lynar and his sons Wolf and Mark, in the year 14—, the day being the eve of St. John. — Adrian, Archiepiscop. et Elector.*"

After her first shock of surprise was over Joan noted carefully the date. It was one year after her own birth, and therefore the like period after the death of her mother, the openly acknowledged Duchess of Hohenstein.

The quick eyes of the woman on the bed had followed hers as they read carefully down the parchment, eagerly and also apprehensively, like those of a mother who for some weighty reason has placed her child in peril.

Joan folded the parchment and handed it back. Then she stood silent waiting for an explanation.

The woman took up her parable calmly, like one who has long comprehended that such a crisis must one day arrive, and who knows her part thoroughly.

"I, who speak to you, am Theresa von Lynar. Your father saw me first at the coronation of our late sovereign, Christian, King of Denmark. And we loved one another. For this cause I moved my brother and his sons to build Castle Lynar on the shores of the Northern Sea. For this cause I accompanied him thither. For many years at Castle Lynar, and also at this place, called the Hermitage of the Dunes, Henry of Kernsberg and I dwelt in such happiness as mortals seldom know. I loved your father, obeyed him, adored him, lived only for him. But there came a spring when my brother, being like your father a hot and passionate man, quarrelled with Duke Henry, threatening to go before the Diet of the Empire if I were not immediately acknowledged Duchess and my son Maurice von Lynar made the heir of Hohenstein. But I, being true to my oath and promise, left my brother and abode here alone with my husband when he could escape from his Dukedom, living like a simple squire and his dame. Those were happy days and made up for much. Then in an evil day I sent my son to my brother to train as his own son in arms and the arts of war. But he, being at enmity with my husband, made ready to carry the lad before the Diet of the Empire, that he might be declared heir to his father. Then, in his anger, Henry the Lion rose and swept Castle Lynar with fire and sword, leaving none alive but this boy only, whom he meant to take back and train with his captains. But on the way home, even as he rode southward through the forest towards Kernsberg, he reeled in the saddle and passed ere he could speak a word, even the name of those he loved. So the boy remained a captive at Kernsberg, called by my brother's name, and knowing even to this day nothing of his father."

And as the woman ceased speaking Werner von Orseln nodded gravely and sadly.

"This thing concerning my lord's death is true," he said; "I was present. These arms received him as he fell. He was dead ere we laid him on the ground!"

Theresa von Lynar raised herself. She had spoken thus far reclining on the bed from which Joan had risen. Now she sat up and for a little space rested her hands on her lap ere she went on.

"Then my son, whom, not knowing, you had taken pity upon and raised to honour, and who is now your faithful servant, sent a secret messenger that you would come to abide secretly with me till a certain dark day had overpassed in Kernsberg. And then there sprang up in my heart a dreadful conceit that he loved you, knowing young blood and hearing the fame of your beauty, and I was afraid for the greatness of the sin—that one should love his sister."

Joan made a quick gesture of dissent, but the woman went on.

"I thought, being a woman alone, and one also, who had given all freely up for love's sake, that he would certainly love you even as I had loved. And when I saw you in my house, so cold and so proud, and when I thought within me that but for you my son would have been a mighty prince, a strange terrible anger and madness came over me, darkening my soul. For a moment I would have slain you. But I could not, because you were asleep. And, even as you stirred, I heard you speak the name of a man, as only one who loves can speak it. I know right well how that is, having listened to it with a glad heart in the night. The name was——"

"Hold!" cried Joan of the Sword Hand. "I believe you—I forgive you!"

"The name," continued Theresa von Lynar, "was *not that of my son*! And now," she went on, slowly rising from the couch to her height, "I am ready. I bid you slay me for the evil deed my heart was willing for a moment to do!"

"I bid you slay me for the evil deed my heart was willing to do."

Joan looked at her full in the eyes for the space of a breath. Then suddenly she held out her hand and answered like her father's daughter.

"Nay," she said, "I only marvel that you did not strike me to the heart, because of your son's loss and my father's sin!"

CHAPTER XXV
BORNE ON THE GREAT WAVE

It chanced that in the chamber from which Werner von Orseln had come so swiftly at the cry of the Wordless Man, Boris and Jorian, after sleeping through the disturbances above them and the first burst of the storm, were waked by the blowing open of the lattice as the wind reached its height. Jorian lay still on his pallet and slily kicked Boris, hoping that he would rise and take upon him the task of shutting it.

Then to Boris, struggling upward to the surface of the ocean of sleep, came the same charitable thought with regard to Jorian. So, both kicking out at the same time, their feet encountered with clash of iron footgear, and then with surly snarls they hent them on their feet, abusing each other in voices which could be heard above the humming of the storm without.

It was tall Boris who, having cursed himself empty, first made his way to the window. The lattice hung by one leathern thong. The other had been torn away, and indeed it was a wonder that the whole framework had not been blown bodily into the room. For the tempest pressed against it straight from the north, and the sticky spray from the waves which broke on the shingle drove stingingly into the eyes of the man-at-arms.

Nevertheless he thrust his head out, looked a moment through half-closed eyelids, and then cried, "Jorian, we are surely lost! The sea is breaking in upon us. It has passed the beach of shingle out there!"

And seizing Jorian by the arm Boris made his way to the door by which they had entered, and, undoing the bolts, they reached the walled courtyard, where, however, they found themselves in the open air, but sheltered from the utmost violence of the tempest. There was a momentary difficulty here, because neither could find the key of the heavy door in the boundary wall. But Boris, ever fertile in expedient, discovered a ladder under a kind of shed, and setting it against the northern wall he climbed to the top. While he remained under the shelter of the wall his body was comfortably warm; only an occasional veering flaw sent a purl downwards of what he was to meet. But the instant his head was above the copestone, and the ice-cold northerly blast met him like a wall, he fairly gasped, for the furious onslaught of the storm seemed to blow every particle of breath clean out of his body.

The spindrift flew smoking past, momentarily white in the constant lightning flashes, and before him, and apparently almost at the foot of the wall, Boris saw a wonderful sight. The sea appeared to be climbing, climbing, climbing upwards over a narrow belt of sand and shingle which separated the scarcely fretted Haff from the tumbling milk of the outer Baltic.

In another moment Jorian was beside him, crouching on the top of the wall to save himself from being carried away. And there, in the steamy smother of the sea, backed by the blue electric flame of the lightning, they saw the slant masts of a vessel labouring to beat against the wind.

"Poor souls, they are gone!" said Boris, trying to shield his eyes with his palm, as the black hull disappeared bodily, and the masts seemed to lurch forward into the milky turmoil. "We shall never see her again."

For one moment all was dark as pitch, and the next a dozen flashes of lightning burst every way, as many appearing to rise upwards as could be seen to fall downwards. A black speck poised itself on the crest of a wave. "It is a boat! It can never live!" cried the two men together, and dropping from the top of the wall they ran down to the shore, going as near as they dared to the surf which arched and fell with ponderous roar on the narrow strip of shingle.

Here Jorian and Boris ran this way and that, trying to pierce the blackness of the sky with their spray-blinded eyes, but nothing more, either of the ship or of the boat which had put out from it, did they see. The mountainous roll and ceaseless iterance of the oncoming breakers hid the surface of the sea from their sight, while the sky, changing with each pulse of the lightning from densest black to green shot with violet, told nothing of the men's lives which were being riven from their bodies beneath it.

"Back, Boris, back!" cried Jorian suddenly, as after a succession of smaller waves a gigantic and majestic roller arched along the whole seaward front, stood for a moment black and imminent above them, and then fell like a whole mountain-range in a snowy avalanche of troubled water which rushed savagely up the beach. The two soldiers, who would have faced unblanched any line of living enemies in the world, fled terror-stricken at that clutching onrush of that sea of milk. The wet sand seemed to catch and hold their feet as they ran, so that they felt in their hearts the terrible sensation of one who flees in dreams from some hideous imagined terror and who finds his powers fail him as his pursuer approaches.

Upward and still upward the wave swept with a soft universal hiss which drowned and dominated the rataplan of the thunder-peals above and the sonorous diapason of the surf around them. It rushed in a creaming smother about their ankles, plucked at their knees, but could rise no higher. Yet so fierce was the back draught, that when the water retreated, dragging the pebbles with it down the shingly shore with the rattle of a million castanets, the two stout captains of Plassenburg were thrown on their faces and lay as dead on the wet and sticky stones, each clutching a double handful of broken shells and oozy sand which streamed through his numbed fingers.

Boris was the first to rise, and finding Jorian still on his face he caught the collar of his doublet and pulled him with little ceremony up the sloping bank out of tide-reach, throwing him down on the shingly summit with as little tenderness or compunction as if he had been a bag of wet salt.

By this time the morning was advancing and the storm growing somewhat less continuous. Instead of the wind bearing a dead weight upon the face, it came now in furious gusts. Instead of one grand roar, multitudinous in voice yet uniform in tone, it hooted and piped overhead as if a whole brood of evil spirits were riding headlong down the tempest-track. Instead of coming on in one solid bank of blackness, the clouds were broken into a wrack of wild and fantastic fragments, the interspaces of which showed alternately paly green and pearly grey. The thunder retreated growling behind the horizon. The violet lightning grew less continuous, and only occasionally rose and fell in vague distant flickerings towards the north, as if some one were lifting a lantern almost to the sea-line and dropping it again before reaching it.

Looking back from the summit of the mound, Boris saw something dark lying high up on the beach amid a wrack of seaweed and broken timber which marked where the great wave had stopped. Something odd about the shape took his eye.

A moment later he was leaping down again towards the shore, taking his longest strides, and sending the pebbles spraying out in front and on all sides of him. He stooped and found the body of a man, tall, well formed, and of manly figure. He was bareheaded and stripped to his breeches and underwear.

Boris stooped and laid his hand upon his heart. Yes, so much was certain. He was not dead. Whereupon the ex-man-at-arms lifted him as well as he could and dragged him by the elbows out of reach of the waves. Then he went back to Jorian and kicked him in the ribs. The rotund man sat up with an execration.

"Come!" cried Boris, "don't lie there like Reynard the Fox waiting for Kayward the Hare. We want no malingering here. There's a man at death's door down on the shingle. Come and help me to carry him to the house."

It was a heavy task, and Jorian's head spun with the shock of the wave and the weight of their burden long before they reached the point where the boundary wall approached nearest to the house.

"We can never hope to get him up that ladder and down the other side," said Boris, shaking his head.

"Even if we had the ladder!" answered Jorian, glad of a chance to grumble; "but, thanks to your stupidity, it is on the other side of the wall."

Without noticing his companion's words, Boris took a handful of small pebbles and threw them up at a lighted window. The head of Werner von Orseln immediately appeared, his grizzled hair blown out like a misty aureole about his temples.

"Come down!" shouted Boris, making a trumpet of his hands to fight the wind withal. "We have found a drowned man on the beach!"

And indeed it seemed literally so, as they carried their burden round the walls to the wicket door and waited. It seemed an interminable time before Werner von Orseln arrived with the dumb man's lantern in his hand.

They carried the body into the great hall, where the Duchess and the old servitor met them. There they laid him on a table. Joan herself lifted the lantern and held it to his face. His fair hair clustered about his head in wet knots and shining twists. The features of his face were white as death and carven like those of a statue. But at the sight the heart of the Duchess leaped wildly within her.

"Conrad!" she cried—that word and no more. And the lantern fell to the floor from her nerveless hand.

There was no doubt in her mind. She could make no mistake. The regular features, the pillar-like neck, the massive shoulders, the strong clean-cut mouth, the broad white brow—and—yes, the slight tonsure of the priest. It was the White Knight of the Courtland lists, the noble Prince of the summer parlour, the red-robed prelate of her marriage-day, Conrad of Courtland, Prince and Cardinal, but to her—"*he*"—the only "he."

CHAPTER XXVI
THE GIRL BENEATH THE LAMP

When Conrad, Cardinal-designate of the Holy Roman Church and Archbishop of Courtland, opened his eyes, it seemed to him that he had passed through warring waters into the serenity of the Life Beyond. His hand, on which still glittered his episcopal ring, lay on a counterpane of faded rose silk, soft as down. Did he dream that another hand had been holding it, that gentlest fingers had rested caressingly on his brow?

A girl, sweet and stately, sat by his bedside. By the door, to which alone he could raise his eyes, stood a tall gaunt man, clad in grey from head to foot, his hands clasped in front of him, and his chin sunk upon his breast.

The Prince-Bishop's eyes rested languidly on the girl's face, on which fell the light of a shaded silver lamp. There was a book in her lap, written upon sheets of thin parchment, bound in gold-embossed leather. But she did not read it. Instead she breathed softly and regularly. She was asleep, with her hand on the coverlet of rosy silk.

Strange fancies passed through the humming brain of the rescued man—as it had been, hunting each other across a stage—visions of perilous endeavour, of fights with wild beasts in shut-in places from which there was no escape, of brutal fisticuffs with savage men. All these again merged into the sense of falling from immense heights only to find that the air upheld him and that, instead of breaking himself to pieces at the bottom, he alighted soft as thistledown on couches of flowers. Strange rich heady scents seemed to rise about him like something palpable. His brain wavered behind his brow like a summer landscape when the sun is hot after a shower. Perfumes, strange and haunting, dwelt in his nostrils. The scent, at once sour and sweet, of bee-hives at night, the richness of honey in the comb, the delicacy of wet banks of violets, full-odoured musk, and the luxury of sun-warmed afternoon beanfields dreamily sweet—these made his very soul swoon within him. Then followed odours of rose gardens, of cool walks drenched in shadow and random scents blown in at open windows. Yes, he knew now; surely he was again in his own chamber in the summer pavilion of the palace in Courtland. He could hear the cool wash of the Alla under its walls, and with the assurance there came somehow a memory of a slim lad with clear-cut features who brought him a message from—was it his sister Margaret, or Louis his brother? He could not remember which.

Of what had he been dreaming? In the endeavour to recall something he harked back on the terrors of the night in which, of all on board the ship, his soul alone had remained serene. He remembered the fury of the storm, the helpless impotence and blank cowardice of the sailor folk, the desertion of the officers in the only seaworthy boat.

Slowly the drifting mists steadied themselves athwart his brain. The actual recomposed itself out of the shreds of dreams. Conrad found himself in a long low room such as he had seen many times in the houses of well-to-do ritters along the Baltic shores. The beams of the roof-tree above were carven and ancient. Arras went everywhere about the halls. Silver candlesticks, with princely crests graven upon them, stood by his bedhead. After each survey his eyes settled on the sleeping girl. She was very young and very beautiful. It was—yet it could not be—the Duchess Joan, whom he himself had married to his brother Louis in the cathedral church of his own archiepiscopal city.

Conrad of Courtland had not been trained a priest, yet, as was common at that age, birth and circumstance had made him early a Prince of the Roman Church. He had been thrust into the hierarchy solely because of his name, for he had succeeded his uncle Adrian in his ecclesiastical posts and emoluments as a legal heir succeeds to an undisputed property. In due time he received his red hat from a pontiff who distributed these among his favourites (or those whom he thought might aggrandise his temporal power) as freely as a groomsman distributes favours at a wedding.

Nevertheless, Conrad of Courtland had all the warm life and imperious impulses of a young man within his breast. Yet he was no Borgia or Della Rovere, cloaking scarlet sins with scarlet vestments. For with the high dignities of his position and the solemn work which lay to his hand in his northern province there had come the resolve to be not less, but more faithful than those martyrs and confessors of whom he read daily in his Breviary. And while, in Rome herself, vice-proud princes, consorting in the foulest alliance with pagan popes, blasphemed the sanctuary and openly scoffed at religion, this finest and most chivalrous of young northern knights had laid down the weapons of his warfare to take up the crucifix, and now had set out joyfully for Rome to receive his cardinal's hat on his knees as the last and greatest gift of the Vicar of Christ.

He had begun his pilgrimage by express command of the Holy Father, who desired to make the youthful Archbishop his Papal assessor among the

Electors of the Empire. But scarcely was he clear of the Courtland shores when there had come the storm, the shipwreck, the wild struggle among the white and foaming breakers—and then, wondrously emergent, like heaven after purgatory, the quiet of this sheltered room and this sleeping girl, with her white hand lying lax and delicate on the rosy silk.

The book slipped suddenly from her fingers, falling on the polished wood of the floor with a startling sound. The eyes of the gaunt man by the door were lifted from the ground, glittered beadily for a moment, and again dropped as before.

The girl did not start, but rather passed immediately into full consciousness with a little shudder and a quick gesture of the hand, as if she pushed something or some one from her. Then, from the pillow on which his head lay, Joan of Hohenstein saw the eyes of the Prince Conrad gazing at her, dark and solemn, from within the purplish rings of recent peril.

"You are my brother's wife!" he said softly, but yet in the same rich and thrilling voice she had listened to with so many heart-stirrings in the summer palace, and had last heard ring through the cathedral church of Courtland on that day when her life had ended.

A chill came over the girl's face at his words.

"I am indeed the Duchess Joan of Hohenstein," she answered. "My father willed that I should wed Prince Louis of Courtland. Well, I married him and rode away. In so much I am your brother's wife."

It was a strange awaking for a man who had passed from death to life, but at least her very impetuosity convinced him that the girl was flesh and blood.

He smiled wanly. The light of the lamp seemed to waver again before his eyes. He saw his companion as it had been transformed and glorified. He heard the rolling of drums in his ears, and merry pipes played sweetly far away. Then came the hush of many waters flowing softly, and last, thrumming on the parched earth, and drunk down gladly by tired flowers, the sound of abundance of rain. The world grew full of sleep and rest and refreshment. There was no longer need to care about anything.

His eyes closed. He seemed about to sink back into unconsciousness, when Joan rose, and with a few drops from Dessauer's phial, which she kept by her in case of need, she called him back from the misty verges of the Things which are Without.

As he struggled painfully upward he seemed to hear Joan's last words repeated and re-repeated to the music of a chime of fairy bells, "*In so much—in so much—I am your brother's wife—your brother's wife!*" He came to himself with a start.

"Will you tell me how I came here, and to whom I am indebted for my life?" he said, as Joan stood up beside him, her shapely head dim and retired in the misty dusk above the lamp, only her chin and the shapely curves of her throat being illumined by the warm lamplight.

"You were picked up for dead on the beach in the midst of the storm," she answered, "and were brought hither by two captains in the service of the Prince of Plassenburg!"

"And where is this place, and when can I leave it to proceed upon my journey?"

The girl's head was turned away from him a trifle more haughtily than before, and she answered coldly, "You are in a certain fortified grange somewhere on the Baltic shore. As to when you can proceed on your journey, that depends neither on you nor on me. I am a prisoner here. And so I fear must you also consider yourself!"

"A prisoner! Then has my brother——?" cried the Prince-Bishop, starting up on his elbow and instantly dropping back again upon the pillow with a groan of mingled pain and weakness. Joan looked at him a moment and then, compressing her lips with quick resolution, went to the bedside and with one hand under his head rearranged the pillow and laid him back in an easier posture.

"You must lie still," she said in a commanding tone, and yet softly; "you are too weak to move. Also you must obey me. I have some skill in leechcraft."

"I am content to be your prisoner," said the Prince-Bishop smiling— "that is, till I am well enough to proceed on my journey to Rome, whither the Holy Father Pope Sixtus hath summoned me by a special messenger."

"I fear me much," answered Joan, "that, spite of the Holy Father, we may be fellow-prisoners of long standing. Those of my own folk who hold me here against my will are hardly likely to let the brother of Prince Louis of Courtland escape with news of my hiding-place and present hermitage!"

The young man seemed as if he would again have started up, but with a gesture smilingly imperious Joan forbade him.

"To-morrow," she said, "perhaps if you are patient I will tell you more. Here comes our hostess. It is time that I should leave you."

Theresa von Lynar came softly to the side of the bed and stood beside Joan. The young Cardinal thought that he had never seen a more queenly pair—Joan resplendent in her girlish strength and beauty, Theresa still in the ripest glory of womanhood. There was a gentler light than before in the elder woman's eyes, and she cast an almost deprecating glance upon Joan. For at the first sound of her approach the girl had stiffened visibly, and now, with only a formal word as to the sick man's condition, and a cold bow to Conrad, she moved away.

Theresa watched her a little sadly as she passed behind the deep curtain. Then she sighed, and turning again to the bedside she looked long at the young man without speaking.

CHAPTER XXVII
WIFE AND PRIEST

"I have a right to call myself the widow of the Duke Henry of Kernsberg and Hohenstein," said Theresa von Lynar, in reply to Conrad's question as to whom he might thank for rescue and shelter.

"And therefore the mother of the Duchess Joan?" he continued.

Theresa shook her head.

"No," she said sadly; "I am not her mother, but—and even that only in a sense—her stepmother. A promise to a dead man has kept me from claiming any privileges save that of living unknown on this desolate isle of sand and mist. My son is an officer in the service of the Duchess Joan."

The face of the Prince-Bishop lighted up instantaneously.

"Most surely, then, I know him. Did he not come to Courtland with my Lord Dessauer, the Ambassador of Plassenburg?"

The lady of Isle Rusgen nodded indifferently.

"Yes," she said; "I believe he went to Courtland with the embassy from Plassenburg."

"Indeed, I was much drawn to him," said the Prince eagerly; "I remember him most vividly. He was of an olive complexion, his features without colour, but graven even as the Greeks cut those of a young god on a gem."

"Yes," said Theresa von Lynar serenely, "he has his father's face and carriage, which are those also of the Duchess Joan."

"And why," said the young man, "if I may ask without offence, is your son not the heir to the Dukedom?"

There was a downcast sadness in the woman's voice and eye as she replied, "Because when I wedded Duke Henry it was agreed between us that aught which might be thereafter should never stand between his daughter and her heritage; and, in spite of deadly wrong done to those of my house, I have kept my word."

The Prince-Cardinal thought long with knitted brow.

"The Duchess is my brother Louis's wife," he said slowly.

"In name!" retorted Theresa, quickly and breathlessly, like one called on unexpectedly to defend an absent friend.

"She is his wife—I married them. I am a priest," he made answer.

A gleam, sharp and quick as lightning jetted from a thunder cloud, sprang into the woman's eye.

"In this matter I, Theresa von Lynar, am wiser than all the priests in the world. Joan of Hohenstein is no more his wife than I am!"

"Holy Church, the mother of us all, made them one!" said the Cardinal sententiously. For such words come easily to dignitaries even when they are young.

She bent towards him and looked long into his eyes.

"No," she said; "you do not know. How indeed is it possible? You are too young to have learned the deep things—too certain of your own righteousness. But you will learn some day. I, Theresa von Lynar, know—aye, though I bear the name of my father and not that of my husband!" And at this imperious word the Prince was silent and thought with gravity upon these things.

Theresa sat motionless and silent by his bed till the day rose cool and untroubled out of the east, softly aglow with the sheen of clouded silk, pearl-grey and delicate. Prince Conrad, being greatly wearied and bruised inwardly with the buffeting of the waves and the stones of the shore, slumbered restlessly, with many tossings and turnings. But as oft as he moved, the hands of the woman who had been a wife were upon him, ordering his bruised limbs with swift knowledgeable tenderness, so that he did not wake, but gradually fell back again into dreamless and refreshing sleep. This was easy to her, because the secret of pain was not hid from Theresa, the widow of the Duke of Hohenstein—though Henry the Lion's daughter, as yet, knew it not.

In the morning Joan came to bid the patient good-morrow, while Werner von Orseln stood in the doorway with his steel cap doffed in his hand, and Boris and Jorian bent the knee for a priestly blessing. But Theresa did not again appear till night and darkness had wrapped the earth. So being all alone he listened to the heavy plunge of the breakers on the beach among which his life had been so nearly sped. The sound grew slower and slower after the storm, until at last only the wavelets of the sheltered sea lapsed on the shingle in a sort of breathing whisper.

"Peace! Peace! Great peace!" they seemed to say hour after hour as they fell on his ear.

And so day passed and came again. Long nights, too, at first with hourly tendance and then presently without. But Joan sat no more with the young man after that first watch, though his soul longed for her, that he might again tell the girl that she was his brother's wife, and urge her to do her duty by him who was her wedded husband. So in her absence Conrad contented himself and salved his conscience by thinking austere thoughts of his mission and high place in the hierarchy of the only Catholic and Apostolic Church. So that presently he would rise up and seek Werner von Orseln in order to persuade him to let him go, that he might proceed to Rome at the command of the Holy Father, whose servant he was.

But Werner only laughed and put him off.

"When we have sure word of what your brother does at Kernsberg, then we will talk of this matter. Till then it cannot be hid from you that no hostage half so valuable can we keep in hold. For if your brother loves my Lord Cardinal, then he will desire to ransom him. On the other hand, if he fear him, then we will keep your Highness alive to threaten him, as the Pope did with Djem, the Sultan's brother!"

So after many days it was permitted to the Prince to walk abroad within the narrow bounds of the Isle Rugen, the Wordless Man guarding him at fifty paces distance, impassive and inevitable as an ambulant rock of the seaboard.

As he went Prince Conrad's eyes glanced this way and that, looking for a means of escape. Yet they saw none, for Werner von Orseln with his ten men of Kernsberg and the two Captains of Plassenburg were not soldiers to make mistakes. There was but one boat on the island, and that was locked in a strong house by the inner shore, and over against it a sentry paced night and day. It chanced, however, upon a warm and gracious afternoon, when the breezes played wanderingly among the garden trees before losing themselves in the solemn aisles of the pines as in a pillared temple, that Conrad, stepping painfully westwards along the beach, arrived at the place of his rescue, and, descending the steep bank of shingle to look for any traces of the disaster, came suddenly upon the Duchess Joan gazing thoughtfully out to sea.

She turned quickly, hearing the sound of footsteps, and at sight of the Prince-Bishop glanced east and west along the shore as if meditating retreat.

But the proximity of Max Ulrich and the encompassing banks of water-worn pebbles convinced her of the awkwardness, if not the impossibility, of escape.

Conrad the prisoner greeted Joan with the sweet gravity which had been characteristic of him as Conrad the prince, and his eyes shone upon her with the same affectionate kindliness that had dwelt in them in the pavilion of the rose garden. But after one glance Joan looked steadily away across the steel-grey sea. Her feet turned instinctively to walk back towards the house, and the Prince turned with her.

"Joan looked steadily across the steel-grey sea."

"If we are two fellow-prisoners," said Conrad, "we ought to see more of each other. Is it not so?"

"That we may concert plans of escape?" said Joan. "You desire to continue your pilgrimage—I to return to my people, who, alas, think themselves better off without me!"

"I do, indeed, greatly desire to see Rome," replied the Prince. "The Holy Father Sixtus has sent me the red biretta, and has commanded me to come to Rome within a year to exchange it for the Cardinal's hat, and also to visit the tombs of the Apostles."

But Joan was not listening. She went on to speak of the matters which occupied her own mind.

"If you were a priest, why did you ride in the great tournament of the Blacks and the Whites at Courtland not a year ago?"

The Prince-Cardinal smiled indulgently.

"I was not then fledged full priest; hardly am I one now, though they have made me a Prince of Holy Church. Yet the tournaying was in a manner, perhaps, what her bridal dress is to a nun ere she takes the veil. But, my Lady Joan, what know you of the strife of Blacks and Whites at Courtland?"

"Your sister, the Princess Margaret, spoke of it, and also the Count von Löen, an officer of mine," answered Joan disingenuously.

"I am indeed a soldier by training and desire," continued the young man. "In Italy I have played at stratagem and countermarch with the Orsini and Colonna. But in this matter the younger son of the house of Courtland has no choice. We are the bulwark of the Church alike against heretic Muscovite to the north and furious Hussite to the south. We of Courtland must stand for the Holy See along all the Baltic edges; and for this reason the Pope has always chosen from amongst us his representative upon the Diet of the Empire, till the office has become almost hereditary."

"Then you are not really a priest?" said Joan, woman-like fixing upon that part of the young man's reply, which somehow had the greatest interest for her.

"In a sense, yes—in truth, no. They say that the Pope, in order to forward the Church's polity, makes and unmakes cardinals every day, some even for money payments; but these are doubtless Hussite lies. Yet though by prescript right and the command of the head of the Church I am both priest and bishop, in my heart I am but Prince Conrad of Courtland and a simple knight, even as I was before."

They paced along together with their eyes on the ground, the Wordless Man keeping a uniform distance behind them. Then the Prince laughed a strange grating laugh, like one who mocks at himself.

"By this time I ought to have been well on my way to the tombs of the Apostles; yet in my heart I cannot be sorry, for—God forgive me!—I had liefer be walking this northern shore, a young man along with a fair maiden."

"A priest walking with his brother's wife!" said Joan, turning quickly upon him and flashing a look into the eyes that regarded her with some wonder at her imperiousness.

"That is true, in a sense," he answered; "yet I am a priest with no consent of my desire—you a wife without love. We are, at least, alike in this—that we are wife and priest chiefly in name."

"Save that you are on your way to take on you the duties of your office, while I am more concerned in evading mine."

The Cardinal meditated deeply.

"The world is ill arranged," he said slowly; "my brother Louis would have made a far better Churchman than I. And strange it is to think that but a year ago the knights and chief councillors of Courtland came to me to propose that, because of his bodily weakness, my brother should be deposed and that I should take over the government and direction of affairs."

He went on without noticing the colour rising in Joan's cheek, smiling a little to himself and talking with more animation.

"Then, had I assented, my brother might have been walking here with tonsured head by your side, while I would doubtless have been knocking at the gates of Kernsberg, seeking at the spear's point for a runaway bride."

"Nay!" cried Joan, with sudden vehemence; "that would you not——"

And as suddenly she stopped, stricken dumb by the sound of her own words.

The Prince turned his head full upon her. He saw a face all suffused with hot blushes, haughtiest pride struggling with angry tears in eyes that fairly blazed upon him, and a slender figure drawn up into an attitude of defiance—at sight of all which something took him instantly by the throat.

"You mean—you mean——" he stammered, and for a moment was silent. "For God's sake, tell me what you mean!"

"I mean nothing at all!" said Joan, stamping her foot in anger.

And turning upon her heel she left him standing fixed in wonder and doubt upon the margin of the sea.

Then the wife of Louis, Prince of Courtland, walked eastward to the house upon the Isle Rugen with her face set as sternly as for battle, but her nether lip quivering—while Conrad, Cardinal and Prince of Holy Church, paced slowly to the west with a bitter and downcast look upon his ordinarily so sunny countenance.

For Fate had been exceeding cruel to these two.

CHAPTER XXVIII
THE RED LION FLIES AT KERNSBERG

And meanwhile right haughtily flew the red lion upon the citadel of Kernsberg. Never had the Lady Duchess, Joan of the Sword Hand, approven herself so brave and determined. In her forester's dress of green velvet, with the links of chain body-armour glinting beneath its frogs and taches, she went everywhere on foot. At all times of the day she was to be seen at the half-moons wherein the cannon were fixed, or on horseback scouring the defenced posts along the city wall. She seemed to know neither fear nor fatigue, and the noise of cheering followed her about the little hill city like her shadow.

Three only there were who knew the truth—Peter Balta, Alt Pikker, and George the Hussite. And when the guards were set, the lamps lit, and the bars drawn, a stupid faithful Hohensteiner set on watch at the turnpike foot with command to let none pass upon his life—then at last the lithe young Sparhawk would undo his belt with huge refreshful gusting of air into his lungs, amid the scarcely subdued laughter of the captains of the host.

"Lord Peter of the Keys!" Von Lynar would cry, "what it is to unbutton and untruss! 'Tis very well to admire it in our pretty Joan, but 'fore the Lord, I would give a thousand crowns if she were not so slender. It cuts a man in two to get within such a girdle. Only Prince Wasp could make a shift to fit it. Give me a goblet of ale, fellows."

"Nay, lad—mead! Mead of ten years alone must thou have, and little enough of that! Ale will make thee fat as mast-fed pigs."

"Or stay," amended George the Hussite; "mead is not comely drink for a maid—I will get thee a little canary and water, scented with millefleurs and rosemary."

"Check your fooling and help to unlace me, all of you," quoth the Sparhawk. "Now there is but a silken cord betwixt me and Paradise. But it prisons me like iron bars. Ah, there"—he blew a great breath, filling and emptying his lungs with huge content—"I wonder why we men breathe with our stomachs and women with their chests?"

"Know you not that much?" cried Alt Pikker. "'Tis because a man's life is in his stomach; and as for women, most part have neither heart, stomach, nor bowels of mercy—and so breathe with whatever it liketh them!"

"No ribaldry in a lady's presence, or in a trice thou shalt have none of these, either!" quoth the false Joan; "help me off with this thrice-accursed chain-mail. I am pocked from head to heel like a Swiss mercenary late come from Venice. Every ring in this foul devil's jerkin is imprinted an inch deep on my hide, and itches worse than a hundred beggars at a church door. Ah! better, better. Yet not well! I had thought our Joan of the Sword Hand a strapping wench, but now a hop-pole is an abbot to her when one comes to wear her *carapace* and *justaucorps!*"

"How went matters to-day on your side?" he went on, speaking to Balta, all the while chafing the calves of his legs and rubbing his pinched feet, having first enwrapped himself in a great loose mantle of red and gold which erstwhile had belonged to Henry the Lion.

"On the whole, not ill," said Peter Balta. "The Muscovites, indeed, drove in our outposts, but could not come nearer than a bowshot from the northern gate, we galled them so with our culverins and bombardels."

"Duke George's famous Fat Peg herself could not have done better than our little leathern vixens," said Alt Pikker, rubbing his grey badger's brush contentedly. "Gott, if we had only provender and water we might keep them out of the city for ever! But in a week they will certainly have cut off our river and sent it down the new channel, and the wells are not enough for half the citizens, to say nothing of the cattle and horses. This is a great fuss to make about a graceless young jackanapes of a Jutlander like you, Master Maurice von Lynar, Count von Löen—wedded wife of his Highness Prince Louis of Courtland. Ha! ha! ha!"

"I would have you know, sirrah," cried the Sparhawk, "that if you do not treat me as your liege lady ought to be treated, I will order you to the deepest dungeon beneath the castle moat! Come and kiss my hand this instant, both of you!"

"Promise not to box our ears, and we will," said Alt Pikker and George the Hussite together.

"Well, I will let you off this time," said Maurice royally, stretching his limbs luxuriously and putting one hosened foot on the mantel-shelf as high as his head. "Heigh-ho! I wonder how long it will last, and when we must surrender."

"Prince Louis must send his Muscovites back beyond the Alla first, and then we will speak with him concerning giving him up his wife!" quoth Peter Balta.

"I wonder what the craven loon will do with her when he gets her," said Alt Pikker. "You must not surrender in your girdle-brace and ring-mail, my liege lady, or you will have to sleep with them on. It would not be seemly to have to call up half a dozen lusty men-at-arms to help untruss her ladyship the Princess of Courtland!"

"Perhaps your goodman will kiss you upon the threshold of the palace as a token of reconciliation!" cackled Hussite George.

"If he does, I will rip him up!" growled Maurice, aghast at the suggestion. "But there is no doubt that at the best I shall be between the thills when they get me once safe in Courtland. To ride the wooden horse all day were a pleasure to it!"

But presently his face lighted up and he murmured some words to himself—

"Yet, after all, there is always the Princess Margaret there. I can confide in her when the worst comes. She will help me in my need—and, what is better still, she may even kiss me!"

And, spite of gloomy anticipations, his ears tingled with happy expectancy, when he thought of opportunities of intimate speech with the lady of his heart.

Nevertheless, in the face of brave words and braver deeds, provisions waxed scarce and dear in Castle Kernsberg, and in the town below women grew gaunt and hollow-cheeked. Then the children acquired eyes that seemed to stand out of hollow purple sockets. Last of all, the stout burghers grew thin. And all three began to dream of the days when the good farm-folk of the blackened country down below them, where now stood the leafy lodges of the Muscovites and the white tents of the Courtlanders, used to come into Kernsberg to market, the great solemn-eyed oxen drawing carts full of country sausages, and brown meal fresh ground from the mill to bake the wholesome bread—or better still when the stout market women brought in the lappered milk and the butter and curds. So the starving folk dreamed and dreamed and woke, and cried out curses on them that had waked them, saying, "Plague take the hands that pulled me back to this gutter-dog's life! For I was just a-sitting down to dinner with a haunch of venison for company, and such a lordly trout, buttered, with green sauce all over him, a loaf of white bread, crisp and crusty, at my elbow, and—Holy

Saint Matthew!—such a noble flagon of Rhenish, holding ten pints at the least."

About this time the Sparhawk began to take counsel with himself, and the issue of his meditations the historian must now relate.

It was in the outer chamber of the Duchess Joan, which looks to the north, that the three captains usually sat—burly Peter Balta, stiff-haired, dry-faced, keen-eyed—Alt Pikker, lean and leathery, the life humour within him all gone to fighting juice, his limbs mere bone and muscle, a certain acrid and caustic wit keeping the corners of his lips on the wicker, and, a little back from these two, George the Hussite, a smaller man, very solemn even when he was making others laugh, but nevertheless with a proud high look, a stiff upper lip, and a moustache so huge that he could tie the ends behind his head on a windy day.

These three had been speaking together at the wide, low window from which one can see the tight little red-roofed town of Kernsberg and the green Kernswater lying like a bright many-looped ribbon at the foot of the hills.

"These three had been speaking together."

To them entered the Sparhawk, a settled frown of gloom upon his brow, and the hunger which he shared equally with the others already sharpening the falcon hook of his nose and whitening his thin nostrils.

At sight of him the three heads drew apart, and Alt Pikker began to speak of the stars that were rising in the eastern dusk.

"The dog-star is white," he said didactically. "In my schooldays I used to read in the Latin tongue that it was red!"

But by their interest in such a matter the Sparhawk knew that they had been speaking of far other things than stars before he burst open the door. For little George the Hussite pulled his pandour moustaches and muttered, "A plague on the dog-star and the foul Latin tongue. They are only fit for the gabble of fat-fed monks. Moreover, you do not see it now, at any rate. For me, I would I were back under the Bohemian pinetrees, where the very wine smacks of resin, and where there is a sheep (your own or another's, it matters not greatly) tied at every true Hussite's door."

"What is this?" cried the Sparhawk. "Do not deceive me. You were none of you talking of stars when I came up the stairs. For I heard Peter Balta's voice say, 'By Heaven! it must come to it, and soon!' And you Hussite George, answered him, 'Six days will settle it.' What do you keep from me? Out with it? Speak up, like three good little men!"

It was Alt Pikker who first found words to answer.

"We spoke indeed of the stars, and said it was six days till the moon should be gone, and that the time would then be ripe for a sally by the—by the—Plassenburg Gate!"

"Pshaw!" cried the Sparhawk. "Lie to your father confessor, not to me. I am not a purblind fool. I have ears, long enough, it is true, but at least they answer to hear withal. You spoke of the wells, I tell you; I saw your heads move apart as I entered; and then, forsooth, that dotard Alt Pikker (who ran away in his youth from a monk's cloister-school with the nun that taught them stocking-mending) must needs furbish up some scraps of Latin and begin to prate about dog-stars red and dog-stars white. Faugh! Open your mouths like men, set truthful hearts behind them, and let me hear the worst!"

Nevertheless the three captains of Kernsberg were silent awhile, for heaviness was upon their souls. Then Peter Balta blurted out, "God help us! There is but ten days more provender in the city, the river is turned, and the wells are almost dried up!"

After this the Sparhawk sat awhile on the low window seat, watching the twinkling fires of the Muscovites and listening to the hum of the town beneath the Castle—all now sullen and subdued, no merry hucksters chaffering about the church porches, no loitering lads and lasses linking arms and bartering kisses in the dusky corners of the linen market, no clattering of hammers in the armourers' bazaar—a muffled buzzing only, as of men talking low to themselves of bitter memories and yet dismaller expectations.

"I have it!" said the Sparhawk at last, his eyes on the misty plain of night, with its twinkling pin-points of fire which were the watch-fires of the enemy.

The three men stirred a little to indicate attention, but did not speak.

"Listen," he said, "and do not interrupt. You must deliver me up. I am the cause of war—I, the Duchess Joan. Hear you? I have a husband who makes war upon me because I contemn his bed and board. He has summoned the Muscovite to help him to woo me. Well, if I am to be given up, it is for us to stipulate that the armies be withdrawn, first beyond the Alla, and then as far as Courtland. I will go with them; they will not find me out—at least, not till they are back in their own land."

"What matter?" cried Balta. "They would return as soon as they discovered the cheat."

"Let us sink or swim together," said Hussite George. "We want no talk of surrender!"

But grey dry Alt Pikker said nothing, weighing all with a judicial mind.

"No, they would not come back," said the Sparhawk; "or, at worst, we would have time—that is, you would have time—to revictual Kernsberg, to fill the tanks and reservoirs, to summon in the hillmen. They would soon learn that there had been no Joan within the city but the one they had carried back with them to Courtland. Plassenburg, slow to move, would have time to bring up its men to protect its borders from the Muscovite. All good chances are possible if only I am out of the way. Surrender me—but by private treaty, and not till you have seen them safe across the fords of the Alla!"

"Nay, God's truth;" cried the three, "that we will not do! They would kill you by slow torture as soon as they found out that they had been tricked."

"Well," said the Sparhawk slowly, "but by that time they *would* have been tricked."

Then Alt Pikker spoke in his turn.

"Men," he said, "this Dane is a man—a better than any of us. There is wisdom in what he says. Ye have heard in church how priests preach concerning One who died for the people. Here is one ready to die—if no better may be—for the people!"

"And for our Duchess Joan!" said the Sparhawk, taking his hat from his head at the name of his mistress.

"Our Lady Joan! Aye, that is it!" said the old man. "We would all gladly die in battle for our lady. We have done more—we have risked our own honour and her favour in order to convey her away from these dangers. Let the boy be given up; and that he go not alone without fit attendance, I will go with him as his chamberlain."

The other two men, Peter Balta and George the Hussite, did not answer for a space, but sat pondering Alt Pikker's counsel. It was George the Hussite who took up the parable.

"I do not see why you, Alt Pikker, and you, Maurice the Dane, should hold such a pother about what you are ready to do for our Lady Joan. So are we all every whit as ready and willing as you can be; and I think, if any are to be given up, we ought to draw lots for who it shall be. You fancy yourselves overmuch, both of you!"

The Sparhawk laughed.

"Great tun-barrelled dolt," he said, clapping Peter on the back, "how sweet and convincing it would be to see you, or that canting ale-faced knave George there, dressed up in the girdle-brace and steel corset of Joan of the Sword Hand! And how would you do as to your beard? Are you smooth as an egg on both cheeks as I am? It would be rare to have a Duchess Joan with an inch of blue-black stubble on her chin by the time she neared the gates of Courtland! Nay, lads, whoever stays—I must go. In this matter of brides I have qualities (how I got them I know not) that the best of you cannot lay claim to. Do you draw lots with Alt Pikker there, an you will, as to who shall accompany me, but leave this present Joan of the Sword Hand to settle her own little differences with him who is her husband by the blessing of Holy Church."

And he threw up his heels upon the table and plaited his knees one above the other.

Then it was Alt Pikker's time.

"Peter Balta, and you, George the Heretic, listen," he cried, vehemently emphasising the points on the palm of his hand. "You, Peter, have a wife that loves you—so, at least, we understand—and your Marion, how would she fare in this hard world without you? Have you laid by a stocking-foot full of gold? Does it hang inside your chimney? I trow not. Well, you at least must bide and earn your pay, for Marion's sake. I have neither kith nor kin, neither sweetheart nor wife, covenanted or uncovenanted. And for you, George, you are a heretic, and if they burn you alive or let out the red sap at your neck, you will go straight to hell-fire. Think of it, George! I, on the other hand, am a true man, and after a paltry year or two in purgatory (just for the experience) will enter straightway into the bosom of patriarchs and apostles, along with our Holy Father the Pope, and our elder brothers the Cardinals Borgia and Delia Rovere!"

"You talk a deal of nothings with your mouth," said George the Hussite. "It is true that I hold not, as you do, that every dishclout in a church is the holy veil, and every old snag of wood with a nail in't a veritable piece of the true cross. But I would have you know that I can do as much for my lady as any one of you—nay, and more, too, Alt Pikker. For a good Hussite is afraid neither of purgatory nor yet of hell-fire, because, if he should chance to die, he will go, without troubling either, straight to the abode of the martyrs and confessors who have been judged worthy to withstand and to conquer."

"And as to what you said concerning Marion," nodded Peter Balta truculently, "she is a soldier's wife and would cut her pretty throat rather than stand in the way of a man's advancement!"

"Specially knowing that so pretty a wench as she is could get a better husband to-morrow an it liked her!" commented Alt Pikker drily.

"Well," cried the Sparhawk, "still your quarrel, gentlemen. At all events, the thing is settled. The only question is *when*? How many days' water is there in the wells?"

Said Peter Balta, "I will go and see."

CHAPTER XXIX
THE GREETING OF THE PRINCESS MARGARET

They were making terms concerning treaty of delivering thus:—

"When the last Muscovite has crossed the Alla, when the men of Courtland stand ready to follow—then, and not sooner, we will deliver up our Lady Joan. For this we shall receive from you, Louis, Prince of Courtland, fifty hogsheads of wine, six hundred wagon-loads of good wheat, and the four great iron cannon now standing before the Stralsund Gate. This all to be completed before we of Kernsberg hand our Lady over."

"It is a thing agreed!" answered Louis of Courtland, who longed to be gone, and, above all, to get his Muscovite allies out of his country. For not only did they take all the best of everything in the field, but, like locusts, they spread themselves over the rear, carrying plunder and rapine through the territories of Courtland itself—treating it, indeed, as so much conquered country, so that men were daily deserting his colours in order to go back to protect their wives and daughters from the Cossacks of the Don and the Strelits of Little Russia.

Moreover, above all, Prince Louis wanted that proud wench, his wife. Without her as his prisoner, he dared not go back to his capital city. He had sworn an oath before the people. For the rest, Kernsberg itself could wait. Without a head it would soon fall in, and, besides, he flattered himself that he would so sway and influence the Duchess, when once he had her safe in his palace by the mouth of Alla, that she would repent her folly, and at no distant day sit knee by knee with him on his throne of state in the audience hall when the suitors came to plead concerning the law.

And even his guest Prince Ivan was complaisant, standing behind Louis's chair and smiling subtly to himself.

"Brother of mine," he would say, "I came to help you to your wife. It is your own affair how you take her and what you do with her when you get her. For me, as soon as you have her safe within the summer palace, and have given me, according to promise, my heart's desire your sister Margaret, so soon will I depart for Moscow. My father, indeed, sends daily posts praying my instant despatch, for he only waits my return to launch a host upon his enemy the King of Polognia."

And Prince Louis, reaching over the arm of his chair, patted his friend's small sweet-scented hand, and thanked him for his most unselfish and generous assistance.

Thus the leaguer of Hohenstein attained its object. Prince Louis had not, it is true, stormed the heights of Kernsberg as he had sworn to do. He had, in fact, left behind him to the traitors who delivered their Duchess a large portion of his stores and munitions of war. Nevertheless, he returned proud in heart to his capital city. For in the midst of his most faithful body of cavalry rode the young Duchess Joan, Princess of Courtland, on a white Neapolitan barb, with reins that jingled like silver bells and rosettes of ribbon on the bosses of her harness.

The beautiful prisoner appeared, as was natural, somewhat wan and anxious. She was clad in a close-fitting gown of pale blue, with inch-wide broidering of gold, laced in front, and with a train which drooped almost to the ground. Over this a cloak of deeper blue was worn, with a hood in which the dark, proud head of the Princess nestled half hidden and half revealed. The folk who crowded to see her go by took this for coquetry. She rode with only the one councillor by her who had dared to share her captivity—one Alt Pikker, a favourite veteran of her little army, and the master-swordsman (they said) who had instructed her in the use of arms.

No indignity had been offered to her. Indeed, as great honour was done her as was possible in the circumstances. Prince Louis had approached and led her by the hand to the steed which awaited her at the fords of the Alla. The soldiers of Courtland elevated their spears and the trumpets of both hosts brayed a salute. Then, without a word spoken, her husband had bowed and withdrawn as a gentleman should. Prince Ivan then approached, and on one knee begged the privilege of kissing her fair hand.

The traitors of Kernsberg, who had bartered their mistress for several tuns of Rhenish, could not meet her eye, but stood gloomily apart with faces sad and downcast, and from within the town came the sound of women weeping. Only George the Hussite stood by with a smile on his face and his thumbs stuck in his waistband.

The captive Princess spoke not at all, as was indeed natural and fitting. A woman conquered does not easily forgive those who have humbled her pride. She talked little even to Alt Pikker, and then only apart. The nearest guide, who had been chosen because of his knowledge of German, could not hear a murmur. With bowed head and eyes that dwelt steadily on the undulating mane of her white barb, Joan swayed her graceful body and compressed her lips like one captured but in nowise vanquished. And the soldiers of the army of Courtland (those of them who were married) whispered one to another, noting her demeanour, "Our good Prince is but at the beginning of his troubles; for, by Brunhild, did you ever see such a wench? They say she can engage any two fencers of her army at one time!"

"Her eye itself is like a rapier thrust," whispered another. "Just now I went near her to look, and she arched an eyebrow at me, no more—and lo! I went cold at my marrow as if I felt the blue steel stand out at my backbone."

"It is the hunger and the anger that have done it," said another; "and, indeed, small wonder! She looked not so pale when I saw her ride along Courtland Street that day to the Dom—the day she was to be married. Then her eyes did not pierce you through, but instead they shone with their own proper light and were very gracious."

"A strange wench, a most strange wench," responded the first, "so soon to change her mind."

"Ha!" laughed his companion, "little do you know if you say so! She is a woman—small doubt of that! Besides, is she not a princess? and wherefore should our Prince's wife not change her mind?"

They entered Courtland, and the flags flew gaily as on the day of wedding. The drums beat, and the populace drank from spigots that foamed red wine. Then Louis the Prince came, with hat in hand, and begged that the Princess Joan would graciously allow him to ride beside her through the streets. He spoke respectfully, and Joan could only bow her head in acquiescence.

Thus they came to the courtyard of the palace, the people shouting behind them. There, on the steps, gowned in white and gold, with bare head overrun with ringlets, stood the Princess Margaret among her women. And at sight of her the heart of the false Princess gave a mighty bound, as Joan of the Sword Hand drew her hood closer about her face and tried to remember in what fashion a lady dismounted from her horse.

"My lady," said Prince Louis, standing hat in hand before her barb, "I commit you to the care of my sister, the Princess Margaret, knowing the ancient friendship that there is between you two. She will speak for me, knowing all my will, and being also herself shortly contracted in marriage to my good friend, Prince Ivan of Muscovy. Open your hearts to each other, I pray you, and be assured that no evil or indignity shall befall one whom I admire as the fairest of women and honour as my wedded wife!"

Joan made no answer, but leaped from her horse without waiting for the hand of Alt Pikker, which many thought strange. In another moment the arms of the Princess Margaret were about her neck, and that impulsive Princess was kissing her heartily on cheek and lips, talking all the while through her tears.

"Quick! Let us get in from all these staring stupid men. You are to lodge in my palace so long as it lists you. My brother hath promised it. Where are your women?"

"I have no women," said Joan, in a low voice, blushing meanwhile; "they would not accompany a poor betrayed prisoner from Kernsberg to a prison cell!"

"Prison cell, indeed! You will find that I have a very comfortable dungeon ready for you! Come—my maidens will assist you. Hasten—pray do make haste!" cried the impetuous little lady, her arm close about the tall Joan.

"I thank you," said the false bride, with some reluctance, "but I am well accustomed to wait on myself."

"Indeed, I do not wonder," cried the ready Princess; "maids are vexatious creatures, well called 'tirewomen.' But come—see the beautiful rooms I have chosen for you! Make haste and take off your cloak, and then I will come to you; I am fairly dying to talk. Ah, why did you not tell me that day? That was ill done. I would have ridden so gladly with you. It was a glorious thing to do, and has made you famous all over the world, they say. I have been thinking ever since what I can do to be upsides with you and make them talk about me. I will give them a surprise one day that shall be great as yours. But perhaps I may not wait till I am married to do it."

And she took her friend by the hand and with a light-hearted skipping motion convoyed her to her summer palace, kissed her again at the door, and shut her in with another imperious adjuration to be speedy.

"I will give you a quarter of an hour," she cried, as she lingered a moment; "then I will come to hear all your story, every word."

Then the false Princess staggered rather than walked to a chair, for brain and eye were reeling.

"God wot," she murmured; "strange things to hear, indeed! Sweet lady, you little know how strange! This is ten thousand times a straiter place to be in than when I played the Count von Löen. Ah, women, women, what you bring a poor innocent man to!"

So, without unhooking her cloak or even throwing back the hood, this sadly bewildered bride sat down and tried to select any hopeful line of action out of the whirling chaos of her thoughts. And even as she sat there a knock came sharply at the door.

CHAPTER XXX
LOVE'S CLEAR EYE

"And now," cried Princess Margaret, clapping her hands together impulsively, "now at last I shall hear everything. Why you went away, and who gave you up, and about the fighting. Ugh! the traitors, to betray you after all! I would have their heads off—and all to save their wretched town and the lives of some score of fat burghers!"

So far the Princess Margaret had never once looked at the Sparhawk in his borrowed plumage, as he stood uneasily enough by the fireplace of the summer palace, leaning an elbow on the mantelshelf. But now she turned quickly to her guest.

"Oh, I love you!" she cried, running to Maurice and throwing her arms about her false sister-in-law in an impulsive little hug. "I think you are so brave. Is my hair sadly tangled? Tell me truly, Joan. The wind hath tumbled it about mine eyes. Not that it matters—with you!"

She said the last words with a little sigh.

Then the Princess Margaret tripped across the polished floor to a dressing-table which had been set out in the angle between the two windows. She turned the combs and brushes over with a contumelious hand.

"Where is your hand-glass?" she cried. "Do not tell me that you have never looked in it since you came to Courtland, or that you can put up with that squinting falsifier up there." She pointed to the oval-framed Venetian mirror which was hung opposite her. "It twists your face all awry, this way and that, like a monkey cracking a nut. 'Twas well enough for our good Conrad, but the Princess Joan is another matter."

"I have never even looked in either!" said the Sparhawk.

Some subtle difference in tone of voice caused the Princess to stop her work of patting into temporary docility her fair clustering ringlets, winding them about her fingers and rearranging to greater advantage the little golden combs which held her sadly rebellious tresses in place. She looked keenly at the Sparhawk, standing with both her shapely arms at the back of her head and holding a long ivory pin with a head of bright green malachite between her small white teeth.

"Your voice is hoarse—somehow you are different," she said, taking the pin from her lips and slipping it through the rebellious plaits with a swift vindictive motion.

"I have caught a cold riding into the city," quoth the Sparhawk hastily, blushing uneasily under her eyes. But for the time being his disguise was safe. Already Margaret of Courtland was thinking of something else.

"Tell me," she began, going to the window and gazing pensively out upon the green white-flecked pour of the Alla, swirling under the beams of the Summer Palace, "how many of your suite have followed you hither?"

"Only Alt Pikker, my second captain!" said the Sparhawk.

Again the tones of his voice seemed to touch her woman's ear with some subtle perplexity even in the midst of her abstraction. Margaret turned her eyes again upon Maurice, and kept them there till he shivered in the flowing, golden-belted dress of velvet which sat so handsomely upon his splendid figure.

"And your chief captain, Von Orseln?" The Princess seemed to be meditating again, her thoughts far from the rush of the Alla beneath and from the throat voice of the false Princess before her.

"Von Orseln has gone to the Baltic Edge to raise on my behalf the folk of the marshes!" answered the Sparhawk warily.

"Then there was——" the Princess hesitated, and her own voice grew a trifle lower—"the young man who came hither as Dessauer's secretary—what of him? The Count von Löen, if I mistake not—that was his name?"

"He is a traitor!"

The Princess turned quickly.

"Nay," she said, "you do not think so. Your voice is kind when you speak of him. Besides, I am sure he is no traitor. Where is he?"

"He is in the place where he most wishes to be—with the woman he loves!"

The light died out of the bright face of the Princess Margaret at the answer, even as a dun snow-cloud wipes the sunshine off a landscape.

"The woman he loves?" she stammered, as if she could not have heard aright.

"Aye," said the false bride, loosening her cloak and casting it behind her. "I swear it. He is with the woman he loves."

But in his heart the Sparhawk was saying, "Steady, Master Maurice von Lynar—or all will be out in five minutes."

The Princess Margaret walked determinedly from the window to the fireplace. She was not so tall by half a head as her guest, but to the eyes of the Sparhawk she towered above him like a young poplar tree. He shrank from her searching glance.

The Princess laid her hand upon the sleeve of the velvet gown. A flush of anger crimsoned her fair face.

"Ah!" she cried, "I see it all now, madam the Princess. You love the Count and you think to blind me. This is the reason of your riding off with him on your wedding day. I saw you go by his side. You sent Count Maurice to bring to you the four hundred lances of Kernsberg. It was for his sake that you left my brother Prince Louis at the church door. Like draws to like, they say, and your eyes even now are as like as peas to those of the Count von Löen."

And this, indeed, could the Sparhawk in no wise deny. The Princess went her angry way.

"There have been many lies told," she cried, raising the pitch of her voice, "but I am not blind. I can see through them. I am a woman and can gauge a woman's pretext. You yourself are in love with the Count von Löen, and yet you tell me that he is with the woman he loves. Bah! he loves you— you, his mistress—next, that is, to his selfish self-seeking self. If he is with the woman he loves, as you say, tell me her name!"

There came a knocking at the door.

"Who is there?" demanded imperiously the Princess Margaret.

"The Prince of Muscovy, to present his duty to the Princess of Courtland!"

"I do not wish to see him—I will not see him!" said the Sparhawk hastily, who felt that one inquisitor at a time was as much as he could hope to deal with.

"Enter!" said the Princess Margaret haughtily.

The Prince opened the door and stood on the threshold bowing to the ladies.

"Well?" queried Margaret of Courtland, without further acknowledgment of his salutation than the slightest and chillest nod.

"My service to both, noble Princesses," the answer came with suave deference. "The Prince Louis sent me to beg of his noble spouse, the Princess Joan, that she would deign to receive him."

"Tell Louis that the Princess will receive him at her own time. He ought to have better manners than to trouble a lady yet weary from a long journey. And as for you, Prince Ivan, you have our leave to go!"

Whilst Margaret was speaking the Prince had fixed his piercing eyes upon the Sparhawk, as if already he had penetrated his secret. But because he was a man Maurice sustained the searching gaze with haughty indifference. The Prince of Muscovy turned upon the Princess Margaret with a bright smile.

"All this makes an ill lesson for you, my fair betrothed," he said, bowing to her; "but—there will be no riding home once we have you in Moscow!"

"True, I shall not need to return, for I shall never ride thither!" retorted the Princess. "Moreover, I would have you remember that I am not your betrothed. The Prince Louis is your betrothed, if you have any in Courtland. You can carry him to Moscow an you will, and comfort each other there."

"That also I may do some day, madam!" flashed Prince Wasp, stirred to quick irritation. "But in the meantime, Princess Joan, does it please you to signify when you will receive your husband?"

"No! no! no!" whispered the Sparhawk in great perturbation.

The Princess Margaret pointed to the door.

"Go!" she said. "I myself will signify to my brother when he can wait upon the Princess."

"My Lady Margaret," the Muscovite purred in answer, "think you it is wise thus to encourage rebellion in the most sacred relations of life?"

The Princess Margaret trilled into merriest laughter and reached back a hand to take Joan's fingers in hers protectingly.

"The homily of the most reverend churchman, Prince Ivan of Muscovy, upon matrimony; Judas condemning treachery, Satan rebuking sin, were nothing to this!"

With all his faults the Prince had humour, the humour of a torture scene in some painted monkish Inferno.

"Agreed," he said, smiling; "and what does the Princess Margaret protecting that pale shrinking flower, Joan of the Sword Hand, remind you of?"

"That the room of Prince Ivan is more welcome to ladies than his company!" retorted Margaret of Courtland, still holding the Sparhawk's hand between both of hers, and keeping her angry eyes and petulant flower face indignantly upon the intruder.

Had Prince Ivan been looking at her companion at that moment he might have penetrated the disguise, so tender and devoted a light of love dwelt on the Sparhawk's countenance and beaconed from his eyes. But he only bowed deferentially and withdrew. Margaret and the Sparhawk were left once more alone.

The two stood thus while the brisk footsteps of Prince Wasp thinned out down the corridor. Then Margaret turned swiftly upon her tall companion and, still keeping her hand, she pulled Maurice over to the window. Then in the fuller light she scanned the Sparhawk's features with a kindling eye and paling lips.

"God in heaven!" she palpitated, holding him at a greater distance, "you are not the Lady Joan; you are—you are— —"

"The man who loves you!" said the Sparhawk, who was very pale.

"The Count von Löen. Oh! Maurice, why did you risk it?" she gasped. "They will kill you, tear you to pieces without remorse, when they find out. And it is a thing that cannot be kept secret. Why did you do it?"

"For your sake, beloved," said the Sparhawk, coming nearer to her; "to look once more on your face—to behold once, if no more, the lips that kissed me in the dark by the river brink!"

"But—but—you may forfeit your life!"

"And a thousand lives!" cried the Sparhawk, nervously pulling at his woman's dress as if ashamed that he must wear it at such a time. "Life without you is naught to Maurice von Lynar!"

A glow of conscious happiness rose warm and pink upon the cheeks of the Princess Margaret.

"Besides," added Maurice, "the captains of Kernsberg considered that thus alone could their mistress be saved."

The glow paled a little.

"What! by sacrificing you? But perhaps you did it for her sake, and not wholly, as you say, for mine!"

There was no such thought in her heart, but she wished to hear him deny it.

"Nay, my one lady," he answered; "I was, indeed, more than ready to come to Courtland, but it was because of the hope that surged through my heart, as flame leaps through tow, that I should see you and hear your voice!"

The Princess held out her hands impulsively and then retracted them as suddenly.

"Now, we must not waste time," she said; "I must save you. They would slay you on the least suspicion. But I will match them. Would to God that Conrad were here. To him I could speak. I could trust him. He would help us. Let me see! Let me see!"

She bent her head and walked slowly to the window. Like every true Courtlander she thought best when she could watch the swirl of the green Alla against its banks. The Sparhawk took a step as if to follow, but instead stood still where he was, drinking in her proud and girlish beauty. To the eye of any spy they were no more than two noble ladies who had quarrelled, the smaller and slighter of whom had turned her back upon the taller!

They were in the same position still, and the white foam-fleck which Margaret was following with her eyes had not vanished from her sight, when the door of the summer palace was rudely thrown open and an officer announced in a loud and strident tone, "The Prince Louis to visit his Princess!"

CHAPTER XXXI
THE ROYAL MINX

Prince Louis entered, flushed and excited. His eyes had lost their furtive meanness and blazed with a kind of reckless fury quite foreign to his nature, for anger affected him as wine might another man.

He spoke first to the Princess Margaret.

"And so, my fair sister," he said, "you would foment rebellion even in my palace and concoct conspiracy with my own married wife. Make ready, madam, for to-morrow you shall find your master. I will marry you to the Prince Ivan of Muscovy. He will carry you to Moscow, where ladies of your breed are taught to obey. And if they will not—why, their delicate skins may chance to be caressed with instruments less tender than lovers' fingers. Go—make you ready. You shall be wed and that immediately. And leave me alone with my wife."

"I will not marry the Prince of Muscovy," his sister answered calmly. "I would rather die by the axe of your public executioner. I would wed with the vilest scullion that squabbles with the swine for gobbets in the gutters of Courtland, rather than sit on a throne with such a man!"

The Prince nodded sagely.

"A pretty spirit—a true Courtland spirit," he said mockingly. "I had the same within my heart when I was young. Conrad hath it now—priest though he be. Nevertheless, he is off to Rome to kiss the Pope's toe. By my faith, Gretchen lass, you show a very pretty spirit!"

He wheeled about and looked towards the false Joan, who was standing gripping nails into palms by the chimney-mantel.

"And you, my lady," he said, "you have had your turn of rebellion. But once is enough. You are conquered now. You are a wedded wife. Your place is with your husband. You sleep in my palace to-night!"

"If I do," muttered the Sparhawk, "I know who will wake in hell to-morrow!"

"My brother Louis," cried the Princess Margaret, running up to him and taking his arm coaxingly, "do not be so hasty with two poor women. Neither of us desire aught but to do your will. But give us time. Spare us, for you are strong. 'A woman's way is the wind's way'—you know our Courtland proverb. You cannot harness the Northern Lights to your chariot-wheels. Woo us—coax us—aye, even deceive us; but do not force us. Louis, Louis, I thought you were wise, and yet I see that you know not the alphabet of love. Here is your lady. Have you ever said a loving word to her, bent the knee, kissed her hand—which, being persisted in, is the true way to kiss the mouth?"

("If he does either," growled the Sparhawk, "my sword will kiss his midriff!")

Prince Louis smiled. He was not used to women's flatteries, and in his present state of exaltation the cajoleries of the Princess suited his mood. He swelled with self-importance, puffing his cheeks and twirling his grey moustache upwards with the finger and thumb of his left hand.

"I know more of women than you think, sister," he made answer. "I have had experiences—in my youth, that is; I am no puppet princeling. By Saint Mark! once on a day I strutted it with the boldest; and to-day—well, now that I have humbled this proud madam and brought her to my own city, why, I will show you that I am no Wendish boor. I can sue a lady's favour as courteously as any man—and, Margaret, if you will promise me to be a good girl and get you ready to be married to-morrow, I promise you that Louis of Courtland will solicit his lady's favour with all grace and observance."

"Gladly will I be married to-morrow," said the Princess, caressing her brother's sleeve—"that is, if I cannot be married to-day!" she added under her breath.

But she paused a few moments as if embarrassed.

Then she went on.

"Brother Louis, I have spoken with my sister here—your wife, the Lady Joan. She hath a scruple concerning matrimony. She would have it resolved before she hath speech with you again. Permit our good Father Clement to advise with her."

"Father Clement—our Conrad's tutor, why he more than another?"

"Well, do you not understand? He is old," pleaded Margaret, "and there are things one can say easiest to an old man. You understand, brother Louis."

The Prince nodded, well pleased. This was pleasant. His mentor, Prince Wasp, did not usually flatter him. Rather he made him chafe on a tight rein.

"And if I send Father Clement to you, chit," he said patting his sister's softly rounded cheek, "will he both persuade you and ease the scruples of my Lady Joan? I am as delicate and understanding as any man. I will not drive a woman when she desires to be led. But led or driven she must be. For to my will she must come at last."

"I knew it, I knew it!" she cried joyously. "Again you are mine own Louis, my dear sweet brother! When will Father Clement come?"

"As soon as he can be sent for," the Prince answered. "He will come directly here to the Summer Palace. And till then you two fair maids can abide together. Princess, my wife, I kiss your noble hand. Margaret, your cheek. Till to-morrow—till to-morrow!"

He went out with an awkward attempt at airy grace curiously grafted on his usually saturnine manners. The door closed behind him. Margaret of Courtland listened a moment with bated breath and finger on lip. A shouted order reached her ear from beneath. Then came the tramp of disciplined feet, and again they heard only the swirl of the Alla fretting about the piles of the Summer Palace.

Then, quickly dropping her lover's fingers, Margaret took hold of her own dress at either side daintily and circled about the Sparhawk in a light-tripping dance.

"Ah, Louis—we will be so good and bidable—to-morrow. To-morrow you will see me a loving and obedient wife. To-morrow I will wed Prince Wasp. Meantime—to-day you and I, Maurice, will consult Father Clement, mine ancient confessor, who will do anything I ask him. To-day we will dance—put your arm about my waist—firmly—so! There, we will dance at a wedding to-day, you and I. For in that brave velvet robe you shall be married!"

"What?" cried the Sparhawk, stopping suddenly. His impulsive sweetheart caught him again into the dance as she swept by in her impetuous career.

"Yes," she nodded, minueting before him. "It is as I say—you are to be married all over again. And when you ride off I will ride with you— no slipping your marriage engagements this time, good sir. I know your Kernsberg manners now. You will not find me so slack as my brother!"

"Margaret!" cried the Sparhawk. And with one bound he had her against his breast.

"Oh!" she cried, with a shrug of her pretty shoulders, as she submitted to his embrace, "I don't love you half as much in that dress. Why, it is like kissing another girl at the convent. Ugh, the cats!"

She was not permitted to say any more. The Alla was heard very clearly in the Summer Palace as it swept the too swift moments with it away towards the sea which is oblivion. Then after a time, and a time and half a time, the Princess Margaret slowly emerged.

"No," she said retrospectively, "it is not like the convent, after all—not a bit."

"Affection is ever seemly, especially between great ladies—also unusual!" said a bass voice, speaking grave and kindly behind them.

The Sparhawk turned quickly round, the crimson rushing instant to his cheek.

"Father—dear Father Clement!" cried Margaret, running to the noble old man who stood by the door and kneeling down for his blessing. He gave it simply and benignantly, and laid his hand a moment on the rippling masses of her fair hair. Then he turned his eyes upon the Sparhawk.

The confusion of his beautiful penitent, the flush which mounted to her neck even as she kneeled, added to a certain level defiance in the glance of her taller companion, told him almost at a glance that which had been so carefully concealed. For the Father was a man of much experience. A man who hears a dozen confessions every day of his life through a wicket in a box grows accustomed to distinguishing the finer differences of sex. His glance travelled back and forth, from the Sparhawk to Margaret, and from Margaret to the Sparhawk.

"Ah!" he said at last, for all comment.

The Princess rose to her feet and approached the priest.

"My Father," she said swiftly, "this is not the Lady Joan, my brother's wife, but a youth marvellously like her, who hath offered himself in her place that she might escape — —"

"Nay," said the Sparhawk, "it was to see you once again, Lady Margaret, that I came to Courtland!"

"Hush! you must not interrupt," she went on, putting him aside with her hand. "He is the Count von Löen, a lord of Kernsberg. And I love him. We want you to marry us now, dear Father—now, without a moment's delay; for if you do not, they will kill him, and I shall have to marry Prince Wasp!"

She clasped her hands about his arm.

"Will you?" she said, looking up beseechingly at him.

The Princess Margaret was a lady who knew her mind and so bent other minds to her own.

The Father stood smiling a little down upon her, more with his eyes than with his lips.

"They will kill him and marry you, if I do. And, moreover, pray tell me, little one, what will they do to me?" he said.

"Father, they would not dare to meddle with you. Your office—your sanctity—Holy Mother Church herself would protect you. If Conrad were here, he would do it for me. I am sure he would marry us. I could tell him everything. But he is far, far away, on his knees at the shrine of Holy Saint Peter, most like."

"And you, young masquerader," said Father Clement, turning to the Sparhawk, "what say you to all this? Is this your wish, as well as that of the Princess Margaret? I must know all before I consent to put my old neck into the halter!"

"I will do whatever the Princess wishes. Her will is mine."

"Do not make a virtue of that, young man," said the priest smiling; "the will of the Princess is also that of most people with whom she comes in contact. Submission is no distinction where our Lady Margaret is concerned. Why, ever since she was so high" (he indicated with his hand), "I declare the minx hath set her own penances and dictated her own absolutions."

"You have indeed been a sweet confessor," murmured Margaret of Courtland, still clasping the Father's arm and looking up fondly into his face. "And you will do as I ask you this once. I will not ask for such a long time again."

The priest laughed a short laugh.

"Nay, if I do marry you to this gentleman, I hope it will serve for a while. I cannot marry Princesses of the Empire to carnival mummers more than once a week!"

A quick frown formed on the brow of Maurice von Lynar. He took a step nearer. The priest put up his hand, with the palm outspread in a sort of counterfeit alarm.

"Nay, I know not if it will last even a week if bride and groom are both so much of the same temper. Gently, good sir, gently and softly. I must go carefully myself. I am bringing my grey hairs unpleasantly near the gallows. I must consider my duty, and you must respect my office."

The Sparhawk dropped on one knee and bent his head.

"Ah, that is better," said the priest, making the sign of benediction above the clustered raven locks. "Rise, sir, I would speak with you a moment apart. My Lady Margaret, will you please to walk on the terrace there while I confer with—the Lady Joan upon obedience, according to the commandment of the Prince."

As he spoke the last words he made a little movement towards the corridor with his hand, at the same moment elevating his voice. The Princess caught his meaning and, before either of her companions could stop her, she tiptoed to the door, set her hand softly to the latch, and suddenly flung it open. Prince Louis stood without, with head bowed to listen.

The Princess shrilled into a little peal of laughter.

"Brother Louis!" she cried, clapping her hands, "we have caught you. You must restrain your youthful, your too ardent affections. Your bride is about to confess. This is no time for mandolins and serenades. You should have tried those beneath her windows in Kernsberg. They might have wooed her better than arbalist and mangonel."

The Prince glared at his *débonnaire* sister as if he could have slain her on the spot.

"I returned," he said formally, speaking to the disguised Maurice, "to inform the Princess that her rooms in the main palace were ready for her whenever she deigns to occupy them."

"I thank you, Prince Louis," returned the false Princess, bowing. In his character of a woman betrayed and led prisoner the Sparhawk was sparing of his words—and for other reasons as well.

"Come, brother, your arm," said the Princess. "You and I must not intrude. We will leave the good Father and his fair penitent. Will you walk with me on the terrace? I, on my part, will listen to your lover's confessions and give you plenary absolution—even for listening at keyholes. Come, dear brother, come!"

And with one gay glance shot backward at the Sparhawk, half over her shoulder, the Lady Margaret took the unwilling arm of her brother and swept out. Verily, as Father Clement had said, she was a royal minx.

CHAPTER XXXII
THE PRINCESS MARGARET IS IN A HURRY

The priest waited till their footsteps died away down the corridor before going to the door to shut it. Then he turned and faced the Sparhawk with a very different countenance to that which he had bent upon the Princess Margaret.

Generally, when women leave a room the thermometer drops suddenly many degrees nearer the zero of verity. There is all the difference between velvet sheath and bare blade, between the courtesies of seconds and the first clash of the steel in the hands of principals. There are, let us say, two men and one woman. The woman is in the midst. Smile answers smile. Masks are up. The sun shines in. She goes—and before the smile of parting has fluttered from her lips, lo! iron answers iron on the faces of the men. Off, ye lendings! Salute! Engage! To the death!

There was nothing, however, very deadly in the encounter of the Sparhawk and Father Clement. It was only as if a couple of carnival maskers had stepped aside out of the whirl of a dance to talk a little business in some quiet alcove. The Father foresaw the difficulty of his task. The Sparhawk was conscious of the awkwardness of maintaining a manly dignity in a woman's gown. He felt, as it were, choked about the legs in another man's presence.

"And now, sir," said the priest abruptly, "who may you be?"

"Father, I am a servant to the Duchess Joan of Hohenstein and Kernsberg. Maurice von Lynar is my name."

"And pray, how came you so like the Duchess that you can pass muster for her?"

"That I know not. It is an affair upon which I was not consulted. But, indeed, I do it but poorly, and succeed only with those who know her little, and who are in addition men without observation. Both the Princess and yourself saw through me easily enough, and I am in fear every moment I am near Prince Ivan."

"How came the Princess to love you?"

"Well, for one thing, I loved her. For another, I told her so!"

"The points are well taken, but of themselves insufficient," smiled the priest. "So also have others better equipped by fortune to win her favour than you. What else?"

Then, with a certain shamefaced and sulky pride, the Sparhawk told Father Clement all the tale of the mission of the Duchess Joan of Courtland, of the liking the Princess had taken to that lady in her secretary's attire, of the kiss exchanged upon the dark river's bank, the fragrant memory of which had drawn him back to Courtland against his will. And the priest listened like a man of many counsels who knows that the strangest things are the truest, and that the naked truth is always incredible.

"It is a pretty tangle you have made between you," said Father Clement when Maurice finished. "I know not how you could more completely have twisted the skein. Every one is somebody else, and the devil is hard upon the hindmost—or Prince Ivan, which is apparently the same thing."

The priest now withdrew in his turn to where he could watch the Alla curving its back a little in mid-stream as the summer floods rushed seaward from the hills. To true Courtland folk its very bubbles brought counsel as they floated down towards the Baltic.

"Let me see! Let me see!" he murmured, stroking his chin.

Then after a long pause he turned again to the Sparhawk.

"You are of sufficient fortune to maintain the Princess as becomes her rank?"

"I am not a rich man," answered Von Lynar, "but by the grace of the Duchess Joan neither am I a poor one. She hath bestowed on me one of her father's titles, with lands to match."

"So," said the priest; "but will Prince Louis and the Muscovites give you leave to enjoy them?"

"The estates are on the borders of Plassenburg," said Maurice, "and I think the Prince of Plassenburg for his own security will provide against any Muscovite invasion."

"Princes are but princes, though I grant you the Executioner's Son is a good one," answered the priest. "Well, better to marry than to burn, sayeth Holy Writ. It is touch and go, in any event. I will marry you and thereafter betake me to the Abbey of Wolgast, where dwells my very good friend the Abbot Tobias. For old sake's sake he will keep me safe there till this thing blows over."

"With my heart I thank you, my Father," said the Sparhawk, kneeling.

"Nay, do not thank me. Rather thank the pretty insistency of your mistress. Yet it is only bringing you both one step nearer destruction. Walking upon egg-shells is child's play to this. But I never could refuse your sweetheart either a comfit or an absolution all my days. To my shame as a servant of God I say it. I will go and call her in."

He went to the door with a curious smile on his face. He opened it, and there, close by the threshold, was the Princess Margaret, her eyes full of a bright mischief.

"Yes, I was listening," she cried, shaking her head defiantly. "I do not care. So would you, Father, if you had been a woman and in love — — "

"God forbid!" said Father Clement, crossing himself.

"You may well make sure of heavenly happiness, my Father, for you will never know what the happiness of earth is!" cried Margaret. "I would rather be a woman and in love, than — than the Pope himself and sit in the chair of St. Peter."

"My daughter, do not be irreverent."

"Father Clement, were you ever in love? No, of course you cannot tell me; but I think you must have been. Your eyes are kind when you look at us. You are going to do what we wish — I know you are. I heard you say so to Maurice. Now begin."

"You speak as if the Holy Sacrament of matrimony were no more than saying 'Abracadabra' over a toadstool to cure warts," said the priest, smiling. "Consider your danger, the evil case in which you will put me when the thing is discovered — — "

"I will consider anything, dear Father, if you will only make haste," said the Princess, with a smiling natural vivacity that killed any verbal disrespect.

"Nay, madcap, be patient. We must have a witness whose head sits on his shoulders beyond the risk of Prince Louis's halter or Prince Ivan's Muscovite dagger. What say you to the High Councillor of Plassenburg, Von Dessauer? He is here on an embassy."

The Princess clapped her hands.

"Yes, yes. He will do it. He will keep our secret. He also likes pretty girls."

"Also?" queried Father Clement, with a grave and demure countenance.

"Yes, Father, you know you do — — "

"It is a thing most strictly forbidden by Holy Church that in fulfilling the duties of sacred office one should be swayed by any merely human considerations," began the priest, the wrinkles puckering about his eyes, though his lips continued grave.

"Oh, please, save the homily till after sacrament, dear Father!" cried the Princess. "You know you like me, and that you cannot help it."

The priest lifted up his hand and glanced upward, as if deprecating the anger of Heaven.

"Alas, it is too true!" he said, and dropped his hand again swiftly to his side.

"I will go and summon Dessauer myself," she went on. "I will run so quick. I cannot bear to wait."

"Abide ye—abide ye, my daughter," said Father Clement; "let us do even this folly decently and in order. The day is far spent. Let us wait till darkness comes. Then when you are rested—and" (he looked towards the Sparhawk) "the Lady Joan also—I will return with High Councillor Dessauer, who, without observance or suspicion, may pay his respects to the Princesses upon their arrival."

"But, Father, I cannot wait," cried the impetuous bride. "Something might happen long before then. My brother might come. Prince Wasp might find out. The Palace itself might fall—and then I should never be married at all!"

And the very impulsive and high-strung daughter of the reigning house of Courtland put a kerchief to her eyes and tapped the floor with the silken point of her slipper.

The holy Father looked at her a moment and turned his eyes to Maurice von Lynar. Then he shook his head gravely at that proximate bridegroom as one who would say, "If you be neither hanged nor yet burnt here in Courtland—if you get safely out of this with your bride—why, then, Heaven have mercy on your soul!"

CHAPTER XXXIII
A WEDDING WITHOUT A BRIDEGROOM

It was very quiet in the river parlour of the Summer Palace. A shaded lamp burned in its niche over the desk of Prince Conrad. Another swung from the ceiling and filled the whole room with dim, rich light. The window was a little open, and the Alla murmured beneath with a soothing sound, like a mother hushing a child to sleep. There was no one in the great chamber save the youth whose masquerading was now well nigh over. The Sparhawk listened intently. Footsteps were approaching. Quick as thought he threw himself upon a couch, and drew about him a light cloak or woollen cloth lined with silk. The footsteps stopped at his door. A hand knocked lightly. The Sparhawk did not answer. There was a long pause, and then footsteps retreated as they had come. The Sparhawk remained motionless. Again the Alla, outside in the mild autumnal gloaming, said, "Hush!"

Tired with anxiety and the strain of the day, the youth passed from musing to real sleep and the stream of unconsciousness, with a long soothing swirl like that of the green water outside among the piles of the Summer Palace, bore him away. He took longer breaths, sighing in his slumbers like a happy tired child.

Again there came footsteps, quicker and lighter this time; then the crisp rustle of silken skirts, a warm breath of scented air, and the door was closed again. No knocking this time. It was some one who entered as of right.

Then the Princess Margaret, with clasped hands and parted lips, stood still and watched the slumber of the man she loved. Though she knew it not, it was one of the crucial moments in the chronicle of love. If a woman's heart melts from tolerant friendship to a kind of motherhood at the sight of a man asleep; if something draws tight about her heart like the strings of an old-fashioned purse; if there is a pulse beating where no pulse should be, a pleasurable lump in the throat, then it is come—the not-to-be-denied, the long-expected, the inevitable. It is a simple test, and one not always to be applied (as it were) without a doctor's prescription; but, when fairly tried, it is infallible. If a woman is happier listening to a man's quiet breathing than she has ever been hearkening to any other's flattery, it is no longer an affair—it is a passion.

The Princess Margaret sat down by the couch of Maurice von Lynar, and, after this manner of which I have told, her heart was moved within her. As she bent a little over the youth and looked into his sleeping face, the likeness to Joan the Duchess came out more strongly than ever, emerging almost startlingly, as a race stamp stands out on the features of the dead. She bent her head still nearer the slightly parted lips. Then she drew back.

"No," she murmured, smiling at her intent, "I will not—at least, not now. I will wait till I hear them coming."

She stole her hand under the cloak which covered the sleeper till her cool fingers rested on Maurice's hand. He stirred a little, and his lips moved. Then his eyelids quivered to the lifting. But they did not rise. The ear of the Princess was very near them now.

"Margaret!" she heard him say, and as the low whisper reached her she sat erect in her chair with a happy sigh. So wonderful is love and so utterly indifferent to time or place, to circumstance or reason.

The Alla also sighed a sigh to think that their hour would pass so swiftly. So Margaret of Courtland, princess and lover, sat contentedly by the pillow of him who had once been a prisoner in the dungeon of Castle Kernsberg.

But in the palace of the Prince of Courtland time ran even more swiftly than the Alla beneath its walls.

Margaret caught a faint sound far away—footsteps, firm footfalls of men who paced slowly together. And as these came nearer, she could distinguish, mixed with them, the sharp tapping of one who leans upon a staff. She did not hesitate a moment now. She bent down upon the sleeper. Her arm glided under his neck. Her lips met his.

"Maurice," she whispered, "wake, dearest. They are coming."

"Margaret!" he would have answered—but could not.

The greetings were soon over. The tale had already been told to Von Dessauer by Father Clement. The pair stood up under the golden glow of the swinging silver lamps. It was a strange scene. For surely never was marriage more wonderfully celebrated on earth than this of two fair maidens (for so they still appeared) taking hands at the bidding of God's priest and vowing the solemn vows, in the presence of a prince's chancellor, to live only for each other in all the world.

Maurice, tall and dark, a red mantle thrown back from his shoulders, confined at the waist and falling again to the feet, stood holding Margaret's hand, while she, younger and slighter, her skin creamily white, her cheek rose-flushed, her eyes brilliant as with fever, watched Father Clement as if she feared he would omit some essential of the service.

"Maurice stood ... holding Margaret's hand."

Von Dessauer, High Councillor of Plassenburg, stood leaning on the head of his staff and watching with a certain gravity of sympathy, mixed with apprehension, the simple ceremonial.

Presently the solemn "Let no man put asunder" was said, the blessing pronounced, and Leopold von Dessauer came forward with his usual courtly grace to salute the newly made Countess von Löen.

He would have kissed her hand, but with a swift gesture she offered her cheek.

"Not hands to-day, good friend," she said. "I am no more a princess, but my husband's wife. They cannot part us now, can they, High Councillor? I have gotten my wish!"

"Dear lady," the Chancellor of Plassenburg answered gently. "I am an old man, and I have observed that Hymen is the most tricksome of the divinities. His omens go mostly by contraries. Where much is expected, little is obtained. When all men speak well of a wedding, and all the prophets prophesy smooth things—my fear is great. Therefore be of good cheer. Though you have chosen the rough road, the perilous venture, the dark night, the deep and untried ford, you will yet come out upon a plain of gladness, into a day of sunshine, and at the eventide reach a home of content."

"So good a fortune from so wise a soothsayer deserves—this!"

And she kissed the Chancellor frankly on the mouth.

"Father Clement," she said, turning about to the priest with a provocative look on her face, "have you a prophecy for us worthy a like guerdon?"

"Avaunt, witch! Get thee behind me, pretty impling! Tempt not an old man to forget his office, or I will set thee such a penance as will take months to perform."

Nevertheless his face softened as he spoke. He saw too plainly the perils which encompassed Maurice von Lynar and his wife. Yet he held out his hand benignantly and they sank on their knees.

"God bring you well through, beloveds!" he said. "May He send His angels to succour the faithful and punish the guilty!"

"I bid you fair good-night!" said Leopold von Dessauer at the threshold. But he added in his heart, "But alas for the to-morrow that must come to you twain!"

"I care for nothing now—I have gotten my will!" said the Princess Margaret, nodding her head to the Father as he went out.

She was standing on the threshold with her husband's hand in hers, and her eyes were full of that which no words can express.

"May that which is so sweet in the mouth now, never prove bitter in the belly!"

That was the Father's last prayer for them.

But neither Margaret nor Maurice von Lynar so much as heard him, for they had turned to one another.

For the golden lamp was burning itself out, and without in the dark the Alla still said, "Hush!" like a mother who soothes her children to sleep.

CHAPTER XXXIV
LITTLE JOHANNES RODE

"But this one day, beloved," the Sparhawk was saying. "What is one day among our enemies? Be brave, and then we will ride away together under cloud of night. Von Dessauer will help us. For love and pity Prince Hugo of Plassenburg will give us an asylum. Or if he will not, by my faith! Helene the Princess will—or her kind heart is sore belied! Fear not!"

"I am not afraid—I have never feared anything in my life," answered the Princess Margaret. "But now I fear for you, Maurice. I would give all I possess a hundred times over—nay, ten years of my life—if only you were safe out of this Courtland!"

"It will not be long," said the Sparhawk soothingly. "To-morrow Von Dessauer goes with all his train. He cannot, indeed, openly give us his protection till we are past the boundaries of the State. But at the Fords of the Alla we must await him. Then, after that, it is but a short and safe journey. A few days will bring us to the borderlands of Plassenburg and the Mark, where we are safe alike from prince brother and prince wooer."

"Maurice—I would it were so, indeed. Do you know I think being married makes one's soul frightened. The one you love grows so terrifyingly precious. It seems such a long time since I was a wild and reckless girl, flouting those who spoke of love, and boasting (oh, so vainly!) that love would never touch me. I used to, not so long ago—though you would not think it now, knowing how weak and foolish I am."

The Sparhawk laughed a little and glanced fondly at his wife. It was a strange look, full of the peculiar joy of man—and that, where the essence of love dwells in him, is his sense of unique possession.

"Do keep still," said the Princess suddenly, stamping her foot. "How can I finish the arraying of your locks, if you twist about thus in your seat? It is fortunate for you, sir, that the Duchess Joan wears her hair short, like a Northman or a bantling troubadour. Otherwise you could not have gone masquerading till yours had grown to be something of this length."

And, with the innocent vanity of a woman preferred, she shook her own head backward till the rich golden tresses, each hair distinct and crisp as a golden wire of infinite thinness, fell over her back and hung down as low as the hollows of her knees.

"Joan could not do that!" she cried triumphantly.

"You are the most beautiful woman in the world," said the Sparhawk, with appreciative reverence, trying to rise from the low stool in front of the Venice mirror upon which he was submitting to having his toilet superintended—for the first time by a thoroughly competent person.

The Princess Margaret bit her lip vixenishly in a pretty way she had when making a pretext of being angry, at the same time sticking the little curved golden comb she was using upon his raven locks viciously into his head.

"Oh, you hurt!" he cried, making a grimace and pretending in his turn.

"And so I will, and much worse," she retorted, "if you do not be still and do as I bid you. How can a self-respecting tire-woman attend to her business under such circumstances? I warn you that you may engage a new maid."

"Wickedest one!" he murmured, gazing fondly up at Margaret, "there is no one like you!"

"Well," she drolled, "I am glad of your opinion, though sorry for your taste. For me, I prefer the Lady Joan."

"And why?"

"Because she is like you, of course!"

So, on the verge perilous, lightly and foolishly they jested as all those who love each other do (which folly is the only wisdom), while the green Alla sped swiftly on to the sea, and the city in which Death waited for Maurice von Lynar began to hum about them.

As yet, however, there fell no suspicion. For Margaret had warned her bowermaidens that the Princess Joan would need no assistance from them. Her own waiting-women were on their way from Castle Kernsberg. In any case she, Margaret of Courtland, would help her sister in person, as well for love as because such service was the guest's right.

And the Courtland maidens, accustomed to the whims and sudden likings of their impetuous mistress, glad also to escape extra duty, hastened their task of arraying Margaret. Never had she been so restless and exacting. Her toilet was not half finished when she rose from her ebony stool, told her favourite Thora of Bornholm that she was too ignorant to be trusted to array so much as the tow-head of a Swedish puppet, endued herself without assistance with a long loose gown of velvet lined with pale blue silk, and flashed out again to revisit her sister-in-law.

"And do you, Thora, and the others, wait my pleasure in the anteroom," she commanded her handmaidens as she swept through the doorway. "Go barter love-compliments with the men-at-arms. It is all such fumblers are good for!"

Behind her back the tiring maids shrugged shoulders and glanced at each other secretly with lifted eyebrow, as they put gowns and broidered slippers back in their places, to signify that if it began thus they were in for a day of it. Nevertheless they obeyed, and, finding certain young gentlemen of Prince Louis's guard waiting for just such an opportunity without, Thora and the others proceeded to carry out to the letter the second part of the instructions of their mistress.

"How now, sweet Thora of the Flaxen Locks?" cried Justus of Grätz, a slender young man who carried the Prince's bannerstaff on saints' days, and practised fencing and the art of love professionally at other times; "has the Princess boxed all your ears this morning, that you come trembling forth, pell-mell, like a flock of geese out of a barn when the farmer's dog is after them?"

There were three under-officers of the guard in the little courtyard. Slim Justus of Grätz, his friend and boon companion Seydelmann, a man of fine presence and empty head, who on wet days could curl the wings of his moustaches round his ears, and, sitting a little apart from these, little Johannes Rode, the only very brave man of the three, a swordsman and a poet, yet one who passed for a ninny and a greenhorn because he chose mostly to be silent. Nevertheless, Thora of Bornholm preferred him to all others in the palace. For the eyes of a woman are quick to discern manhood—so long, that is, as she is not in love. After that, God wot, there is no eyeless fish so blind in all the caverns of the Hartz.

With the Northwoman Thora in her tendance of the Princess there were joined Anna and Martha Pappenheim, two maids quicker of speech and more restless in demeanour—Franconians, like all their name, of their persons little and lithe and gay. The Princess had brought them back with her when at the last Diet she visited Ratisbon with her brother.

"Ah, Thora, fairest of maids! Hath an east wind made you sulky this morning, that you will not answer?" languished Justus. "Then I warrant so are not Anna and Martha. My service to you, noble dames!"

"Noble 'dames' indeed—and to us!" they answered in alternate jets of speech. "As if we were apple-women or the fat house-frows of Courtlandish burghers. Get away—you have no manners! You sop your wits in sour beer. You eat frogs-meat out of your Baltic marshes. A dozen dozen of you were not worth one lively lad out of sweet Franconia!"

"Swe-e-et Franconia!" mocked Justus; "why, then, did you not stop there? Of a verity no lover carried you off to Courtland across his saddle-bow, that I warrant! He had repented his pains and killed his horse long ere he smelt the Baltic brine."

"The most that such louts as you Courtlanders could carry off would be a screeching pullet from a farmyard, when the goodman is from home. There is no spirit in the North—save, I grant, among the women. There is our Princess and her new sister the Lady Joan of the Sword Hand. Where will you see their match? Small wonder they will have nothing to say to such men as they can find hereabouts! But how they love each other! 'Tis as good as a love tale to see them——"

"Aye, and a very miracle to boot!" interjected Thora of Bornholm.

The Pappenheims, as before, went on antiphonally, each answering and anticipating the other.

"The Princesses need not any man to make them happy! Their affection for each other is past telling," said Martha.

"How their eyes shine when they look at each other!" sighed Anna, while Thora said nothing for a little, but watched Johannes Rode keenly. She saw he had something on his mind. The Northwoman was not of the opinion which Anna Pappenheim attributed to the Princesses. For the fair-skinned daughters of the Goth, being wise, hold that there is but one kind of love, as there is but one kind of gold. Also they believe that they carry with them the philosopher's stone wherewith to procure that fine ore. After a while Thora spoke.

"This morning it was 'The Princess needs not your help—I myself will be her tire-woman!' I wot Margaret is as jealous of any other serving the Lady Joan——"

"As you would be if we made love to Johannes Rode there!" laughed Martha Pappenheim, getting behind a pillar and peeping roguishly round in order that the poet might have an opportunity of seeing the pretty turn of her ankle.

But little Johannes, who with a nail was scratching a line or two of a catch on a smooth stone, hardly even smiled. He minded maids of honour, their gabble and their ankles, no more than jackdaws crying in the crevices of the gable—that is, all except Thora, who was so large and fair and white that he could not get her quite out of his mind. But even with Thora of Bornholm he did his best.

"That is all very well *now*," put in vain Fritz Seydelmann, stroking his handsome beard and smiling vacantly; "but wait till these same Princesses have had husbands of their own for a year. Then they will spit at each other and scratch—like cats. All women are cats, and maids of honour the worst of all!"

"How so, Sir Wiseman—because they do not like puppies? You have found out that?" Anna Pappenheim struck back demurely.

"You ask me why maids of honour are like cats," returned Seydelmann complacently (he had been making up this speech all night). "Do they not arch their backs when they are stroked? Do they not purr? Have you not seen them lie about the house all day, doing nothing and looking as saintly as so many abbots at High Mass? But at night and on the tiles—phew! 'tis another matter then."

And having thus said vain moustached Seydelmann, who plumed himself upon his wit, dragged at his moustache horns and simpered bovinely down upon the girls.

Anna Pappenheim turned to Thora, who was looking steadily through the self-satisfied Fritz, much as if she could see a spider crawling on the wall behind him.

"Do they let things like that run about loose here in Courtland?" she asked, with some anxiety on her face. "We have sties built for them at home in Franconia!"

But Thora was in no mood for the rough jesting of officers-in-waiting and princesses' tirewomen. She continued to watch the spider.

Then little Johannes Rode spoke for the first time.

"I wager," he said slowly, "that the Princesses will be less inseparable by this time to-morrow."

"What do you mean, Johannes Rode?" said Thora, with instant challenge in her voice, turning the wide-eyed directness of her gaze full upon him.

The young man did not look at her. He merely continued the carving of his couplet upon the lower stone of the sundial, whistling the air as he did so.

"Well," he answered slowly, "the Muscovite guard of Prince Ivan have packed their own baggage (together with a good deal that is not their own), and the minster priests are warned to hold themselves at the Prince's bidding all day. That means a wedding, and I warrant you our noble Louis does not mean to marry his Princess all over again in the Dom-Kirch of Courtland. They are going to marry the Russ to our Princess Margaret!"

Blonde Fritz laughed loud and long and tugged at his moustache.

"Out, you fool!" he cried; "this is a saint's day! I saw it in the chaplain's Breviary. The Prince goes to shrive himself, and right wisely he judges. I would not only confess, but receive extreme unction as well, before I attempted to come nigh Joan of the Sword Hand in the way of love! What say you, Justus?"

But before his companion could reply, Thora of Bornholm had risen and stolen quietly within.

CHAPTER XXXV
A PERILOUS HONEYMOON

Never was day so largely and gloriously blue since Courtland was a city as the first morning of the married life of Maurice and Margaret von Lynar, Count and Countess von Löen. The summer floods had subsided, and the tawny dye had gone clean out of the Alla, which was now as clear as aquamarine, and laved rather than fretted the dark green piles of the Summer Palace.

The Princesses (so they said without) were more than ever inseparable. They were constantly talking confidentially together, for all the world like schoolgirls with a secret. Doubtless Prince Louis's fair sister was persuading the unruly wife to return to her duty. Doubtless it was so—ah, yes, doubtless!

"Better that Prince Louis should do his own embassage in such a matter in his proper person," said the good-wives of Thorn. "For me, I would not listen to any sister if my man came not to my feet himself. The Lady Joan is in the right of it—a feckless lover, no true man!"

"Aye," said the men, agreeing for once, "a paper-backed princeling! God wot, were it our Conrad we should soon hear other of it! There would be none of this shilly-shallying back-and-forth work then! We would give half a year's income in golden gulden for a good lusty heir to the Principalities— with that foul Muscovite Ivan yearning to lay the knout across our backs!"

"There is something toward to-day," said a decent widow woman who lived in the Königstrasse to her neighbour. "My son, who as you know is a chorister, is gone to practise the Wedding Hymn in the cathedral. I am going thither to get a good place. I will not miss it, whatever it is. Perhaps they are going to make the Princess Joan do penance for her fault, in a white sheet with a candle in her hand a yard long! That would be rare sport. I would not miss it for so much as four farthings!"

And with that the chorister's mother hobbled off, telling everybody she met the same story. And so in half an hour the news had spread all over the city, and there began to be the makings of quite a respectable crowd in the Dom Platz of Courtland.

It was half-past eleven when the archers of the guard appeared at the entrance of the square which leads from the palace. Behind them, rank upon rank, could be seen the lances of the wild Cossacks of Prince Ivan's escort who had remained behind when the Muscovite army went back to the Russian plains. Their dusky goat-hair tents, which had long covered the banks of the Alla, had now been struck and were laded upon baggage-horses and sumpter mules.

"The Prince of Muscovy delays only for the ceremony, whatever it may be!" the people said, admiring at their own prevision.

And the better sort added privately, "We shall be well rid of him!" But the baser grieved for the loss of the largesse which he scattered abroad in good Muscovite silver, unclipped and unalloyed, with the mint-master's hammer-stroke clean and clear to the margin. For with such Prince Ivan knew how to make himself beloved, holding man's honour and woman's love at the price of so few and so many gold pieces, and thinking well or ill of them according to their own valuation. The rabble of Courtland, whose price was only silver, he counted as no better than the trodden dirt of the highway.

Meanwhile, in the river parlour of the Summer Palace, the two Princesses were talking together even as the people had said. The Princess Margaret sat on a low stool, leaning her elbow on her companion's knee and gazing up at him. And though she sometimes looked away, it was not for long, and Maurice, meeting her ever-recurrent regard, found that a new thing had come into her eyes.

Presently a low tapping was heard at the inner door, from which a passage communicated with the rooms of the Princess Margaret. The Sparhawk would have risen, for the moment forgetful of his disguise, but with a slight pressure of her arm upon his knee the Princess restrained him.

"Enter!" she called aloud in her clear imperious voice.

Thora entered hurriedly, and, closing the door behind her, she stood with the latch in her hand. "My Princess," she said in a voice that was little more than a whisper, "I have heard ill news. They are making the cathedral ready for a wedding. The Cossacks have struck their tents. I think a plot is on foot to marry you this day to Prince Ivan, and to carry you off with him to Moscow."

The Sparhawk sprang to his feet and laid his hand on the place where his sword-hilt should have been.

"Never," he cried; "it is impossible! The Princess is——"

He was about to add, "She is married already," but with a quick gesture of warning Margaret stopped him.

"Who told you this?" she queried, turning again to Thora of Bornholm.

"Johannes Rode of the Prince's guard told me a moment ago," she answered. "He has just returned from the Muscovite camp."

"I thank you, Thora—I shall not forget this faithfulness," said Margaret. "Now you have my leave to go!" The Princess spoke calmly, and to the ear even a little coldly.

The door closed upon the Swedish maiden. Margaret and Maurice turned to each other with one pregnant instinct and took hands.

"Already!" said Margaret faintly, going back into the woman; "they might have left us alone a little longer. How shall we meet this? What shall we do? I had counted on this one day."

"Margaret," answered the Sparhawk impulsively, "this shall not daunt us. We would have told your brother Louis one day. We will tell him now. Duchess Joan is safe out of his reach, Kernsberg is revictualled, the Muscovite army returned. There is no need to keep up the masquerade any longer. Whatever may come of it, let us go to your brother. That will end it swiftly, at all events."

The Princess put away his restraining clasp and came closer to him.

"No—no," she cried: "you must not. You do not know my brother. He is wholly under the influence of Ivan of Muscovy. Louis would slay you for having cheated him of his bride—Ivan for having forestalled him with me."

"But you cannot marry Ivan. That were an outrage against the laws of God and man!"

"Marry Ivan!" she cried, to the full as impulsively as her lover; "not though they set ravens to pick the live flesh off my bones! But it is the thought of torture and death for you—that I cannot abide. We must continue to deceive them. Let me think!—let me think!"

Hastily she barred the door which led out upon the corridor. Then taking Maurice's hand once more she led him over to the window, from which she could see the green Alla cutting its way through the city bounds and presently escaping into the yet greener corn lands on its way to the sea.

"It is for this one day's delay that we must plan. To-night we will certainly escape. I can trust certain of those of my household. I have tried them before.... I have it. Maurice, you must be taken ill—lie down on this couch away from the light. There is a rumour of the Black Death in the city—we must build on that. They say an Astrakhan trader is dead of it already. For one day we may stave it off with this. It is the poor best we can do. Lie down, I will call Thora. She is staunch and fully to be trusted."

The Princess Margaret went to the inner door and clapped her hands sharply.

The fair-haired Swedish maiden came running to her. She had been waiting for such a signal.

"Thora," said her mistress in a quick whisper, "we must put off this marriage. I would sooner die than marry Ivan. You have that drug you spoke of—that which gives the appearance of sickness unto death without the reality. The Lady Joan must be ill, very ill. You understand, we must deceive even the Prince's physicians."

The girl nodded with quick understanding, and, turning, she sped away up the inner stair to her own sleeping-chamber, the key of which (as was the custom in Courtland) she carried in her pocket.

"This will keep you from being suspected—as in public places you would have been," whispered Margaret to her young husband. "What Thora thinks or knows does not matter. I can trust Thora with my life—nay, what is far more, with yours."

A light tap and the girl re-entered, a tall phial in her hand. With a swift look at her mistress to obtain permission, she went up to the couch upon which the Sparhawk had lain down. Then with a deft hand she opened the bottle, and pouring a little of a colourless liquid into a cup she gave it him to drink. In a few minutes a sickly pallor slowly overspread Maurice von Lynar's brow. His eyes appeared injected, the lips paled to a grey white, beads of perspiration stood on the forehead, and his whole countenance took on the hue and expression of mortal sickness.

"Now," said Thora, when she had finished, "will the noble lady deign to swallow one of these pellicles, and in ten minutes not a leech in the country will be able to pronounce that she is not suffering from a dangerous disease."

"You are sure, Thora," said the Princess Margaret almost fiercely, laying her hand on her tirewoman's wrist, "that there is no harm in all this? Remember, on your life be it!"

The placid, flaxen-haired woman turned with the little silver box in her hand.

"Danger there is, dear mistress," she said softly, "but not, I think, so great danger as we are already in. But I will prove my honesty——"

She took first a little of the liquid, and immediately after swallowed one of the white pellicles she had given Maurice.

"It will be as well," she said, "when the Prince's wiseacre physicians come, that they should find another sickening of the same disease."

Thora of Bornholm passed about the couch and took up a waiting-maid's station some way behind.

"All is ready," she said softly.

"We will forestall them," answered the Princess. "Thora, send and bid Prince Louis come hither quickly."

"And shall I also ask him to send hither his most skilled doctors of healing?" added the girl. "I will despatch Johannes Rode. He will go quickly and answer as I bid him with discretion—and without asking questions."

And with the noiseless tread peculiar to most blonde women of large physique, Thora disappeared through the private door by which she had entered.

The Princess Margaret kneeled down by the couch and looked into the face of the Sparhawk. Even she who had seen the wonder was amazed and almost frightened by the ghastly effect the drug had wrought in such short space.

"You are sure that you do not feel any ill effects—you are perfectly well?" she said, with tremulous anxiety in her voice.

The Sparhawk smiled and nodded reassuringly up at her.

"Never better," he said. "My nerves are iron, my muscles steel. I feel as if, for my Margaret's sake, I could vanquish an army of Prince Ivan's single-handed!"

The Princess rose from her place and unlocked the main door.

"We will be ready for them," she said. "All must appear as though we had no motive for concealment."

And, having drawn the curtains somewhat closer, she kneeled down again by the couch. There was no sound in the room as the youthful husband and wife thus waited their fate hand in hand, save only the soft continuous sibilance of their whispered converse, and from without the deeper note of the Alla sapping the Palace walls.

CHAPTER XXXVI
THE BLACK DEATH

The Princes of Courtland and Muscovy, inseparable as the Princesses, were on the pleasant creeper-shaded terrace which looks over the rose garden of the palace of Courtland down upon the sea plain of the Baltic, now stretching blue black from verge to verge under the imminent sun of noon.

Prince Louis moved restlessly to and fro, now biting his lip, now frowning and fumbling with his sword-hilt, and anon half drawing his jewelled dagger from its sheath and allowing it to slip back again with the faintly musical click of perfectly fitting steel. Ivan of Muscovy, on the other hand, lounged listlessly in the angle of an embrasure, alternately contemplating his red-pointed toes shod in Cordovan leather, and glancing keenly from under his eyelids at his nervous companion as often as his back was turned in the course of his ceaseless perambulations.

"You would desert me, Ivan," Prince Louis was saying in a tone at once appealing and childishly aggressive: "you would leave me in the hour of my need. You would take away from me my sister Margaret, who alone has influence with the Princess, my wife!"

"But you do not try to court the lady with any proper fervour," objected Ivan, half humouring and half irritating his companion; "you observe none of the rules. Speak her soft, praise her eyelashes—surely they are worthy of all praise; give her a pet lamb for a playmate. Feed her with conserves of honey and spice. Surely such comfits would mollify even Joan of the Sword Hand!"

"Tush!—you flout me, Ivan—even you. Every one despises me since— since she flouted me. The woman is a tigress, I tell you. Every time she looks at me her eyes flick across me like a whip-lash!"

"That is but her maiden modesty. How often is it assumed to cover love!" murmured Ivan, demurely smiling at his shoe point, which nodded automatically before him. "So doth the glance of my sweet bride of to-day, your own sister Margaret. To all seeming she loves me as little as the Lady Joan does you. Yet I am not afraid. I know women. Before I have her a month in Moscow she will run that she may be allowed to pull my shoes off and on. She will be out of breath with hasting to fetch my slippers—together with other little domestic offices of that sort, all very profitable for women's souls to perform. Take pattern by me, Louis, and teach the tigress to bring your shoes and tie your hose points. In a little while she will like it and hold up her cheek to be kissed for a sufficient reward."

At this point an officer came swiftly across the parterre and stood with uncovered head by the steps of the terrace, waiting permission to ascend. The Prince summoned him with a movement of his hand.

"What news?" he said; "have the ladies yet left the Summer Palace?"

"No, my lord," answered the officer earnestly; "but Johannes Rode of the Princess Margaret's household has come with a message that the plague has broken out there, and that the Lady Princess is the first stricken!"

"Which Princess?" demanded Ivan, with an instant incision of tone.

"The Lady Joan, Princess of Courtland, your Highness," replied the man, without, however, looking at the Prince of Muscovy.

"The Lady Joan?" cried the Prince Louis. "She is ill? She has brought the Black Death with her from Kernsberg! She is stricken with the plague? How fortunate that, so far, I— —"

He clapped his hand upon his brow and shut his eyes as if giving thanks.

"I see it all now!" he cried. "This is the reason the Kernsberg traitors were so willing to give her up. It is all a plot against my life. I will not go near. Let the court physicians be sent! Cause the doors of the Summer Palace to be sealed! Set double guards! Permit none to pass either way, save the doctors only! And let them change their clothes and perfume themselves with the smoke of sulphur before they come out!"

His voice mounted higher and higher as he spoke, and Ivan of Muscovy watched him without speaking, as with hands thrust out and distended nostrils he screamed and gesticulated.

Prince Ivan had never seen a thorough coward before, and the breed interested him. But when he had let the Prince run on far enough to shame him before his own officer, he rose quietly and stood in front of him.

"Louis," he said, in a low voice, "listen to me—this is but a report. It is like enough to be false; it is certain to be exaggerated. Let us go at once and find out."

Prince Louis threw out his hands with a gesture of despair.

"Not I—not I!" he cried. "You may go if you like, if you do not value your life. But I—I do not feel well even now. Yesterday I kissed her hand. Ah, would to God that I had not! That is it. I wondered what ailed me this morning. Go—stop the court physicians! Do not let them go to the Summer Palace; bring them here to me first. Your arm, officer; I think I will go to my room—I am not well."

Prince Ivan's countenance grew mottled and greyish, and his teeth showed in the sun like a thin line of dazzling white. He grasped the poltroon by the wrist with a hand of steel.

"Listen," he said—"no more of this; I will not have it! I will not waste my own time and the blood of my father's soldiers for naught. This is but some woman's trick to delay the marriage—I know it. Hearken! I fear neither Black Death nor black devil; I will have the Lady Margaret to-day if I have to wed her on her death-bed! Now, I cannot enter your wife's chamber alone. Yet go I must, if only to see what all this means, and you shall accompany me. Do you hear, Prince Louis? I swear you shall go with me to the Summer Palace if I have to drag you there step by step!"

His grasp lay like a tightening circle of iron about the wrist of Prince Louis; his steady glance dominated the weaker man. Louis drew in his breath with a choking noise.

"I will," he gasped; "if it must—I will go. But the Death—the Black Death! I am sick—truly, Ivan, I am very sick!"

"So am I!" said Prince Ivan, smiling grimly. "But bring his Highness a cup of wine, and send hither Alexis the Deacon, my own physician."

The officer went out cursing the Muscovite ears that had listened to such things, and also high Heaven for giving such a Prince to his true German fatherland.

Prince Ivan and Prince Louis stood at the door of the river parlour. The peculiar moving hush and tepidly stagnant air of a sick-room penetrated even through the panels. Ivan still kept hold of his friend, but now by the hand, not compulsively, but rather like one who in time of trouble comforts another's sorrow.

At either end of the corridor could be seen a guard of Cossacks keeping it against all intrusion from without or exodus from within. So Prince Ivan had ordered it. His fellows were used to the plague, he said.

At the Princess's door Prince Ivan tapped gently and inclined his ear to listen. Louis fumbled with his golden crucifix, and as the Muscovite turned away his head he pressed it furtively to his lips. Ever since he set foot in the Summer Palace he had been muttering the prayers of the Church in a rapid undertone.

"The Prince Louis to see the Princess Joan!" Ivan answered the low-voiced challenge from within. The door opened slightly and then more widely. Ivan pushed his friend forward and they entered, Louis dragging one foot after the other towards the shaded couch by which knelt the Princess Margaret. Thora of Bornholm, pallid and blue-lipped, stood beside her, swaying a little, but still holding, half unconsciously, as it seemed, a silver basin, into which Margaret dipped a fine linen cloth, before touching with it the foam-flecked lips of the sufferer. Prince Ivan remained a little back, near to where the court physicians were conferring together in stage whispers. As he passed, a tall grey-skirted long-bearded man, girt about the middle with a silver chain, detached himself from the official group and approached Prince Ivan. After an instinctive cringing movement of homage and salutation, he bent to the young man's ear and whispered half a dozen words. Prince Ivan nodded very slightly and the man stole away as he had come. No one in the room had noticed the incident.

Meanwhile Louis of Courtland, almost as pale as Thora herself, his lips blue, his teeth chattering, his fingers clammy with perspiration, stood by the bedside clutching the crucifix. Presently a hand was laid upon his arm. He started violently at the touch.

"It is true—a bad case," said Ivan in his ear. "Let us get away; I must speak with you at once. The physicians have given their verdict. They can do nothing!"

With a gasp of relief Prince Louis faced about, and as he turned he tottered.

"Steady, friend Louis!" said Prince Ivan in his ear, and passed his arm about his waist.

He began to fear lest he should have frightened his dupe too thoroughly.

"See how he loves her!" murmured the doctors of healing, still conferring with their heads together. "Who would have believed it possible?"

"Nay, he is only much afraid," said Alexis the Deacon, the Muscovite doctor; "and small blame to him, now that the Black Death has come to Courtland. In half an hour we shall hear the death-rattle!"

"Then there is no need of us staying," said more than one learned doctor, and they moved softly towards the door. But Ivan had possessed himself of the key, and even as the hand of the first was on the latchet bar the bolt was shot in his face. And the eyes of Alexis the Deacon glowed between his narrow red lids like sparks in tinder as he glanced at the whitening faces of the learned men of Courtland.

Without the door Ivan fixed Prince Louis with his will.

"Now," he said, speaking in low trenchant tones, "if this be indeed the Black Death (and it is like it), there is no safety for us here. We must get without the walls. In an hour there will be such a panic in the city as has not been for centuries. I offer you a way of escape. My Cossacks stand horsed and ready without. Let us go with them. But the Princess Margaret must come also!"

"She cannot—she cannot. I will not permit it. She may already be infected!" gasped Prince Louis.

"There is no infection till the crisis of the disease is passed," said Prince Ivan firmly. "We have had many plagues in Holy Russia, and know the symptoms."

("Indeed," he added to himself, "my physician, Alexis the Deacon, can produce them!")

"But—but—but——" Louis still objected, "the Princess Joan—she may die. It will reflect upon my honour if we all desert her. My sister must continue to attend her. They are friends. I will go with you.... Margaret can remain and nurse her!"

A light like a spear point glittered momentarily under the dark brows of the Muscovite.

"Listen, Prince Louis," he said. "Your honour is your honour. Joan of the Sword Hand and her Black Plagues are your own affair. She is your wife, not mine. I have helped you to get her back—no more. But the Princess Margaret is my business. I have bought her with a price. And look you, sir, I will not ride back to Russia empty-handed, that every petty boyar and starveling serf may scoff at me, saying, 'He helped the Prince of Courtland to win his wife, but he could not bring back one himself.' The whole city, the whole country from here to Moscow know for what cause I have so long sojourned in your capital. No, Prince Louis, will you have me go as your friend or as your enemy?"

"Ivan—Ivan, you are my friend. Do not speak to me so! Who else is my friend if you desert me?"

"Then give me your sister!"

The Prince cast up his hand with a little gesture of despair.

"Ah," he sighed, "you do not know Margaret! She is not in my gift, or you should have had her long ago! Oh, these troubles, these troubles! When will they be at an end?"

"They are at an end now," said Prince Ivan consolingly. "Call your sister out of the chamber on a pretext. In ten minutes we shall be at the cathedral gates. In another ten she and I can be wedded according to your Roman custom. In half an hour we shall all be outside the walls. If you fear the infection you need not once come near her. I will do all that is necessary. And what more natural? We will be gone before the panic breaks—you to one of your hill castles—if you do not wish to come with us to Moscow."

"And the Princess Joan——?" faltered the coward.

"She is in good hands," said the Prince, truthfully for once. "I pledge you my word of honour she is in no danger. Call your sister!"

Even as he spoke he tapped lightly, turned the key in the lock and whispered, "Now!" to the Prince of Courtland.

"Tell the Princess Margaret I would speak with her!" said Prince Louis. "For a moment only!" he added, fearing that otherwise she might not come.

There was a stir in the sick chamber and then quick steps were heard coming lightly across the floor. The face of the Princess appeared at the door.

"Well?" she said haughtily to her brother. Prince Ivan she did not see, for he had stepped back into the dusk of the corridor. Louis beckoned his sister without.

"I must speak a word with you," he said. "I would not have these fellows hear us!" She stepped out unsuspectingly. Instantly the door was closed behind her. A dark figure slid between. Prince Ivan turned the key and laid his hand upon her arm.

"Help!" she cried, struggling; "help me! For God's grace, let me go!"

But from behind came four Cossacks of the Prince's retinue who half-carried, half-forced her along towards the gates at which the Muscovite horses stood ready saddled. And as Margaret was carried down the passage the alarmed servitors stood aloof from her cries, seeing that Prince Louis himself was with her. Yet she cried out unceasingly in her anger and fear, "To me, men of Courtland! The Cossacks carry me off—I will not go! O God, that Conrad were here! I will not be silent! Maurice, save me!"

But the people only shrugged their shoulders even when they heard—as did also the guards and the gentlemen-in-waiting, the underlings and the very porters at the Palace gates. For they said, "They are strange folk, these

Courtland princes and princesses of ours, with their marriages and givings in marriage. They can neither wed nor bed like other people, but must make all this fuss about it. Well—happily it is no business of ours!"

Then at the stair foot she sank suddenly down by the sundial, almost fainting with the sudden alarm and fear, crying for the last time and yet more piercingly, "Maurice! Maurice! Come to me, Maurice!" Then above them in the Palace there began a mighty clamour, the noise of blows stricken and the roar of many voices. But Ivan of Muscovy was neither to be hurried nor flurried. Impassive and determined, he swung himself into the saddle. His black charger changed his feet to take his weight and looked about to welcome him—for he, too, knew his master.

"Give the Princess to me," he commanded. "Now assist Prince Louis into his saddle. To the cathedral, all of you!"

CHAPTER XXXVII
THE DROPPING OF A CLOAK

And so, with the mounted guard of his own Cossacks before him and behind, Prince Ivan carried his bride to church through the streets of her native city. And the folk thronged and marvelled at this new custom of marrying. But none interfered by word or sign, and the obsequious rabble shouted, "Long live Prince Ivan!"

Even some of the better disposed, who had no liking for the Muscovite alliance, said within their hearts, looking at the calm set face of the Prince, "He is a man! Would to God that our own Prince were more like him!"

Also many women nodded their heads and ran to find their dearest gossips. "You will see," they said, "this one will have no ridings away. He takes his wife before him upon his saddle-bow as a man should. And she will pretend that she does not like it. But secretly—ah, we know!"

And they smiled at each other. For there is that in most women which will never be civilised. They love not men who walk softly, and still in their heart of hearts they prefer to be wooed by the primitive method of capture. For if a woman be not afraid of a man she will never love him truly. And that is a true word among all peoples.

So they came at last to the Dom and the groups of wondering folks, thinly scattered here and there—women mostly. For there had been such long delay at the Summer Palace that the men had gone back to their shavings and cooperage tubs or were quaffing tankards in the city ale-cellars.

The great doors of the cathedral had been thrown wide open and the leathern curtains withdrawn. The sun was checkering the vast tesselated pavement with blurs of purple and red and glorious blue shot through the western window of the nave. In gloomy chapel and recessed nook marble princes and battered Crusaders of the line of Courtland seemed to blink and turn their faces to the wall away from the unaccustomed glare. The altar candles and the lamps a-swing in the choir winked no brighter than yellow willow leaves seen through an autumnal fog. But as the *cortège* dismounted the organ began to roll, and the people within rose with a hush like that which follows the opening of a window at night above the Alla.

The sonorous diapason of the great instrument disgorged itself through the doorway in wave upon wave of sound. The Princess Margaret found herself again on her feet, upheld on either side by brother and lover. She was at first somewhat dazed with the rush of accumulate disasters. Slowly her mind came back. The Dom Platz whirled more slowly about her. With a fresh-dawning surprise she heard the choir sing within. She began to understand the speech of men. The great black square of the open doorway slowed and finally stopped before her. She was on the steps of the cathedral. What had come to her? Was it the Duchess Joan's wedding day? Surely no! Then what was the matter? Had she fainted?

Maurice—where was Maurice? She turned about. The small glittering eyes of Prince Ivan, black as sloes, were looking into hers. She remembered now. It was her own wedding. These two, her brother and her enemy, were carrying out their threat. They had brought her to the cathedral to wed her, against her will, to the man she hated. But they could not. She would tell them. Already she was a—but then, if she told them that, they would ride back and kill him. Better that she should perjure herself, condemn herself to hell, than that. Better anything than that. But what was she to do? Was ever a poor girl so driven?

And there, in the hour of her extremity, her eye fell upon a young man in the crowd beneath, a youth in a 'prentice's blue jerkin. He was passing his arm softly about a girl's waist—slily also, lest her mother should see. And the maid, first starting with a pretence of not knowing whence came the pressure, presently looked up and smiled at him, nestling a moment closer to his shoulder before removing his hand, only to hold it covertly under her apron till her mother showed signs of turning round.

"Ah! why was I born a princess?" moaned the poor driven girl.

"Margaret, you must come with us into the cathedral." It was the voice of her brother. "It is necessary that the Prince should wed you now. It has too long been promised, and now he can delay no longer. Besides, the Black Death is in the city, and this is the only hope of escape. Come!"

It was on the tip of Margaret's tongue to cry out with wild words even as she had done at the door at the river parlour. But the thought of Maurice, of the torture and the death, silenced her. She lifted her eyes, and there, at the top of the steps, were the dignitaries of the cathedral waiting to lead the solemn procession.

"I will go!" she said.

And at her words the Prince Ivan smiled under his thin moustache.

She laid her hand on her brother's arm and began the ascent of the long flight of stairs. But even as she did so, behind her there broke a wave of sound—the crying of many people, confused and multitudinous like the warning which runs along a crowded thoroughfare when a wild charger escaped from bonds threshes along with frantic flying harness. Then came the clatter of horses' hoofs, the clang of doors shut in haste as decent burghers got them in out of harm's way! And lo! at the foot of the steps, clad from head to foot in a cloak, the sick Princess Joan, she whom the Black Death had stricken, leaped from her foaming steed, and drawing sword followed fiercely up the stairway after the marriage procession. The Cossacks of the Muscovite guard looked at each other, not knowing whether to stand in her way or no.

"The Princess Joan!" they said from one to the other.

"Joan of the Sword Hand!" whispered the burghers of Courtland. "The disease has gone to her brain. Look at the madness in her eye!"

And their lips parted a little as is the wont of those who, having come to view a comedy, find themselves unexpectedly in the midst of high tragedy.

"Hold, there!" the pursuer shouted, as she set foot on the lowest step.

"Lord! Surely that is no woman's voice!" whispered the people who stood nearest, and their lower jaws dropped a little further in sheer wonderment.

The Princes turned on the threshold of the cathedral, with Margaret still between them, the belly of the church black behind them, and the processional priests first halting and then peering over each other's shoulders in their eagerness to see.

Up the wide steps of the Dom flew the tall woman in the flowing cloak. Her face was pallid as death, but her eyes were brilliant and her lips red. At the sight of the naked sword Prince Ivan plucked the blade from his side and Louis shrank a little behind his sister.

"Treason!" he faltered. "What is this? Is it sudden madness or the frenzy of the Black Death?"

"The Princess Margaret cannot be married!" cried the seeming Princess. "To me, Margaret! I will slay the man who lays a hand on you!"

Obedient to that word, Margaret of Courtland broke from between her brother and Prince Ivan and ran to the tall woman, laying her brow on her breast. The Prince of Muscovy continued calm and immovable.

"And why?" he asked in a tone full of contempt. "Why cannot the Princess Margaret be married?"

"Because," said the woman in the long cloak, fingering a string at her neck, "she is married already. *I am her husband!*"

The long blue cloak fell to the ground, and the Sparhawk, clad in close-fitting squire's dress, stood before their astonished eyes.

A long low murmur, gathering and sinking, surged about the square. Prince Louis gasped. Margaret clung to her lover's arm, and for the space of a score of seconds the whole world stopped breathing.

Prince Ivan twisted his moustache as if he would pull it out by the roots.

"So," he said, "the Princess is married, is she? And you are her husband? 'Whom God hath joined'—and the rest of it. Well, we shall see, we shall see!"

He spoke gently, meditatively, almost caressingly.

"Yes," cried the Sparhawk defiantly, "we were married yesterday by Father Clement, the Prince's chaplain, in the presence of the most noble Leopold von Dessauer, High Councillor of Plassenburg!"

"And my wife—the Princess Joan, where is she?" gasped Prince Louis, so greatly bewildered that he had not yet begun to be angry.

Ivan of Muscovy put out his hand.

"Gently, friend," he said; "I will unmask this play-acting springald. This is not your wife, not the woman you wedded and fought for, not the Lady Joan of Hohenstein, but some baseborn brother, who, having her face, hath played her part, in order to mock and cheat and deceive us both!"

He turned again to Maurice von Lynar.

"I think we have met before, Sir Masquer," he said with his usual suave courtesy; "I have, therefore, a double debt to pay. Hither!" He beckoned to the guards who lined the approaches. "I presume, sir, so true a courtier will not brawl before ladies. You recognise that you are in our power. Your sword, sir!"

The Sparhawk looked all about the crowded square. Then he snapped his sword over his knee and threw the pieces down on the stone steps.

"You are right; I will not fight vainly here," he said. "I know well it is useless. But"—he raised his voice—"be it known to all men that my name is Maurice, Count von Löen, and that the Princess Margaret is my lawfully wedded wife. She cannot then marry Ivan of Muscovy!"

The Prince laughed easily and spread his hand with gentle deprecation, as the guards seized the Sparhawk and forced him a little space away from the clinging hands of the Princess.

"I am an easy man," he said gently, as he clicked his dagger to and fro in its sheath. "When I like a woman, I would as lief marry her widow as maid!"

CHAPTER XXXVIII
THE RETURN OF THE BRIDE

"Prince Louis," continued Ivan, turning to the Prince, "we are keeping these holy men needlessly, as well as disappointing the good folk of Courtland of their spectacle. There is no need that we should stand here any longer. We have matters to discuss with this gentleman and—his wife. Have I your leave to bring them together in the Palace? We may have something to say to them more at leisure."

But the Prince of Courtland made no answer. His late fears of the Black Death, the astonishing turn affairs had taken, the discovery that his wife was not his wife, the slowly percolating thought that his invasion of Kernsberg, his victories there, and his triumphal re-entry into his capital, had all been in vain, united with his absorbing fear of ridicule to deprive him of speech. He moved his hand angrily and began to descend the stairs towards the waiting horses.

Prince Ivan turned towards Maurice von Lynar.

"You will come with me to the Palace under escort of these gentlemen of my staff," he said, with smiling equality of courtesy; "there is no need to discuss intimate family affairs before half the rabble of Courtland."

He bowed to Maurice as if he had been inviting him to a feast. Maurice looked about the crowded square, and over the pennons of the Cossacks. He knew there was no hope either in flight or in resistance. All the approaches to the square had been filled up with armed men.

"I will follow!" he answered briefly.

The Prince swept his plumed hat to the ground.

"Nay," he said; "lead, not follow. You must go with your wife. The Prince of Muscovy does not precede a lady, a princess,—and a bride!"

So it came about that Margaret, after all, descended the cathedral steps on her husband's arm.

And as the cavalcade rode back to the Palace the Princess was in the midst between the Sparhawk and Prince Wasp, Louis of Courtland pacing moodily ahead, his bridle reins loose upon his horse's neck, his chin sunk on his breast, while the rabble cried ever, "Largesse! largesse!" and ran before them casting brightly coloured silken scarves in the way.

Then Prince Ivan, summoning his almoner to his side, took from him a bag of coin. He dipped his fingers deeply in and scattered the coins with a free hand, crying loudly, "To the health and long life of the Princess Margaret and her husband! Health and riches and offspring!"

And the mob taking the word from him shouted all along the narrow streets, "To the Princess and her husband!"

But from the hooded dormers of the city, from the lofty gable spy-holes, from the narrow windows of Baltic staircase-towers the good wives of Courtland looked down to see the great folk pass. And their comment was not that of the rabble. "Married, is she?" they said among themselves. "Well, God bless her comely face! It minds me of my own wedding. But, by my faith, I looked more at my Fritz than she doth at the Muscovite. I declare all her eyes are for that handsome lad who rides at her left elbow— —"

"Nay, he is not handsome—look at his face. It is as white as a new-washen clout hung on a drying line. Who can he be?"

"Minds me o' the Prince's wife, the proud lady that flouted him, mightily he doth—I should not wonder if he were her brother."

"Yes, by my faith, dame—hast hit it! So he doth. And here was I racking my brains to think where I had seen him before, and then, after all, I never *had* seen him before!"

"A miracle it is, gossip, and right pale he looks! Yet I should not wonder if our Margaret loves him the most. Her eyes seek to him. Women among the great are not like us. They say they never like their own husbands the best. What wouldst thou do, good neighbour Bette, if I loved your Hans better than mine own stupid old Fritz! Pull the strings off my cap, dame, sayst thou? That shows thee no great lady. For if thou wast of the great, thou wouldst no more than wave thy hand and say, 'A good riddance and a heartsome change!'—and with that begin to make love to the next young lad that came by with his thumbs in his armholes and a feather in his cap!"

"And what o' the childer—the house-bairns—what o' them? With all this mixing about, what comes o' them—answer me that, good dame!"

"What, Gossip Bette—have you never heard? The childer of the great, they suck not their own mothers' milk—they are not dandled in their own mothers' arms. They learn not their Duty from their mothers' lips. When they are fractious, a stranger beats them till they be good— —"

"Ah," cried the court of matrons all in unison, "I would like to catch one of the fremit lay a hand on my Karl—my Kirsten—that I would! I would comb their hair for them, tear the pinner off their backs—that I would!" "And I!" "And I!"

"Nay, good gossips all," out of the chorus the voice of the dame learned in the ways of the great asserted itself; "that, again, proves you all no better than burgherish town-folk—not truly of the noble of the land. For a right great lady, when she meets a foster-nurse with a baby at the breast, will go near and say—I have heard 'em—'La! the pretty thing—a poppet! Well-a-well, 'tis pretty, for sure! And whose baby may this be?'

"'Thine own, lady, thine own!'"

At this long and loud echoed the derision of the good wives of Courtland. Their gossip laughed and reasserted. But no, they would not hear a word more. She had overstepped the limit of their belief.

"What, not to know her child—her own flesh and blood? Out on her!" cried every mother who had felt about her neck the clasp of tiny hands, or upon her breast the easing pressure of little blind lips. "Good dame, no; you shall not hoodwink us. Were she deaf and dumb and doting, a mother would yet know her child. 'Tis not in nature else! Well, thanks be to Mary Mother—she who knew both wife-pain and mother-joy, we, at least, are not of the great. We may hush our own bairns to sleep, dance with them when they frolic, and correct them when they be naughty-minded. Nevertheless, a good luck go with our noble lady this day! May she have many fair children and a husband to love her even as if she were a common woman and no princess!"

So in little jerks of blessing and with much head-shaking the good wives of Courtland continued their congress, long after the last Cossack lance with its fluttering pennon had been lost to view down the winding street.

For, indeed, well might the gossips thank the Virgin and their patron saints that they were not as the poor Princess Margaret, and that their worst troubles concerned only whether Hans or Fritz tarried a little over-long in the town wine-cellars, or wagered the fraction of a penny too much on a neighbour's cock-fight, and so returned home somewhat crusty because the wrong bird had won the main.

But in the Prince's palace other things were going forward. Hitherto we have had to do with the Summer Palace by the river, a building of no strength, and built more as a pleasure house for the princely family than as a place of permanent habitation. But the Castle of Courtland was a structure of another sort.

Set on a low rock in the centre of the town, its walls rose continuous with its foundations, equally massive and impregnable, to the height of over seventy feet. For the first twenty-five neither window nor grating broke the grim uniformity of those mighty walls of mortared rock. Above that line only a few small openings half-closed with iron bars evidenced the fact that a great prince had his dwelling within. The main entrance to the Castle was through a gateway closed by a grim iron-toothed portcullis. Then a short tunnel led to another and yet stronger defence—a deep natural fosse which surrounded the rock on all sides, and over which a drawbridge conducted into the courtyard of the fortress.

The Sparhawk knew very well that he was going to his death as he rode through the streets of the city of Courtland, but none would have discovered from his bearing that there was aught upon his mind of graver concern than the fit of a doublet or, perhaps, the favour of a pretty maid-of-honour. But with the Princess Margaret it was different. In these last crowded hours she had quite lost her old gay defiance. Her whole heart was fixed on Maurice, and the tears would not be bitten back when she thought of the fate to which he was going with so manly a courage and so fine an air.

They dismounted in the gloomy courtyard, and Maurice, slipping quickly from his saddle, caught Margaret in his arms before the Muscovite could interfere. She clung to him closely, knowing that it might be for the last time.

"Maurice, Maurice," she murmured, "can you forgive me? I have brought you to this!"

"Hush, sweetheart," he answered in her ear; "be my own dear princess. Do not let them see. Be my brave girl. They cannot divide our love!"

"Come, I beg of you," came the dulcet voice of Prince Ivan behind them; "I would not for all Courtland break in upon the billing and cooing of such turtle-doves, were it not that their affection blinds them to the fact that the men-at-arms and scullions are witnesses to these pretty demonstrations. Tarry a little, sweet valentines—time and place wait for all things."

The Princess commanded herself quickly. In another moment she was once more Margaret of Courtland.

"Even the Prince of Muscovy might spare a lady his insults at such a time!" she said.

The Prince bared his head and bowed low.

"Nay," he said very courteously; "you mistake, Princess Margaret. I insult you not. I may regret your taste—but that is a different matter. Yet even that may in time amend. My quarrel is with this gentleman, and it is one of some standing, I believe."

"My sword is at your service, sir!" said Maurice von Lynar firmly.

"Again you mistake," returned the Prince more suavely than ever; "you have no sword. A prisoner, and (if I may say so without offence) a spy taken red-hand, cannot fight duels. The Prince of Courtland must settle this matter. When his Justiciar is satisfied, I shall most willingly take up my quarrel with—whatever is left of the most noble Count Maurice von Lynar."

To this Maurice did not reply, but with Margaret still beside him he followed Prince Louis up the narrow ancient stairway called from its shape the couch, into the gloomy audience chamber of the Castle of Courtland.

They reached the hall, and then at last, as though restored to power by his surroundings, Prince Louis found his tongue.

"A guard!" he cried; "hither Berghoff, Kampenfeldt! Conduct the Princess to her privy chamber and do not permit her to leave it without my permission. I would speak with this fellow alone."

Ivan hastily crossed over to Prince Louis and whispered in his ear.

In the meantime, ere the soldiers of the guard could approach, Margaret cried out in a loud clear voice, "I take you all to witness that I, Margaret of Courtland, am the wife of this man, Maurice von Lynar, Count von Löen. He is my wedded husband, and I love him with all my heart! According to God's holy ordinance he is mine!"

"You have forgotten the rest, fair Princess," suggested Prince Ivan subtly—"*till death you do part!*"

CHAPTER XXXIX
PRINCE WASP STINGS

Margaret did not answer her tormentor's taunt. Her arms went about Maurice's neck, and her lips, salt with the overflowing of tears, sought his in a last kiss. The officer of the Prince's guard touched her on the shoulder. She shook him haughtily off, and then, having completed her farewells, she loosened her hands and went slowly backward towards the further end of the hall with her eyes still upon the man she loved.

"Stay, Berghoff," said Prince Louis suddenly; "let the Princess remain where she is. Cross your swords in front of her. I desire that she shall hear what I have to say to this young gentleman."

"And also," added Prince Ivan, "I desire the noble Princess to remember that this has been granted by the Prince upon my intercession. In the future, it may gain me more of her favour than I have had the good fortune to enjoy in the past!"

Maurice stood alone, his tall slender figure supple and erect. One hand rested easily upon his swordless thigh, while the other still held the plumed hat he snatched up as in frantic haste he had followed Margaret from the Summer Palace.

There ensued a long silence in which the Sparhawk eyed his captors haughtily, while Prince Louis watched him from under the grey penthouse of his eyebrows.

Then three several times the Prince essayed to speak, and as often utterance was choked within him. His feelings could only find vent in muttered imprecations, half smothered by a consuming rage. Then Prince Ivan crossed over and laid his hand restrainingly on his arm. The touch seemed to calm his friend, and, after swallowing several times as there had been a knot in his throat, at last he spoke.

For the second time in his life Maurice von Lynar stood alone among his enemies; but this time in peril far deadlier than among the roisterous pleasantries of Castle Kernsberg. Yet he was as little daunted now as then. Once on a time a duchess had saved him. Now a princess loved him. And even if she could not save him, still that was better.

"So," cried Prince Louis, in the curiously uneven voice of a coward lashing himself into a fury, "you have played out your treachery upon a reigning Prince of Courtland. You cheated me at Castle Kernsberg. Now you have made me a laughing-stock throughout the Empire. You have shamed a maiden of my house, my sister, the daughter of my father. What have you to say ere I order you to be flung out from the battlements of the western tower?"

"Ere it comes to that I shall have something to say, Prince Louis," interrupted Prince Wasp, smiling. "We must not waste such dainty powers of masquerade on anything so vulgar as the hangman's rope."

"Gentlemen and princes," Maurice von Lynar answered, "that which I have done I have done for the sake of my mistress, the Lady Joan, and I am not afraid. Prince Louis, it was her will and intent never to come to Courtland as your wife. She would not have been taken alive. It was therefore the duty of her servants to preserve her life, and I offered myself in her stead. My life was hers already, for she had preserved it. She had given. It was hers to take. With the chief captains of Kernsberg I plotted that she should be seized and carried to a place of refuge wherein no foe could even find her. There she abides with chosen men to guard her. I took her place and was delivered up that Kernsberg might be cleared of its enemies. Gladly I came that I might pay a little of my debt to my sovran lady and liege mistress, Joan Duchess of Kernsberg and Hohenstein."

"Nobly perorated!" cried Prince Ivan, clapping his hands. "Right sonorously ended. Faith, a paladin, a deliverer of oppressed damsels, a very carnival masquerader! He will play you the dragon, this fellow, or he will act Saint George with a sword of lath! He will amble you the hobby-horse, or be the Holy Virgin in a miracle play. Well, he shall play in one more good scene ere I have done with him. But, listen, Sir Mummer, in all this there is no word of the Princess Margaret. How comes it that you so loudly proclaim having given yourself a noble sacrifice for one fair lady, when at the same time you are secretly married to another? Are you a deliverer of ladies by wholesale? Speak to this point. Let us have another noble period — its subject my affianced bride. Already we have heard of your high devotion to Prince Louis's wife. Well—next!"

But it was the Princess who spoke from where she stood behind the crossed swords of her guards.

"That *I* will answer. I am a woman, and weak in your hands, princes both. You have set the grasp of rude men-at-arms upon the wrist of a Princess of Courtland. But you can never compel her soul. Brother Louis, my father committed me to you as a little child—have I not been a loving and a faithful sister to you? And till this Muscovite came between, were you not good to me? Wherefore have you changed? Why has he made you cruel to your little Margaret?"

Prince Louis turned towards his sister, moving his hands uncertainly and even deprecatingly.

Ivan moved quickly to his side and whispered something which instantly rekindled the light of anger in the weakling's eyes.

"You are no sister of mine," he said; "you have disgraced your family and yourself. Whether it be true or no that you are married to this man matters little!"

"It is true; I do not lie!" said Margaret recovering herself.

"So much the worse, then, and he shall suffer for it. At least I can hide, if I cannot prevent, your shame!"

"I will never give him up; nothing on earth shall part our love!"

Prince Ivan smiled delicately, turning to where she stood at the end of the hall.

"Sweet Princess," he said, "divorce is, I understand, contrary to your holy Roman faith. But in my land we have discovered a readier way than any papal bull. Be good enough to observe this"—he held a dagger in his hand. "It is a little blade of steel, but a span long, and narrow as one of your dainty fingers, yet it will divorce the best married pair in the world."

"But neither dagger nor the hate of enemies can sever love," Margaret answered proudly. "You may slay my husband, but he is mine still. You cannot twain our souls."

The Prince shrugged his shoulder and opened his palms deprecatingly.

"Madam," he said, "I shall be satisfied with twaining your bodies. In holy Russia we are plain men. We have a saying, 'No one hath ever seen a soul. Let the body content you!' When this gentleman is—what I shall make him, he is welcome to any communion of souls with you to which he can attain. I promise you that, so far as he is concerned, you shall find me neither exigent lover nor jealous husband!"

The Princess looked at Maurice. Her eyes had dwelt defiantly on the Prince of Muscovy whilst he was speaking, but now a softer light, gentle yet brave, crept into them.

"Fear not, my husband," she said. "If the steel divide us, the steel can also unite. They cannot watch so close, or bind so tight, but that I can find a way. Or, if iron will not pierce, fire burn, or water drown, I have a drug that will open the door which leads to you. Fear not, dearest, I shall yet meet you unashamed, and as your loyal wife, without soil or stain, look into your true eyes."

"I declare you have taught your mistress the trick of words!" cried the Prince delightedly. "Count von Löen, the Lady Margaret has quite your manner. She speaks to slow music."

But even the sneers of Prince Ivan could not filch the greatness out of their loves, and Prince Louis was obviously wavering. Ivan's quick eye noted this and he instantly administered a fillip.

"Are you not moved, Louis?" he said. "How shamelessly hard is your heart! This handsome youth, whom any part sets like a wedding favour and fits like his own delicate skin, condescends to become your relative. Where is your welcome, your kinsmanlike manners? Go, fall upon his neck! Kiss him on either cheek. Is he not your heir? He hath only sequestrated your wife, married your sister. Your only brother is a childless priest. There needs only your decease to set him on the throne of the Princedom. Give him time. How easily he has compassed all this! He will manage the rest as easily. And then—listen to the shouting in the streets. I can hear it already. 'Long live Maurice the Bastard, Prince of Courtland!'"

And the Prince of Muscovy laughed loud and long. But Prince Louis did not laugh. His eyes glared upon the prisoner like those of a wild beast caught in a corner whence it wishes to flee but cannot.

"He shall die—this day shall be his last. I swear it!" he cried. "He hath mocked me, and I will slay him with my hand."

He drew the dagger from his belt. But in the centre of the hall the Sparhawk stood so still and quiet that Prince Louis hesitated. Ivan laid a soft hand upon his wrist and as gently drew the dagger out of his grasp.

"Nay, my Prince, we will give him a worthier passing than that. So noble a knight-errant must die no common death. What say you to the Ukraine Cross, the Cross of Steeds? I have here four horses, all wild from the steppes. This squire of dames, this woman-mummer, hath, as now we know, four several limbs. By a strange coincidence I have a wild horse for each of these. Let limbs and steeds be severally attached, my Cossacks know how. Upon each flank let the lash be laid—and—well, the Princess Margaret is welcome to her liege lord's soul. I warrant she will not desire his fair body any more."

At this Margaret tottered, her knees giving way beneath her, so that her guards stood nearer to catch her if she should fall.

"Louis—my brother," she cried, "do not listen to the monster. Kill my husband if you must—because I love him. But do not torture him. By the last words of our mother, by the memory of our father, by your faith in the Most Pitiful Son of God, I charge you—do not this devilry."

Prince Ivan did not give Louis of Courtland time to reply to his sister's appeal.

"The most noble Princess mistakes," he murmured suavely. "Death by the Cross of Steeds is no torture. It is the easiest and swiftest of deaths. I have witnessed it often. In my country it is reserved for the greatest and the most distinguished. No common felon dies by the Cross of Steeds, but men whose pride it is to die greatly. Ere long we will show you on the plain across the river that I speak the truth. It is a noble sight, and all Courtland shall be there. What say you, Louis? Shall this springald seat himself in your princely chair, or—shall we try the Cross of the Ukraine?"

"Have it your own way, Prince Ivan!" said Louis, and went out without another word. The Muscovite stood a moment looking from Maurice to Margaret and back again. He was smiling his inscrutable Oriental smile.

"The Prince has given me discretion," he said at last. "I might order you both to separate dungeons, but I am an easy man and delight in the domestic affections. I would see the parting of two such faithful lovers. I may learn somewhat that shall stand me in good stead in the future. It is my ill-fortune that till now I have had little experience of the gentler emotions."

He raised his hand.

"Let the Princess pass," he cried.

The guards dropped their swords to their sides. They had been restraining her with as much gentleness as their duty would permit.

Instantly the Princess Margaret ran forward with eager appeal on her face. She dropped on her knees before the Prince of Muscovy and clasped her hands in supplication.

"Prince Ivan," she said, "I pray you for the love of God to spare him, to let him go. I promise never to see him more. I will go to a nunnery. I will look no more upon the face of day."

"That, above all things, I cannot allow," said the Prince. "So fair a face must see many suns—soon, I trust, in Moscow city, and by my side."

"Margaret," said the Sparhawk, "it is useless to plead. Do not abase yourself in the presence of our enemy. You cannot touch a man's heart when his breast covers a stone. Bid me goodbye and be brave. The time will not be long."

From the place where Margaret the loving woman had kneeled Margaret the Princess rose to her feet at the word of her husband. Without deigning even to glance at Ivan, who had stooped to assist her, she passed him by and went to Von Lynar. He held out both his hands and took her little trembling ones in a strong assured clasp.

The Prince watched the pair with a chill smile.

"Margaret," said Maurice, "this will not be for long. What matters the ford, so that we both pass over the river. Be brave, little wife. The crossing will not be wide, nor the water deep. They cannot take from us that which is ours. And He who joined us, whose priest blessed us, will unite us anew when and where it seemeth good to Him!"

"Maurice, I cannot let you die—and by such a terrible death!"

"Dearest, what does it matter? I am yours. Wherever my spirit may wander, I am yours alone. I will think of you when the Black Water shallows to the brink. On the further side I will wait a day and then you will meet me there. To you it may seem years. It will be but a day to me. And I shall be there. So, little Margaret, good-night. Do not forget that I love you. I would have made you very happy, if I had had time—ah, if I had had time!"

Like a child after its bedside prayer she lifted up her face to be kissed.

"Good-night, Maurice," she said simply. "Wait for me; I shall not be long after!"

She laid her brow a moment on his breast. Then she lifted her head and walked slowly and proudly out of the hall. The guard fell in behind her, and Maurice von Lynar was left alone with the Prince of Muscovy.

As the door closed upon the Princess a sudden devilish grimace of fury distorted the countenance of Prince Ivan. Hitherto he had been studiously and even caressingly courteous. But now he strode swiftly up to his captive and smote him across the mouth with the back of his gauntleted hand.

"That!" he said furiously, "that for the lips which have kissed hers! Soon, soon I shall pay the rest of my debt. Yes, by the most high God, I will pay it—with usury thereto!"

A thin thread of scarlet showed upon the white of Maurice von Lynar's chin and trickled slowly downwards. But he uttered no word. Only he looked his enemy very straightly in the eyes, and those of the Muscovite dropped before that defiant fierce regard.

CHAPTER XL
THE LOVES OF PRIEST AND WIFE

It remains to tell briefly how certain great things came to pass. We must return to Isle Rugen and to the lonely grange on the spit of sand which separates the Baltic from the waters of the Freshwater Haff.

Many things have happened there since Conrad of Courtland, Cardinal and Archbishop, awaked to find by his bedside the sleeping girl who was his brother's wife.

On Isle Rugen, where the pines grew dense and green, gripping and settling the thin sandy soil with their prehensile roots, Joan and Conrad found themselves much alone. The lady of the grange was seldom to be seen, save when all were gathered together at meals. Werner von Orseln and the Plassenburg captains, Jorian and Boris, played cards and flung harmless dice for white stones of a certain size picked from the beach. Dumb Max Ulrich went about his work like a shadow. The ten soldiers mounted guard and looked out to sea with their elbows on their knees in the intervals. Three times a week the solitary boat, with Max Ulrich at the oars, crossed to the landing-place on the mainland and returned laden with provisions. The outer sea was empty before their eyes, generally deep blue and restless with foam caps. Behind them the Haff lay vacant and still as oil in a kitchen basin.

But it was not dull on Isle Rugen.

The osprey flashed and fell in the clear waters of the Haff, presently to re-emerge with a fish in his beak, the drops running like a broken string of pearls from his scales. Rough-legged buzzards screamed their harsh and melancholy cry as on slanted wings they glided down inclines of sunshine or lay out motionless upon the viewless glorious air. Wild geese swept overhead out of the north in V-shaped flocks. The sea-gulls tacked and balanced. All-graceful terns swung thwartways the blue sky, or plunged headlong into the long green swells with the curve and speed of falling stars.

It was a place of forgetting, and in the autumn time it is good to forget. For winter is nigh, when there will be time and enough to think all manner of sad thoughts.

So in the September weather Joan and Conrad walked much together. And as Joan forgat Kernsberg and her revenge, Rome and his mission receded into the background of the young man's thoughts. Soon they met undisguisedly without fear or shame. This Isle Rugen was a place apart—a haven of refuge not of their seeking. Mars had driven one there, Neptune the other.

Yet when Conrad woke in his little north-looking room in the lucid pearl-grey dawn he had some bad moments. His vows, his priesthood, his princedom of Holy Church were written in fire before his eyes. His heart weighed heavy as if cinctured with lead. And, deeper yet, a rat seemed to gnaw sharp-toothed at the springs of his life.

Also, when the falling seas, combing the pebbly beaches with foamy teeth, rattled the wet shingle, Joan would ofttimes wake from sleep and lie staring wide-eyed at the casement. Black reproach of self brooded upon her spirit, as if a foul bird of night had fluttered through the open window and settled upon her breast. The poor folk of Kernsberg—her fatherland invaded and desolate, the Sparhawk, the man who ought to have been the ruler she was not worthy to be, the leader in war, the lawgiver in peace— these reproachful shapes filled her mind so that sleep fled and she lay pondering plans of escape and deliverance.

But of one thing she never thought—of the cathedral of Courtland and the husband to whose face she had but once lifted her eyes.

The sun looked through between the red cloud bars. These he soon left behind, turning them from fiery islands to banks of fleecy wool. The shadows shot swiftly westward and then began slowly to shorten. In his chamber Prince Conrad rose and went to the window. A rose-coloured light lay along the sea horizon, darting between the dark pine stems and transmuting the bare sand-dunes into dreamy marvels, till they touched the heart like glimpses of a lost Eden seen in dreams. The black bird of night flapped its way behind the belting trees. There was not such a thing as a ghostly rat to gnaw unseen the heart of man. The blue dome of sky overhead was better than the holy shrine of Peter across the tawny flood of Tiber, and Isle Rugen more to be desired than the seven-hilled city itself. Yea, better than lifted chalice and wafted incense, Joan's hand in his— —

And Conrad the lover turned from the window with a defiant heart.

At her casement, which opened to the east, stood at the same moment the young Duchess of Hohenstein. Her lips were parted and the mystery of the new day dwelt in her eyes like the memory of a benediction. Southward lay the world, striving, warring, sinning, repenting, elevating the Host, slaying the living, and burying the dead. But between her and that world stretched a wide water not to be crossed, a fixed gulf not to be passed over. It was the new day, and there beneath her was the strip of silver sand where he and she had walked yestereven, when the moon was full and the wavelets of that sheltered sea crisped in silver at their feet.

An hour afterwards these two met and gave each other a hand silently. Then, facing the sunrise, they walked eastward along the shore, while from the dusk of the garden gate Theresa von Lynar watched them with a sad smile upon her face.

"She is learning the lesson even as I learned it," she murmured, unconsciously thinking aloud. "Well, that which the father taught it is meet that the daughter should learn. Let her eat the fruit, the bitter fruit of love— even as I have eaten it!"

She watched a little longer, standing there with the pruning-knife in her hand. She saw Conrad turn towards Joan as they descended a little dell among the eastern sand-hills. And though she could not see, she knew that two hands met, and that they stood still for a moment, ere their feet climbed the opposite slope of dew-drenched sand. A swift sob took her unexpectedly by the throat.

"And yet," she said, "were all to do over, would not Theresa von Lynar again learn that lesson from Alpha to Omega, eat the Dead Sea fruit to its bitterest kernel, in order that once more the bud might open and love's flower be hers?"

Theresa von Lynar at her garden door spoke truth. For even then among the sand-hills the bud was opening, though the year was on the wane and the winter nigh.

"Happy Isle Rugen!" said Joan, drawing a breath like a sigh. "Why were we born to princedoms, Conrad, you and I?"

"I at least was not," answered her companion. "Dumb Max's jerkin of blue fits me better than any robe royal."

They stood on the highest part of the island. Joan was leaning on the crumbling wall of an ancient fort, which, being set on a promontory from which the pinetrees drew back a little, formed at once a place of observation and a point objective for their walks. She turned at his words and looked at him. Conrad, indeed, never looked better or more princely than in that rough jerkin of blue, together with the corded forester's breeches and knitted hose which he had borrowed from Theresa's dumb servitor.

"Conrad," said Joan, suddenly standing erect and looking directly at the young man, "if I were to tell you that I had resolved never to return to Kernsberg, but to remain here on Isle Rugen, what would you answer?"

"I should ask to be your companion—or, if not, your bailiff!" said the Prince-Bishop promptly.

"That would be to forget your holy office!"

A certain gentle sadness passed over the features of the young man.

"I leave many things undone for the sake of mine office," he said; "but the canons of the Church do not forbid poverty, or yet manual labour."

"But you have told me a hundred times," urged Joan, smiling in spite of herself, "that necessity and not choice made you a Churchman. Does that necessity no longer exist?"

"Nay," answered Conrad readily as before; "but smaller necessities yield to greater?"

"And the greater?"

"Why," he answered, "what say you to the tempest that drove me hither—the thews and stout hearts of Werner von Orseln and his men, not to speak of Captains Boris and Jorian there? Are they not sufficient reasons for my remaining here?"

He paused as if he had more to say.

"Well?" said Joan, and waited for him to continue.

"There is something else," he said. "It is—it is—that I cannot bear to leave you! God knows I could not leave you if I would!"

Joan of Hohenstein started. The words had been spoken in a low tone, yet with suppressed vehemence, as though driven from the young man's lips against his will. But there was no mistaking their purport. Yet they were spoken so hopelessly, and withal so gently, that she could not be angry.

"Conrad—Conrad," she murmured reproachfully, "I thought I could have trusted you. You promised never again to forget what we must both remember!"

"In so thinking you did well," he replied; "you may trust me to the end. But the privilege of speech and testimony is not denied even to the criminal upon the scaffold."

A wave of pity passed over Joan. A month before she would have withdrawn herself in hot anger. But Isle Rugen had gentled all her ways. The peace of that ancient fortalice, the wash of its ambient waters, the very lack of incident, the sense of the mysteries of tragic life which surrounded her on all sides, the deep thoughts she had been thinking alone with herself, the companionship of this man whom she loved—all these had wrought a new spirit in Joan of the Sword Hand. Women who cannot be pitiful are but half women. They have never yet entered upon their inheritance. But now Joan was coming to her own again. For to pity of Theresa von Lynar she was adding pity for Conrad of Courtland and—Joan of Hohenstein.

"Speak," she said very gently. "Do not be afraid; tell me all that is in your heart."

Joan was not disinclined to hear any words that the young man might speak. She believed that she could listen unmoved even to his most passionate declarations of love. Like the wise physician, she would listen, understand, prescribe—and administer the remedy.

But the pines of Isle Rugen stood between this woman and the girl who had ridden away so proudly from the doors of the Kernsberg minster at the head of her four hundred lances. Besides, she had not forgotten the tournament and the slim secretary who had once stood before this man in the river parlour of the Summer Palace.

Then Conrad spoke in a low voice, very distinct and even in its modulation.

"Joan," he said, "once on a time I dreamed of being loved—dreamed that among all the world of women there might be one woman for me. Such things must come when deep sleep falleth upon a young man. Waking I put them from me, even as I put arms and warfare aside. I believed that I had conquered the lust of the eye. Now I know that I can never again be true priest, never serve the altar with a clean heart.

"Listen, my Lady Joan! I love you—there is no use in hiding it. Doubtless you yourself have already seen it. I love you so greatly that vows, promises, priesthoods, cardinalates are no more to me than the crying of the seabirds out yonder. Let a worthier than I receive and hold them. They are not for a weak and sinful man. My bishopric let another take. I would rather be your groom, your servitor, your lacquey, than reign on the Seven Hills and sit in Holy Peter's chair!"

Joan leaned against the crumbling battlement, and the words of Conrad were very sweet in her ear. They filled her with pity, while at the same time her heart was strong within her. None had dared to speak such things to her before in all her life, and she was a woman. The Princess Margaret, had she loved a man as Joan did this man, would have given back vow for vow, renunciation for renunciation, and, it might be, have bartered kiss for kiss.

But Joan of the Sword Hand was never stronger, never more serene, never surer of herself than when she listened to the words she loved best to hear, from the lips of the man whom of all others she desired to speak them. At first she had been looking out upon the sea, but now she permitted her eyes to rest with a great kindliness upon the young man. Even as he spoke Conrad divined the thing that was in her heart.

"Mark you," he said, "do me the justice to remember that I ask for nothing. I expect nothing. I hope for nothing in return. I thought once that I could love Divine things wholly. Now I know that my heart is too earthly. But instead I love the noblest and most gracious woman in all the world. And I love her, too, with a love not wholly unworthy of her."

"You do me overmuch honour," said Joan quietly. "I, too, am weak and sinful. Or how else would I, your brother's wife, listen to such words from any man—least of all from you?"

"Nay," said Conrad; "you only listen out of your great pitifulness. But I am no worthy priest. I will not take upon me the yet greater things for which I am so manifestly unfitted. I will not sully the holy garments with my earthliness. Conrad of Courtland, Bishop and Cardinal, died out there among the breakers.

"He will never go to Rome, never kneel at the tombs of the Apostles. From this day forth he is a servitor, a servant of servants in the train of the Duchess Joan. Save those with us here, our hostess and the three captains (who for your sake will hold their peace), none know that Conrad of Courtland escaped the waters that swallowed up his companions. They and you will keep the secret. This shaven crown will speedily thatch itself again, a beard grow upon these shaveling cheeks. A dash of walnut juice, and who will guess that under the tan of Conrad the serf there is concealed a prince of Holy Church?"

He paused, almost smiling. The picture of his renunciation had grown real to him even as he spoke. But Joan did not smile. She waited a space to see if he had aught further to say. But he was silent, waiting for her answer.

"Conrad," she said very gently, "that I have listened to you, and that I have not been angry, may be deadly sin for us both. Yet I cannot be angry. God forgive me! I have tried and I cannot be angry. And why should I? Even as I lay a babe in the cradle, I was wedded. If a woman must suffer, she ought at least to be permitted to choose the instrument of her torture."

"It is verity," he replied; "you are no more true wife than I am true priest."

"Yet because you have dispensed holy bread, and I knelt before the altar as a bride, we must keep faith, you and I. We are bound by our nobility. If we sin, let it be the greater and rarer sin—the sin of the spirit only. Conrad, I love you. Nay, stand still where you are and listen to me—to me, Joan, your brother's wife. For I, too, once for all will clear my soul. I loved you long ere your eyes fell on me. I came as Dessauer's secretary to the city of Courtland. I determined to see the man I was to wed. I saw the prince—my prince as I thought—storm through the lists on his white horse. I saw him bare his head and receive the crown of victory. I stood before him, ashamed yet glad, hosed and doubleted like a boy, in the Summer Pavilion. I heard his gracious words. I loved my prince, who so soon was to be wholly mine. The months slipped past, and I was ever the gladder the faster they sped. The woman stirred within the stripling girl. In half a year, in twenty weeks—in five—in one—in a day—an hour, I would put my hand, my life, myself into his keeping! Then came the glad tumult of the rejoicing folk, the hush of the crowded cathedral. I said, 'Oh, not yet—I will not lift my eyes to my prince until— —' We stopped. I lifted my eyes. And lo! the prince was not my prince!"

There was a long and solemn pause between these two on the old watchtower. Never was declaration of love so given and so taken. Conrad remained still as a statue, only his eyes growing great and full of light. Joan stood looking at him, unashamed and fearless. Yet neither moved an inch toward either. A brave woman's will, to do right greatly, stood between them.

She went on.

"Now you know all, my Conrad," she said. "Isle Rugen can never more be the isle of peace to us. You and I have shivered the cup of our happiness. We must part. We can never be merely friends. I must abide because I am a prisoner. You will keep my counsel, promising me to be silent, and together we will contrive a way of escape."

When Conrad answered her again his voice was hoarse and broken, almost like one rheumed with sleeping out on a winter's night. His words whistled in his windpipe, flying from treble to bass and back again.

"Joan, Joan!" he said, and the third time "Joan!" And for the moment he could say no more.

"True love," she said, and her voice was almost caressing, "you and I are barriered from each other. Yet we belong—you to me—I to you! I will not touch your hand, nor you mine. Not even as we have hitherto done. Let ours be the higher, perhaps deadlier sin—the sin of soul and soul. Do you go back to your office, your electorate, while I stay here to do my duty."

"And why not you to your duchy?" said Conrad, who had begun to recover himself.

"Because," she answered, "if I refuse to abide by one of my father's bargains, I have no right to hold by the other. He would have made me your brother's wife. That I have refused. He disinherited his lawful son that I might take the dukedom with me as my dowry. Can I keep that which was only given me in trust for another? Maurice von Lynar shall be Duke Maurice, and Theresa von Lynar shall have her true place as the widow of Henry the Lion!"

And she stood up tall and straight, like a princess indeed.

"And you?" he said very low. "What will you do, Joan?"

"For me, I will abide on Isle Rugen. Nunneries are not for me. There are doubtless one or two who will abide with me for the sake of old days— Werner von Orseln for one, Peter Balta for another. I shall not be lonely."

She smiled upon him with a peculiar trustful sweetness and continued—

"And once a year, in the autumn, you will come from your high office. You will lay aside the princely scarlet, and don the curt hose and blue jerkin, even as now you stand. You will gather blackberries and help me to preserve them. You will split wood and carry water. Then, when the day is well spent, you and I shall walk hither in the high afternoon and tell each other how we stand and all the things that have filled our hearts in the year's interspace. Thus will we keep tryst, you and I—not priest and wedded wife, but man and woman speaking the truth eye to eye without fear and without stain. Do you promise?"

And for all answer the Prince-Cardinal kneeled down, and taking the hem of her dress he kissed it humbly and reverently.

CHAPTER XLI
THERESA KEEPS TROTH

But they had reckoned without Theresa von Lynar.

Conrad and Joan came back from the ruined fortification, silent mostly, but thrilled with the thoughts of that which their eyes had seen, their ears heard. Each had listened to the beating of the other's heart. Both knew they were beloved. Nothing could alter *that* any more for ever. As they had gone out with Theresa watching them from the dusk of the garden arcades, their hands had drawn together. Eyes had sought answering eyes at each dip of the path. They had listened for the finest shades of meaning in one another's voices, and taken courage or lost hope from the droop of an eyelid or the quiver of a syllable.

Now all was changed. They knew that which they knew.

The orchard of the lonely grange on Isle Rugen was curiously out of keeping with its barren surroundings. Enclosed within the same wall as the dwelling-house, it was the special care of the Wordless Man, whose many years of pruning and digging and watering, undertaken each at its proper season, had resulted in a golden harvest of September fruit. When Joan and Conrad came to the portal which gave entrance from without, lo! it stood open. The sun had been shining in their eyes, and the place looked very slumberous in the white hazy glory of a northern day. The path which led out of the orchard was splashed with cool shade. Green leaves shrined fair globes of fruitage fast ripening in the blowing airs and steadfast sun. Up the path towards them as they stood together came Theresa von Lynar. There was a smile on her face, a large and kindly graciousness in her splendid eyes. Her hair was piled and circled about her head, and drawn back in ruddy golden masses from the broad white forehead. Autumn was Theresa's season, and in such surroundings she might well have stood for Ceres or Pomona, with apron full enough of fruit for many a horn of plenty.

Such large-limbed simple-natured women as Theresa von Lynar appear to greatest advantage in autumn. It is their time when the day of apple-blossom and spring-flourish is overpast, and when that which these foreshadowed is at length fulfilled. Then to see such an one emerge from an orchard close, and approach softly smiling out of the shadow of fruit trees, is to catch a glimpse of the elder gods. Spring, on the other hand, is for merry maidens, slips of unripe grace, buds from the schools. Summer is the season of languorous dryads at rest in the green gloom of forests, fanning sunburnt cheeks with leafy boughs, their dark eyes full of the height of living. Winter is the time of swift lithe-limbed girls with heads proudly set, who through the white weather carry them like Dian the Huntress, their dainty chins dimpling out of softening furs. To each is her time and supremacy, though a certain favoured few are the mistresses of all. They move like a part of the spring when cherry blossoms are set against a sky of changeful April blue. They rejoice when dark-eyed summer wears scarlet flowers in her hair, shaded by green leaves and fanned by soft airs. Well-bosomed Ceres herself, smiling luxuriant with ripe lips, is not fairer than they at the time of apple-gathering, nor yet dainty Winter, footing it lightly over the frozen snow.

Joan, an it liked her, could have triumphed in all these, but her nature was too simple to care about the impression she made, while Conrad was too deep in love to notice any difference in her perfections.

And now Theresa von Lynar, the woman who had given her beauty and her life like a little Saint Valentine's gift into the hand of the man she loved, content that he should take or throw away as pleased him best— Theresa von Lynar met these two, who in their new glory of renunciation thought that they had plumbed the abysses of love, when as yet they had taken no more than a single sounding in the narrow seas. She stood looking at them as they came towards her, with a sympathy that was deeper far than mere tolerance.

"Our Joan of the Sword Hand is growing into a woman," she murmured; and something she had thought buried deep heaved in her breast, shaking her as Enceladus the Giant shakes Etna when he turns in his sleep. For she saw in the girl her father's likeness more strongly than she had ever seen it in her own son.

"You have faced the sunshine!" Thus she greeted them as they came. "Sit awhile with me in the shade. I have here a bower where Maurice loved to play—before he left me. None save I hath entered it since that day."

So saying, she led the way along an alley of pleached green, at the far end of which they could see the solitary figure of Max Ulrich, in the full sun, bending his back to his gardening tasks, yet at the same time, as was his custom, keeping so near his mistress that a fluttering kerchief or a lifted hand would bring him instantly to her side.

It was a small rustic eight-sided lodge, thatched with heather, its latticed windows wide open and creeper-grown, to which Theresa led them. It had been well kept; and when Joan found herself within, a sudden access of tenderness for this lonely mother, who for love's sake had offered herself like a sacrifice upon an altar, took possession of her.

For about the walls was fastened a child's pitiful armoury. Home-made swords of lath, arrows winged with the cast feathers of the woodland, crooked bows, the broken crockery of a hundred imagined banquets— these, and many more, were carefully kept in place with immediate and loving care. Maurice would be back again presently, they seemed to say, and would take up his play just where he left it.

No cobwebs hung from the roof; the bows were duly unstrung; and though wooden platters and rough kitchen equipage were mingled with warlike accoutrements upon the floor, there was not a particle of dust to be seen anywhere. As they sat down at the mother's bidding, it was hard to persuade themselves that Maurice von Lynar was far off, enduring the hardships of war or in deadly peril for his mistress. He might have been even then in hiding in the brushwood, ready to cry bo-peep at them through the open door.

There was silence in the arbour for a space, a silence which no one of the three was anxious to break. For Joan thought of her promise, Conrad of Joan, and Theresa of her son. It was the last who spoke.

"Somehow to-day it is borne in upon me that Kernsberg has fallen, and that my son is in his enemy's hands!"

Joan started to her feet and thrust her hands a little out in front of her as if to ward off a blow.

"How can you know that?" she cried. "Who——No; it cannot be. Kernsberg was victualled for a year. It was filled with brave men. My captains are staunch. The thing is impossible."

Theresa von Lynar, with her eyes on the waving foliage which alternately revealed and eclipsed the ruddy globes of the apples on the orchard trees, slowly shook her head.

"I cannot tell you how I know," she said; "nevertheless I know. Here is something which tells me." She laid her hand upon her heart. "Those who are long alone beside the sea hear voices and see visions."

"But it is impossible," urged Joan; "or, if it be true, why am I kept here? I will go and die with my people!"

"It is my son's will," said Theresa—"the will of the son of Henry the Lion. He is like his father—therefore women do his will!"

The words were not spoken bitterly, but as a simple statement of fact.

Joan looked at this woman and understood for the first time that she was the strongest spirit of all—greater than her father, better than herself. And perhaps because of this, nobility and sacrifice stirred emulously in her own breast.

"Madam," she said, looking directly at Theresa von Lynar, "it is time that you and I understood each other. I hold myself no true Duchess of Hohenstein so long as your son lives. My father's compact and condition are of no effect. The Diet of the Empire would cancel them in a moment. I will therefore take no rest till this thing is made clear. I swear that your son shall be Duke Maurice and sit in his father's place, as is right and fitting. For me, I ask nothing but the daughter's portion—a grange such as this, as solitary and as peaceful, a garden to delve and a beach to wander upon at eve!"

As she spoke, Theresa's eyes suddenly brightened. A proud high look sat on the fulness of her lips, which gradually faded as some other thought asserted its supremacy. She rose, and going straight to Joan, for the first time she kissed her on the brow.

"Now do I know," she said, "that you are Henry the Lion's daughter. That is spoken as he would have spoken it. It is greatly thought. Yet it cannot be."

"It shall be!" cried Joan imperiously.

"Nay," returned Theresa von Lynar. "Once on a time I would have given my right hand that for half a day, for one hour, men might have said of me that I was Henry the Lion's wife, and my son his son! It would have been right sweet. Ah God, how sweet it would have been!" She paused a moment as if consulting some unseen presence. "No, I have vowed my vow. Here was I bidden to stay and here will I abide. For me there was no sorrow in any hard condition, so long as *he* laid it upon me. For have I not tasted with him the glory of life, and with him plucked out the heart of the mystery? That for which I paid, I received. My lips have tasted both of the Tree of Knowledge and of the Tree of Life—for these two grow very close together, the one to the other, upon the banks of the River of Death. But for my son, this thing is harder to give up. For on him lies the stain, though the joy and the sin were mine alone."

"Maurice of Hohenstein shall sit in his father's seat," said Joan firmly. "I have sworn it. If I live I will see him settled there with my captains about him. Werner von Orseln is an honest man. He will do him justice. Von Dessauer shall get him recognised, and Hugo of Plassenburg shall stand his sponsor before the Diet of the Empire."

"I would it could be so," said Theresa wistfully. "If my death could cause this thing righteously to come to pass, how gladly would I end life! But I am bound by an oath, and my son is bound because I am bound. The tribunal is not the Diet of Ratisbon, but the faithfulness of a woman's heart. Have I been loyal to my prince these many years, so that now shame itself sits on my brow as gladly as a crown of bay, that I should fail him now? Low he lies, and I may never stand beside his sepulchre. No son of mine shall sit in his high chair. But if in any sphere of sinful or imperfect spirits, be it hell or purgatory, he and I shall encounter, think you that for an empire I would meet him shamed. And when he says, 'Woman of my love, hast thou kept thy troth?' shall I be compelled to answer 'No?'"

"But," urged Joan, "this thing is your son's birthright. My father, for purposes of state, bound my happiness to a man I loathe. I have cast that band to the winds. The fathers cannot bind the children, no more can you disinherit your son."

Theresa von Lynar smiled a sad wise smile, infinitely patient, infinitely remote.

"Ah," she said, "you think so? You are young. You have never loved. You are his daughter, not his wife. One day you shall know, if God is good to you!"

At this Joan smiled in her turn. She knew what she knew.

"You may think you know," returned Theresa, her calm eyes on the girl's face, "but what I mean by loving is another matter. The band you broke you did not make. I keep the vow I made. With clear eye, undulled brain, willing hand I made it—because he willed it. Let my son Maurice break it, if he can, if he will—as you have broken yours. Only let him never more call Theresa von Lynar mother!"

Joan rose to depart. Her intent had not been shaken, though she was impressed by the noble heart of the woman who had been her father's wife. But she also had vowed a vow, and that vow she would keep. The Sparhawk should yet be the Eagle of Kernsberg, and she, Joan, a home-keeping housewife nested in quietness, a barn-door fowl about the orchards of Isle Rugen.

"Madam," she said, "your word is your word. But so is that of Joan of Kernsberg. It may be that out of the unseen there may leap a chance which shall bring all to pass, the things which we both desire—without breaking of vows or loosing of the bands of obligation. For me, being no more than a daughter, I will keep Duke Henry's will only in that which is just!"

"And I," said Theresa von Lynar, "will keep it, just or unjust!"

Yet Joan smiled as she went out. For she had been countered and checkmated in sacrifice. She had met a nature greater than her own, and that with the truly noble is the pleasure of pleasures. In such things only the small are small, only the worms of the earth delight to crawl upon the earth. The great and the wise look up and worship the sun above them. And if by chance their special sun prove after all to be but a star, they say, "Ah, if we had only been near enough it would have been a sun!"

All the while Conrad sat very still, listening with full heart to that which it did not concern him to interrupt. But within his heart he said, "Woman, when she is true woman, is greater, worthier, fuller than any man—aye, were it the Holy Father himself. Perhaps because they draw near Christ the Son through Mary the Mother!"

But Theresa von Lynar sat silent, and watched the girl as she went down the long path, the leafy branches spattering alternate light and shadow upon her slender figure. Then she turned sharply upon Conrad.

"And now, my Lord Cardinal," she said, "what have you been saying to my husband's daughter?"

"I have been telling her that I love her!" answered Conrad simply. He felt that what he had listened to gave this woman a right to be answered.

"And what, I pray you, have princes of Holy Church to do with love? They seek after heavenly things, do they not? Like the angels, they neither marry nor are given in marriage."

"I know," said Conrad humbly, and without taking the least offence. "I know it well. But I have put off the armour I had not proven. The burden is too great for me. I am a soldier—I was trained a soldier—yet because I was born after my brother Louis, I must perforce become both priest and cardinal. Rather a thousand times would I be a man-at-arms and carry a pike!"

"Then am I to understand that as a soldier you told the Duchess Joan that you loved her, and that as a priest you forbade the banns? Or did you wholly forget the little circumstance that once on a time you yourself married her to your brother?"

"I did indeed forget," said Conrad, with sincere penitence; "yet you must not blame me too sorely. I was carried out of myself——"

"The Duchess, then, rejected your suit with contumely?"

Conrad was silent.

"How should a great lady listen to her husband's brother—and he a priest?" Theresa went on remorseless. "What said the Lady Joan when you told her that you loved her?"

"The words she spoke I cannot repeat, but when she ended I set my lips to her garment's hem as reverently as ever to holy bread."

The slow smile came again over the face of Theresa von Lynar, the smile of a warworn veteran who watches the children at their drill.

"You do not need to tell me what she answered, my lord," she said, for the first time leaving out the ecclesiastic title. "I know!"

Conrad stared at the woman.

"She told you that she loved you from the first."

"How know you that?" he faltered. "None must hear that secret—none must guess it!"

Theresa von Lynar laughed a little mellow laugh, in which a keen ear might have detected how richly and pleasantly her laugh must once have sounded to her lover when all her pulses beat to the tune of gladness and the unbound heart.

"Do you think to deceive me, Theresa, whom Henry the Lion loved? Have I been these many weeks with you two in the house and not seen this? Prince Conrad, I knew it that night of the storm when she bent her over the couch on which you lay. 'I love,' you say boldly, and you think great things of your love. But she loved first as she will love most, and your boasted love will never overtake hers—no, not though you love her all your life.... Well, what do you propose to do?"

Conrad stood a moment mutely wrestling with himself. He had never felt Joan's first instinctive aversion to this woman, a dislike even yet scarcely overcome—for women distrust women till they have proven themselves innocent, and often even then.

"My lady," he said, "the Duchess Joan has showed me the better way. Like a man, I knew not what I asked, nor dared to express all that I desired. But I have learned how souls can be united, though bodies are separated. I will not touch her hand; I will not kiss her lips. Once a year only will I see her in the flesh. I shall carry out my duty, made at least less unworthy by her example——"

"And think you," said Theresa, "that in the night watches you will keep this charge? Will not her face come between you and the altar? Will not her image float before you as you kneel at the shrine? Will it not blot out the lines as you read your daily office?"

"I know it—I know it too well!" said Conrad, sinking his head on his breast. "I am not worthy."

"What, then, will you do? Can you serve two masters?" persisted the inquisitor. "Your Scripture says not."

A larger self seemed to flame and dilate within the young man.

"One thing I can do," he said—"like you, I can obey. She bade me go back and do my duty. I cannot bind my thought; I cannot change my heart; I cannot cast my love out. I have heard that which I have heard, and I cannot forget; but at least with the body I can obey. I will perform my vow; I will keep my charge to the letter, every jot and tittle. And if God condemn me for a hypocrite—well, let Him! He, and not I, put this love into my heart. My body may be my priesthood's—I will strive to keep it clean—but my soul is my lady's. For that let Him cast both soul and body into hell-fire if He will!"

Theresa von Lynar did not smile any more. She held out her hand to Conrad of Courtland, priest and prince.

"Yes," she said, "you do know what love is. In so far as I can I will help you to your heart's desire."

And in her turn she rose and passed down through the leafy avenues of the orchard, over which the westering sun was already casting rood-long shadows.

CHAPTER XLII
THE WORDLESS MAN TAKES A PRISONER

It was the hour of the evening meal at Isle Rugen. The September day piped on to its melancholy close, and the wild geese overhead called down unseen from the upper air a warning that the storm followed hard upon their backs. At the table-head sat Theresa von Lynar, her largely moulded and beautiful face showing no sign of emotion. Only great quiet dwelt upon it, with knowledge and the sympathy of the proven for the untried. On either side of her were Joan and Prince Conrad—not sad, neither avoiding nor seeking the contingence of eye and eye, but yet, in spite of all, so strange a thing is love once declared, consciously happy within their heart of hearts.

Then, after a space dutifully left unoccupied, came Captains Boris and Jorian; while at the table-foot, opposite to their hostess, towered Werner von Orseln, whose grey beard had wagged at the more riotous board of Henry the Lion of Hohenstein.

Werner was telling an interminable story of the old wars, with many a "Thus said I" and "So did he," ending thus: "There lay I on my back, with thirty pagan Wends ready to slit my hals as soon as they could get their knives between my gorget and headpiece. Gott! but I said every prayer that I knew—they were not many in those days—all in two minutes' space, as I lay looking at the sky through my visor bars and waiting for the first prick of the Wendish knife-points.

"But even as I looked up, lo! some one bestrode me, and the voice I loved best in all the world—no, not a woman's, God send him rest" ("Amen!" interjected the Lady Joan)—"cried, 'To me, Hohenstein! To me, Kernsberg!' And though my head was ringing with the shock of falling, and my body weak from many wounds, I strove to answer that call, as I saw my master's sword flicker this way and that over my head. I rose half from the ground, my hilt still in my hand—I had no more left after the fight I had fought. But Henry the Lion gave me a stamp down with his foot. 'Lie still, man,' he said; 'do not interfere in a little business of this kind!' And with his one point he kept a score at bay, crying all the time, 'To me, Hohenstein! To me, Kernsbergers all!'

"And when the enemy fled, did he wait till the bearers came? Well I wot, hardly! Instead, he caught me over his shoulder like an empty sack when one goes a-foraging—me, Werner von Orseln, that am built like a donjon tower. And with his sword still red in his right hand he bore me in, only turning aside a little to threaten a Wendish archer who would have sent an arrow through me on the way. By the knights who sit round Karl's table, he was a man!"

And then to their feet sprang Boris and Jorian, who were judges of men.

"To Prince Henry the Lion—*hoch!*" they cried. "Drink it deep to his memory!"

And with tankard and wreathed wine-cup they quaffed to the great dead. Standing up, they drank—his daughter also—all save Theresa von Lynar. She sat unmoved, as if the toast had been her own and in a moment more she must rise to give them thanks. For the look on her face said, "After all, what is there so strange in that? Was he not Henry the Lion—and mine?"

For there is no joy like that which you may see on a woman's face when a great deed is told of the man she loves.

The Kernsberg soldiers who had been trained to serve at table, had stopped and stood fixed, their duties in complete oblivion during the tale, but now they resumed them and the simple feast continued. Meanwhile it had been growing wilder and wilder without, and the shrill lament of the wind was distinctly heard in the wide chimney-top. Now and then in a lull, broad splashes of rain fell solidly into the red embers with a sound like musket balls "spatting" on a wall.

Then Theresa von Lynar looked up.

"Where is Max Ulrich?" she said; "why does he delay?"

"My lady," one of the men of Kernsberg answered, saluting; "he is gone across the Haff in the boat, and has not yet returned."

"I will go and look for him—nay, do not rise, my lord. I would go forth alone!"

So, snatching a cloak from the prong of an antler in the hall, Theresa went out into the irregular hooting of the storm. It was not yet the deepest gloaming, but dull grey clouds like hunted cattle scoured across the sky, and the rising thunder of the waves on the shingle prophesied a night of storm. Theresa stood a long time bare-headed, enjoying the thresh of the broad drops as they struck against her face and cooled her throbbing eyes. Then she pulled the hood of the cloak over her head.

The dead was conquering the quick within her.

"I have known a *man*!" she said; "what need I more with life now? The man I loved is dead. I thank God that I served him—aye, as his dog served him. And shall I grow disobedient now? No, not that my son might sit on the throne of the Kaiser!"

Theresa stood upon the inner curve of the Haff at the place where Max Ulrich was wont to pull his boat ashore. The wind was behind her, and though the waves increased as the distance widened from the pebbly bank on which she stood, the water at her feet was only ruffled and pitted with little dimples under the shocks of the wind. Theresa looked long southward under her hand, but for the moment could see nothing.

Then she settled herself to keep watch, with the storm riding slack-rein overhead. Towards the mainland the whoop and roar with which it assaulted the pine forests deafened her ears. But her face was younger than we have ever seen it, for Werner's story had moved her strongly. Once more she was by a great man's side. She moved her hand swiftly, first out of the shelter of the cloak as if seeking furtively to nestle it in another's, and then, as the raindrops plashed cold upon it, she drew it slowly back to her again.

And though Theresa von Lynar was yet in the prime of her glorious beauty, one could see what she must have been in the days of her girlhood. And as memory caused her eyes to grow misty, and the smile of love and trust eternal came upon her lips, twenty years were shorn away; and the woman's face which had looked anxiously across the darkening Haff changed to that of the girl who from the gate of Castle Lynar had watched for the coming of Duke Henry.

She was gazing steadfastly southward, but it was not for Max the Wordless that she waited. Towards Kernsberg, where he whose sleep she had so often watched, rested all alone, she looked and kissed a hand.

"Dear," she murmured, "you have not forgotten Theresa! You know she keeps troth! Aye, and will keep it till God grows kind, and your true wife can follow—to tell you how well she hath kept her charge!"

Awhile she was silent, and then she went on in the low even voice of self-communing.

"What to me is it to become a princess? Did not he, for whose words alone I cared, call me his queen? And I was his queen. In the black blank day of my uttermost need he made me his wife. And I am his wife. What want I more with dignities?"

Theresa von Lynar was silent awhile and then she added—

"Yet the young Duchess, his daughter, means well. She has her father's spirit. And my son—why should my vow bind him? Let him be Duke, if so the Fates direct and Providence allow. But for me, I will not stir finger or utter word to help him. There shall be neither anger nor sadness in my husband's eyes when I tell him how I have observed the bond!"

Again she kissed a hand towards the dead man who lay so deep under the ponderous marble at Kernsberg. Then with a gracious gesture, lingeringly and with the misty eyes of loving womanhood, she said her lonely farewells.

"To you, beloved," she murmured, and her voice was low and very rich, "to you, beloved, where far off you lie! Sleep sound, nor think the time long till Theresa comes to you!"

She turned and walked back facing the storm. Her hood had long ago been blown from her head by the furious gusts of wind. But she heeded not. She had forgotten poor Max Ulrich and Joan, and even herself. She had forgotten her son. Her hand was out in the storm now. She did not draw it back, though the water ran from her fingertips. For it was clasped in an unseen grasp and in an ear that surely heard she was whispering her heart's troth. "God give it to me to do one deed—one only before I die—that, worthy and unashamed, I may meet my King."

When Theresa re-entered the hall of the grange the company still sat as she had left them. Only at the lower end of the board the three captains conferred together in low voices, while at the upper Joan and Prince Conrad sat gazing full at each other as if souls could be drunk in through the eyes.

With a certain reluctance which yet had no shame in it, they plucked glance from glance as she entered, as it were with difficulty detaching spirits which had been joined. At which Theresa, recalled to herself, smiled.

"In all that touches not my vow I will help you two!" she thought, as she looked at them. For true love came closer to her than anything else in the world.

"There is no sign of Max," she said aloud, to break the first silence of constraint; "perhaps he has waited at the landing-place on the mainland till the storm should abate—though that were scarce like him, either."

She sat down, with one large movement of her arm casting her wet cloak over the back of a wooden settle, which fronted a fireplace where green pine knots crackled and explosive jets of steam rushed spitefully outwards into the hall with a hissing sound.

"You have been down at the landing-place—on such a night?" said Joan, with some remains of that curious awkwardness which marks the interruption of a more interesting conversation.

"Yes," said Theresa, smiling indulgently (for she had been in like case— such a great while ago, when her brothers used to intrude). "Yes, I have been at the landing-place. But as yet the storm is nothing, though the waves will be fierce enough if Max Ulrich is coming home with a laden boat to pull in the wind's eye."

It mattered little what she said. She had helped them to pass the bar, and the conversation could now proceed over smooth waters.

Yet there is no need to report it. Joan and Conrad remained and spoke they scarce knew what, all for the pleasure of eye answering eye, and the subtle flattery of voices that altered by the millionth of a tone each time they answered each other. Theresa spoke vaguely but sufficiently, and allowed herself to dream, till to her yearning gaze honest, sturdy Werner grew misty and his bluff figure resolved itself into that one nobler and more kingly which for years had fronted her at the table's end where now the chief captain sat.

Meanwhile Jorian and Boris exchanged meaning and covert glances, asking each other when this dull dinner parade would be over, so that they might loosen leathern points, undo buttons, and stretch legs on benches with a tankard of ale at each right elbow, according to the wont of stout war-captains not quite so young as they once were.

Thus they were sitting when there came a clamour at the outer door, the noise of voices, then a soldier's challenge, and, on the back of that, Max Ulrich's weird answer—a sound almost like the howl of a wolf cut off short in his throat by the hand that strangles him.

"There he is at last!" cried all in the dining-hall of the grange.

"Thank God!" murmured Theresa. For the man wanting words had known Henry the Lion.

They waited a long moment of suspense till the door behind Werner was thrust open and the dumb man came in, drenched and dripping. He was holding one by the arm, a man as tall as himself, grey and gaunt, who fronted the company with eyes bandaged and hands tied behind his back. Max Ulrich had a sharp knife in his hand with a thin and slightly curved blade, and as he thrust the pinioned man before him into the full light of the candles, he made signs that, if his lady wished it, he was prepared to despatch his prisoner on the spot. His lips moved rapidly and he seemed to be forming words and sentences. His mistress followed these movements with the closest attention.

"He says," she began to translate, "that he met this man on the further side. He said that he had a message for Isle Rugen, and refused to turn back on any condition. So Max blindfolded, bound, and gagged him, he being willing to be bound. And now he waits our pleasure."

"Let him be unloosed," said Joan, gazing eagerly at the prisoner, and Theresa made the sign.

Stolidly Ulrich unbound the broad bandage from the man's eyes, and a grey badger's brush of upright stubble rose slowly erect above a high narrow brow, like laid corn that dries in the sun.

"Alt Pikker!" said Joan of the Sword Hand, starting to her feet.

"Alt Pikker!" cried in varied tones of wonderment Werner von Orseln and the two captains of Plassenburg, Jorian and Boris.

And Alt Pikker it surely was.

CHAPTER XLIII
TO THE RESCUE

But the late prisoner did not speak at once, though his captor stood back as though to permit him to explain himself. He was still bound and gagged. Discovering which, Max in a very philosophical and leisurely manner assisted him to relieve himself of a rolled kerchief which had been placed in his mouth.

Even then his throat refused its office till Werner von Orseln handed him a great cup of wine from which he drank deeply.

"Speak!" said Joan. "What disaster has brought you here? Is Kernsberg taken?"

"The Eagle's Nest is harried, my lady, but that is not what hath brought me hither!"

"Have they found out this my—prison? Are they coming to capture me?"

"Neither," returned Alt Pikker. "Maurice von Lynar is in the hands of his cruel enemies, and on the day after to-morrow, at sunrise, he is to be torn to pieces by wild horses."

"Why?" "Wherefore?" "In what place?" "Who would dare?" came from all about the table; but the mother of the young man sat silent as if she had not heard.

"To save Kernsberg from sack by the Muscovites, Maurice von Lynar went to Courtland in the guise of the Lady Joan. At the fords of the Alla we delivered him up!"

"You delivered him up?" cried Theresa suddenly. "Then you shall die! Max Ulrich, your knife!"

The dumb man gave the knife in a moment, but Theresa had not time to approach.

"I went with him," said Alt Pikker calmly.

"You went with him," repeated his mother after a moment, not understanding.

"Could I let the young man go alone into the midst of his enemies?"

"He went for my sake!" moaned Joan. "He is to die for me!"

"Nay," corrected Alt Pikker, "he is to die for wedding the Princess Margaret of Courtland!"

Again they cried out upon him in utmost astonishment—that is, all the men.

"Maurice von Lynar has married the Princess Margaret of Courtland? Impossible!"

"And why should he not?" his mother cried out.

"I expected it from the first!" quoth Joan of the Sword Hand, disdainful of their masculine ignorance.

"Well," put in Alt Pikker, "at all events, he hath married the Princess. Or she has married him, which is the same thing!"

"But why? We knew nothing of this! He told us nothing. We thought he went for our lady's sake to Courtland! Why did he marry her?" cried severally Von Orseln and the Plassenburg captains.

"Why?" said Theresa the mother, with assurance. "Because he loved her doubtless. How? Because he was his father's son!"

And Theresa being calm and stilling the others, Alt Pikker got time to tell his tale. There was silence in the grange of Isle Rugen while it was being told, and even when it was ended for a space none spoke. But Theresa smiled well pleased and said in her heart, "I thank God! My son also shall meet Henry the Lion face to face and not be ashamed."

After that they made their plans.

"I will go," said Conrad, "for I have influence with my brother—or, if not with him, at least with the folk of Courtland. We will stop this heathenish abomination."

"I will go," said Theresa, "because he is my son. God will show me a way to help him."

"We will all go," chorussed the captains; "that is—all save Werner——"

"All except Boris——!"

"All except Jorian——!"

"Who will remain here on Isle Rugen with the Duchess Joan?" They looked at each other as they spoke.

"You need not trouble yourselves! I will not remain on Isle Rugen—not an hour," said Joan. "Whoever stays, I go. Think you that I will permit this man to die in my stead? We will all go to Courtland. We will tell Prince Louis that I am no duchess, but only the sister of a duke. We will prove to him that my father's bond of heritage-brotherhood is null and void. And then we will see whether he is willing to turn the princedom upside down for such a dowerless wife as I!"

"For such a wife," thought Conrad, "I would turn the universe upside down, though she stood in a beggar's kirtle!"

But being loyally bound by his promise he said nothing.

It was Theresa von Lynar who put the matter practically.

"At a farm on the mainland, hidden among the salt marshes, there are horses—those you brought with you and others. They are in waiting for such an emergency. Max will bring them to the landing-place. Three or four of your guard must accompany him. The rest will make ready, and at the first hint of dawn we will set out. There is yet time to save my son!"

She added in her heart, "Or, if not, then to avenge him."

Strangely enough, Theresa was the least downcast of the party. Death seemed a thing so little to her, even so desirable, that though the matter concerned her son's life, she commanded herself and laid her plans as coolly as if she had been preparing a dinner in the grange of Isle Rugen.

But her heart was proud within her with a great pride.

"He is Henry the Lion's son. He was born a duke. He has married a princess. He has tasted love and known sacrifice. If he dies it will be for the sake of his sister's honour. 'Tis no bad record for twenty years. These things *he* will count high above fame and length of days!"

The little company which set out from Isle Rugen to ride to Courtland had no thought or intention of rescuing Maurice von Lynar by force of arms. They knew their own impotence far too exactly. Yet each of the leaders had a plan of action thought out, to be pursued when the city was reached.

If her renunciation of her dignities were laughed at, as she feared, there was nothing for Joan but to deliver herself to Prince Louis. She had resolved to promise to be his wife and princess in all that it concerned the outer world to see. Their provinces would be united, Kernsberg and Hohenstein delivered unconditionally into his hand.

On his part, Werner von Orseln was prepared to point out to the Prince of Courtland that with Joan as his wife and the armies and levies of Hohenstein added to his own under the Sparhawk's leadership, he would be in a position to do without the aid of the Prince of Muscovy altogether. Further, that in case of attack from the north, not only Plassenburg and the Mark, but all the Teutonic Bond must rally to his side.

Boris and Jorian, being stout-hearted captains of men-at-arms, were ready for anything. But though their swords were loosened in their sheaths to be prepared for any assault, they were resolved also to give what official dignity they could to their mission by a free use of the names of their master and mistress, the Prince Hugo and Princess Helene of Plassenburg. They were sorry now that they had left their credentials behind them, at Kernsberg, but they meant to make confidence and assured countenances go as far as they would.

Conrad, who was intimately acquainted with the character of his brother, and who knew how entirely he was under the dominion of Prince Ivan, had resolved to use all powers, ecclesiastical and secular, which his position as titular Prince of the Church put within his reach. To save the Sparhawk from a bloody and disgraceful death he would invoke upon Courtland even the dread curse of the Greater Excommunication. With his faithful priests around him he would seek his brother, and, if necessary, on the very execution place itself, or from the high altar of the cathedral, pronounce the dread "Anathema sit." He knew his brother well enough to be sure that this threat would shake his soul with terror, and that such a curse laid on a city like Courtland, not too subservient at any time, would provoke a rebellion which would shake the power of princes far more securely seated than Prince Louis.

The only one of the party wholly without a settled plan was the woman most deeply interested. Theresa von Lynar simply rode to Courtland to save her son or to die with him. She alone had no influence with Prince Ivan, no weapon to use against him except her woman's wit.

As the cavalcade rode on, though few, they made a not ungallant show. For Theresa had clad Prince Conrad in a coat of mail which had once belonged to Henry the Lion. Joan glittered by his side in a corselet of steel rings, while Werner von Orseln and the two captains of Plassenburg followed fully armed, their accoutrements shining with the burnishing of many idle weeks. These, with the men-at-arms behind them, made up such an equipage as few princes could ride abroad with. But to all of them the journey was naught, a mere race against time—so neither horse nor man was spared. And the two women held out best of all.

But when in the morning light of the second day they came in sight of Courtland, and saw on the green plain of the Alla a great concourse, it did not need Alt Pikker's shout to urge them forward at a gallop, lest after all they should arrive too late.

"They have brought him out to die," cried Joan. "Ride, for the young man's life!"

CHAPTER XLIV
THE UKRAINE CROSS

Upon the green plain beside the Alla a great multitude was assembled. They had come together to witness a sight never seen in Courtland before— the dread punishment of the Ukraine Cross. It was to be done, they said, upon the body of the handsome youth with whom the Princess Margaret was secretly in love—some even whispered married to him.

The townsfolk murmured among themselves. This was certainly the beginning of the end. Who knew what would come next? If the barbarous Muscovite punishments began in Courtland, it would end in all of them being made slaves, liable at any moment to knout and plet. Ivan had bewitched the Prince. That was clear, and for a certainty the Princess Margaret wept night and day. In this fashion ran the bruit of that which was to be.

"Torn to pieces by wild horses!" It was a thing often talked about, but one which none had seen in a civilised country for a thousand years. Where was it to be done? It was shocking, terrible; but—it would be worth seeing. So all the city went out, the men with weapons under their cloaks pressing as near as the soldiers would allow them, while the women, being more pitiful, stood afar off and wept into their aprons—only putting aside the corners that they might see clearly and miss nothing.

At ten a great green square of riverside grass was held by the archers of Courtland. The people extended as far back as the shrine of the Virgin, where at the city entrance travellers are wont to give thanks for a favourable journey. At eleven the lances of Prince Ivan's Cossacks were seen topping the city wall. On the high bank of the Alla the people were craning their necks and looking over each other's shoulders.

The wild music of the Cossacks came nearer, each man with the butt of his lance set upon his thigh, and the pennon of blue and white waving above. Then a long pitying "A—a—h!" went up from the people. For now the Sparhawk was in sight, and at the first glimpse of him they swayed from the Riga Gate to the shrine of John Evangelist, like a willow copse stricken by a squall from off the Baltic, so that it shows the under-grey of its leaves.

"The poor lad! So handsome, so young!"

The first soft universal hush of pity broke presently into a myriad exclamations of anger and deprecation. "How high he holds his head! See! They have opened his shirt at the neck. Poor Princess, how she must love him! His hands are tied behind his back. He rides in that jolting cart as if he were a conqueror in a triumphal procession, instead of a victim going to his doom."

"Pity, pity that one so young should die such a death! They say she is to be carried up to the top of the Castle wall that she may see. Ah, here he comes! He is smiling! God forgive the butchers, who by strength of brute beasts would tear asunder those comely limbs that are fitted to be a woman's joy! Down with all false and cruel princes, say I! Nay, mistress, I will not be silent. And there are many here who will back me, if I be called in question. Who is the Muscovite, that he should bring his abominations into Courtland? If I had my way, Prince Conrad——"

"Hush, hush! Here they come! Side by side, as usual, the devil and his dupe. Aha! there is no sound of cheering! Let but a man shout, 'Long live the Prince!' and I will slit his wizzand. I, Henry the coppersmith, will do it! He shall sleep with pennies on his eyes this night!"

So through the lane by which the city gate communicated with the tapestried stand set apart for the greater spectators, the Princes Louis and Ivan, fool and knave, servant and master, took their way. And they had scarce passed when the people, mutinous and muttering, surged black behind the archers' guard.

"Back there—stand back! Way for their Excellencies—way!"

"Stand back yourselves," came the growling answer. "We be free men of Courtland. You will find we are no Muscovite serfs, and that or the day be done. Karl Wendelin, think shame—thou that art my sister's son—to be aiding and abetting such heathen cruelty to a Christen man, all that you may eat a great man's meat and wear a jerkin purfled with gold."

Such cries and others worse pursued the Princes' train as it went.

"Cossack—Cossack! You are no Courtlanders, you archers! Not a girl in the city will look at you after this! Butchers' slaughtermen every one? Whipped hounds that are afraid of ten score Muscovites! Down, dogs, knock your foreheads on the ground! Here comes a Muscovite!"

Thus angrily ran taunt and jeer, till the Courtland guard, mostly young fellows with relatives and sweethearts among the crowd, grew well-nigh frantic with rage and shame. The rabble, which had hung on the Prince of Muscovy so long as he scattered his largesse, had now wheeled about with characteristic fickleness.

"See yonder! What are they doing? Peter Altmaar, what are they doing? Tell us, thou long man! Of what use is your great fathom of pump-water? Can you do nothing for your meat but reach down black puddings from the rafters?"

At this all eyes turned to Peter, a lanky overgrown lad with a keen eye, a weak mouth, and the gift of words.png—-\C.M Pg325 png—-\C.M Pg325 png—-\C.M Pg325 png—-\C.M Pg325 png—-\C.M Pg325

"Speak up, Peter! Aye, listen to Peter—a good lad, Peter, as ever was!"

"Strong Jan the smith, take him up on your back so that he may see the better!"

"Hush, there! Stop that woman weeping. We cannot hear for her noise. She says he is like her son, does she? Well then, there will be time enough to weep for him afterwards."

"They are bringing up four horses from the Muscovite camp. The folk are getting as far off as they can from their heels," began Peter Altmaar, looking under his hand over the people's heads. "Half a score of men are at each brute's head. How they plunge! They will never stand still a moment. Ah, they are tethering them to the great posts of stone in the middle of the green square. Between, there is a table—no, a kind of square wooden stand like a priest's platform in Lent when he tells us our sins outside the church."

"The Princes are sitting their horses, watching. Bravo, that was well done. We came near to seeing the colour of the Muscovite brains that time. One of the wild horses spread his hoofs on either side of Prince Ivan's head!"

"God send him a better aim next time! Tell on, Peter! Aye, get on, good Peter!"

"The Princes have gone up into their balcony. They are laughing and talking as if it were a raree-show!"

"What of him, good Peter? How takes he all this?"

"What of whom?" queried Peter, who, like all great talkers, was rapidly growing testy under questioning.

"There is but one 'he' to-day, man. The young lad, the Princess Margaret's sweetheart."

"They have brought him down from the cart. The Cossacks are close about him. They have put all the Courtland men far back."

"Aye, aye; they dare not trust them. Oh, for an hour of Prince Conrad! If we of the city trades had but a leader, this shame should not blot our name throughout all Christendom! What now, Peter?"

"The Muscovites are binding the lad to a wooden frame like the empty lintels of a door. He stands erect, his hands in the corners above, and his feet in the corners below. They have stripped him to the waist."

"Hold me higher up, Jan the smith! I would see this out, that you may tell your children and your children's children. Aye—ah, so it is. It is true. Sainted Virgin! I can see his body white in the sunshine. It shines slender as a peeled willow wand."

Then the woman who had wept began again. Her wailing angered the people.

"He is like my son—save him! He is the very make and image of my Kaspar. Slender as a young willow, supple as an ash, eyes like the berries of the sloe-thorn. Give me a sword! Give an old woman a sword, and I will deliver him myself, for my Kaspar's sake. God's grace—Is there never a man amongst you?"

And as her voice rose into a shriek there ran through all the multitude the strange shiver of fear with which a great crowd expects a horror. A hush fell broad and equal as dew out of a clear sky. A mighty silence lay on all the folk. Peter Altmaar's lips moved, but no sound came from them. For now Maurice was set on high, so that all could see for themselves. White against the sky of noon, making the cross of Saint Andrew within the oblong framework to which he was lashed, they could discern the slim body of the young man who was about to be torn in sunder. The executioners held him up thus a minute or two for a spectacle, and then, their arrangements completed, they lowered that living crucifix till it lay flat upon its little platform, with the limbs extended stark and tense towards the heels of the wild plunging horses of the Ukraine.

"Maurice was set on high."

Then again the voice of Peter Altmaar was heard, now ringing false like an untuned fiddle. "They are welding the manacles upon his ankles and wrists. Listen to the strokes of the hammer."

And in the hush which followed, faintly and musically they could hear iron ring on iron, like anvil strokes in some village smithy heard in the hush of a summer's afternoon.

"Blessed Virgin! they are casting loose the horses! A Cossack with a cruel whip stands by each to lash him to fury! They are slipping the platform from under him. God in heaven! What is this?"

Hitherto the eyes of the great multitude, which on three sides surrounded the place of execution, had been turned inward. But now with one accord they were gazing, not on the terrible preparations which were coming so near their bloody consummation, but over the green tree-studded Alla meads towards a group of horsemen who were approaching at a swift hand-gallop.

Whereupon immediately Peter, the lank giant, was in greater request than ever.

"What do they look at, good Peter—tell us quickly? Will the horses not pull? Will the irons not hold? Have the ropes broken? Is it a miracle? Is it a rescue? Thunder-weather, man! Do not stand and gape. Speak—tell us what you see, or we will prod you behind with our daggers!"

"Half a dozen riding fast towards the Princes' stand, and holding up their hands—nay, there are a dozen. The Princes are standing up to look. The men have stopped casting loose the wild horses. The man on the frame is lying very still, but the chains from his ankles and arms are not yet fastened to the traces."

"Go on, Peter! How slow you are, Peter! Stupid Peter!"

"There is a woman among those who ride—no, two of them! They are getting near the skirts of the crowd. Men are shouting and throwing up their hands in the air. I cannot tell what for. The soldiers have their hats on the tops of their pikes. They, too, are shouting!"

As Peter paused the confused noise of a multitude crying out, every man for himself, was borne across the crowd on the wind. As when a great stone is cast into a little hill-set tarn, and the wavelet runs round, swamping the margin's pebbles and swaying the reeds, so there ran a shiver, and then a mighty tidal wave of excitement through all that ring which surrounded the crucified man, the deadly platform, and the tethered horses.

Men shouted sympathetically without knowing why, and the noise they made was half a suppressed groan, so eager were they to take part in that which should be done next. They thrust their womenkind behind them, shouldering their way into the thick of the press that they might see the more clearly. Instinctively every weaponed man fingered that which he chanced to carry. Yet none in all that mighty assembly had the least conception of what was really about to happen.

By this time there was no more need of Peter Altmaar. The ring was rapidly closing now all about, save upon the meadow side, where a lane was kept open. Through this living alley came a knight and a lady—the latter in riding habit and broad velvet cap, the knight with his visor up, but armed from head to foot, a dozen squires and men-at-arms following in a compact little cloud; and as they came they were greeted with the enthusiastic acclaim of all that mighty concourse.

About them eddied the people, overflowing and sweeping away the Cossacks, carrying the Courtland archers with them in a mad frenzy of fraternisation. In the stand above Prince Louis could be seen shrilling commands, yet dumb show was all he could achieve, so universal the clamour beneath him. But the Princess Margaret heard the shouting and her heart leaped.

"Prince Conrad—our own Prince Conrad, he has come back, our true Prince? We knew he was no priest! Courtland for ever! Down with Louis of the craven heart! Down with the Muscovite! The young man shall not die! The Princess shall have her sweetheart!"

And as soon as the cavalcade had come within the square the living wave broke black over all. The riders could not dismount, so thick the press. The halters of the wild horses were cut, and right speedily they made a way for themselves, the people falling back and closing again so soon as they had passed out across the plain with necks arched to their knees and a wild flourish of unanimous hoofs.

Then the cries began again. Swords and bare fists were shaken at the grand stand, where, white as death, Prince Louis still kept his place.

"Prince Conrad and the Lady Joan!"

"Kill the Muscovite, the torturer!"

"Death to Prince Louis, the traitor and coward!"

"We will save the lad alive!"

About the centre platform whereon the living cross was extended the crush grew first oppressive and then dangerous.

"Back there—you are killing him! Back, I say!"

Then strong men took staves and halberts out of the hands of dazed soldiermen, and by force of brawny arms and sharp pricking steel pressed the people back breast high. The smiths who had riveted the wristlets and ankle-rings were already busy with their files. The lashings were cast loose from the frames. A hundred palms chafed the white swollen limbs. A burgher back in the crowd slipped his cloak. It was passed overhead on a thousand eager hands and thrown across the young man's body.

At last all was done, and dazed and blinded, but unshaken in his soul, Maurice von Lynar stood totteringly upon his feet.

"Lift him up! Lift him up! Let us see him! If he be dead, we will slay Prince Louis and crucify the Muscovite in his place!"

"Bah!" another would cry, "Louis is no longer ruler! Conrad is the true Prince!"

"Down with the Russ, the Cossack! Where are they? Pursue them! Kill them!"

So ran the fierce shouts, and as the rescuers raised the Sparhawk high on their plaited hands that all men might see, on the far skirts of the crowd Ivan of Muscovy, with a bitter smile on his face, gathered together his scattered horsemen. One by one they had struggled out of the press while all men's eyes were fixed upon the vivid centrepiece of that mighty whirlpool.

"Set Prince Louis in your midst and ride for your lives!" he cried. "To the frontier, where bides the army of the Czar!"

With a flash of pennons and a tossing of horses' heads they obeyed, but Prince Ivan himself paused upon the top of a little swelling rise and looked back towards the Alla bank.

The delivered prisoner was being held high upon men's arms. The burgher's cloak was wrapped about him like a royal robe.

Prince Ivan gnashed his teeth in impotent anger.

"It is your day. Make the most of it," he muttered. "In three weeks I will come back! And then, by Michael the Archangel, I will crucify one of you at every street corner and cross-road through all the land of Courtland! And that which I would have done to my lady's lover shall not be named beside that which I shall yet do to those who rescued him!"

And he turned and rode after his men, in the midst of whom was Prince Louis, his head twisted in fear and apprehension over his shoulder, and his slack hands scarce able to hold the reins.

After this manner was the Sparhawk brought out from the jaws of death, and thus came Joan of the Sword Hand the second time to Courtland.

But the end was not yet.

CHAPTER XLV
THE TRUTH-SPEAKING OF BORIS AND JORIAN

This is the report verbal of Captains Boris and Jorian, which they gave in face of their sovereigns in the garden pleasaunce of the palace of Plassenburg. Hugo and Helene sat at opposite ends of a seat of twisted branches. Hugo crossed his legs and whistled low with his thumbs in the slashing of his doublet, a habit of which Helene had long striven in vain to cure him. The Princess was busy broidering the coronated double eagle of a new banner, but occasionally she raised her eyes to where on the green slope beneath, under the wing of a sage woman of experience, the youthful hope of Plassenburg led his mimic armies to battle against the lilies by the orchard wall, or laid lance in rest to storm the too easy fortress of his nurse's lap.

"Boris," whispered Jorian, "remember! Do not lie, Boris. 'Tis too dangerous. You remember the last time?"

"Aye," growled Boris. "I have good cause to remember! What a liar our Hugo must have been in his time, so readily to suspect two honest soldiers!"

"Speak out your minds, good lads!" said Hugo, leaning a little further back.

"Aye, tell us all," assented Helene, pausing to shake her head at the antics of the young Prince Karl; "tell us how you delivered the Sparhawk, as you call him, the officer of the Duchess Joan!"

So Boris saluted and began.

"The tale is a long one, Prince and Princess," he said. "Of our many and difficult endeavours to keep the peace and prevent quarrelling I will say nothing——"

"Better so!" interjected Hugo, with a gleam in his eye. Jorian coughed and growled to himself, "That long fool will make a mess of it!"

"I will pass on to our entry into Courtland. It was like the home-coming of a long-lost true prince. There was no fighting—alack, not so much as a stroke after all that pother of shouting!"

"Boris!" said the Princess warningly.

"Give him rope!" muttered Prince Hugo. "He will tangle himself rarely or all be done!"

"I mean by the blessing of Heaven there was no bloodshed," Boris corrected himself. "There was, as I say, no fighting. There was none to fight with. Prince Louis had not a friend in his own capital city, saving the Muscovite. And at that moment Prince Ivan the Wasp was glad enough to win clear off to the frontier with his Cossacks at his tail. It was a God's pity we could not ride them down. But though Jorian and I did all that men could——"

"Ahem!" said Jorian, as if a fly had flown into his mouth and tickled his throat.

"I mean, your Highnesses, we did whatever men could to keep the populace within bounds. But they broke through and leaped upon us, throwing their arms about our horses' necks, crying out, 'Our saviours!' 'Our deliverers!' God wot, we might as well have tried to charge through the billows of the Baltic when it blows a norther right from the Gulf of Bothnia! But it almost broke my heart to see them ride off with never so much as a spear thrust through one single Muscovite belly-band!"

Here Jorian had a fit of coughing which caused the Princess to look severely upon him. Boris, recalled to himself, proceeded more carefully.

"It was all we could do to open up a way to where the young man Maurice lay stretched on the Cross of Death. They had loosed the wild horses before we arrived, and these had galloped off after their companions. A pity! Oh, a great pity!

"Then came the young man's mother near, she who was our hostess at Isle Rugen——"

"Why did you not abide at Kernsberg as you were instructed?" put in Hugo at this point.

"Never mind—go on—tell the tale!" cried Helene, who was listening breathlessly.

"We thought it our duty to accompany the Duchess Joan," said Boris, deftly enough; "where the king is, there is the court!"

And at this point the two captains saluted very dutifully and respectfully, like machines moved by one spring.

"Well said for once, thou overly long one," growled Jorian under his breath.

"Go on!" commanded Helene.

"The young man's mother came near and threw a cloak across his naked body. Then Jorian and I unbound him and chafed his limbs, first removing the gag from his mouth; but so tightly had the cords been bound about him that for long he could not stand upright. Then, from the royal pavilion, where she had been brought for cruel sport to see the death, the Princess Margaret came running— —"

"Oh, wickedness!" cried Helene, "to make her look on at her lover's death!"

"She came furiously, though a dainty princess, thrusting strong men aside. 'Way there!' she cried, 'on your lives make way! I will go to him. I am the Princess Margaret. Give me a dagger and I will prick me a way.'"

"And, by Saint Stephen the holy martyr—if she did not snatch a bodkin from the belt of a tailor in the High Street and with it open up her way as featly as though she were handling a Cossack lance."

"And what happened when she got to him—when she found her husband?" cried Helene, her eyes sparkling. And she put out a hand to touch her own, just to be sure that he was there.

"Truth, a very wondrous thing happened!" said Jorian, whose fingers also had been twitching, "a mightily wondrous thing. Thus it was— —"

"Hold your tongue, sausage-bag!" growled Boris, very low; "who tells this tale, you or I?"

"Get on, then," answered in like fashion Captain Jorian, "you are as long-winded and wheezy as a smith's bellows!"

"Yes, a strange thing it was. I was standing by Maurice von Lynar, undoing the cord from his neck. His mother was chafing an arm. The Lady Joan was bending to speak softly to him, for she had dismounted from her horse, when, all in the snapping of a twig, the Princess Margaret came bursting through the ring which Jorian and the Kernsbergers were keeping with their lance-butts. She thrust us all aside. By my faith, me she sent spinning like the young Prince's top there!"

"God save his Excellency!" quoth Jorian, not to be left out entirely.

"Silence!" cried Helene, with an imperious stamp of her little foot; "and do you, Boris, tell the tale without comparisons. What happened then?"

"Only the boy's mother kept her ground! She went on chafing his arm without so much as raising her eyes."

"Did the Princess serve Joan of the Sword Hand as she served you?" interposed Hugo.

"Marry, worse!" cried Boris, growing excited for the first time. "She thrust her aside like a kitchen wench, and our lady took it as meekly as— as——"

"Go on! Did I not tell you to spare us your comparatives?" cried Helene the Princess, letting her broidery slip to the ground in her consuming interest.

"Well," said Boris, quickly sobered, "it was in truth a mighty quaint thing to see. The Princess Margaret took the young man in her arms and caught him to her. The Lady Theresa kept hold of his wrist. They looked at each other a moment without speech, eye countering eye like knights at a——"

"Go on!" the Princess thundered, if indeed a silvern voice can be said to thunder.

"'Give him up to me! He is mine!' cried the Princess.

"'He is mine!' answered very haughtily the lady of the Isle Rugen— 'Who are you?' 'And you?' cried both at once, flinging their heads back, but never for a moment letting go with their hands. The youth, being dazed, said nothing, nor so much as moved.

"'I am his mother!' said the Lady Theresa, speaking first.

"'I am his wife!' said the Princess.

"Then the woman who had borne the young man gave him into his wife's arms without a word, and the Princess gathered him to her bosom and crooned over him, that being her right. But his mother stepped back among the crowd and drew the hood of her cloak over her head that no man might look upon her face."

"Bravo!" cried Helene, clapping her hands, "it was her right!"

"Little one," said her husband, pointing to the boy on the terrace beneath, who was lashing a toy horse of wood with all his baby might, "I wonder if you will think so when another woman takes *him* from you!"

The Princess Helene caught her breath sharply.

"That would be different!" she said, "yes, very different!"

"Ah!" said Hugo the Prince, her husband.

CHAPTER XLVI
THE FEAR THAT IS IN LOVE

Thus the climax came about in the twinkling of an eye, but the universal turmoil and wild jubilation in which Prince Louis's power and government were swept away had really been preparing for years, though the end fell sharp as the thunderclap that breaks the weather after a season of parching heat.

For all that the trouble was only deferred, not removed. The cruel death of Maurice von Lynar had been rendered impossible by the opportune arrival of Prince Conrad and the sudden revolution which the sight of his noble and beloved form, clad in armour, produced among the disgusted and impulsive Courtlanders.

Yet the arch-foe had only recoiled in order that he might the further leap. The great army of the White Czar was encamped just across the frontier, nominally on the march to Poland, but capable of being in a moment diverted upon the Princedom of Courtland. Here was a pretext of invasion ripe to Prince Ivan's hand. So he kept Louis, the dethroned and extruded prince, close beside him. He urged his father, by every tie of friendship and interest, to replace that prince upon his throne. And the Czar Paul, well knowing that the restoration of Louis meant nothing less than the incorporation of Courtland with his empire, hastened to carry out his son's advice.

In Courtland itself there was no confusion. A certain grim determination took possession of the people. They had made their choice, and they would abide by it. They had chosen Conrad to be their ruler, as he had long been their only hope; and they knew that now Louis was for ever impossible, save as a cloak for a Muscovite dominion.

It had been the first act of Conrad to summon to him all the archpriests and heads of chapels and monasteries by virtue of his office as Cardinal-Archbishop. He represented to them the imminent danger to Holy Church of yielding to the domination of the Greek heretic. Whoever might be spared, the Muscovite would assuredly make an end of them. He promised absolution from the Holy Father to all who would assist in bulwarking religion and the Church of Peter against invasion and destruction. He himself would for the time being lay aside his office and fight as a soldier in the sacred war which was before them. Every consideration must give way to that. Then he would lay the whole matter at the feet of the Holy Father in Rome.

So throughout every town and village in Courtland the war of the Faith was preached. No presbytery but became a recruiting office. Every pulpit was a trumpet proclaiming a righteous war. There was to be no salvation for any Courtlander save in defending his faith and country. It was agreed by all that there was no hope save in the blessed rule of Prince Conrad, at once worthy Prince of the Blood, Prince of Holy Church, and defender of our blessed religion. Prince Louis was a deserter and a heretic. The Pope would depose him, even as (most likely) he had cursed him already.

So, thus encouraged, the country rose behind the retiring Muscovite, and Prince Louis was conducted across the boundary of his princedom under the bitter thunder of cannon and the hiss of Courtland arrows. And the craven trembled as he listened to the shouted maledictions of his own people, and begged for a common coat, lest his archer guard should distinguish their late Prince and wing their clothyard shafts at him as he cowered a little behind Prince Ivan's shoulder.

Meanwhile Joan, casting aside with an exultant leap of the heart her intent to make of herself an obedient wife, rode back to Kernsberg in order to organise all the forces there to meet the common foe. It was to be the last fight of the Teuton Northland for freedom and faith.

The Muscovite does not go back, and if Courtland were conquered Kernsberg could not long stand. To Plassenburg (as we have seen) rode Boris and Jorian to plead for help from their Prince and Princess. Dessauer had already preceded them, and the armies, disciplined and equipped by Prince Karl, were already on the march to defend their frontiers—it might be to go farther and fight shoulder to shoulder with Courtland and Kernsberg against the common foe.

And if all this did not happen, it would not be the fault of those honest soldiers and admirable diplomatists, Captains Boris and Jorian, captains of the Palace Guard of Plassenburg.

The presence of Prince Conrad in the city of Courtland seemed to change entirely the character of the people. From being somewhat frivolous they became at once devoted to the severest military discipline. Nothing was heard but words of command and the ordered tramp of marching feet. The country barons and knights brought in their forces, and their tents, all gay with banners and fluttering pennons, stretched white along the Alla for a mile or more.

The word was on every lip, "When will they come?"

For already the Muscovite allies of Prince Louis had crossed the frontier and were moving towards Courtland, destroying everything in their track.

The day after the deliverance of the Sparhawk, Joan had announced her intention of riding on the morrow to Kernsberg. Maurice von Lynar and Von Orseln would accompany her.

"Then," cried Margaret instantly, "I will go, too!"

"The ride would be over toilsome for you," said Joan, pausing to touch her friend's hair as she looked forth from the window of the Castle of Courtland at the Sparhawk ordering about a company of stout countrymen in the courtyard beneath.

"I *will* go!" said Margaret wilfully. "I shall never let him out of my sight again!"

"We shall be back within the week! You will be both safer and more comfortable here!"

The Princess Margaret withdrew her head from the open window, momentarily losing sight of her husband and, in so doing, making vain her last words.

"Ah, Joan," she said reproachfully, "you are wise and strong—there is no one like you. But you do not know what it is to be married. You never were in love. How, then, can you understand the feelings of a wife?"

She looked out of the window again and waved a kerchief.

"Oh, Joan," she looked back again with a mournful countenance, "I do believe that Maurice does not love me as I love him. He never took the least notice of me when I waved to him!"

"How could he," demanded Joan, the soldier's daughter, sharply, "he was on duty?"

"Well," answered Margaret, still resentful and unconsoled, "he would not have done that *before* we were married! And it is only the first day we have been together, too, since—since——"

And she buried her head in her kerchief.

Joan looked at the Princess a moment with a tender smile. Then she gave a little sigh and went over to her friend. She laid her hand on her shoulder and knelt down beside her.

"Margaret," she whispered, "you used to be so brave. When I was here, and had to fight the Sparhawk's battles with Prince Wasp, you were as headstrong as any young squire desiring to win his spurs. You wished to see us fight, do you remember?"

The Princess took one corner of her white and dainty kerchief away from her eyes in order to look yet more reproachfully at her friend.

"Ah," she said, "that shows! Of course, I knew. You were not *he*, you see; I knew that in a moment."

Joan restrained a smile. She did not remind her friend that then she had never seen "him." The Princess Margaret went on.

"Joan," she cried suddenly, "I wish to ask you something!"

She clasped her hands with a sweet petitionary grace.

"Say on, little one!" said Joan smiling.

"There will be a battle, Joan, will there not?"

Joan of the Sword Hand nodded. She took a long breath and drew her head further back. Margaret noted the action.

"It is very well for you, Joan," she said; "I know you are more than half a man. Every one says so. And then you do not love any one, and you like fighting. But—you may laugh if you will—I am not going to let my husband fight. I want you to let him go to Plassenburg till it is over!"

Joan laughed aloud.

"And you?" she said, still smiling good-naturedly.

It was now Margaret's turn to draw herself up.

"You are not kind!" she said. "I am asking you a favour for my husband, not for myself. Of course I should accompany him! *I* at least am free to come and go!"

"My dear, my dear," said Joan gently, "you are at liberty to propose this to your husband! If he comes and asks me, he shall not lack permission."

"You mean he would not go to Plassenburg even if I asked him?"

"I know he would not—he, the bravest soldier, the best knight——"

There came a knocking at the door.

"Enter!" cried Joan imperiously, yet not a little glad of the interruption.

Werner von Orseln stood in the portal. Joan waited for him to speak.

"My lady," he said, "will you bid the Count von Löen leave his work and take some rest and sustenance. He thinks of nothing but his drill."

"Oh, yes, he does," cried the Princess Margaret; "how dare you say it, fellow! He thinks of me! Why, even now——"

She looked once more out of the window, a smile upon her face. Instantly she drew in her head again and sprang to her feet.

"Oh, he is gone! I cannot see him anywhere!" she cried, "and I never so much as heard them go! Joan, I am going to find him. He should not have gone away without bidding me goodbye! It was cruel!"

She flashed out of the room, and without waiting for tiring maid or coverture, she ran downstairs, dressed as she was in her light summer attire.

Joan stood a moment silent, looking after her with eyes in which flashed a tender light. Werner von Orseln smiled broadly—the dry smile of an ancient war-captain who puts no bounds to the vagaries of women. It was an experienced smile.

"'Tis well for Kernsberg, my lady," said Werner grimly, "that you are not the Princess Margaret."

"And why!" said Joan a little haughtily. For she did not like Conrad's sister to be treated lightly even by her chief captain.

"Ah, love—love," said Werner, nodding his head sententiously. "It is well, my lady, that I ever trained you up to care for none of these things. Teach a maid to fence, and her honour needs no champion. Give her sword-cunning and you keep her from making a fool of herself about the first man who crosses her path. Strengthen her wrist, teach her to lunge and parry, and you strengthen her head. But you do credit to *your* instructor. You have never troubled about the follies of love. Therefore are you our own Joan of the Sword Hand!"

Joan sighed another sigh, very softly this time, and her eyes, being turned away from Von Orseln, were soft and indefinitely hazy.

"Yes," she answered, "I am Joan of the Sword Hand, and I never think of these things!"

"Of course not," he cried cheerfully; "why should you? Ah, if only the Princess Margaret had had an ancient Werner von Orseln to teach her how to drill a hole in a fluttering jackanapes! Then we would have had less of this meauling apron-string business!"

"Silence," said Joan quickly. "She is here."

And the Princess came running in with joy in her face. Instinctively Werner drew back into the shadow of the window curtain, and the smile on his face grew more grimly experienced than ever.

"Oh, Joan," cried the Princess breathlessly, "he had not really gone off without bidding me goodbye. You remember I said that I could not believe it of him, and you see I was right. One cannot be mistaken about one's husband!"

"No?" said Joan interrogatively.

"Never—so long as he loves you, that is!" said Margaret, breathless with her haste; "but when you really love any one, you cannot help getting anxious about them. And then Ivan or Louis might have sent some one to carry him off again to tear him to pieces. Oh, Joan, you cannot know all I suffered. You must be patient with me. I think it was seeing him bound and about to die that has made me like this!"

"Margaret!"

Joan went quickly towards her friend, touched with compunction for her lack of sympathy, and resolved to comfort her if she could. It was true, after all, that while she and Conrad had been happy together on Isle Rugen, this girl had been suffering.

Margaret came towards her, smiling through her tears.

"But I have thought of something," she said, brightening still more; "such a splendid plan. I know Maurice would not want to go away when there was fighting—though I believe, if I had him by himself for an hour, I could persuade him even to that, for my sake."

A stifled grunt came from behind the curtains, which represented the injury done to the feelings of Werner von Orseln by such unworthy sentiments.

The Princess looked over in the direction of the sound, but could see nothing. Joan moved quietly round, so that her friend's back was towards the window, behind the curtains of which stood the war captain.

"This is my thought," the Princess went on more calmly. "Do you, Joan, send Maurice on an embassy to Plassenburg till this trouble is over. Then he will be safe. I will find means of keeping him there——"

A stifled groan of rage came from the window. Margaret turned sharply about.

"What is that?" she cried, taking hold of her skirts, as the habit of women is.

"Some one without in the courtyard," said Joan hastily; "a dog, a cat, a rat in the wainscot—anything!"

"It sounded like something," answered the Princess, "but surely not like anything! Let us look."

"Margaret," said Joan, gently taking her by the arm and walking with her towards the door, "Maurice von Lynar is a soldier and a soldier's son. You would break his heart if you took him away from his duty. He would not love you the same; you would not love him the same."

"Oh, yes, I would," said Margaret, showing signs that her sorrow might break out afresh. "I would love him more for taking care of his life for my sake!"

"You know you would not, Margaret," Joan persisted. "No woman can truly and fully love a man whom she is not proud of."

"Oh, that is before they are married!" cried the Princess indignantly. "Afterwards it is different. You find out things then—and love them all the same. But, of course, how should I expect you to help me? You have never loved; you do not understand!" And, without another word, Margaret of Courtland, who had once been so heart-free and *débonnaire*, went out sobbing like a fretted child. Hardly had the door closed upon her when the sound of stifled laughter broke from the window-seat. Joan indignantly drew the curtains aside and revealed Werner von Orseln shaking all over and vainly striving to govern his mirth with his hands pressed against his sides.

"Joan indignantly drew the curtain aside."

At sight of the face of his mistress, which was very grave, and even stern, his laughter instantly shut itself off. As it seemed, with a single movement, he raised himself to his feet and saluted. Joan stood looking at him a moment without speech.

"Your mirth is exceedingly ill-timed," she said slowly. "On a future occasion, pray remember that the Lady Margaret is a Princess and my friend. You can go! We ride out to-morrow morning at five. See that everything is arranged."

Once more Von Orseln saluted, with a face expressionless as a stone. He marched to the door, turned and saluted a third time, and with heavy footsteps descended the stairs communing with himself as he went.

"That was salt, Werner. Faith, but she gave you the back of the sword-hand that time, old kerl! Yet, 'twas most wondrous humorsome. Ha! ha! But I must not laugh—at least, not here, for if she catches me the Kernsbergers will want a new chief captain. Ha! ha! No, I will not laugh. Werner, you old fool, be quiet! God's grace, but she looked right royal! It is worth a dressing down to see her in a rage. Faith, I would rather face a regiment of Muscovites single-handed than cross our Joan in one of her tantrums!"

He was now at the outer door. Prince Conrad was dismounting. The two men saluted each other.

"Is the Duchess Joan within?" said Conrad, concealing his eagerness under the hauteur natural to a Prince.

"I have just left her!" answered the chief captain.

Without a word Conrad sprang up the steps three at a time. Werner turned about and watched the young man's firm lithe figure till it had disappeared.

"Faith of Saint Anthony!" he murmured, "I am right glad our lady cares not for love. If she did, and if you had not been a priest—well, there might have been trouble."

CHAPTER XLVII
THE BROKEN BOND

Above, in the dusky light of the upper hall, Conrad and Joan stood holding each other's hands. It was the first time they had been alone together since the day on which they had walked along the sand-dunes of Rugen.

Since then they seemed to have grown inexplicably closer together. To Joan, Conrad now seemed much more her own—the man who loved her, whom she loved—than he had been on the Island. To watch day by day for his passing in martial attire brought back the knight of the tournament whose white plume she had seen storm through the lists on the day when, a slim secretary, she had stood with beating heart and shining eyes behind the chair of Leopold von Dessauer, Ambassador of Plassenburg.

For almost five minutes they stood thus without speech; then Joan drew away her hands.

"You forget," she said smiling, "that was forbidden in the bond."

"My lady," he said, "was not the bond for Isle Rugen alone? Here we are comrades in the strife. We must save our fatherland. I have laid aside my priesthood. If I live, I shall appeal to the Holy Father to loose me wholly from my vows."

Smilingly she put his eager argument by.

"It was of another vow I spoke. I am not the Holy Father, and for this I will not give you absolution. We are comrades, it is true—that and no more! To-morrow I ride to Kernsberg, where I will muster every man, call down the shepherds from the hills, and be back with you by the Alla before the Muscovite can attack you. I, Joan of the Sword Hand, promise it!"

She stamped her foot, half in earnest and half in mockery of the sonorous name by which she was known.

"I would rather you were Joan of the Grange at Isle Rugen, and I your jerkined servitor, cleaving the wood that you might bake the bread."

"Conrad," said Joan, shaking her head wistfully, "such thoughts are not wise for you and me to harbour. I may indeed be no duchess and you no prince, but we must stand to our dignities now when the enemy threatens and the people need us. Afterwards, an it like us, we may step down together. But, indeed, I need not to argue, for I think better of you, my comrade, than to suppose you would ever imagine anything else."

"Joan," said Conrad very gravely, "do not fear for me. I have turned once for all from a career I never chose. Death alone shall turn me back this time."

"I know it," she answered; "I never doubted it. But what shall we do with this poor lovesick bride of ours?"

And she told him of her interview that morning with his sister. Conrad laughed gently, yet with sympathy; Margaret had always been his "little girl," and her very petulances were dear to him.

"It had been well if she would have consented to remain here," he said; "and yet I do not know. She is not built for rough weather, our Gretchen. We are near the enemy, and many things may happen. Our soldiers are mostly levies in Courtland, and the land has been long at peace. The burghers and country folk are willing enough, but—well, perhaps she will be better with you."

"She swears she will not go without her husband," said Joan. "Yet he ought to remain with you. I do not need him; Werner will be enough."

"Leave me Von Orseln, and do you take the young man," said Conrad; "then Margaret will go with you willingly and gladly."

"But she will want to return—that is, if Maurice comes, too."

"Isle Rugen?" suggested Conrad, smilingly. "Send your ten men who know the road. If they could carry off Joan of the Sword Hand, they should have no difficulty with little Margaret of Courtland."

Joan clapped her hands with pleasure and relief, all unconscious that immediately behind her Margaret had entered softly and now stood arrested by the sound of her own name.

"Oh, they will have no trouble, will they not?" she said in her own heart, and smiled. "Isle Rugen? Thank you, my very dear brother and sister. You would get rid of me, separate me from Maurice while he is fighting for your precious princedoms. What is a country in comparison with a husband? I would not care a doit which country I belonged to, so long as I had Maurice with me!"

A moment or two Conrad and Joan discussed the details of the capture, while more softly than before Margaret retired to the door. She would have slipped out altogether but that something happened just then which froze her to the spot.

A trumpet blew without—once, twice, and thrice, in short and stirring blasts. Hardly had the echoes died away when she heard her brother say, "Adieu, best-beloved! It is the signal that tells me that Prince Ivan is within a day's march of Courtland. I bid you goodbye, and if—if we should never meet again, do not forget that I loved you—loved you as none else could love!"

He held out his hand. Joan stood rooted to the spot, her lips moving, but no words coming forth. Then Margaret heard a hoarse cry break from her who had contemned love.

"I cannot let you go thus!" she cried. "I cannot keep the vow! It is too hard for me! Conrad!—I am but a weak woman after all!"

And in a moment the Princess Margaret saw Joan the cold, Joan of the Sword Hand, Joan Duchess of Kernsberg and Hohenstein, in the arms of her brother.

Whereupon, not being of set purpose an eavesdropper, Margaret went out and shut the door softly. The lovers had neither heard her come nor go. And the wife of Maurice von Lynar was smiling very sweetly as she went, but in her eyes lurked mischief.

Conrad descended the stair from the apartments of the Duchess Joan, divided between the certainty that his lips had tasted the unutterable joy and the fear lest his soul had sinned the unpardonable sin.

A moment Joan steadied herself by the window, with her hand to her breast as if to still the flying pulses of her heart. She took a step forward that she might look once more upon him ere he went. But, changing her purpose in the very act, she turned about and found herself face to face with the Princess Margaret, who was still smiling subtly.

"You have granted my request?" she said softly.

Joan commanded herself with difficulty.

"What request?" she asked, for she indeed had forgotten.

"That Maurice and I should first go with you to Kernsberg and afterwards to Plassenburg."

"Let me think—let me think—give me time!" said Joan, sinking into a chair and looking straight before her. The world was suddenly filled with whirling vapour and her brain turned with it.

"I am in the midst of troubles. I know not what to do!" she murmured.

"Ah, it was quieter at Isle Rugen, was it not?" suggested Margaret, who had not forgiven the project of kidnapping her and carrying her off from her husband.

But Joan was thinking too deeply to answer or even to notice any taunt.

"I cannot go," she murmured, thinking aloud. "I cannot ride to Kernsberg and leave him in the front of danger!"

"A woman's place is at home!" said Margaret in a low tone, maliciously quoting Joan's words.

"He must not fight this battle alone. Perhaps I shall never see him again!"

"A man must not be hampered by affection in the hour of danger!"

At this point Joan looked down upon Margaret as she might have done at a puppy that worried a stick to attract her attention.

"Do you know," she said, "that Prince Ivan and his Muscovites are within a day's march of Courtland, and that Prince Conrad has already gone forth to meet them?"

"What!" cried Margaret, "within a day's march of the city? I must go and find my husband."

"Wait!" said Joan. "I see my way. Your husband shall come hither."

She went to the door and clapped her hands. An attendant appeared, one of the faithful Kernsberg ten to whom so much had been committed upon the Isle Rugen.

"Send hither instantly Werner von Orseln, Alt Pikker, and the Count von Löen!"

She waited with the latch of the door in her hand till she heard their footsteps upon the stair. They entered together and saluted. Margaret moved instinctively nearer to her husband. Indeed, only the feeling that the moment was a critical one kept her from running at once to him. As for Maurice, he had not yet grown ashamed of his wife's open manifestations of affection.

"Gentlemen," said Joan, "the enemy is at the gate of the city. We shall need every man. Who will ride to Kernsberg and bring back succour?"

"Alt Pikker will go!" said Maurice instantly; "he is in charge of the levies!"

"The Count von Löen is young. He will ride fastest!" said the chief captain.

"Werner von Orseln, of course!" said Alt Pikker, "he is in chief command."

"What? You do not wish to go?" said Joan a little haughtily, looking from one to the other of them. It was Werner von Orseln who answered.

"Your Highness," he said respectfully, "if the enemy be so near, and a battle imminent, the man is no soldier who would willingly be absent. But we are your servants. Choose you one to go; or, if it seem good to you, more than one. Bid us go, and on our heads it shall be to escort you safely to Kernsberg and bring back reinforcements."

The Princess came closer to Joan and slipped a hand into hers. The witty wrinkle at the corner of Werner von Orseln's mouth twitched.

"Von Lynar shall go!" said Joan.

Whereat Maurice held down his head, Margaret clapped her hands, and the other two stood stolidly awaiting instructions, as became their position.

"At what hour shall I depart, my lady?" said Maurice.

"Now! So soon as you can get the horses ready?"

"But your Grace must have time to make her preparations!"

"I am not going to Kernsberg. I stay here!" said Joan, stating a fact.

Werner von Orseln was just going out of the door, jubilantly confiding to Alt Pikker that as soon as he saw the Princess put her hand in their lady's he knew they were safe. At the sound of Joan's words he was startled into crying out loudly, "What?" At the same time he faced about with the frown on his face which he wore when he corrected an irregularity in the ranks.

"I am not going to Kernsberg. I bide here!" Joan repeated calmly. "Have you anything to say to that, Chief Captain von Orseln?"

"But, my lady——"

"There are no buts in the matter. Go to your quarters and see that the arms and armour are all in good case!"

"Madam, the arms and armour are always in good case," said Werner, with dignity; "but go to Kernsberg you must. The enemy is near to the city, and your Highness might fall into their hands."

"You have heard what I have said!" Joan tapped the oaken floor with her foot.

"But, madam, let me beseech you——"

Joan turned from her chief captain impatiently and walked towards the door of her private apartments. Werner followed his mistress, with his hands a little outstretched and a look of eager entreaty on his face.

"My lady," he said, "thirty years I was the faithful servant of your father—ten I have served you. By the memory of those years, if ever I have served you faithfully—"

"My father taught you but little, if after thirty years you have not learned to obey. Go to your post!"

Werner von Orseln drew himself up and saluted. Then he wheeled about and clanked out without adding a word more.

"Faith," he confided to Alt Pikker, "the wench is her father all over again. If I had gone a step further, I swear she would have beat me with the flat of my own sword. I saw her eye full on the hilt of it."

"Faith, I too, wished that I had been better helmeted!" chuckled Alt Pikker.

"Well," said Werner, like one who makes the best of ill fortune, "we must keep the closer to her, you and I, that in the stress of battle she come not to a mischief. Yet I confess that I am not deeply sorry. I began to fear that Isle Rugen had sapped our lass's spirit. To my mind, she seemed somewhat over content to abide there."

"Ah," nodded Alt Pikker, "that is because, after all, our Joan is a woman. No one can know the secret of a woman's heart."

"And those who think they know most, know the least!" concurred the much experienced Werner.

For a moment, after the door closed upon the men, Joan and Margaret stood in silence regarding each other.

"I must go and make me ready," said Margaret, speaking like one who is thinking deeply. Joan stood still, conscious that something was about to happen, uncertain what it might be.

"I shall see you before I depart," Margaret was saying, with her hand on the latch.

Suddenly she dropped the handle of the door and ran impulsively to Joan, clasping her about the neck.

"*I know!*" she said, looking up into her face.

With a great leap the blood flew to Joan's neck and brow, then as slowly faded away, leaving her paler than before.

"What do you know?" she faltered; and she feared, yet desired, to hear.

"That you love him!" said Margaret very low. "I came in—I could not help it—I did not know—when Conrad was bidding you goodbye. Joan, I am so glad—so glad! Now you will understand; now you will not think me foolish any more!"

"Margaret, I am shamed for ever—it is sin!" whispered Joan, with her arms about her friend.

"It is love!" said the wife of Maurice von Lynar, with glowing eyes and pride in her voice.

"I hope I shall die in battle— —"

"Joan!"

"I a wife, and love a priest—the brother of the man who is my husband! I pray God that He will take my life to atone for the sin of loving him. Yet He knows that I could neither help it nor yet hinder."

"Joan, you will yet be happy."

The Duchess shook her head.

"It were best for us both that I should die—that is what I pray for."

"May Heaven avert this thing—you know not what you say. And yet," Margaret continued in a more meditative tone, "I am not sure. If he were there with you, death itself would not be so hard; at all events, it were better than living without each other."

And the two women went into the attiring-room with arms still locked about each other's waists. And as often as their eyes encountered they lingered a little, as if tasting the sweet new knowledge which they had in common. Then those of Joan of the Sword Hand were averted and she blushed.

CHAPTER XLVIII
JOAN GOVERNS THE CITY

It was night in the city of Courtland, and a time of great fear. The watchmen went to and fro on the walls, staring into the blank dark. The Alla, running low with the droughts, lapped gently about the piles of the Summer Palace and lisped against the bounding walls of the city.

But ever and anon from the east, where lay the camps of the opposed forces, there came a sound, heavy and sonorous, like distant thunder. Whereat the frighted wives of the burghers of Courtland said, "I wonder what mother's son lies a-dying now. Hearken to the talking of Great Peg, the Margraf's cannon!"

At the western or Brandenberg gate there was yet greater fear. For the news had spread athwart the city that a great body of horsemen had paused in front of it, and were being held in parley by the guard on duty, till the Lady Joan, Governor of the city, should be made aware.

"They swear that they are friends"—so ran the report—"which is proof that they are enemies. For how can there be friends who are not Courtlanders. And these speak an outland speech, clacking in their throats, hissing their s's, and laughing 'Ho! ho!' instead of 'Hoch! hoch!' as all good Christians do!"

The Governor of the city, roused from a rare slumber, leaped on her horse and went clattering off with an escort through the unsleeping streets. When first she came the folk had cheered her as she went. But they were too jaded and saddened now.

"Our Governor, the Princess Joan!" they used to call her with pride. But for all that she found not the same devotion among these easy Courtlanders as among her hardy men of Hohenstein. To these she was indeed the Princess Joan. But to those in Castle Kernsberg she was Joan of the Sword Hand.

When at last she came to the Brandenburg gate she found before it a great gathering of the townsfolk. The city guard manned the walls, fretted with haste and falling over each other in their uncertainty. There was yet no strictness of discipline among these raw train-bands, and, instead of waiting for an officer to hail the horsemen in front, every soldier, hackbutman, and halberdier was shouting his loudest, till not a word of the reply could be heard.

But all this turmoil vanished before the first fierce gust of Joan's wrath like leaves blown away by the blasts of January.

"To your posts, every man! I will have the first man spitted with arrows who disobeys—aye, or takes more upon himself than simple obedience to orders. Let such as are officers only abide here with me. Silence beneath in the tower there."

Looking out, Joan could see a dark mass of horsemen, while above them glinted in the pale starlight a forest of spearheads.

"Whence come you, strangers?" cried Joan, in the loud, clear voice which carried so far.

"From Plassenburg we are!" came back the answer.

"Who leads you?"

"Captains Boris and Jorian, officers of the Prince's bodyguard."

"Let Captains Boris and Jorian approach and deliver their message."

"With whom are we in speech?" cried the unmistakable voice of Boris, the long man.

"With the Princess Joan of Hohenstein, Governor of the city of Courtland," said Joan firmly.

"Come on, Boris; those Courtland knaves will not shoot us now. That is the voice of Joan of the Sword Hand. There can be no treachery where she is."

"Ho, below there!" cried Joan. "Shine a light on them from the upper sally port."

The lanterns flashed out, and there, immediately below her, Joan beheld Boris and Jorian saluting as of old, with the simultaneous gesture which had grown so familiar to her during the days at Isle Rugen. She was moved to smile in spite of the soberness of the circumstances.

"What news bring you, good envoys?"

"The best of news," they said with one accord, but stopped there as if they had no more to say.

"And that news is——"

"First, we are here to fight. Pray you tell us if it is all over!"

Joan of the Sword Hand | 279

"It is not over; would to Heaven it were!" said Joan.

"Thank God for that!" cried Boris and Jorian, with quite remarkable unanimity of piety.

"Is that all your tidings?"

"Nay, we have brought the most part of the Palace Guard with us—five hundred good lances and all hungry-bellied for victuals and all monstrously thirsty in their throats. Besides which, Prince Hugo raises Plassenburg and the Mark, and in ten days he will be on the march for Courtland."

"God send him speed! I fear me in ten days it will be over indeed," said Joan, listening for the dull recurrent thunder down towards the Alla mouth.

"What, does the Muscovite press you so hard?"

"He has thousands to our hundreds, so that he can hem us in on every side."

"Never fear," cried Boris confidently; "we will hold him in check for you till our good Hugo comes to take him on the flank."

Then Joan bade the gates be opened, and the horsemen of Plassenburg, strong men on huge horses, trampled in. She held out a hand for the captains to kiss, and sent the burgomaster to assign them billets in the town.

Then, without resting, she went to the wool market, which had been turned into a soldiers' hospital. Here she found Theresa von Lynar, going from bed to bed smoothing pillows, anointing wounded limbs, and assisting the surgeons in the care of those who had been brought back from the fatal battlefields of the Alla.

Theresa von Lynar rose to meet Joan as she entered, with all the respect due to the city's Governor. Silently the young girl beckoned her to follow, and they went out between long lines of pallets. Here and there a torch glimmered in a sconce against the wall, or a surgeon with a candle in his hand paused at a bedside. The sough of moaning came from all about, and in a distant window-bay, unseen, a man distract with fever jabbered and fought fitfully.

Never had Joan realised so nearly the reverse of war. Never had she so longed for the peace of Isle Rugen. She could govern a city. She could lead a foray. She was not afraid to ride into battle, lance in rest or sword in hand. But she owned to herself that she could not do what this woman was doing.

"Remember, when all is over I shall keep my vow!" Joan began, as they paused and looked down the long alley of stained pillows, tossing heads, and torn limbs lying very still on palliasses of straw. Without, some of the riotous youth of the city were playing martial airs on twanging instruments.

"And I also will keep mine!" responded Theresa briefly.

"I am Duchess and city Governor only till the invader is driven out," Joan continued. "Then Isle Rugen is to be mine, and your son shall sit in the seat of Henry the Lion!"

"Isle Rugen shall be yours!" answered Theresa.

"And when you are tired of Castle Kernsberg you will cross the wastes and take boat to visit me, even as at the first I came to you!" said Joan, kindling at the thought of a definite sacrifice. It seemed like an atonement for her soul's sin.

"And what of Prince Conrad!" said Theresa quietly.

Joan was silent for a space, then she answered with her eyes on the ground.

"Prince Conrad shall rule this land as is his duty—Cardinal, Archbishop, Prince he shall be; there shall be none to deny him so soon as the power of the Muscovite is broken. He will be in full alliance with Hohenstein. He will form a blood bond with Plassenburg. And when he dies, all that is his shall belong to the children of Duke Maurice and his wife Margaret!"

Theresa von Lynar stood a moment weighing Joan's words, and when she spoke it was a question that she asked.

"Where is Maurice to-night?" she asked.

"He commands the Kernsbergers in the camp. Prince Conrad has made him provost-marshal."

"And the Princess Margaret?"

"She abides in the river gate of the city, which Maurice passes often upon his rounds!"

A strange smile passed over the face of Theresa von Lynar.

"There are many kinds of love," she said; "but not after this fashion did I, that am a Dane, love Henry the Lion. Wherefore should a woman hamper a man in his wars? Sooner would I have died by his hand!"

"She loves him," said Joan, with a new sympathy. "She is a princess and wilful. Moreover, not even a woman can prophesy what love will make another woman do!"

"Aye!" retorted Theresa, "I am with you there. But to help a man, not to hinder. Let her strip herself naked that he may go forth clad. Let her fall on the sharp wayside stones that he may march to victory. Let her efface herself that no breath may sully his great name. Let her die unknown—nay, make of herself a living death—that he may increase and fill the mouths of men. That is love—the love of women as I have imagined it. But this love that takes and will not give, that hampers and sends not forth to conquer, that keeps a man within call like a dog straining upon a leash—pah! that is not the love I know!"

She turned sharply upon Joan, all her body quivering with excitement.

"No, nor yet is it your way of love, my Lady Joan!"

"I shall never be so tried, like Margaret," answered Joan, willing to change her mood. "I shall never love any man with the love of wife!"

"God forbid," said Theresa, looking at her, "that such a woman as you should die without living!"

CHAPTER XLIX
THE WOOING OF BORIS AND JORIAN

"Jorian," said Boris, adjusting his soft underjerkin before putting on his body armour, "thou art the greatest fool in the world!"

"Hold hard, Boris," answered Jorian. "Honour to whom honour—thou art greater by at least a foot than I!"

"Well," said the long man, "let us not quarrel about the breadth of a finger-nail. At any rate, we two are the greatest fools in the world."

"There are others," said Jorian, jerking his thumb over his shoulder in the direction of the women's apartments.

"None so rounded and tun-bellied with folly!" cried Boris, with decision. "No two donkeys so thistle-fed as we—to have the command of five hundred good horsemen, and the chances of as warm a fight as ever closed——"

"That is just it," cried Jorian; "our Hugo had no business to forbid us to engage in the open before he should come."

"'Hold the city.' quoth he, shaking that great head of his. 'I know not the sort of general this priest-knight may be, and till I know I will not have my Palace Guard flung like a can of dirty water in the face of the Muscovites. Therefore counsel the Prince to stand on the defensive till I come.'"

"And rightly spoke the son of the Red Axe," assented Boris; "only our good Hugo should have sent other men than you and me to command in such a campaign. We never could let well alone all the days of us."

"Save in the matter of marriage or no marriage!" smiled Boris grimly.

"A plague on all women!" growled the little fat man, his rubicund and shining face lined with unaccustomed discontent. "A plague on all women, I say! What can this Theresa von Lynar want in the Muscovite camp, that we must promise to convey her safe through the fortifications, and then put her into Prince Wasp's hands?"

"Think you that for some hatred of our Joan—you remember that night at Isle Rugen—or some purpose of her own (she loves not the Princess Margaret either), this Theresa would betray the city to the enemy?"

"Tush!" Jorian had lost his temper and answered crossly. "In that case, would she have called us in? It were easy enough to find some traitor among these Courtlanders, who, to obtain the favour of Prince Louis, would help to bring the Muscovite in. But what, if she were thrice a traitress, would cause her to fix on the two men who of all others would never turn knave and spoil-sport—no, not for a hundred vats of Rhenish bottled by Noah the year after the Flood!"

"Well," sighed his companion, "'tis well enough said, my excellent Jorian, but all this does not advance us an inch. We have promised, and at eleven o' the clock we must go. What hinders, though, that we have a bottle of Rhenish now, even though the vintage be younger than you say? Perhaps, however, the patron was more respectable!"

Thus in the hall of the men-at-arms in the Castle of Courtland spoke the two captains of Plassenburg. All this time they were busy with their attiring, Boris in especial making great play with a tortoiseshell comb among his tangled locks. Somewhat more spruce was the arraying of our twin comrades-in-arms than we have seen it. Perhaps it was the thought of the dangerous escort duty upon which they had promised to venture forth that night; perhaps— —

"May we come in?" cried an arch voice from the doorway. "Ah, we have caught you! There—we knew it! So said I to my sister not an hour agone. Women may be vain as peacocks, but for prinking, dandifying vanity, commend me to a pair of foreign war-captains. My lords, have you blacked your eyelashes yet, touched up your eyebrows, scented and waxed those *beautiful* moustaches? Sister, can you look and live?"

And to the two soldiers, standing stiff as at attention, with their combs in their hands, enter the sisters Anna and Martha Pappenheim, more full of mischief than ever, and entirely unsubdued by the presence of the invader at their gates.

"Russ or Turk, Courtlander or Franconian, Jew, proselyte, or dweller in Mesopotamia, all is one to us. So be they are men, we will engage to tie them about our little fingers!"

"Why," cried Martha, "whence this grand toilet? We knew not that you had friends in the city. And yet they tell me you have been in Courtland before, Sir Boris?"

"Marthe," cried Anna Pappenheim, with vast pretence of indignation, "what has gotten into you, girl? Can you have forgotten that martial carriage, those limbs incomparably knit, that readiness of retort and delicate sparkle of Wendish wit, which set all the table in a roar, and yet never once brought the blush to maiden's cheek? For shame, Marthe!"

"Ha! ha!" laughed Jorian suddenly, short and sharp, as if a string had been pulled somewhere.

"Ho! ho!" thus more sonorously Boris.

Anna Pappenheim caught her skirts in her hand and spun round on her heel on pretence of looking behind her.

"Sister, what was that?" she cried, spying beneath the settles and up the wide throat of the chimney. "Methought a dog barked."

"Or a grey goose cackled!"

"Or a donkey sang!"

"Ladies," said Jorian, who, being vastly discomposed, must perforce try to speak with an affectation of being at his ease, "you are pleased to be witty."

"Heaven mend our wit or your judgment!"

"And we are right glad to be your butts. Yet have we been accounted fellows of some humour in our own country and among men— —"

"Why, then, did you not stay there?" inquired Martha pointedly.

"It was not Boris and I who could not stay without," retorted Jorian, somewhat nettled, nodding towards the door of the guard-room.

"Well said!" cried frank Anna. "He had you there, Marthe. Pricked in the white! Faith, Sir Jorian pinked us both, for indeed it was we who intruded into these gentlemen's dressing-room. Our excuse is that we are tirewomen, and would fain practise our office when and where we can. Our Princess hath been wedded and needs us but once a week. Noble Wendish gentlemen, will not you engage us?"

She clasped her hands, going a step or two nearer Boris as if in appeal.

"Do, kind sirs," she said, "have pity on two poor girls who have no work to do. Think—we are orphans and far from home!"

The smiles on the faces of the war-captains broadened. "Ho! ho! Good!" burst out Boris.

"Ha! ha! Excellent!" assented Jorian, nodding, with his eyes on Martha.

Anna Pappenheim ran quickly on tip-toe round to Boris's back and peered between his shoulders. Then she ran her eyes down to his heels.

"Sister," she cried, "*they* do it. That dreadful noise comes from somewhere about them. I distinctly saw their jaws waggle. They must of a surety be wound up like an arbalist. Yet I cannot find the string and trigger! Do come and help me, good Marthe! If you find it, I will dance at your wedding in my stocking-feet!"

And the gay Franconian reached up and pulled a stray tag of Boris's jerkin, which hung down his back. The knot slipped, and a circlet of red and gold, ragged at the lower edges, came off in her hand, revealing the fact that Boris's noble *soubreveste* was no more than a fringe of broidered collar.

"Ha! ha! ha!" laughed Jorian irrepressibly. For Boris looked mightily crestfallen to have his magnificence so rudely dealt with.

Anna von Pappenheim clapped her hands.

"I have found it," she cried. "It goes like this. You touch off the trigger of one, and the other explodes!"

Boris wheeled about with fell intent on his face. He would have caught the teasing minx in his arms, but Anna skipped round behind a chair and threatened him with her finger.

"Not till you engage us," she cried. "Hands off, there! We are to array you—not you to disarray us!"

Whereat the two gamesome Southlanders stood together in ludicrous imitation of Boris and Jorian's military stiffness, folding their hands meekly and casting their eyes downward like a pair of most ingenuous novices listening to the monitions of their Lady Superior. Then Anna's voice was heard speaking with almost incredible humility.

"Will my lord with the hook nose so great and noble deign to express a preference which of us shall be his handmaid?"

But they had ventured an inch too far. The string was effectually pulled now.

"I will have this one—she is so merry!" cried solemn Boris, seizing Anna Pappenheim about the waist.

"And I this! She pretendeth melancholy, yet has tricks like a monkey!" said Jorian, quickly following his example. The girls fended them gallantly, yet, as mayhap they desired, their case was hopeless.

"Hands off! I will not be called 'this one,'" cried Anna, though she did not struggle too vehemently.

"Nor I a monkey! Let me go, great Wend!" chimed Martha, resigning herself as soon as she had said it.

In this prosperous estate was the courtship of Franconia and Plassenburg, when some instinct drew the eyes of Jorian to the door of the officers' guard-room, which Anna had carefully left open at her entrance, in order to secure their retreat.

The Duchess Joan stood there silent and regardant.

"Boris!" cried Jorian warningly. Boris lifted his eyes from the smiling challenge upon Anna's upturned lips, which, after the manner of your war-captains, he was stooping to kiss.

Unwillingly Boris lifted his eyes. The next moment both the late envoys of Plassenburg were saluting as stiffly as if they had still been men-at-arms, while Anna and Martha, blushing divinely, were busy with their needlework in the corner, as demure as cats caught sipping cream.

Joan looked at the four for a while without speaking.

"Captains Boris and Jorian," she said sternly, "a messenger has come from Prince Conrad to say that the Muscovites press him hard. He asks for instant reinforcements. There is not a man fit for duty within the city saving your command. Will you take them to the Prince's assistance immediately? Werner von Orseln fights by his side. Maurice and my Kernsbergers are already on their way."

The countenances of the two Plassenburg captains fell as the leathern screen drops across a cathedral door through which the evening sunshine has been streaming.

"My lady, it is heartbreaking, but we cannot," said Boris dolefully. "Our Lord Prince Hugo bade us keep the city till he should arrive!"

"But I am Governor. I will keep the city," cried Joan; "the women will mount halberd and carry pike. Go to the Prince! Were Hugo of Plassenburg here he would be the first to march! Go, I order you! Go, I beseech you!"

She said the last words in so changed a tone that Boris looked at her in surprise.

But still he shook his head.

"It is certain that if Prince Hugo were here he would be the first to ride to the rescue. But Prince Hugo is not here, and my comrade and I are soldiers under orders!"

"Cowards!" flashed Joan, "I will go myself. The cripples, the halt, and the blind shall follow me. Thora of Bornheim and these maidens there, they shall follow me to the rescue of their Prince. Do you, brave men of Plassenburg, cower behind the walls while the Muscovite overwhelms all and the true Prince is slain!"

And at this her voice broke and she sobbed out, "Cowards! cowards! cowards! God preserve me from cowardly men!"

For at such times and in such a cause no woman is just. For which high Heaven be thanked!

Boris looked at Jorian. Jorian looked at Boris.

"No, madam," said Boris gravely; "your servants are no cowards. It is true that we were commanded by our master to keep his Palace Guard within the city walls, and these must stay. But we two are in some sense still Envoys Extraordinary, and not strictly of the Prince's Palace Guard. As Envoys, therefore, charged with a free commission in the interests of peace, we can without wrongdoing accompany you whither you will. Eh, Jorian?"

"Aye," quoth Jorian; "we are at her Highness's service till ten o' the clock."

"And why till ten?" asked Joan, turning to go out.

"Oh," returned Jorian, "there is guard-changing and other matters to see to. But there is time for a wealth of fighting before ten. Lead on, madam. We follow your Highness!"

CHAPTER L
THE DIN OF BATTLE

It was a strange uncouth band that Joan had got together in a handful of minutes in order to accompany her to the field upon which, sullenly retiring before a vastly more numerous enemy, Conrad and his little army stood at bay. Raw lathy lads, wide-hammed from sitting cross-legged in tailors' workshops; prentices too wambly and knock-kneed to be taken at the first draft; old men who had long leaned against street corners and rubbed the doorways of the cathedral smooth with their backs; a sprinkling of stout citizens, reluctant and much afraid, but still more afraid of the wrath of Joan of the Sword Hand.

Joan was still scouring the lanes and intricate passages for laggards when Boris and Jorian entered the little square where this company were assembled, most of them embracing their arbalists as if they had been sweeping besoms, and the rest holding their halberds as if they feared they would do themselves an injury.

The nose of fat Jorian went so high into the air that, without intending it, he found himself looking up at Boris; and at that moment Boris chanced to be glancing at Jorian down the side of his high arched beak.

To the herd of the uncouth soldiery it simply appeared as though the two war-captains of Plassenburg looked at each other. An observer on the opposite side would have noted, however, that the right eye of Jorian and the left eye of Boris simultaneously closed.

Yet when they turned their regard upon the last levy of the city of Courtland their faces were grave.

"Whence come these churchyard scourings, these skulls and crossbones set up on end?" cried Jorian in face of them all. And this saying from so stout a man made their legs wamble more than ever.

"Rotboss rascals, rogues in grain," Boris took up the tale, "faith, it makes a man scratch only to look at them! Did you ever see their marrow?"

The two captains turned away in disgust. They walked to and fro a little apart, and Boris, who loved all animals, kicked a dog that came his way. Boris was unhappy. He avoided Jorian's eye. At last he broke out.

"We cannot let our Lady Joan set forth for field with such a compost of mumpers and tun-barrels as these!" he said.

Boris confided this, as it were to the housetops. Jorian apparently did not listen. He was clicking his dagger in its sheath, but from his next word it was evident that his mind had not been inactive.

"What excuse could we make to Hugo, our Prince?" he said at last. "Scarcely did he believe us the last time. And on this occasion we have his direct orders."

"Are we not still Envoys?" queried Boris.

"Extraordinary!" twinkled Jorian, catching his comrade's idea as a bush of heather catches moorburn.

"And as Envoys of a great principality like Plassenburg—representatives of the most noble Prince and Princess in this Empire, should we not ride with retinue due and fitting? That is not taking the Palace Guard into battle. It is only affording due protection to their Excellencies' representatives."

"That sounds well enough," answered Boris doubtfully, "but will it stand probation, think you, when Hugo scowls at us from under his brows, and you see the bar of the fifteen Red Axes of the Wolfmark stand red across his forehead?"

"Tut, man, his anger is naught to that of Karl the Miller's Son. You and I have stood that. Why should we fear our quiet Hugo?"

"Aye, aye; in our day we have tried one thing and then another upon Karl and have borne up under his anger. But then Karl only cursed and used great horned words, suchlike as in his youth he had heard the waggoners use to encourage their horses up the mill brae. But Hugo—when he is angry he says nought, only the red bar comes up slowly, and as it grows dark and fiery you wish he would order you to the scaffold at once, and be done with it!"

"Well," said Jorian, "at all events, there is always our Helene. I opine, whatever we do, she will not forget old days—the night at the earth-houses belike and other things. I think we may risk it!"

"True," meditated Boris, "you say well. There is always Helene. The Little Playmate will not let our necks be stretched! Not at least for succouring a Princess in distress."

"And a woman in love?" added Jorian, who, though he followed the lead of the long man in great things, had a shrewder eye for some more intimate matters.

"Eh, what's that you say?" said Boris, turning quickly upon him. He had been regarding with interest a shackled-kneed varlet holding a halberd in his arms as if it had been a fractious bairn.

But Jorian was already addressing the company before him.

"Here, ye unbaked potsherds—dismiss, if ye know what that means. Get ye to the walls, and if ye cannot stand erect, lean against them, and hold brooms in your hands that the Muscovite may take them for muskets and you for men if he comes nigh enough. Our Lady is not Joan of the Dishclout, that such draught-house ragpickers as you should be pinned to her tail. Set bolsters stuffed with bran on the walls! Man the gates with faggots. Cleave beech billets half in two and set them athwart wooden horses for officers. But insult not the sunshine by letting your shadows fall outside the city. Break off! Dismiss! Go! Get out o' this!"

As Jorian stood before the levies and vomited his insults upon them, a gleam of joy passed across chops hitherto white like fish-bellies with the fear of death. Bleared eyes flashed with relief. And there ran a murmur through the ragged ranks which sounded like "Thank you, great captain!"

In a short quarter of an hour the drums of the Plassenburg Palace Guard had beaten to arms. From gate to gate the light sea-wind had borne the cheerful trumpet call, and when Joan returned, heartless and downcast, with half a dozen more mouldy rascals, smelling of muck-rakes and damp stable straw, she found before her more than half the horsemen of Plassenburg armed cap-a-pie in burnished steel. Whereat she could only look at Boris in astonishment.

"Your Highness," said that captain, saluting gravely, "we are only able to accompany you as Envoys Extraordinary of the Prince and Princess of Plassenburg. But as such we feel it our duty in order properly to support our state, to take with us a suitable attendance. We are sure that neither Prince Hugo nor yet his Princess Helene would wish it otherwise!"

Before Joan could reply a messenger came springing up the long narrow streets along which the disbanded levies, so vigorously contemned of Jorian, were hurrying to their places upon the walls with a detail of the Plassenburg men behind them, driving them like sheep.

Joan took the letter and opened it with a jerk.

"From High Captain von Orseln to the Princess Joan.

"Come with all speed, if you would be in time. We are hard beset. The enemy are all about us. Prince Conrad has ordered a charge!"

The face of the woman whitened as she read, but at the same moment the fingers of Joan of the Sword Hand tightened upon the hilt. She read the letter aloud. There was no comment. Boris cried an order, Jorian dropped to the rear, and the retinue of the Envoys Extraordinary swung out on the road towards the great battle.

Outnumbered and beaten back by the locust flock which spread to either side, far outflanking and sometimes completely enfolding his small army, Prince Conrad still maintained himself by good generalship and the high personal courage which stimulated his followers. The hardy Kernsbergers, both horse and foot, whom Maurice had brought up, proved the backbone of the defence. Besides which Werner von Orseln had striven by rebuke and chastening, as well as by appeals to their honour, to impart some steadiness into the Courtland ranks. But save the free knights from the landward parts, who were driven wild by the sight of the ever-spreading Muscovite desolation, there was little stamina among the burghers. They were, indeed, loud and turbulent upon occasion, but they understood but ill any concerted action. In this they differed conspicuously from their fellows of the Hansa League, or even from the clothweavers of the Netherland cities.

As Joan and the war-captains of Plassenburg came nearer they heard a low growling roar like the distant sound of the breakers on the outer shore at Isle Rugen. It rose and fell as the fitful wind bore it towards them, but it never entirely ceased.

They dashed through the fords of the Alla, the three hundred lances of the Plassenburg Guard clattering eagerly behind them. Joan led, on a black horse which Conrad had given her. The two war-captains with one mind set their steel caps more firmly on their heads, and as his steed breasted the river bank Jorian laughed aloud. Angrily Joan turned in her saddle to see what the little man was laughing at. But with quick instinct she perceived that he laughed only as the war-horse neighs when he scents the battle from afar. He was once more the born fighter of men. Jorian and his mate would never be generals, but they were the best tools any general could have.

They came nearer. A few wreaths of smoke, hanging over the yet distant field, told where Russ and Teuton met in battle array. A solemn slumberous reverberation heard at intervals split the dull general roar apart. It was the new cannon which had come from the Margraf George to help beat back the common foe. Again and again broke in upon their advance that appalling sound, which set the inward parts of men quivering. Presently they began to pass limping men hasting cityward, then fleeing and panic-stricken wretches who looked over their shoulders as if they saw steel flashing at their backs.

A camp-marshal or two was trying to stay these, beating them over the head and shoulders with the flat of their swords; but not a man of the Plassenburgers even looked towards them. Their eyes were on that distant tossing line dimly seen amid clouds of dust, and those strange wreaths of white smoke going upward from the cannons' mouths. The roar grew louder; there were gaps in the fighting line; a banner went down amid great shouting. They could see the glinting of sunshine upon armour.

"Kernsberg!" cried Joan, her sword high in the air as she set spurs in her black stallion and swept onward a good twenty yards before the rush of the horsemen of Plassenburg.

Now they began to see the arching arrow-hail, grey against the skyline like gnat swarms dancing in the dusk of summer trees. The quarrels buzzed. The great catapults, still used by the Muscovites, twanged like the breaking of viol cords.

The horses instinctively quickened their pace to take the wounded in their stride. There—there was the thickest of the fray, where the great cannon of the Margraf George thundered and were instantly wrapped in their own white pall.

Joan's quick glance about her for Conrad told her nothing of his whereabouts. But the two war-captains, more experienced, perceived that the Muscovites were already everywhere victorious. Their horsemen outflanked and overlapped the slender array of Courtland. Only about the cannon and on the far right did any seem to be making a stand.

"There!" cried Jorian, couching his lance, "there by the cannon is where we will get our bellyful of fighting."

He pointed where, amid a confusion of fighting-men, wounded and struggling horses, and the great black tubes of the Margraf's cannon, they saw the sturdy form of Werner von Orseln, grown larger through the smoke and dusty smother, bestriding the body of a fallen knight. He fought as one fights a swarm of angry bees, striking every way with a desperate courage.

**"The sturdy form of Werner von Orseln,
bestriding the body of a fallen knight."**

The charging squadrons of Plassenburg divided to pass right and left of the cannon. Joan first of all, with her sword lifted and crying not Kernsberg now, but "Conrad! Conrad!" drave straight into the heart of the Cossack swarm. At the trampling of the horses' feet the Muscovites lifted their eyes. They had been too intent to kill to waste a thought on any possible succour.

Joan felt herself strike right and left. Her heart was crazed within her so that she set spurs to her steed and rode him forward, plunging and furious. Then a blowing wisp of white plume was swept aside, and through a helmet (broken as a nut shell is cracked and falls apart) Joan saw the fair head of her Prince. A trickle of blood wetted a clinging curl on his forehead and stole down his pale cheek. Werner von Orseln, begrimed and drunken with battle, bestrode the body of Prince Conrad. His defiance rose above the din of battle.

"Come on, cowards of the North! Taste good German steel! To me, Kernsberg! To me, Hohenstein! Curs of Courtland, would ye desert your Prince? Curses on you all, swart hounds of the Baltic! Let me out of this and never a dog of you shall ever bite bread again!"

And so, foaming in his battle anger, the ancient war-captain would have stricken down his mistress. For he saw all things red and his heart was bitter within him.

With all the power that was in her, right and left Joan smote to clear her way to Conrad, praying that if she could not save him she might at least die with him.

But by this time Captains Boris and Jorian, leaving their horsemen to ride at the second line, had wheeled and now came thrusting their lances freely into Cossack backs. These last, finding themselves thus taken in the rear, turned and fled.

"Hey, Werner, good lad, do not slay your comrades! Down blade, old Thirsty. Hast thou not drunken enough blood this morning?" So cried the war-captains as Werner dashed the blood and tears out of his eyes.

"Back! back!" he cried, as soon as he knew with whom he had to do. "Go back! Conrad is slain or hath a broken head. They were lashing at him as he lay to kill him outright? Ah, viper, would you sting?" (He thrust a wounded Muscovite through as he was crawling nearer to Conrad with a broad knife in his hand.) "These beaten curs of Courtlanders broke at the first attack. Get him to horse! Quick, I say. My Lady Joan, what do you do in this place?"

For even while he spoke Joan had dismounted and was holding Conrad's head on her lap. With the soft white kerchief which she wore on her helm as a favour she wiped the wound on his scalp. It was long, but did not appear to be very deep.

As Werner stood astonished, gazing at his mistress, Boris summoned the trumpeter who had wheeled with him.

"Sound the recall!" he bade him. And in a moment clear notes rang out.

"He is not dead! Lift him up, you two!" Joan cried suddenly. "No, I will take him on my steed. It is the strongest, and I the lightest. I alone will bear him in."

And before any could speak she sprang into the saddle without assistance with all her old lightness of action, most like that of a lithe lad who chases the colts in his father's croft that he may ride them bareback.

So Werner von Orseln lifted the head and Boris the feet, bearing him tenderly that they might set him upon Joan's horse. And so firm was her seat (for she rode as the Maid rode into Orleans with Dunois on one side and Gilles de Rais on the other), that she did not even quiver as she received the weight. The noble black looked round once, and then, as if understanding the thing that was required of him, he gentled himself and began to pace slow and stately towards the city. On either side walked tall Boris and sturdy Werner, who steadied the unconscious Prince with the palms of their hands.

Meanwhile the Palace Guard, with Jorian at its head, defended the slow retreat, while on the flanks Maurice and his staunch Kernsbergers checked the victorious advance of the Muscovites. Yet the disaster was complete. They left the dead, they left the camp, they left the munitions of war. They abandoned the Margraf's cannon and all his great store of powder. And there were many that wept and some that only ground teeth and cursed as they fell back, and heard the wailing of the women and saw the fear whitening on the faces they loved.

Only the Kernsbergers bit their lips and watched the eye of Maurice, by whose side a slim page in chain-mail had ridden all day with visor down. And the men of the Palace Guard prayed for Prince Hugo to come.

As for Joan, she cared nothing for victory or defeat, loss or gain, because that the man she loved leaned on her breast, bleeding and very still.

Yet with great gentleness she gave him down into loving hands, and afterwards stood marble-pale beside the couch while Theresa von Lynar unlaced his armour and washed his wounds. Then, nerving herself to see him suffer, she murmured over to herself, once, twice, and a hundred times, "God help me to do so and more also to those who have wrought this—specially to Louis of Courtland and Ivan of Muscovy."

"Abide ye, little one—be patient. Vengeance will come to both!" said Theresa. "I, who do not promise lightly, promise it you!"

And she laid her hand on the girl's shoulder. Never before had the Duchess Joan been called "little one!" Yet for all her brave deeds she laid her head on Theresa's shoulder, murmuring, "Save him—save him! I cannot bear to lose him. Pray for him and me!"

Theresa kissed her brow.

"Ah," she said, "the prayers of such as Theresa von Lynar would avail little. Yet she may be a weapon in the hand of the God of vengeance. Is it not written that they that take the sword shall perish by the sword?"

But already Joan had forgotten vengeance. For now the surgeons of Courtland stood about, and she murmured, "Must he die? Tell me, will he die?"

And as the wise men silently shook their heads, the crying of the victorious Muscovites could be heard outside the wall.

Then ensued a long silence, through which broke a gust of iron-throated laughter. It was the roar of the Margraf's captured cannon firing the salvo of victory.

CHAPTER LI
THERESA'S TREACHERY

That night the whole city of Courtland cowered in fear before its triumphant enemy. At the nearest posts the Muscovites were in great strength, and the sight of their burnings fretted the souls of the citizens on guard. Some came near enough to cry insults up to the defenders.

"You would not have your own true Prince. Now ye shall have ours. We will see how you like the exchange!"

This was the cry of some renegade Courtlander, or of a Muscovite learned (as ofttimes they are) in the speech of the West.

But within the walls and at the gates the men of Kernsberg and Hohenstein rubbed their hands and nudged each other.

"Brisk lads," one said, "let us make our wills and send them by pigeon post. I am leaving Gretchen my Book of Prayers, my Lives of the Saints, my rosary, and my belt pounced with golden eye-holes——"

"Methinks that last will do thy Gretchen most service," said his companion, "since the others have gone to the vintner's long ago!"

"Thou art the greater knave to say so," retorted his companion; "and if by God's grace we come safe out of this I will break thy head for thy roguery!"

The Muscovites had dragged the captured cannon in front of the Plassenburg Gate, and now they fired occasionally, mostly great balls of quarried stone, but afterward, as the day wore later, any piece of metal or rock they could find. And the crash of wooden galleries and stone machicolations followed, together with the scuttling of the Courtland levies from the post of danger. A few of the younger citizens, indeed, were staunch, but for the most part the Plassenburgers and Kernsbergers were left to bite their lips and confide to each other what their Prince Hugo or their Joan of the Hand Sword would have done to bring such cowards to reason and right discipline.

"An it were not for our own borders and that brave priest-prince, no shaveling he," they said, "faith, such curs were best left to the Muscovite. The plet and the knout were made for such as they!"

"Not so," said he who had maligned Gretchen; "the Courtlanders are yea-for-soothing knaves, truly; but they are Germans, and need only to know they must, to be brave enough. One or two of our Karl's hostelries, with thirteen lodgings on either side, every guest upright and a-swing by the neck—these would make of the Courtlanders as good soldiers as thyself, Hans Finck!"

But at that moment came Captain Boris by and rebuked them sharply for the loudness of their speech. It was approaching ten of the clock. Boris and Jorian had already visited all the posts, and were now ready to make their venture with Theresa von Lynar.

"No fools like old fools!" grumbled Jorian sententiously, as he buckled on his carinated breastplate, that could shed aside bolts, quarrels, and even bullets from powder guns as the prow of a vessel sheds the waves to either side in a good northerly wind.

"'Tis you should know," retorted Boris, "being both old and a fool."

"A man is known by the company he keeps!" answered Jorian, adjusting the lining of his steel cap, which was somewhat in disarray after the battle of the morning.

"Ah!" sighed his companion. "I would that I had the choosing of the company I am to keep this night!"

"And I!" assented Jorian, looking solemn for once as he thought of pretty Martha Pappenheim.

"Well, we do it from a good motive," said Boris; "that is one comfort. And if we lose our lives, Prince Conrad will order many masses (they will need to be very many) for your soul's peace and good quittance from purgatory!"

"Humph!" said Jorian, as if he did not see much comfort in that, "I would rather have a box on the ear from Martha Pappenheim than all the matins of all the priests that ever sung laud!"

"Canst have that and welcome—if her sister will do as well!" cried Anna, as the two men went out into the long passage. And she suited the deed to the word.

"Oh! I have hurt my hand against that hard helmet. It serves me right for listening! Marthe!"—she looked about for her sister before turning to the soldiers—"see, I have hurt my hand," she added.

Then she made the tears well up in her eyes by an art of the tongue in the throat she had.

"Kiss it well, Marthe!" she said, looking up at her sister as she came along the passage swinging a lantern as carelessly as if there were not a Muscovite in the world.

But Boris forestalled the newcomer and caught up the small white hand in the soft leathern grip of his palm where the ring-mail stopped.

"*I* will do that better than any sister!" he said.

"That, indeed, you cannot; for only the kiss of love can make a hurt better!"

Anna glanced up at him with wet eyes, a little maid full of innocence and simplicity. Most certainly she was all unconscious of the danger in which she was putting herself.

"Well, then, I love you!" said Boris, who did his wooing plainly.

And did not kiss her hand.

Meanwhile the others had wandered to the end of the passage and now stood at the turnpike staircase, the light of Martha Pappenheim's lantern making a dim haze of light about them.

Anna looked at Boris as often as she could.

"You really love me?" she questioned. "No, you cannot; you have known me too brief a time. Besides, this is no time to speak of love, with the enemy at the gates!"

"Tush!" said Boris, with the roughness which Anna had looked for in vain among all the youth of Courtland. "I tell you, girl, it is the time. You and I are no Courtlanders, God be thanked! In a little while I shall ride back to Plassenburg, which is a place where men live. I shall not go alone. You, little Anna, shall come, too!"

"You are not deceiving me?" she murmured, looking up upon occasion. "There is none at Plassenburg whom you love at all?"

"I have never loved any woman but you!" said Boris, settling his conscience by adding mentally, "though I may have thought I did when I told them so."

"Nor I any man!" said Anna, softly meditative, making, however, a similar addition.

Thus Greek met Greek, and both were very happy in the belief that their own was the only mental reservation.

"But you are going out?" pouted Anna, after a while. "Why cannot you stay in the Castle to-night?"

"To-night of all nights it is impossible," said Boris. "We must make the rounds and see that the gates are guarded. The safety of the city is in our hands."

"You are sure that you will not run into any danger!" said Anna anxiously. She remembered a certain precariousness of tenure among some of her previous—mental reservations. There was Fritz Wünch, who had laughed at the red beard of a Prussian baron; Wilhelm of Bautzen, who went once too often on a foray with his uncle, Fighting Max of Castelnau——

For answer the staunch war-captain kissed her, and the girl clung to her lover, this time in real tears. Martha's candle had gone out, and the two had perforce to go down the stair in the dark. They reached the foot at last.

"None of them were quite like him," she owned that night to her sister. "He takes you up as if he would break you in his arms. And he could, too. It is good to feel!"

"Jorian also is just like that—so satisfactory!" answered Martha. Which shows the use Jorian must have made of his time at the stairhead, and why Martha Pappenheim's light went out.

"He swears he has never loved any woman before."

"Jorian does just the same."

"I suppose we must never tell them——"

"Marthe—if you should dare, I will—— Besides, you were just as bad!"

"Anna, as if I would dream of such a thing!"

And the two innocents fell into each other's arms and embraced after the manner of women, each in her own heart thinking how much she preferred "the way of a man with a maid"—at least that form of it cultivated by stout war-captains of Plassenburg.

Without, Boris and Jorian trampled along through a furious gusting of Baltic rain, which came in driving sheets from the north and splashed its thumb-board drops equally upon the red roofs of Courtland, the tented Muscovites drinking victory, and upon the dead men lying afield. Worse still, it fell on many wounded, and to such even the thrust of the thievish camp-follower's tolle-knife was merciful. Never could monks more fitly have chanted, "Blessed are the dead!" than concerning those who lay stiff and unconscious on the field where they had fought, to whose ears the Alla sang in vain.

Attired in her cloak of blue, with the hood pulled low over her face, Theresa von Lynar was waiting for Boris and Jorian at the door of the market-hospital.

"I thank you for your fidelity," she said quickly. "I have sore need of you. I put a great secret into your hands. I could not ask one of the followers of Prince Conrad, nor yet a soldier of the Duchess Joan, lest when that is done which shall be done to-night the Prince or the Duchess should be held blameworthy, having most to gain or lose thereto. But you are of Plassenburg and will bear me witness!"

Boris and Jorian silently signified their obedience and readiness to serve her. Then she gave them their instructions.

"You will conduct me past the city guards, out through the gates, and take me towards the camp of the Prince of Muscovy. There you will leave me, and I shall be met by one who in like manner will lead me through the enemy's posts."

"And when will you return, my Lady Theresa? We shall wait for you!"

"Thank you, gentlemen. You need not wait. I shall not return!"

"Not return?" cried Jorian and Boris together, greatly astonished.

"No," said Theresa very slowly and quietly, her eyes set on the darkness. "Hear ye, Captains of Plassenburg—I will give you my mind. You are trusty men, and can, as I have proved, hold your own counsel."

Boris and Jorian nodded. There was no difficulty about that.

"Good!" they said together as of old.

As they grew older it became more and more easy to be silent. Silence had always been easier to them than speech, and the habit clave to them even when they were in love.

"Listen, then," Theresa went on. "You know, and I know, that unless quick succour come, the city is doomed. You are men and soldiers, and whether ye make an end amid the din of battle, or escape for this time, is a matter wherewith ye do not trouble your minds till the time comes. But for me, be it known to you that I am the widow of Henry the Lion of Kernsberg. My son Maurice is the true heir to the Dukedom. Yet, being bound by an oath sworn to the man who made me his wife, I have never claimed the throne for him. But now Joan his sister knows, and out of her great heart she swears that she will give up the Duchy to him. If, therefore, the city is taken, the Muscovite will slay my son, slay him by their hellish tortures, as they have sworn to do for the despite he put upon Prince Ivan. And his wife, the Princess Margaret, will die of grief when they carry her to Moscow to make a bride out of a widow. Joan will be a prisoner, Conrad either dead or a priest, and Kernsberg, the heritage of Henry the Lion, a fief of the Czar. There is no help in any. Your Prince would succour, but it takes time to raise the country, and long ere he can cross the frontier the Russian will have worked his will in Courtland. Now I see a way—a woman's way. And if I fall in the doing of it, well—I but go to meet him for the sake of whose children I freely give my life. In this bear me witness."

"Madam," said Boris, gravely, "we are but plain soldiers. We pretend not to understand the great matters of State of which you speak. But rest assured that we will serve you with our lives, bear true witness, and in all things obey your word implicitly."

Without difficulty they passed through the streets and warded gates. Werner von Orseln, indeed, tramping the inner rounds, cried "Whither away?" Then, seeing the lady cloaked between them, he added after his manner, "By my faith, you Plassenburgers beat the world. Hang me to a gooseberry bush if I do not tell Anna Pappenheim of it ere to-morrow's sunset. As I know, she will forgive inconstancy only in herself!"

They plunged into the darkness of the outer night. As soon as they were beyond the gates the wind drave past them hissing level. The black trees roared overhead. At first in the swirl of the storm the three could see nothing; but gradually the watchfires of the Muscovite came out thicksown like stars along the rising grounds on both sides of the Alla. Boris strode on ahead, peering anxiously into the night, and a little behind Jorian gave Theresa his hand over the rough and uneven ground. A pair of ranging stragglers, vultures that accompany the advance of all great armies, came near and examined the party, but retreated promptly as they caught the glint of the firelight upon the armour of the war-captains. Presently they began to descend into the valley, the iron-shod feet of the men clinking upon the stones. Theresa walked silently, steeped in thought, laying a hand on arm or shoulder as she had occasion. Suddenly tall Boris stopped dead and with a sweep of his arm halted the others.

"There!" he whispered, pointing upward.

And against the glow thrown from behind a ridge they could see a pair of Cossacks riding to and fro ceaselessly, dark against the ruddy sky.

"Gott, would that I had my arbalist! I could put gimlet holes in these knaves!" whispered Jorian over Boris's shoulder.

"Hush!" muttered Boris; "it is lucky for Martha Pappenheim that you left it at home!"

"Captains Boris and Jorian," Theresa was speaking with quietness, raising her voice just enough to make herself heard over the roar of the wind overhead, for the nook in which they presently found themselves was sheltered, "I bid you adieu—it may be farewell. You have done nobly and like two valiant captains who were fit to war with Henry the Lion. I thank you. You will bear me faithful witness in the things of which I have spoken to you. Take this ring from me, not in recompense, but in memory. It is a bauble worth any lady's acceptance. And you this dagger." She took two from within her mantle, and gave one to Jorian. "It is good steel and will not fail you. The fellow of it I will keep!"

She motioned them backward with her hand.

"Abide there among the bushes till you see a man come out to meet me. Then depart, and till you have good reason keep the last secret of Theresa, wife of Henry the Lion, Duke of Kernsberg and Hohenstein!"

Boris and Jorian bowed themselves as low as the straitness of their armour would permit.

"We thank you, madam," they said; "as you have commanded, so will we do!"

And as they had been bidden they withdrew into a clump of willow and alder whose leaves clashed together and snapped like whips in the wind.

"Yonder woman is braver than you or I, Jorian," said Boris, as crouching they watched her climb the ridge. "Which of us would do as much for any on the earth?"

"After all, it is for her son. If you had children, who can say——?"

"Whether I may have children or no concerns you not," returned Boris, who seemed unaccountably ruffled. "I only know that I would not throw away my life for a baker's dozen of them!"

Upon the skyline Theresa von Lynar stood a moment looking backward to make sure that her late escort was hidden. Then she took a whistle from her gown and blew upon it shrilly in a lull of the storm. At the sound the war-captains could see the Cossacks drop their lances and pause in their unwearying ride. They appeared to listen eagerly, and upon the whistle being repeated one of them threw up a hand. Then between them and on foot the watchers saw another man stand, a dark shadow against the watchfires. The sentinels leaned down to speak with him, and then, lifting their lances, they permitted him to pass between them. He was a tall man, clad in a long caftan which flapped about his feet, a sheepskin posteen or winter jacket, and a round cap of fur, high-crowned and flat-topped, upon his head.

He came straight towards Theresa as if he expected a visitor.

The two men in hiding saw him take her hand as a host might that of an honoured guest, kiss it reverently, and then lead her up the little hill to where the sentinels waited motionless on their horses. So soon as the pair had passed within the lines, their figures and the Cossack salute momentarily silhouetted against the watchfires, the twin horsemen resumed their monotonous ride.

By this time Jorian's head was above the bushes and his eyes stood well nigh out of his head.

"Down, fool!" growled Boris, taking him by the legs and pulling him flat; "the Cossacks will see you!"

"Boris," gasped Jorian, who had descended so rapidly that the fall and the weight of his plate had driven the wind out of him, "I know that fellow. I have seen him before. It is Prince Wasp's physician, Alexis the Deacon. I remember him in Courtland when first we came thither!"

"Well, and what of that?" grunted Boris, staring at the little detached tongues of willow-leaf flame which were blown upward from the Muscovite watchfires.

"What of that, man?" retorted Boris. "Why, only this. We have been duped. She was a traitress, after all. This has been planned a long while."

"Traitress or saint, it is none of our business," said Boris grimly. "We had better get ourselves within the walls of Courtland, and say nothing to any of this night's work!"

"At any rate," added the long man as an afterthought, "I have the ring. It will be a rare gift for Anna."

Jorian looked ruefully at his dagger, holding it between the rustling alder leaves, so as to catch the light from the watchfires. The red glow fell on a jewel in the hilt.

"'Tis a pretty toy enough, but how can I give that to Marthe? It is not a fit keepsake for a lady!"

"Well," said Boris, suddenly appeased, "I will swop you for it. I am not so sure that my pretty spitfire would not rather have it than any ring I could give her. Shall we exchange?"

"But we promised to keep them as souvenirs?" urged Jorian, whose conscience smote him slightly. "One does not tell lies to a lady—at least where one can help it."

"It depends upon the lady!" said Boris practically. "You can tell your Marthe the truth. I will please myself with Anna. Hand over the dagger."

So wholly devoid of sentiment are war-captains when they deal with keepsakes.

CHAPTER LII
THE MARGRAF'S POWDER CHESTS

It was indeed Alexis the Deacon who met the Lady Theresa. And the matter had been arranged, just as Boris said. Alexis the Deacon, a wise man of many disguises, remained in Courtland after the abrupt departure of Prince Ivan. Theresa had found him in the hospital, where, sheltered by a curtain, she heard him talk with a dying man—the son of a Greek merchant domiciled in Courtland, whose talent for languages and quick intelligence had induced Prince Conrad to place him on his immediate staff of officers.

"I bid you reveal to me the plans and intents of the Prince," Theresa heard Alexis say, "otherwise I cannot give you absolution. I am priest as well as doctor."

At this the young Greek groaned and turned aside his head, for he loved the Prince. Nevertheless, he spoke into the ear of the physician all he knew, and as reward received a sleeping draught, which induced the sleep from which none waken.

And afterwards Theresa had spoken also.

So it was this same Alexis—spy, priest, surgeon, assassin, and chief confidant of Ivan Prince of Muscovy—who, in front of the watchfires, bent over the hand of Theresa von Lynar on that stormy night which succeeded the crowning victory of the Russian arms in Courtland.

"This way, madam. Fear not. The Prince is eagerly awaiting you—both Princes, indeed," Alexis said, as he led her into the camp through lines of lighted tents and curious eyes looking at them from the darkness. "Only tell them all that you have to tell, and, trust me, there shall be no bounds to the gratitude of the Prince, or of Alexis the Deacon, his most humble servant."

Theresa thought of what this boundless gratitude had obtained for the young Greek, and smiled. They came to an open space before a lighted pavilion. Before the door stood a pair of officers trying in vain to shield their gay attire under scanty shoulder cloaks from the hurtling inclemency of the night. Their ready swords, however, barred the way.

"To see the Prince—his Highness expects us," said Alexis, without any salute. And with no further objection the two officers stood aside, staring eagerly and curiously however under the hood of the lady's cloak whom Alexis brought so late to the tent of their master.

"Ha!" muttered one of them confidentially as the pair passed within, "I often wondered what kept our Ivan so long in Courtland. It was more than his wooing of the Princess Margaret, I will wager!"

"Curse the wet!" growled his fellow, turning away. He felt that it was no time for speculative scandal.

Theresa and her conductor stood within the tent of the commander of the Muscovite army. The glow of light, though it came only from candles set within lanterns of horn, was great enough to be dazzling to her eyes. She found herself in the immediate presence of Prince Ivan, who rose with his usual lithe grace to greet her. An older man, with a grey pinched face, sat listlessly with his elbow on the small camp table. He leaned his forehead on his palm, and looked down. Behind, in the half dark of the tent, a low wide divan with cushions was revealed, and all the upper end of the tent was filled up with a huge and shadowy pile of kegs and boxes, only half concealed behind a curtain.

"I bid you welcome, my lady," said Prince Ivan, taking her hand. "Surely never did ally come welcomer than you to our camp to-night. My servant Alexis has told me of your goodwill—both towards ourselves and to Prince Louis." (He indicated the silent sitting figure with a little movement of his hand sufficiently contemptuous.) "Let us hear your news, and then will we find you such lodging and welcome as may be among rough soldiers and in a camp of war."

As he was speaking Theresa von Lynar loosened her long cloak of blue, its straight folds dank and heavy with the rains. The eyes of the Prince of Muscovy grew wider. Hitherto this woman had been to him but a common traitress, possessed of great secrets, doubtless to be flattered a little, and then—afterwards—thrown aside. Now he stood gazing at her his hands resting easily on the table, his body a little bent. As she revealed herself to him the pupils of his eyes dilated, and amber gleams seemed to shoot across the irises. He thought he had never seen so beautiful a woman. As he stood there, sharpening his features and moistening his lips, Prince Ivan looked exceedingly like a beast of prey looking out of his hole upon a quarry which comes of its own accord within reach of his claws.

But in a moment he had recovered himself, and came forward with renewed reverence.

"Madam," he said, bowing low, "will you be pleased to sit down? You are wet and tired."

He went to the flap of the pavilion and pushed aside the dripping flap.

"Alexis!" he cried, "call up my people. Bid them bring a brazier, and tell these lazy fellows to serve supper in half an hour on peril of their heads!"

He returned and stood before Theresa, who had sunk back as if fatigued on an ottoman covered with thick furs. Her feet nestled in the bearskins which covered the floor. The Prince looked anxiously down.

"Pardon me, your shoes are wet," he said. "We are but Muscovite boors, but we know how to make ladies comfortable. Permit me!"

And before Theresa could murmur a negative the Prince had knelt down and was unloosing the latchets of her shoes.

"A moment!" he said, as he sprang again to his feet with the lithe alertness which distinguished him. Prince Ivan ran to a corner where, with the brusque hand of a master, he had tossed a score of priceless furs to the ground. He rose again and came towards Theresa with a flash of something scarlet in his hand.

"You will pardon us, madam," he said, "you are our guest—the sole lady in our camp. I lay it upon your good nature to forgive our rude makeshifts."

And again Prince Ivan knelt. He encased Theresa's feet in dainty Oriental slippers, small as her own, and placed them delicately and respectfully on the couch.

"There, that is better!" he said, standing over her tenderly.

"I thank you, Prince." She answered the action more than the words, smiling upon him with her large graciousness; "I am not worthy of so great favour."

"My lady," said the Prince, "it is a proverb of our house that though one day Muscovy shall rule the world, a woman will always rule Muscovy. I am as my fathers were!"

Theresa did not answer. She only smiled at the Prince, leaning a little further back and resting her head easily upon the palm of her hand. The servitors brought in more lamps, which they slung along the ridge-pole of the roof, and these shedding down a mellow light enhanced the ripe splendour of Theresa's beauty.

Prince Ivan acknowledged to himself that he had spoken the truth when he said that he had never seen a woman so beautiful. Margaret?—ah, Margaret was well enough; Margaret was a princess, a political necessity, but this woman was of a nobler fashion, after a mode more truly Russ. And the Prince of Muscovy, who loved his fruit with the least touch of over-ripeness, would not admit to himself that this woman was one hour past the prime of her glorious beauty. And indeed there was much to be said for this judgment.

Theresa's splendid head was set against the dusky skins. Her rich hair of Venice gold, escaping a little from the massy carefulness of its ordered coils, had been blown into wet curls that clung closely to her white neck and tendrilled about her broad low brow. The warmth of the tent and the soft luxury of the rich rugs had brought a flush of red to a cheek which yet tingled with the volleying of the Baltic raindrops.

"Alexis never told me this woman was so beautiful," he said to himself. "Who is she? She cannot be of Courtland. Such a marvel could not have been hidden from me during all my stay there!"

So he addressed himself to making the discovery.

"My lady," he said, "you are our guest. Will you deign to tell us how more formally we may address you? You are no Courtlander, as all may see!"

"I am a Dane," she answered smiling; "I am called the Lady Theresa. For the present let that suffice. I am venturing much to come to you thus! My father and brothers built a castle upon the Baltic shore on land that has been the inheritance of my mother. Then came the reivers of Kernsberg and burned the castle to the ground. They burned it with fire from cellar to roof-tree. And they slackened the fire with the blood of my nearest kindred!"

As she spoke Theresa's eyes glittered and altered. The Prince read easily the meaning of that excitement. How was he to know all that lay behind?

"And so," he said, "you have no good-will to the Princess Joan of Hohenstein—and Courtland. Or to any of her favourers?" he added after a pause.

At the name the grey-headed man, who had been sitting unmoved by the table with his elbow on the board, raised a strangely wizened face to Theresa's.

"What"—he said, in broken accents, stammering in his speech and grappling with the words as if, like a wrestler at a fair, he must throw each one severally—"what—who has a word to say against the Lady Joan, Princess of Courtland? Whoso wrongs her has me to reckon with—aye, were it my brother Ivan himself!"

"Not I, certainly, my good Louis," answered Ivan easily. "I would not wrong the lady by word or deed for all Germany from Bor-Russia to the Rhine-fall!"

He turned to Alexis the Deacon, who was at his elbow.

"Fill up his cup—remember what I bade you!" he said sharply in an undertone.

"His cup is full, he will drink no more. He pushes it from him!" answered Alexis in the same half-whisper. But neither, as it seemed, took any particular pains to prevent their words carrying to the ear of Prince Louis. And, indeed, they had rightly judged. For swiftly as it had come the momentary flash of manhood died out on the meagre face. The arm upon which he had leaned swerved limply aside, and the grey beard fell helplessly forward upon the table.

"So much domestic affection is somewhat belated," said Prince Ivan, regarding Louis of Courtland with disgust. "Look at him! Who can wonder at the lady's taste? He is a pretty Prince of a great province. But if he live he will do well enough to fill a chair and hold a golden rod. Take him away, Alexis!"

"Nay," said Theresa, with quick alarm, "let him stay. There are many things to speak of. We may need to consult Prince Louis later."

"I fear the Prince will not be of great use to us," smiled Prince Ivan. "If only I had known, I would have conserved his princely senses more carefully. But for heads like his the light wine of our country is dangerously strong."

He glanced about the pavilion. The servants had not yet retired.

"Convey his Highness to the rear, and lay him upon the powder barrels!" He indicated with his hand the array of boxes and kegs piled in the dusk of the tent. The servitors did as they were told; they lifted Prince Louis and would have carried him to that grim couch, but, struck with some peculiarity, Alexis the Deacon suddenly bent over his lax body and thrust his hand into the bosom of his princely habit, now tarnished thick with wine stains and spilled meats.

"Excellency," he said, turning to his master, "the Prince is dead! His heart does not beat. It is the stroke! I warned you it would come!"

Prince Ivan strode hastily towards the body of Louis of Courtland.

"Surely not?" he cried, in seeming astonishment. "This may prove very inconvenient. Yet, after all, what does it matter? With your assistance, madam, the city is ours. And then, what matters dead prince or living prince? A garrison in every fort, a squadron of good Cossacks pricking across every plain, a tax-collector in every village—these are the best securities of princedom. But this is like our good Louis. He never did anything at a right time all his life."

Theresa stood on the other side of the dead man as the servitors lowered him for the inspection of their lord. The weary wrinkled face had been smoothed as with the passage of a hand. Only the left corner of the mouth was drawn down, but not so much as to be disfiguring.

"I am glad he spoke kindly of his wife at the last," she murmured. And she added to herself, "This falls out well—it relieves me of a necessity."

"Spoken like a woman!" cried Prince Ivan, looking admiringly at her. "Pray forgive my bitter speech, and remember that I have borne long with this man!"

He turned to the servitors and directed them with a motion of his hand towards the back of the pavilion.

"Drop the curtain," he said.

And as the silken folds rustled heavily down the curtain fell upon the career and regality of Louis, Prince of Courtland, hereditary Defender of the Holy See.

The men did not bear him far. They placed him upon the boxes of the powder for the Margraf's cannon, which for safety and dryness Ivan had bade them bring to his own pavilion. The dead man lay in the dark, open-eyed, staring at the circling shadows as the servitors moved athwart the supper table, at which a woman sat eating and drinking with her enemy.

Theresa von Lynar sat directly opposite the Prince of Muscovy. The board sparkled with mellow lights reflected from many lanterns. The servitors had departed. Only the measured tread of the sentinels was heard without. They were alone.

And then Theresa spoke. Very fully she told what she had learned of the defences of the place, which gates were guarded by the Kernsbergers, which by the men of Plassenburg, which by the remnants of the broken army of Courtland. She spoke in a hushed voice, the Prince sipping and nodding as he looked into her eyes. She gave the passwords of the inner and outer defences, the numbers of the defenders at each gate, the plans for bringing provisions up the Alla—indeed, everything that a besieging general needs to know.

And so soon as she had told the passwords the Prince asked her to pardon him a moment. He struck a silver bell and with scarce a moment's delay Alexis entered.

"Go," said the Prince; "send one of our fellows familiar with the speech of Courtland into the city by the Plassenburg Gate. The passwords are '*Henry the Lion*' at the outer gate and '*Remember*' at the inner port. Let the man be dressed in the habit of a countryman, and carry with him some wine and provend. Follow him and report immediately."

While the Prince was speaking he had never taken his eyes off Theresa von Lynar, though he had appeared to be regarding Alexis the Deacon. Theresa did not blanch. Not a muscle of her face quivered. And within his Muscovite heart, full of treachery as an egg of meat, Prince Ivan said, "She is no traitress, this dame; but a simpleton with all her beauty. The woman is speaking the truth."

And Theresa was speaking the truth. She had expected some such test and was prepared; but she only told the defenders' plans to one man; and as for the passwords, she had arranged with Boris that at the earliest dawn they were to be changed and the forces redistributed.

While these two waited for the return of Alexis, the Prince encouraged Theresa to speak of her wrongs. He watched with approbation the sparkle of her eye as he spoke of Joan of the Sword Hand. He noted how she shut down her lips when Henry the Lion was mentioned, how her voice shook as she recounted the cruel end of her kin.

Though at ordinary times most sober, the Prince now added cup to cup, and like a Muscovite he grew more bitter as the wine mounted to his head. He leaned forward and laid his hand upon his companion's white wrist. Theresa quivered a little, but did not take it away. The Prince was becoming confidential.

"Yes," he said, leaning towards her, "you have suffered great wrongs, and do well to hate with the hate that craves vengeance. But even you shall be satisfied. To-morrow and to-morrow's to-morrow you and I shall have out our hearts' desire upon our enemies. Yes, for many days. Sweet—sweet it shall be—sweet, and very slow; for I, too, have wrongs, as you shall hear."

"Truly, I did well to come to you!" said Theresa, giving her hand willingly into his. He clasped her fingers and would have kissed her but for the table between.

"You speak truth." He hissed the words bitterly. "Indeed, you did better than well. I also have wrongs, and Ivan of Muscovy will show you a Muscovite vengeance.

"This Prince Conrad of theirs baulked me of my revenge and drove me from the city. Him will I take and burn at the stake in his priest's robes, as if he were saying mass—or, better still, in the red of the cardinal's habit with his hat upon his head. And ere he dies he shall see his paramour carried to her funeral. For I will give you the life of the woman for whose sake he thwarted Ivan of Muscovy. If you will it, no hand but yours shall have the shedding of the blood of your house's enemy. Is not this your vengeance already sweet in prospect?"

"It is sweet indeed!" answered Theresa.

"Your Highness!" said the voice of Alexis at the tent door, "am I permitted to speak?"

"Speak on!" cried Ivan, without relaxing his clasp upon the hand of Theresa von Lynar. Indeed, momentarily it became a grip.

"The man went safely through at the Plassenburg Gate. The passwords were correct. The man who challenged spoke with a Kernsberg accent!"

The Prince's grasp relaxed.

"It is well," he said. "Now go to the captains and tell them to be in their posts about the city according to the plan—the main assault to be delivered by the gate of the sea. At dawn I will be with you! Go! Above all, do not forget the passwords—first 'Henry the Lion!' then 'Remember!'"

Alexis the Deacon saluted and went.

The Prince rose and came about the table nearer to Theresa von Lynar. She drew her breath quickly and checked it as sharply with a kind of sob. Her left hand went down to her side as naturally as a nun's to her rosary. But it was no rosary her fingers touched. The action steadied her, and she threw back her head and smiled up at her companion debonairly as though she had no care in the world.

Theresa repeated the passwords slowly and audibly.

"'Henry the Lion!' 'Remember!' Ah!" (she broke off with a laugh) "I am not likely to forget." Ivan laid his hand on her shoulder, glad to see her so resolute.

"All in good time," he said, sitting down on a stool at her feet and taking her hand—her right hand. The other he did not see. Then he spoke confidentially.

"One other revenge I have which I shall keep till the last. It shall be as sweet to me as yours to you. I shall draw it out lingeringly that I may drain all its sweetness. It concerns the upstart springald whom the Princess

Margaret had the bad taste to prefer to me. Not that I cared a jot for the Princess. My taste is far other" (here he looked up tenderly); "but the Princess I must wed, as maid or widow I care not. I take her provinces, not herself; and these must be mine by right of fief and succession as well as by right of conquest. The way is clear. That piece of carrion which men called by a prince's name was carried out a while ago. Conrad the priest, who is a man, shall die like a man. And I, Ivan, and Holy Russia shall enter in. By the right of Margaret, sole heir of Courtland, city and province shall be mine; Kernsberg shall be mine; Hohenstein shall be mine. Then mayhap I will try a fall for Plassenburg and the Mark with the Executioner's Son and his little housewife. But sweeter than all shall be my revenge upon the man I hate— upon him who took his betrothed wife from Ivan of Muscovy."

"Ah," said Theresa von Lynar, "it will indeed be sweet! And what shall be your worthy and terrible revenge?"

"I have thought of it long—I have turned it over, this and that have I thought—of the smearing with honey and the anthill, of trepanning and the worms on the brain—but I have fixed at last upon something that will make the ears of the world tingle— —"

He leaned forward and whispered into the ear of Theresa von Lynar the terrible death he had prepared for her only son. She nodded calmly as she listened, but a wonderful joy lit up the woman's face.

"I am glad I came hither," she murmured, "it is worth it all."

Prince Ivan took her hand in both of his and pressed it fondly.

"And you shall be gladder yet," he said, "my Lady Theresa. I have something to say. I had not thought that there lived in the world any woman so like-minded, even as I knew not that there lived any woman so beautiful. Together you and I might rule the world. Shall it be together?"

"But, Prince Ivan," she interposed quickly, but still smiling, "what is this? I thought you were set on wedding the Princess Margaret. You were to make her first widow and then wife."

"Theresa," he said, looking amorously up at her, "I marry for a kingdom. But I wed the woman who is my mate. It is our custom. I must give the left hand, it is true, but with it the heart, my Theresa!"

He was on his knees before her now, still clasping her fingers.

"You consent?" he said, with triumph already in his tone.

"I do not say you nay!" she answered, with a sigh.

He kissed her hand and rose to his feet. He would have taken her in his arms, but a noise in the pavilion disturbed him. He went quickly to the curtain and peeped through.

"It is nothing," he said, "only the men come to fetch the powder for the Margraf's cannon. But the night speeds apace. In an hour we assault."

With an eager look on his face he came nearer to her.

"Theresa," he said, "a soldier's wooing must needs be brisk and speedy. Yours and mine yet swifter. Our revenge beckons us on. Do you abide here till I return—with those good friends whose names we have mentioned. But now, ere I go forth, pledge me but once your love. This is our true betrothal. Say, 'I love you, Ivan!' that I may keep it in my heart till my return!"

Again he would have taken her in his arms, but Theresa turned quickly, finger on lip. She looked anxiously towards the back of the tent where lay the dead prince. "Hush! I hear something!" she said.

Then she smiled upon him—a sudden radiance like sunshine through rain-clouds.

"Come with me—I am afraid of the dark!" she said, almost like a child. For great is the guile of woman when her all is at stake.

Theresa von Lynar opened the latch of a horn lantern which dangled at a pole and took the taper in her left. She gave her right hand with a certain gesture of surrender to Prince Ivan.

"Come!" she said, and led him within the inner pavilion. A dim light sifted through the open flap by which the men had gone out with their load of powder. Day was breaking and a broad crimson bar lay across the path of the yet unrisen sun. Theresa and Prince Ivan stood beside the dead. He had been roughly thrown down on the pile of boxes which contained the powder manufactured by the Margraf's alchemists according to the famous receipt of Bertholdus Schwartz. The lid of the largest chest stood open, as if the men were returning for yet another burden.

"Quick!" she said, "here in the presence of the dead, I will whisper it here, here and not elsewhere."

She brought him close to her with the gentle compulsion of her hand till he stood in a little angle where the red light of the dawn shone on his dark handsome face. Then she put an arm strong as a wrestler's about him, pinioning him where he stood. Yet the gracious smile on the woman's lips held him acquiescent and content.

She bent her head.

"Listen," she said, "this have I never done for any man before—no, not so much as this! And for you will I do much more. Prince Ivan, you speak true—death alone must part you and me. You ask me for a love pledge. I will give it. Ivan of Muscovy, you have plotted death and torture—the death of the innocent. Listen! I am the wife of Henry of Kernsberg, the mother of the young man Maurice von Lynar whom you would slay by horrid devices. Prince, truly you and I shall die together—and the time is *now*!"

Vehemently for his life struggled Prince Ivan, twisting like a serpent, and crying, "Help! Help! Treachery! Witch, let me go, or I will stab you where you stand." Once his hand touched his dagger. But before he could draw it there came a sound of rushing feet. The forms of many men stumbled up out of the gleaming blood-red of the dawn.

Then Theresa von Lynar laughed aloud as she held him helpless in her grasp.

"The password, Prince—do not forget the password! You will need it to-night at both inner and outer guard! I, Theresa, have not forgotten. It is *'Henry the Lion*! Remember!'"

"'The password, Prince—do not forget the password!'"

And Theresa dropped the naked candle she had been holding aloft into the great chest of dull black grains which stood open by her side.

And after that it mattered little that at the same moment beyond the Alla the trumpets of Hugo, Prince of Plassenburg, blew their first awakening blast.

CHAPTER LIII
THE HEAD OF THE CHURCH VISIBLE

"So," said Pope Sixtus amicably, "your brother was killed by the great explosion of Friar Roger's powder in the camp of the enemy! Truly, as I have often said, God is not with the Greek Church. They are schismatics if not plain heretics!"

He was a little bored with this young man from the North, and began to remember the various distractions which were waiting for him in his own private wing of the Vatican. Still, the Church needed such young war-gods as this Prince Conrad. There were signs, too, that in a little she might need them even more.

The Pope's mind travelled fast. He had a way of murmuring broken sentences to himself which to his intimates showed how far his thoughts had wandered.

It was the Vatican garden in the month of April. Holy Week was past, and the mind of the Vicar of Christ dwelt contentedly upon the great gifts and offerings which had flowed into his treasury. Conrad could not have arrived more opportunely. Beneath, the eye travelled over the hundred churches of Rome and the red roofs of her palaces—to the Tiber no longer tawny, but well-nigh as blue as the Alla itself; then further still to the grey Campagna and the blue Alban Hills. But the Pope's eye was directed to something nearer at hand.

In an elevated platform garden they sat in a bower sipping their after-dinner wine. Beyond answering questions Conrad said little. He was too greatly astonished. He had expected a saint, and he had found himself quietly talking politics and scandal with an Italian Prince. The Holy Father's face was placid. His lips moved. Now and then a word or two escaped him. Yet he seemed to be listening to something else.

That which he looked at was an excavation over which thousands of men crawled, thick as ants about a mound when you thrust your stick among their piled pine-needles on Isle Rugen. Already at more than one point massive walls began to rise. Architects with parchment rolls in their hands went to and fro talking to overseers and foremen. These were clad in black coats reaching below the waist, which made inky blots on the white earth-glare and contrasted with the striped blouses of the overseers and the naked bodies and red loin-cloths of the workmen.

Conrad blessed his former sojourns in Italy which enabled him to follow the fast-running river of the Pontiff's half-unconscious meditation, which was couched not in crabbed monkish Latin, but in the free Italic to which as a boy the Head of the Church had been accustomed.

"So your brother is dead!—(Yes, yes, he told me so before.) And a blessing of God, too. I never liked my brothers. Nephews and nieces are better, so be they are handsome. What, you have none? Then you are the heir to the kingdom—you must marry—you must marry!"

Conrad suddenly flushed fiery red.

"Holy Father," he said nervously, his eyes on the Alban Hills, "it was concerning this that I made pilgrimage to Rome—that I might consult your Holiness!"

The Pontiff nodded amicably and looked about him. At the far end of the garden, in a second creeper-enclosed arbour similar to that in which they sat, the Pope's personal attendants congregated. These were mostly gay young men in parti-coloured raiment, who jested and laughed without much regard for appearances, or at all fearing the displeasure of the Church's Head. As Conrad looked, one of them stood up and tossed over the wall a delicately folded missive, winged like a dart and tied with a ribbon of fluttering blue. Then, the moment afterwards, from beneath came the sound of girlish laughter, whereat all the young men, save one, craned their necks over the wall and shouted jests down to the unseen ladies on the balcony below.

All save one—and he, a tall stern-faced dark young man in a plain black soutane, walked up and down in the sun, with his eyes on the ground and his hands knotting themselves behind his back. The fingers were twisting nervously, and he pursed his lips in meditation. He did not waste even one contemptuous glance on the riotous crew in the arbour.

"Aha—you came to consult me about your marriage," chuckled the Holy Father. "Well, what have you been doing? Young blood—young blood! Once I was young myself. But young blood must pay. I am your father confessor. Now, proceed. (This may be useful—better, better, better!)"

And with a wholly different air of interest, the Pope poured himself a glass of the rich wine and leaned back, contemplating the young man now with a sort of paternal kindliness. The thought that he had certain peccadillos to confess was a relish to the rich Sicilian vintage, and created, as it were, a common interest between them. For the first time Pope Sixtus felt thoroughly at ease with his guest.

"I have, indeed, much to confess, Holy Father, much I could not pour into any ears but thine."

"Yes—yes—I am all attention," murmured the Pontiff, his ears pricking and twitching with anticipation, and the famous likeness to a goat coming out in his face. "Go on! Go on, my son. Confession is the breathing health of the soul! (If this young man can tell me aught I do not know—by Peter, I will make him my private chaplain!)."

Then Conrad summoned up all his courage and put his soul's sickness into the sentence which he had been conning all the way from the city of Courtland.

"My father," he said, very low, his head bent down, "I, who am a priest, have loved the Lady Joan, my brother's wife!"

"Ha," said Sixtus, pursing his lips, "that is bad—very bad. (Bones of Saint Anthony! I did not think he had the spirit!) Penance must be done— yes, penance and payment! But hath the matter been secret? There has, I hope, been no open scandal; and of course it cannot continue now that your brother is dead. While he was alive all was well; but dead—oh, that is different! You have now no cloak for your sin! These open sores do the Church much harm! I have always avoided such myself!"

The young man listened with a swiftly lowering brow.

"Holy Father," he said; "I think you mistake me. I spoke not of sin committed. The Princess Joan is pure as an angel, unstained by evil or the thought of it! She sits above the reach of scandalous tongues!"

("Humph—what, then, is the man talking about? Some cold northern snowdrift! Strange, strange! I thought he had been a lad of spirit!")

But aloud Sixtus said, with a surprised accent, "Then why do you come to me?"

"Sire, I am a priest, and even the thought of love is sin!"

"Tut-tut; you are a prince-cardinal. In Rome at least that is a very different thing!"

He turned half round in his seat and looked with a certain indulgent fondness upon the gay young men who were conducting a battle of flowers with the laughing girls beneath them. Two of them had laid hold of another by the legs and were holding him over the trellised flowers that he might kiss a girl whom her companions were elevating from below for a like purpose. As their young lips met the Pontiff slapped the purple silk on his thigh and laughed aloud.

"Ah, rascals, merry rascals!" (here he sighed). "What it is to be young! Take an old man's advice, Live while you are young. Yes, live and leave penance, for old age is sufficient penance in itself. (Tut—what am I saying? Let his pocket do penance!) He who kissed was my nephew Girolamo, ever the flower of the flock, my dear Girolamo. I think you said, Prince Conrad, that you were a cardinal. Well, most of these young men are cardinals (or will be, so soon as I can get the gold to set them up. They spend too much money, the rascals)."

"These are cardinals? And priests?" queried Conrad, vastly astonished.

The Holy Father nodded and took another sip of the perfumed Sicilian.

"To be a cardinal is nothing," he said calmly. "It is a step—nothing more. The high road of advancement, the spirit of the time. When I have princedoms for them all, why, they must marry and settle—raise dynasties, found princely houses. So it shall be with you, son Conrad. Your brother was alive, Prince of Courtland, married to this fair lady (what was her name? Yes, yes, Joanna). You, a younger son, must be provided for, the Church supported. Therefore you received that which was the hereditary right of your family—the usual payments to Holy Church being made. You were Archbishop, Cardinal, Prince of the Church. In time you would have been Elector of the Empire and my assessor at the Imperial Diet. That was your course. What harm, then, that you should make love to your brother's wife? Natural—perfectly natural. Fortunate, indeed, that you had a brother so complaisant— —"

"Sir," said Conrad, half rising from his seat, "I have already had the honour of informing you— —"

"Yes, yes, I forgot—pardon an old man. (Ah, the rascal, would he? Served him right! Ha, ha, well smitten—a good girl!)"

Another had tried the trick of being held over the balcony, but this time the maiden below was coy, and, instead of a kiss, the youth had received only a sound smack on the cheek fairly struck with the palm of a willing hand.

"Yes, I remember. It was but a sin of the soul. (Stupid fellow! stupid fellow! Girolamo is a true Delia Rovere. He would not have been served so.) Yes, a sin of the soul. And now you wish to marry? Well, I will receive back your hat. I will annul your orders—the usual payments being made to Holy Church. I have so many expenses—my building, the decorations of my chapel, these young rascals—ah, little do you know the difficulties of a Pope. But whom do you wish to marry? What, your brother's widow? Ah, that is bad—why could you not be content— —? Pardon, your pardon, my mind is again wandering."

"Tsut—tsut—this is a sad business, a matter infinitely more difficult, forbidden by the Church. What? They parted at the church door? A wench of spirit, I declare. I doubt not like that one who smote Pietro just now. I wonder not at you, save at your moderation—that is, if you speak the truth."

"I do speak the truth!" said Conrad, with northern directness, beginning to flush again.

"Gently—gently," said Sixtus; "there are many minutes in a year, many people go to make a world. I have never seen a man like you before. Be patient, then, with me. I am giving you a great deal of my time. It will be difficult, this marriage—difficult, but not impossible. Peter's coffers are very empty, my son."

The Pontiff paused to give Conrad time to speak.

"I will pay into the treasury of the Holy Father on the day of my marriage a hundred thousand ducats," said Conrad, blushing deeply. It seemed like bribing God.

The Vicegerent of Christ stretched out a smooth white hand, and his smile was almost as gracious as when he turned it upon his nephew Girolamo.

"Spoken like a true prince," he cried, "a son of the Church indeed. Her works—the propagation of the Faith, the Holy Office—these shall benefit by your generosity."

He turned about again and beckoned to the tall young man in the black soutane.

"Guliano, come hither!" he cried, and as he came he explained in his low tones, "My nephew, between ourselves, a dull dog, but will be great. He choked a ruffian who attacked him on the street; so, one day, he will choke this Italy between his hands. He will sit in this chair. Ah, there is one thing that I am thankful for, and it is that I shall be dead when our Julian is Pope. I know not where I shall be—but anything were preferable to being in Rome under Julian—purgatory or— —Yes, my dear nephew, Prince Conrad of Courtland! You are to go and prepare documents concerning this noble prince. I will instruct you as to their nature presently. Await me in the hither library."

The young man had been looking steadily at Conrad while his uncle was speaking. It was a firm and manly look, but there was cruelty lurking in the curve of the upper lip. Guliano della Rovere looked more *condottiere* than priest. Nevertheless, without a word he bowed and retired.

When he was gone the Pope sat a moment absorbed in thought.

"I will send him to Courtland with you. (Yes, yes, he is staunch and to be trusted with money.) He will marry you and bring back the—the—benefaction. Your hand, my son. I am an old man and need help. May you be happy! Live well and honour Holy Church. Be not too nice. The commons like not a precisian. And, besides, you cannot live your youth over. Girolamo! Girolamo! Where is that rascal? Ah, there you are. I saw you kiss yonder pretty minx! Shame, sir, shame! You shall do penance—I myself will prescribe it. What kept you so long when I called you? Some fresh rascality, I will wager!"

"No, my father," said Girolamo readily. "I went to the dungeons of the Holy Office to see if they had finished off that ranting philosopher who stirred up the people yesterday!"

"Well, and have they?" asked the Pontiff.

"Yes, the fellow has confessed that six thousand pieces are hidden under the hearthstone of his country house. So all is well ended. He is to be burned to-morrow."

"Good—good. So perish all Jews, heretics, and enemies of Holy Church!" said Pope Sixtus piously. "And now I bid you adieu, son Conrad! You set out to-morrow. The papers shall be ready. A hundred thousand ducats, I think you said—*and* the fees for secularisation. These will amount to fifty thousand more. Is it not so, my son?"

Conrad bowed assent. He thought it was well that Courtland was rich and his brother Louis a careful man.

"Good—good, my son. You are a true standard-bearer of the Church. I will throw in a perpetual indulgence—with blanks which you may fill up. No, do not refuse! You think that you will never want it, because you do not want it now. But you may—you may!"

He stretched out his hand. The blessed ring of Saint Peter shone upon it. Conrad fell on his knees.

"*Pater Domini nostri Jesu Christi benedicat te in omni benedictione spirituali. Amen!*"

EPILOGUE OF EXPLICATION

It was the morning of a white day. The princely banner flew from every tower in Castle Kernsberg, for that day it was to lose a duchess and gain a duke. It was Joan's second wedding-day—the day of her first marriage.

Never had the little hill town seen so brave a gathering since the northern princes laid Henry the Lion in his grave. In the great vault where he slept there was a new tomb, a plain marble slab with the inscription—

"THERESA, WIFE OF HENRY,
DUKE OF KERNSBERG AND HOHENSTEIN."

And underneath, and in Latin, the words—

"AFTER THE TEMPEST, PEACE!"

For strangely enough, by the wonder of Providence or some freak of the exploding powder, they had found Theresa fallen where she had stood, blackened indeed but scarce marred in face or figure. So from that burnt-out hell they had brought her here that at the last she might rest near the man whom her soul loved.

And as they moved away and left her, little Johannes Rode, the scholar, murmured the words, *"Post tempestatem, tranquillitas!"*

Prince Conrad heard him, and he it was who had them engraven on her tomb.

But on this morning of gladness only Joan thought of the dead woman.

"To-day I will do the thing she wished," the Duchess thought, as she looked from the window towards her father's tomb. "She would take nothing for herself, yet shall her son sit in my place and rule where his father ruled. I am glad!"

Here she blushed.

"Yet, why should I vaunt? It is no sacrifice, for I shall be—what I would rather a thousand times be. Small thanks, then, that I give up freely what is worth nothing to me now!"

And with the arm that had wielded a sword so often and so valiantly, Joan the bride went on arraying her hair and making her beautiful for the eyes of her lord.

"My lord!" she said, and again with a different accent. "*My* lord!"

And when these her living eyes met those others in the Venice mirror, lo! either pair was smiling a new smile.

Meantime, beneath in her chamber, the Princess Margaret was making her husband's life a burden to him, or rather, first quarrelling with him and the next moment throwing her arms about his neck in a passion of remorse. For that is the wont of dainty Princess Margarets who are sick and know not yet what aileth them.

"Maurice," she was saying, "is it not enough to make me throw me over the battlements that they should all forsake me, on this day of all others, when you are to be made a Duke in the presence of the Pope's Legate and the Emperor's *Alter*—what is it?—*Alter ego*? What a silly word! And you might have told it to me prettily and without laughing at me. Yes, you did, and you also are in league against me. And I will not go to the wedding; no, not if Joan were to beg of me on my knees! I will not have any of these minxes in to do my hair. Nay, do not you touch it. I am nobody, it seems, and Joan everything. Joan—Joan! It is Joan this and Joan that! Tush, I am sick of your Joans.

"She gives up the duchy to us—well, that is no great gift. She is getting Courtland for it, and my brother. Even he will not love me any more. Conrad is like the rest. He eats, drinks, sleeps, wakes, talks Joan. He is silent, and thinks Joan. So, I believe, do you. You are only sorry that she did not love you best!

"Well, if you *are* her brother, I do not care. Who was speaking about marrying her? And, at any rate, you did not know she was your sister. You might very well have loved her. And I believe you did. You do not love me, at all events. *That* I do know!

"No, I will not 'hush,' nor will I come upon your knee and be petted. I am not a baby! '*What is the matter betwixt me and the maidens?*' If you had let me explain I would have told you long ago. But I never get speaking a word. I am not crying, and I shall cry if I choose. Oh yes, I will tell you, Duke Maurice, if you care to hear, why I am angry with the maids. Well, then, first it was that Anna Pappenheim. She tugged my hair out by the roots in handfuls, and when I scolded her I saw there were tears in her eyes. I asked her why, and for long she would not tell me. Then all at once she acknowledged that she had promised to marry that great overgrown chimney-pot, Captain Boris, and must hie her to Plassenburg, if I pleased. I did not please, and when I said that surely Marthe was not so foolish thus to throw herself away, the wretched Marthe came bawling and wringing hands, and owned that she was in like case with Jorian.

"So I sent them out very quickly, being justly angry that they should thus desert me. And I called for Thora of Bornholm, and began easing my mind concerning their ingratitude, when the Swede said calmly, 'I fear me, madam, I am not able to find any fault with Anna and Martha. For I am even as they, or worse. I have been married for over six months.'

"'And to whom?' I cried; 'tell me, and he shall hang as surely as I am a Princess of Courtland.' For I was somewhat disturbed.

"'To-day your Highness is Duchess of Kernsberg,' said the minx, as calmly as if at sacrament. 'My husband's name is Johannes Rode!'

"And when I have told you, instead of being sorry for me, you do nothing but laugh. I will indeed fling me over the window!"

And the fiery little Princess ran to the window and pretended to cast herself headlong. But her husband did not move. He stood leaning against the mantelshelf and smiling at her quietly and lovingly.

Hearing no rush of anxious feet, and finding no restraining arm cast about her, Margaret turned, and with fresh fire in her gesture stamped her foot at Maurice.

"That just proves it! Little do you care whether or no I kill myself. You wish I would, so that you might marry somebody else. You dare not deny it!"

Maurice knew better than to deny it, nor did he move till the Princess cast herself down on the coverlet and sobbed her heart out, with her face on the pillow and her hair spraying in linked tendrils about her white neck and shoulders. Then he went gently to her and laid his hand on her head, regardless of the petulant shrug of her shoulders as he touched her. He gathered her up and sat down with her in his arms.

"Little one," he said, "I want you to be good. This is a great and a glad day. To-day my sister finds the happiness that you and I have found. To-day I am to sit in my father's seat and to have henceforth my own name among men. You must help me. Will you, little one? For this once let me be your tire-woman. I have often done my own tiring when, in old days, I dared death in women's garments for your sweet sake. Dearest, do not hurt my heart any more, but help me."

His wife smiled suddenly through her tears, and cast her arms about his neck.

"Oh, I am bad—bad—bad," she cried vehemently. "It were no wonder if you did not love me. But do keep loving me. I should die else. I will be better—I will—I will! I do not know why I should be so bad. Sometimes I think I cannot help it."

But Maurice kissed her and smiled as if he knew.

"We will live like plain and honest country folk, you and I," he said. "Let Anna and Martha follow their war-captains. Thora at least will remain with us, and we will make Johannes Rode our almoner and court poet. Now smile at me, little one! Ah, that is better."

In Margaret's April eyes the sun shone out again, and she clung lovingly to her husband a long moment before she would let him go.

Then she thrust him a little away from her, that she might see his face, as she asked the question of all loving and tempestuous Princess Margarets, "Are you sure you love me just the same, even when I am naughty?"

Maurice was sure.

And taking his face between her hands in a fierce little clutch, she asked a further assurance. "Are you quite, quite sure?" she said.

And Maurice was quite, quite sure.

Not in a vast and solemn cathedral was Joan married, but in the old church of Kernsberg, which had so often raised the protest of the Church against the exactions of her ancestors. The bridal escort was of her own tried soldiery, now to be hers no more, and all of them a little sad for that. Hugo and Helene of Plassenburg had come—Hugo because he was the representative of the Emperor, and Helene because she was a sweet and loving woman who delighted to rejoice in another's joy.

With these also arrived, and with these was to depart, the dark-faced stern young cardinal of San Pietro in Vincoli. He must have good escort, he said, for he carried many precious relics and tokens of the affection of the faithful for the Church's Head. The simple priesthood of Kernsberg shrank from his fiery glances, and were glad when he was gone. But, save at the hour of bridal itself, he spent all his time with the treasurer of the Princedom of Courtland.

When at last they came down the aisle together, and the sweet-voiced choristers sang, and the white-robed maidens scattered flowers for their feet to walk upon, the bride found opportunity to whisper to her husband, "I fear me I shall never be Joan of the Sword Hand any more!"

He smiled back at her as they came out upon the tears and laughter and acclaim of the many-coloured throng that filled the little square.

"Be never afraid, beloved," he said, and his eyes were very glad and proud, "only be Joan to me, and I will be your Sword Hand!"